Also avai

Ti
Mickey C

HEARTS ON HOLD

CHARISH REID

carina
press

carina
press®

Recycling programs
for this product may
not exist in your area.

ISBN-13: 978-1-335-89591-2

Hearts on Hold

First published in 2020. This edition published in 2024.

Copyright © 2020 by Charish Reid

For questions and comments about the quality of this book,
please contact us at CustomerService@Harlequin.com.

® is a trademark of Harlequin Enterprises ULC.

Carina Press
22 Adelaide St. West, 41st Floor
Toronto, Ontario M5H 4E3, Canada
www.CarinaPress.com

Printed in U.S.A.

Support your local library.

Chapter One

"I think it's a cute idea, Ms. Reese," Kenneth Williams droned on. "But your library internship excludes the remainder of our English students; those who aren't bound for Kiddie Lit or Early Education careers."

Victoria straightened her back and fought the urge to break the pencil in her clenched fist. *A cute idea* was how Victoria might describe Halloween party crafts, not a library internship meant to advance the visibility of Pembroke University's English Department. She had prepared herself for condescension, but her face grew warm all the same. If Kenneth could get past his disdain for change, he would see what Victoria saw: opportunity.

When the president announced that faculty and staff create low-cost ideas to boost enrollment, she took the proposed Four-Week Initiative seriously. As did every other university worker. She had to make certain hers stood out from the pack, since only the best five would be implemented in the spring semester. So far, she had a preliminary idea, a list of possible benefits, and a desire to be recognized as a changemaker.

"Thank you, Kenneth," she said in a sweet tone. "I'm glad you think it's a cute idea. But I fail to see how all English students couldn't benefit from an experience like this. Contrary to your beliefs, many of our students *do* go on to a Library Science graduate program, this kind of experience could be a tremendous help."

If she were proposing something as exciting as rock wall in the rec center or ice-cream Thursdays in the quad, she wouldn't have to plead her case to Kenneth. But since her idea actually involved educational development, she was stuck climbing the chain of command. Victoria knew that bringing her case to the Curriculum and Policy Committee would be rough with her boss acting as their chair. He would lead the small group for an entire academic year, so his approval would be necessary. The other professors, who presided over curriculum business, deferred most decisions to him in hopes of ending the meeting earlier. Her peers sat at a large round table in one of the meeting rooms of Stevenson Hall, some watching the clock tick away the seconds. If the shape of the table was supposed to be a metaphor for an equal division of power, it was a laughable attempt with Williams acting as their leader. Democracy was not his style.

Kenneth shifted in his seat and looked to the others for help. He wore the smug grin she was used to, but he appeared to be running out of viable excuses. "An M.A. in Library Science is hardly what our department wants to be known for. Those are the students who couldn't hack it in literature."

The focus of their department *was* literature, but times were changing. Technical writing, journalism, and education needed to muscle their way into the discourse if students had a fighting chance to succeed with a degree in English. While Kenneth and Victoria had been lucky to earn doctorates in Literature Studies *and* score jobs, their students would have a struggling economy to contend with. Before she could open her mouth to object, Sydney Spellman, from the Biology department, jumped in. "Kenneth, I wouldn't be so harsh on the students who aren't following your literary path."

He shrugged. "I just think that in this climate, we should be wary of spreading our already thin resources on a graduate program that we don't even have."

"Now that's an idea," said Marcus Pierce, from Social Work. "We could start a Library Sciences program. I heard online enrollment can be pretty decent. Plus, there's a new trend of social workers helping people within local library systems..." He wrote the idea down in a notepad. Victoria snuck a covert glance at his notes. *4 Week Ideas.*

Apparently, Victoria had misread the room. She was convinced that no one would aid in talking Williams down. Apparently, Kenneth's small-scale megalomania rubbed people the wrong way, even outside their department. She sprung on the chance for a possible mutiny. "That's certainly a possibility, Marcus. At the very least, we can send students to Farmingdale Public Library to help patrons with job applications, resumés, or adult learning."

Marcus nodded and continued writing notes. "Exactly."

Williams peered at her with narrowed eyes. "Don't get ahead of yourself, Ms. Reese."

"I don't believe the university is opposed to expanding programs to accommodate increased enrollment," Victoria said.

"But before we create make-believe programs out of thin air, let's consider how this internship benefits some faculty members over others. Kiddie Lit will see an increase of warm bodies in their classes."

"Just three quick things, Kenneth." She fought to keep her voice calm. "First, it's called *Children's Literature*. Second, the *warm bodies* you're talking about are our students. They need a fighting chance to find employment in their struggling fields. Lastly, any additional opportunities to the department are a benefit to *all* faculty."

"If I can't get institutional support for a Globe Theater trip from that stingy new president, I don't know how she can support all of these new ideas. Sure, back in the day, Bob would have signed off on anything, but we're not there anymore."

Victoria sighed and buried her head in her hands. Didn't he understand that the school was currently in a pickle *because* the former president, Bob Sheldon, had signed off on everything? "Kenneth, you're completely missing the point. A pilgrimage to England would have been a financial burden to the handful of students who could sign up. This"—she pointed to her proposal— "wouldn't cost them anything. In fact, it's practical work experience that will prepare them for the future."

"I'm sorry that I'm not concerned enough about *practical work experience*, as you put it," Williams said in an irritated voice. "I'm more concerned about programs dragging the prestige of Pembroke University to the level of a...community college, Ms. Reese."

Victoria sat stiffly in her chair. There it was: classism at its finest. These were the obtuse situations she spent so much time preparing herself for; old men who demanded she justify her existence in their hallowed institutions. "You've called me Ms. Reese three times so far," she said through a clenched jaw. "I shouldn't have to remind you that I have the same qualifications as you do, but here we are. It's Dr. Reese or Victoria."

The silence that settled over the room was thick. Only a nervous cough from Marcus broke the tension long enough for Williams to give a thin-lipped smile. "I didn't think pedigree was important to anyone in this room. We're all professionals, *Victoria.*"

Victoria was livid. "It would be nice if you showed that professionalism towards your scholarly peer."

"Yes, well, the committee will get to your business when the time comes. In the meantime, we've got more pressing issues to address."

She ignored him and directed her attention to the rest of the committee. "Who among you has a question regarding my proposal? You will see that it benefits the university with no additional cost to the students or our budget, and it will strengthen community ties. If students can give their time to the public library, it will cover their service hours and prepare them for future careers in literacy.

"You never know if one of these students decides to further their education in Social Work, Political Science, or even Biology. These subjects are not mutually exclusive, right? Pembroke insists on teaching students about interdisciplinary studies; why not start with the library?"

When she finished, they looked from her to the proposal she gave them. "I really don't see what the problem is," Sydney said. "I show up to these committee meetings every week and deal with more complexities in brand new courses. This is pretty simple."

Victoria gave her a small smile before turning to Marcus. "What do you think?"

Marcus shrugged. "I agree with Sydney. There's nothing controversial about letting kids work at a library."

"We can't approve anything without Linda from History," Williams said in a flat voice. "It's not fair to her."

Victoria tried to hide her grin as she pulled an email from her folder. "I've already reached out to her. She's interested."

Williams took the email and pulled out his reading glasses to glance through it. "Even if we give the go-ahead, that doesn't mean that the provost will approve it."

He was losing ground and it was making him uncomfortable. Victoria knew quiet desperation when she saw it. "I'm well aware of the process, Kenneth. But I'm planning a meeting with both the provost and President regarding the Four-Week Initiative."

Williams removed his glasses and gave Victoria a cold stare. "I move that we table this issue and come back to it next time we meet."

"And when is that?"

"In two weeks, I believe."

By that time, twenty people would have beaten her to the punch and the school would be stuck with some frivolous initiative like a new dodgeball team. Victoria gathered her emotions and stuffed them deep down in the pit of anger she seldom released. "What's to stop you from signing off on it now?" she asked, clenching her fists under the table.

"One of us, I'll decide who, will have to research current internships and analyze their learning objectives. If you've done your job properly, your goals should fall within the guidelines. Once that stage is complete, we can push it to the provost's desk. If he finds it useful,

I'm sure he'll turn it over to President Kowalski." Williams paused. "I'm afraid we must follow proper procedure and protocol."

Victoria did what she was good at; she held her tongue. The mask that she was accustomed to wearing settled over her face, covering any emotions that could betray her. Later, she could deal with those feelings, but in this moment, she would pretend Kenneth Williams didn't hurt her by stomping all over her ideas. "Well, that sounds like a deal," she said with a bright smile. "Thank you all for letting me sit in on this meeting. I'll follow up with you soon."

Williams gave her a placid smile. "Or we'll follow up you."

She swallowed. "A reminder couldn't hurt. I'll follow up." Victoria stood up and took her leave before he could lob her another insult, before she could lose her temper. Once she closed the door behind her, she leaned against the outside wall.

Williams's faint voice drifted through the door. "I don't know why she's in such a hurry…"

Victoria made it back to the safety of her office before she broke down in quiet tears. Williams humiliated her for sport. He must of have sensed some hesitance in her voice and he jumped on her weakness. She retraced her memory for something, anything that could have tipped him off. She arrived to their meeting with a pleasant smile, she was perfectly groomed, and spoke like a professional…

She had played the game and it hadn't worked.

Williams had cut her down and succeeded in making her ideas feel small. She'd been knocked off course even before meeting with the Farmingdale Public Library. Victoria now had to wait two weeks for the committee's approval, which cut into the Four-Week Initiative. As anger replaced her sadness, she began to plot her next approach. She would need to show up with something better than a mock-up proposal. She'd better have the whole darn thing—long-term effects, projected costs, and exact learning goals that paired with the library's job description. Victoria dried her face and began furiously scribbling on color-coded sticky notes. She would show Kenneth.

When her phone rang, she considered not answering it. What was the point of having her own office if she couldn't plot her revenge in peace? She wanted to be left alone. After digging into her jacket pocket for her phone, she saw that she wouldn't have that opportunity. Her weekly phone call with Katherine Reese was about to happen and Victoria was not prepared.

Dang it.

She sat up in her chair, as if her mother would hear the slouch in her shoulders. "Ma'am," she said.

Skipping the pleasantries, Katherine got to the point. "I'm throwing a gala!"

G.D. it.

Her mother's excitement only meant extra work for her. A gala, as she liked to call them, was simply a retirement ball for another aging Marine in their social circle. Even after Victoria's father had retired from military service, Katherine still managed to maintain her busy schedule with Chicago's chapter of Marine Wives. Whether it was brunch or community service events or retirement ceremonies, her mother was there with her battalion of ladies, armed with sheet cake and balloons.

Victoria would normally get on a train and make an appearance, but it was October: the busiest part of fall semester outside of finals week. She had midterms to plan, committee meetings to crash, and initiatives to shove down Kenneth Williams's throat. "I wonder if I could skip that," she asked, toying around with the loose corner of her desk calendar. Most of its squares were being steadily filled with tasks and reminders that had nothing to do with military galas.

"You want to skip it?" Katherine asked in a familiar key of aghast and hurt. "Why on earth would you do that?"

"Because I don't think I'll have time, ma'am."

Her mother sighed. "I don't have time is an excuse for the lazy. Only when we die, do we no longer have time. What have I told you about keeping a decent schedule? You're not going to get where you need to go—"

"—without a good plan," Victoria finished. Her mother's mantra was a response to everything that went wrong in Victoria's life. Lost your scarf? Forgot to replace the milk? Didn't make the Dean's List? *You should have had a plan, Victoria.* "I know. I just don't think I can squeeze it in at the moment."

"What's there to squeeze in?" her mother asked. "All you need to do is get on a train and in two hours you're here. If you're still having trouble prioritizing your tasks, you need to admit it."

Victoria swallowed. "Why do you need me to be there?"

Katherine's tone softened. "Your father and I haven't seen you in several months. Jeffrey Robbins is finally retiring; he's like an uncle to you. It would mean so much to him and Janet if you came to support him." Her mother paused. "Of course, we'd love to see you as well."

Victoria nibbled on her thumbnail as she listened to her mother scrape together an excuse for a party. It was nice to be needed by her parents, but she knew that Katherine would be hell on wheels during a large event. Her mother loved her, but when it came to planning parties, her critical nature stole the limelight. She would inevitably find something wrong with the way Victoria held a fork, stood without an invisible stack of books on her head, or how much skin she showed. "Is this black tie?"

Katherine laughed. "Of course it is, silly. Mark your calendar for October 25th, 18:00, at the Drake Hotel."

Victoria rolled her eyes as she wrote the word *gala* on her desk calendar. "And what comes after the reception? Will there be another thing?"

"We're having brunch the next day, dear."

Of course there was brunch. Uncle Jeffrey wouldn't get off that easily. He and his wife would sit with her family to trot out memories of the old days while Victoria kept her elbows off the table. "So, we're talking one night?"

"One night wouldn't kill you, Victoria. Honestly, you act like teaching is the end-all, be-all of your existence. Just don't assign the children homework over the weekend and you'll be fine."

After all these years, she had the idea that Victoria was a grade school marm. "I don't just teach, ma'am," she said. "I wish it was just teaching."

Katherine breezed past her point. "Well, you can put it on hold for a little while."

"I'm glad you think so."

"And while you're here, I'm going to introduce you to Linda's boy," her mother said in an excited voice.

"Who's Linda?"

"You've met Linda; she's another officer's wife. Her son, Matthew, is a lawyer at some firm or another, here in the city."

Victoria frowned. "Are you trying to set me up on a date?"

"If we're lucky!" Katherine said. "His divorce just cleared."

"I'm not interested," she said, dropping her head to the desk's surface.

"Don't say what you're not interested in until you've got all the answers, Victoria," Katherine scolded. "If you want to talk about not having time, you'd better start with your ovaries, little lady. Thirty-four and single is the epitome of running out of time."

She was going to get all of the greatest hits on this phone call. Katherine's favorite being unwed and child-less. "Mother…"

"Your gradebook isn't going to keep you warm at night."

"I will come to Chicago on one huge condition: Please do not pawn me off on a divorced lawyer."

"Well it's not as if you've got someone to bring. I don't want you to be the lonesome single woman, all pitiful and bookish."

"I'm sure it would reflect poorly on you," Victoria said.

"You know what I meant. Like I said, you don't have anyone to bring, do you?"

Nope, unwed and childless Victoria Reese didn't have

a date. "Whether I do or not, you can't meddle in my life like that," she said in a tired voice.

"What you call meddling, I call concerned and attentive," Katherine said. "Matthew will be there and I'd like you to at least speak to him, like a lady."

Like a lady...

"I'll be there, but I'm not promising anything." It was the best response to get her mother off the phone. Flat-out nos were not allowed in their relationship. If she let her mother believe there was a small chance of controlling the situation, they were better off for it.

"Excellent."

She could hear her mother's grin. "I'll see you on Friday night," Victoria said.

"Arrive early at the house and we'll all go to The Drake together."

"Sure." When she hung up, Victoria was exhausted.

Chapter Two

It had been a full twenty-four hours since John Donovan had to trade in his title of "Fun Uncle Johnny" for
the role of full-time father figure to his niece, Becca.
And it wasn't going well. After an awkwardly silent
dinner of Chinese takeout, the twelve-year-old had retired to her bedroom, leaving John to watch television
by himself. As he lounged on the couch, he tried to decide if he should call Becca's mother for advice or talk
to Becca himself. After a sixteen hour flight, his sister,
Jessi, would most likely be exhausted. If he tried his
hand at talking to Becca, he might come away learning
very little about what bothered her. He could only assume that her mother leaving for a work trip was only
part of it. The other part was that communication with
her father went quiet soon after Jessi filed for a divorce.

Unbeknownst to Becca, all hell had broken out several months ago when Jessi had discovered Allen's infi-
delities...*plural*. When John found out, he hadn't reacted
with the most tact, but he did feel that a swift punch to
the jaw was justified. He didn't know where Becca's father was at the moment, but he knew the man wasn't in
a hurry to visit his daughter. Not while she stayed with
John. Not all of the details were explained to Becca:

not the secretary or the young recording star that Allen was an agent for, nor the punch John landed at a church cookout. All she knew was that her parents were divorcing and her mother was making efforts to advance her career by traveling to Sweden for two months. Becca wasn't happy about that either.

So John had to decide what to do. Talk to the girl or talk to his stepsister.

Indecision was a common problem for him. When too many things were on his plate, he became anxious and ultimately did nothing. The thought of acting swirled and tangled with the other responsibilities he was charged with. Talk to Becca, talk to Jessi, finish the budget reports for the library, schedule reading groups for the children's department, follow up with the local university regarding some student internship thing... The more he thought about the list, the tighter his chest became. A workout was what he needed. If his niece wasn't in the guestroom, he would have put on his sneakers and gone to the gym. A couple rounds on the heavy bag and he would have been able to focus his mind on a solution.

"Uncle Johnny?" said a small voice from behind him.

He twisted around to find Becca in her pajamas and satin bonnet. Her face, a mirror image of her mother's, was tired and pinched with anxiety. "Hey honey, what's up?"

She stood there, wringing her hands at the waist, before circling the couch and asking, "Can I use your phone?"

"Sure," he said, pulling his phone from his back pocket. "But you might want to give your mom another hour. I think her plane just landed."

"I'm not calling her," Becca said in a solemn voice. "I want to call my dad."

John hesitated before handing the phone over. "Yeah?"

"He's not answering," she said. "I thought that if I could use your phone…"

Jessi had made it clear to him that he was not to speak ill of Allen, but John was finding it difficult to stay mum when the man couldn't even make an effort. He couldn't deny Becca, he would have to let her find out for herself. "Here," he said.

She dialed, and they waited through each ring, until finally, Allen's voicemail indicated he would not be taking calls that evening. John let out a breath and silently cursed his brother-in-law. A simple "hey, honey, I can't talk right now, but can I call you back later?" would have worked. To say she looked defeated was an understatement. Her brown eyes watered, but in the same stubbornness she shared with her mother, she did not cry. "He's busy," she said with more diplomacy than was necessary.

"Call your mom."

"But you said—"

"I know, but you need to talk to her," John said softly.

Becca tried again and successfully reached her mother in three rings. The phone's screen lit up with Jessi's beaming face. "Is that my little pumpkin?" she asked loudly.

His niece's tears receded as a smile spread across her face. "Hi, Mom, are you in Sweden yet?"

"Just got to my hotel, baby," Jessi said. "I've already bought you a flag, a soccer jersey, and a Viking helmet. Is Uncle Johnny there?"

"I'm here."

"Johnny, I got you a bottle of elderflower schnapps."

He pulled a disgusted face at Becca, who smirked. "Thanks, sis."

"How are you doing, kiddo?"

"I'm okay," she said. John waited for her to mention her father, but Becca continued down a different road. "I just wanted to say hi before I go to bed."

"Well, *hej*, honey. That's how they say hello here," Jessi said. John could hear something was off in his sister's voice. It sounded strained and overly cheery.

Becca gave a tense smile. "Okay, I love you, Mom."

"I love you too, pumpkin. Sleep well."

John motioned for her to give him the phone. "Let me talk to your mom," he said, moving from the couch. He gave her a hug and watched her slouch off to her room before he turned his attention to his sister.

Jessi's smile dropped. "Oh god, is she okay?" she asked in a lower voice.

He carried the phone upstairs to his bedroom for more privacy. "She's still trying to adjust," he admitted. "But I'm also concerned about how my step-twin is doing."

When John's parents divorced and his father remarried Jessi's mother, he had made an effort to get to know the bookworm in his AP Bio class. Sure, it was awkward at first—*hey, my dad is your dad now*—but they quickly became the best of friends. Jessi's expressive face was often easy to read, and John had trained himself to interpret every crease of her brow, every clenched jaw. She was exhausted and stressed.

"I'm fine," she said with a tremulous smile.

"You lie."

Jessi shrugged her shoulders. "You caught me. I'm just worried about Becca."

"She'll be fine," John said in a firm voice. "I've been taking her to school and feeding her."

"Yes, I know you're doing all of that. Thank you for watching her while I'm gone. It's just…" She pursed her lips and frowned. "I hated leaving her, that's all. I've never taken a work trip like this, but it felt like an opportunity I couldn't pass up."

She was right; she couldn't pass up this opportunity. After Allen had moved out of the house, Jessi set out to write a grant for an international trip. She had wanted to advance her career as a civil engineer, and make improvements to Farmingdale by studying city planning in Scandinavia. John had encouraged her to take the plunge and he would hold down the fort on his end.

"I'm glad I'm doing it," she continued. "But I worry I left Becca in a lurch."

"You have a job to do. And Becca's not without a group of people to love her while you're gone. She's got me, and our moms when I eventually fuck up. Her grandmother is really good at first aid…"

His stepsister laughed. "Which grandmother? Your mother passes out at the sight of blood."

"The point is, Becca belongs to the Donovan clan. We've got her back."

"Speaking of people having her back…any word from Allen?"

He shook his head. "She's been trying to call him."

Jessi rolled her eyes upward and heaved a sigh. "I wish he could just give a damn."

"Any idea where he's at?"

"In LA maybe? That's where the divorce papers were being forwarded."

"When do you think you're going to have a talk with

her about her father? Don't you think it's time she knows the full story?"

"The full story? How explicit should I get with a twelve-year-old who still thinks her father is a hero?" she asked. "Where would I even start?"

As "Fun Uncle Johnny," he didn't know the answer to that question. His job was to be a goofball, but Becca didn't seem all that receptive to his usual shenanigans. "I can't say, but it's going to get harder and harder to explain his silence. I know she has questions, Jess. It's not going to take her long to start asking them."

"I know, I know," his stepsister said, rubbing her temple. "I'm fairly new to this too."

They sat on the line in silence before John took a deep breath. "It's okay. I'll continue to treat the subject with kid gloves."

"I'd appreciate it," she said with a nod. "Let's change subjects okay?"

"Yeah," he said with a half smile. "I've got a long list of shit to do and I'm not doing any of it."

"Perfect," she said. "Have you written the list down?"

"Nope."

"Is there something you can work on tonight?"

John chuckled. This is what his stepsister lived for. When John's ADD made it difficult to concentrate, she always had helpful suggestions to jump-start his brain. "The library director passed a university project to me. Some internship I didn't finish reading about."

"Okay, so let's finish reading the email first."

"I think I can do that," John said with another laugh. "Sometimes it feels like you're patronizing me."

"I never want it to sound like that, Johnny. I just know that it's difficult for you to focus on more than one thing at a time. Especially if you're stressed out. Just finish reading the email and then you can start some really broad research, nothing too in-depth."

"It's just the fall rush. There are more children's activities to plan and Halloween is coming up. Plus, the budget numbers are due—"

"One thing at a time," Jessi reminded him. "Right now, you read the email."

"Right. Well, maybe I should let you go so I can do that."

"I love you, bro. Good luck with my little pumpkin."

"Love you too. Stay safe."

When he hung up, he plopped onto his back and took a deep breath. Without realizing it, he had marked at least one thing off his list: Talk to Jessi. He was still unsure how to deal with the Allen/Becca problem, but he'd do his best to stay the current course. Staying mum until his sister could deal with it. For now, John would take her advice and read the message from his director.

He pulled it up on his phone and reviewed it. Pembroke English department, internship, Dr. Victoria Reese, forming valuable community ties, etc. Director Wegman had already expressed his interest, which meant John *had* to investigate. He wasn't the head of the Children's Department for nothing. He would just add this task to his already full plate.

Chapter Three

Subject: Collaboration with Pembroke University's English Department

Victoria,
I look forward to meeting w/ you re: internship. Might be a bit late. Btw, looks like you got an overdue book w/ massive fines...
For the Duke's Convenience?
We might need to discuss ;)
Cheers,
John

Even as her face burned with embarrassment, Victoria managed to read the email twice before staring out the window of her office. Three p.m. on Pembroke's campus was cloudy with a stiff wind blowing the scarves and jackets of students who hurried to their next class. The beginning of October was colder than folks had anticipated, since Illinois had experienced a scorching summer. But Farmingdale was dealing with a cold snap that forced Pembroke University students to change out their flip-flops for UGG boots. The chill that burrowed its way into Victoria's meager office was replaced with

a furnace in her chest. She glanced back at the email
and read it once more. Her eyes settled on the book title
and narrowed.

For the Duke's Convenience.

"I returned that," she whispered to her computer
screen. As she calculated the length of time it had been
since her last visit to the Farmingdale library, she clicked
on their website. Her account was flagged with a fine.
Victoria's eyes went round. $27.10. "Jesus, effin' Christ."

Perspiration prickled her scalp and under her arms
while she searched for answers. The account information didn't tell her much, but the amount was alarming
enough. She clicked back to John Donovan's email and
tried to read his tone. Joking, laid-back, and late. He
would be tardy to their first meeting, which was just
as annoying as the overdue book comment. Her time
was precious and getting more scarce by the day. After
their meeting, she had to gather the graduate students
for an emergency meeting regarding the writing center.
Later that evening, she'd have to start on the first wave
of grading. She'd made the mistake of assigning papers
to two classes only two days apart. On top of all that,
she'd stolen a library book.

Victoria needed some air.

She gathered herself and shook out her arms in a
desperate attempt to cool her armpits. A dull headache
joined the itchy sensation of her too-tight braids. She resisted the urge to scratch, since she'd only gotten them
done yesterday and still wanted them to have that fresh
look. Oh, but she could have used an ibuprofen. Victoria swung her glossy black braids, some decorated
with cowrie shells and gold cuffs, behind her shoulder
and smoothed down her skirt before leaving her office.

In the hallway, she glanced at the open doors and spotted Paula's office. Paula Michaels was an adjunct who shared workspace with two other part-time lecturers. When she wasn't lesson planning, the rest of her time was spent writing romance novels that made women flush and swoon. Victoria admired her friend's passion to create and grade papers at the same time. She peeked in Paula's work station and saw her friend with her feet on her desk, balancing a pencil between her lip and nose.

"Workin' hard or hardly workin'?" Victoria asked, wiggling her eyebrows.

Paula glanced up, letting the pencil fall from her face. "A bit of both," she said with a grin.

Paula was alone with a small measure of privacy, so Victoria invited herself in and sat at her desk. "What are you working hard on and what are you slacking on?"

Her friend put her sneakered feet on the floor and straightened up in her chair. After she stuck the pencil in her short afro, she swung her computer monitor around to face Victoria. "Read that," she said, pointing a bubblegum-pink fingernail at the screen.

Victoria squinted and leaned forward. "Billy yanked her panties down her thighs…"

"To yourself," Paula said.

"Is this your new book?"

"Hm-hmm."

Victoria skimmed the page before resting her chin on her knuckles. "Mmh."

"Is that a good 'mmh' or a bad 'mmh'?"

"Do you have to say the p-word so much?"

Paula let out an exaggerated sigh and rolled her eyes.

"My readers love the p-word. What else am I going to call it?"

Victoria shrugged her shoulders, her hair ornaments clattering. "I don't know," she said. "The books I read have more subtle words like mound and womanhood."

"Too much hedging. A lot of women like to get straight to the point, girl. If I labored over the millions of different ways to say pussy, I wouldn't have time to write what Billy does to it." She pointed to the second page, forcing Victoria to continue reading.

Victoria raised a brow as her face burned. "Jeez, Paula. Do guys even do that?"

Paula raised her own brow in response. "Ooh, baby, what is you doing?"

"Not that," she said, nodding to the screen. Although, Victoria did have to do some mental calculation to re-member the last time any man had shared her bed. Thirty-three and now thirty-four were particularly dry years since her break up with Kevin. Not that he did any-thing mind-blowing when they did share a bed. Lights off, missionary, and quick was Kevin's style. His brand of lovemaking wasn't even long enough for her to think of a theme for the next day's lecture.

"Well we need to fix that," Paula said, turning the monitor back. "Any prospects?"

"You sound like my mom."

"Don't tell me that," her friend said with a barking laugh. "Your mom is a piece of work and I don't want to be associated with her."

Victoria debated whether to tell Paula about the strange email she received from John Donovan. Since Paula signed on for the fall semester, it had been easier to face the stressful culture of Pembroke University.

Victoria didn't have very many people to talk to in the English department even though she'd worked there for four years. But because of the exclusive air of the private institution, a fear of judgement made it difficult to share one's ideas or problems with equally competitive professors. But this was Paula, her former graduate school buddy and the third member of The Write Bitches Gang. Their other member, Regina Crawford, refused higher education for a life in finance. If there was anyone on Pembroke's campus she could trust, it was her girl. "Can I talk to you about administration?" Victoria asked, casting a nervous glance over her shoulder.

Paula typed something before pressing backspace several times. "Girl, yes. Who's being messy today?"

"Did you get a chance to go to that all-campus meeting last Thursday?"

"Adjuncts don't have to go," her friend said with a smile.

Victoria nodded. "Right. So the new president corralled us in an auditorium like Stalin would and told us that the university is basically broke."

Paula looked up from her work. "What?"

"The last president had been playing the stocks with university money and he lost big," Victoria said in a low voice.

"Did they tell you this?" Paula asked. She folded her arms over her ample bosom, obscuring the Free Angela graphic on her T-shirt with her brown arms.

"They didn't have to," Victoria said with a sigh. "We all knew they had a ton of investments. But that's not quite the problem. President Kowalski wants faculty and staff to make up the enrollment numbers. I mean, they're already increasing tuition for next year, but we need to put our heads down and push for higher numbers."

Paula frowned. "How?"

"Well, I'll say this about the president, she's business savvy—"

"Is she?"

"—she's starting a new open-door policy that might work," Victoria finished.

Her friend remained unimpressed. "Open-door policies are bullshit."

"Be that as it may, the Four-Week Initiative might work. Kowalski is giving us four weeks to come up with innovative programs to attract incoming freshmen. They have to be low-cost of course, but also something that generates excitement."

Paula fixed her mouth and sighed. "What have you come up with, Vicki?"

Victoria grew excited. "Okay, so I'm thinking of a library internship for the English department students. We'll partner with the Farmingdale Public Library to give students a real-world learning experience that can carry over to graduate school or outside of academia. What do you think?"

There was a pregnant pause that made her tense. When Paula finally spoke, she gave her a pitying smile. "Girl, I think that's a great idea. A library internship is going to help give students a leg up in any discipline they choose."

Eyeing her smile, Victoria leaned forward. "But?"

Paula's shoulders slumped. "But I worry that you think you always have to save someone. It's like graduate school all over again. Reggi and I had to talk you off a ledge every time you piled too much on your plate.

Hearts on Hold

The president's problems aren't your problems and you don't have to work yourself into a lather over mismanaged funds."

Victoria frowned. "I'm not working myself into a lather."

"You don't see it until your elaborate plans are near the end. Afterward, you tell us that you'll never work that hard on bullshit projects. This is not your problem."

She shook her head. "That's where you're wrong, Paula. Pembroke's problems *are* my problems. I chose this path because I wanted to teach and research. If my school goes under, how am I supposed to do either?"

"I get it, girl. I have the luxury of not needing this job, so I take it for granted. But you're going to work yourself into an early grave if you keep this up. Being the mule that Zora wrote about is not sustainable."

Victoria swallowed. Whenever Paula made literary references during debates, she meant business. Throwing Zora Neale Hurston into the conversation made her both irritated and hesitant to defend her school. Sure, Victoria liked pulling her weight, sometimes even a couple extra pounds, if it meant tasks got done and boxes got checked. But if history was any indication of how this project would turn out, she might want to pace herself. "I hear you loud and clear," she said. "But I'm going to try my best anyway."

Paula reached out and took her hand. "And that's what I love about you," she said in a softer tone. "Your work ethic is something I'd like to bottle up and take twice daily. But I just wish you'd rest."

Victoria squeezed her friend's hand. "I'll rest when I reach my goals," she said with a chuckle.

"Bitch, please. That sounds like Katherine talking."

Victoria pulled away. "We'll see if any of this actually gets off the ground. Today, I'm supposed to have a meeting with a librarian and he's already going to be late. I don't know how that can bode well."

"Aww, he's probably an elderly dude who's just trying to make his way across town," her friend said with a grin.

Victoria didn't get the sense that John Donovan was a doddering old man. The tone of his email suggested that he might be closer to her age. Originally, she addressed her email to the library's aging director, Howard Wegman. She was surprised that it was Donovan who replied to her. He was terribly informal and familiar with his message, making her nervous. *What if he doesn't take the project seriously? What if he is incompetent?* "He also informed me of an overdue library book," she said.

"Stealing books, are we?"

"No, I definitely returned it," Victoria said absently. She wondered what she had been doing several months ago that would warrant a missing book. "I just find it weird that he would put that in an email regarding our meeting today."

"Did he sound mad?"

"No," Victoria said slowly. "He wrote it with a wink face emoticon."

"Hmm."

"Is that a good 'hmm' or a bad 'hmm'?" Victoria asked.

Paula shrugged. "Depends on what the book was."

She sighed and averted her gaze. "*For the Duke's Convenience.*"

Paula burst into laughter. "Goddamn, Vicki…"

"I definitely returned it."

Her laughter had not yet abated as she wiped tears from her eyes. "Oh my god... You are still reading the historical stuff? That's why the p-word is foreign to your virgin ears!"

"It's titillating without the vulgarity."

Paula doubled over. "Oh man, I needed that," she said, taking a breath. "It feels so good to laugh."

"You're welcome," Victoria said in a dry voice.

"Girl, you were always averse to 'vulgarity,' as you like to call it. I'd hate to think that the prim, rule-abiding girl inside you doesn't want to get her back broke with some great dick. Also, did it ever occur to you that John Donovan might be flirting with you?"

Victoria frowned. The idea had *not* occurred to her. Paula was just thinking with her romance writer's brain. To her, there was always something sexy just around the corner. "That's not professional at all."

"People get by all the time without being professional. How do you think I got here?"

Victoria sat back in her chair. Comparatively, the two friends had always stood on opposite sides of what one would deem "professional." Paula and her cute afro, jeans, and sneakers attracted others with her charm and humor. Things seemed to come easy to the one member of The Write Bitches who always remained herself. Even through grad school. Regina and Victoria had stayed in line, choosing fields that required giving up a piece of their personality. Reggi had gone for a career in banking, even though she was an editor for the university newspaper, while Victoria was aiming to make it in academia. Her four years at Pembroke had been devoted to making tenure and she was determined to fight tooth and nail for it. "I'm not here for that, Paula," she said. "I plan to stay the course. I've got an outline and everything."

Paula gave her a knowing smile. "She's got an outline and everything… Baby, it might be time to let your hair down."

"My hair is fine right where it is."

"True," Paula said, narrowing her eyes. "Did Reggi do those braids? Because they look hella cute."

Victoria rolled her eyes. Her head was still aching. "Forty dollars and you have to bring the bundles."

"Okay, that's what's up."

She smiled. No matter how she disagreed with her friends, they could always switch it up and make light of most situations. "I'm going to wait for Donovan in my office. I'll talk to you later?"

"Sure," Paula said, returning to her screen. "Let me know if I need to bail you out of book jail."

Chapter Four

"You're late."

It was the greeting John expected, but when he looked into his young niece's eyes, he saw a glimpse of her mother's wrath. The twelve-year-old wasn't having it today and John was going to get an earful about it. "You don't know the half of it," he said.

Becca stood on the school's sidewalk, not making any moves to get into his truck. Her large brown eyes narrowed to slits as her pointed chin jutted at him. "Mom is never late."

John leaned against his steering wheel and sighed. "I know, honey. Your mom is incredibly responsible and I'm just a substitute until she gets back. But if you don't get in the truck, I'm going to be late for the next thing. And so on and so forth."

His lateness was actually starting to spiral. He woke up late that morning, knowing that it was his day off, but forgetting that his niece was living with him. Apparently little girls needed to go to school. They'd been late to school, he was late picking her up, and now he was going to be late getting to the university.

Their stalemate was interrupted by a school administrator who had been waiting off to the side. The older woman approached his vehicle with a disapproving glare, looking from Becca to John, and back to Becca. "Hello? What's going on here?" the she asked. Her voice was reedy and filled with judgement.

"Just trying to grab this little one," John said with a friendly wave.

Nope. That came out wrong.

Behind thick glasses, her magnified blue eyes widened. She clutched a walkie-talkie, threatening to call for backup. "Excuse me?"

John glanced at Becca, who was thoroughly enjoying herself. "Becca, please tell the nice lady that I'm here to get you."

His niece smirked.

"Sir, do you have clearance to receive this child?"

John sighed again and retrieved his wallet. "Yes, ma'am. She's my niece, and her mother is in Europe. Becca will be my ward for two months." He reached across the passenger's side to hand the confused woman his driver's license.

He understood the woman's bewilderment. Becca's burnt sienna skin and curly afro puffs bore no resemblance to John's white skin and green eyes. He stared at his niece with a perturbed expression, silently willing her to speak. She rolled her eyes and let out a huff.

"Yeah," she finally said. "This is my uncle Johnny and he's late…as usual."

The school marm relaxed the grip on her walkie-talkie and took another sneaking glance at the two. Of course she had questions, but was too polite to voice them. "I see, well, Mr. Donovan… I encourage you to be mindful of the time in the future."

"I'll do my best, ma'am," John said, starting the en-

gine. The roar of his busted muffler filled the school
parking lot preventing anymore conversation.

Becca scooted past the administrator and climbed
into the pickup. As they rolled out of the parking lot
and on to Center Street, John glanced down at the girl
and scowled.

"You know better than to pull that," he said.

"How else will you learn to be on time?"

Oh, the mouth on this one... "Let's start over. Hey
kiddo, how was school today? What did you learn?"

Silence filled the cab as they stopped at a red light.
Then sniffles. A drag of a jacket sleeve across the nose.
John looked down again to see a quiet stream of tears
roll down Becca's cheeks.

Okay, so it was a bad day. John caved under the pressure of seeing his niece's tears. "What is it, honey?"

"Nothing," she muttered.

"No, not nothing. I've known enough women to understand what 'nothing' means. Now what's wrong?"

"I miss Mom," Becca snapped. "I hate school and
Dad won't talk to me."

John's stomach knotted from the girl's words. When
the light turned green, he pulled off, and thought about
how to stop these tears. He'd never taken up the father
title and only knew his niece as a fun time he could drop
off at the end of the day. Uncle Johnny got to toss children around and feed them candy until they got sick.
Sick kids eventually went home to their real parents.
Now he had to wander the minefield of twelve-year-old
girl emotions without help. One false step and boom.

"Honey, your mom—"

"Yeah, I get it," Becca said. "You don't have to explain it. Can't I just be mad?"

Boom.

They drew closer to the library and Uncle Johnny was running out of time to put a bandage on this situation. "Your mom didn't just up and leave you. She loves you and she loves helping others, yeah? Because women can what?"

Becca's dark watery eyes met his. "Because women can do anything."

John smiled. "That's right. She can love you and work at the same time. Now, your father is working though some things at the moment." This was harder to articulate, but he'd try to push through. "Divorce is difficult for moms and dads."

He got no response and wasn't surprised. If they were actually blood-related, John would say Becca got her ability to hold a grudge from him.

"Your dad…he's got a lot on his mind," he said. He knew that his attempt to save his brother-in-law was a lame one, but his sister wanted him to try. "He'll reach out when he's ready, but until then you have to continue being great."

John drove them to the entrance of the library parking lot and cut the engine. Becca clutched her backpack to her chest and stared out the window. "I guess."

He reached across the space and took her tear-stained face in his large hand, pulling her gaze towards him. "Hey, honey, you've got this," he said, wiping her cheek with his thumb. "I wouldn't lie to you."

Becca's face crumpled into a fresh sob. "I feel like everyone's lying to me."

The tightness in his chest was familiar. *Everyone's lying to me…* "It's a confusing time for you. I know what this feels like."

"Because of Granddad?"

John nodded. "My parents divorced when I was your age and Granddad found your nana and your mom. I was angry just like you are, but the anger goes away."

Eventually.

Becca took a deep breath and wiped her eyes on her jacket sleeve. "Okay."

"Your mom became my sister and that was the greatest gift I could have received. That is...until you came along."

This made her smile, which was a relief. "So it gets better?"

John undid his seatbelt and gathered her into his arms. "Of course, honey." When her arms wrapped around his torso, he knew he'd diffused the bomb for now. "It *does* get better."

She sniffed against his shirt. "Okay."

When John released her, he swiped his palm down her wet face and tweaked her button nose. "I'll pick you up this evening and we're going to talk about school."

A cloud settled over her face. "Okay," Becca said cautiously.

"I'll be back in a couple of hours. Check in with the front desk and do your homework in my office."

She opened the door and hopped out of the cab. "Fine."

"Do it, Becca."

She slammed the door. "Fine!"

John would settle for her attitude, for now, if it meant he could take a break from her. He watched her march into the library before starting the engine. His watch showed he was twenty minutes late. He hoped the rushed

email he sent Victoria Reese would give him some lee-
way, but he wasn't trying to push it.

After his sister directed him to read his email and do
some light research, John had focused up and scoured
the internet for any traces of the woman who was connected to Pembroke University and found nothing outside of her published articles and university profile page.
Immediately, he saw she was an assistant professor in the
English department and specialized in African American literature. John had inferred the rest based on her
profile photo. Her sharp cheekbones and pointed chin
were almost as sharp as her piercing brown eyes. They
stared down the camera with a defiance that intrigued
him. Her brown skin shined like bronze against photography lights, her full lips painted oxblood red. *Power
color.* Her photo, alone, told him to proceed with caution, but it also stirred something in him that few women
had managed in the past couple years. Sure, she was
beautiful, but her expressive eyes spoke volumes. John
could have been reaching, but he saw wit, fierceness,
and stubbornness…

Back on the streets of Farmingdale, he drove carefully around jay-walking college students as they ambled
towards the many eateries near the downtown area, or
found a loitering spot on the quad. He envied the kids
of Pembroke, many living charmed lives inside a private
university bubble, blissfully unaware of the real-world
challenges waiting for them. As he searched for Stevenson Hall, Victoria's building, he checked himself over
in his rearview mirror and lamented how casually he'd
dressed. When he was a teenager, destined for a life of
publicly-funded college, he recalled how unobtainable
Pembroke Girls had been. They hailed from wealthy

families and went home to the Chicago suburbs during summer break. Pembroke Girls never had time for the corn-fed boys of Downstate Illinois. And certainly not one like John, whose father worked at the Illinois Farm Bureau.

There was no telling if Victoria was a Pembroke Girl. She was a professor, after all, and John was no longer a teenager. He was a librarian now, and she was in need of his services. No matter what he wore, he was going to work with a woman who needed his expertise. With that in mind, he gave himself a firm nod in the mirror. John knew one thing about Professor Victoria Reese: she was in possession of an overdue library book.

For the Duke's Convenience.

He probably shouldn't have, but he added that humorous nugget of information in his email. Surely she could take a joke.

Chapter Five

Twenty-seven minutes late.

Victoria glanced at the clock sitting on her desk, while she outlined her library internship proposal. So far, it was a list of possible questions she had for John. So far, there were only two items on the list. Her concentration was elsewhere, but she still knew that her proposal had to be immaculate before she presented anything to the president. It would help if the man she was to work with arrived on time to start this process.

Twenty-eight minutes late.

She stopped typing to tap her fingernails against her desk. This was a poor start and a bad omen. Victoria didn't know how John Donovan ran things down at the Farmingdale Public Library, but here at Pembroke, things ran like clockwork. Emails were timely, meetings ran according to the Robert's Rules of Order, and people arrived to said meetings on time.

While she stewed in her righteous indignation, a knock at her door interrupted her thoughts. Victoria sat up straight in her chair, pulled at the lapels of her gray blazer, and smoothed her green silk blouse down. She took an extra step and ran her tongue over her teeth, rubbing at any red lipstick, and swung her braids over her shoulder. She didn't know why she was taking careful measures for a man who couldn't bother to arrive on time. "Come in," she called.

The man who walked in was unlike any children's librarian she'd ever met. Since the library website only offered his contact information and no photograph, Victoria couldn't have prepared for this moment.

Mr. Donovan was positively gorgeous.

He closed the door behind him and flashed her a bashful smile. The air was sucked from the room like someone had smashed open a port window in her space capsule. Oxygen was plummeting to critically low levels.

"Dr. Reese," he started. His voice matched his body: a masculine rumble from his chest, rough and hearty. From behind her desk, she tried to gauge his height and Victoria speculated he might tower over her by nearly a foot. *He's a G.D. Viking...*

Mr. Donovan dressed casually to this meeting. His faded denim button-down was slightly wrinkled and his sleeves were rolled to the elbow, revealing a brilliant assortment of colorful tattoos snaking down muscular forearms. His olive green pants hugged his trunk-like thighs and tapered at a pair of worn Timberland boots. He was a brunette with strands of blond streaked by the sun. Most of it was gathered in a bun at the back of his head, but some locks framed his face. Something about those locks bothered Victoria. She didn't know why her fingers itched to smooth them back or pulled the whole bun loose. Perhaps loose hair went better with the well-groomed beard that covered his angular jaw.

"My apologies for being tardy."

Victoria jumped from her seat and crossed the room. What drove her to be so quick with her greeting, she didn't quite know. A magnetism drew her to him, made her extend her hand, and look up at him in wonder. "Mr. Donovan."

His green eyes twinkled with humor as he took her hand in his. A calloused thumb swept over her fingers, sending a shiver up her arm. "It's nice to meet you," he said softly.

Victoria reluctantly pulled away and gestured to the chair before her desk. "Please, take a seat and let's get started." She was conscious of the way she moved as she made her way behind the large metal desk, back to the safety of her chair. She quieted the swing of her hips as she walked. She noticed he waited until she was seated before taking his own. He looked entirely too large for the chair used for guests and students. Really, he was too large for her small office. His energy flooded every square inch of the room, mingling with her own nervous energy. Yes, he was attractive, but it didn't have to rattle Victoria like it did. She was still a professional in the face of such blatant handsomeness.

Business first. Jesus, business only. She took a breath and gave him a polite smile. "Traffic delay?" Being passive aggressive was one of her many gifts. She got it from her mother. If she could keep a little haughtiness in her voice, perhaps the words wouldn't come out so shaky.

John shook his head. "Nope, pretty light out there."

He didn't sound like he was going to explain his tardiness. "Right."

"So you're Professor Reese…"

Victoria narrowed her eyes, focusing on his face and not his body. The tiny lines at the corners of his eyes became visible every time he smiled. His jaw quirking at an angle as his full lips pursed. He was trying to size her up. Pin her down. The very thought made Victoria squeeze her thighs together. "Were you expecting someone else?" she asked, immediately feeling defensive.

"No," he said. "I saw your picture earlier. Meeting you in person, though…you seem a bit younger than I expected."

She shifted in her chair. "I assure you, Mr. Donovan—"

"Johnny, please," he interrupted, with that same wry grin. "Mr. John Donovan was my father."

Victoria's mouth snapped shut before she could find her footing. "Forgive me, but I think formalities are good enough for now, *Mr. Donovan*."

His broad shoulders gave an easy shrug. "For now."

Victoria searched for something on her desk to occupy her idle hands. She discreetly grabbed an ink pen and tapped it against her desk calendar. "Right, well, I know this is short notice and I certainly appreciate you getting back to me. I'd like to talk about a possible partnership—"

"I'm listening."

"—between the Farmingdale Public Library and Pembroke University. As I said in my email, I think it would be an excellent opportunity to unite our two academic institutions."

"Sure," John said.

"I'm currently trying to convince my department chair that this program could work. Do you think the library director would be amendable to such a partnership?"

"It depends on what you're proposing," he said, the grin returning. His answers were too short for her to tell if he was serious or interested.

"I… I'm hoping that students of our department could benefit from learning about children's literacy by working with you." She was growing nervous, which was unusual. Meetings like these tended to work in her favor since she knew her audience. Working with academics was fairly easy; she knew their insecurities and ticks. Victoria didn't know this man. Her brain, usually alert, was slowly turning into mush as she stared at him.

He gave another shrug. "Sounds great to me. Let's do it."

She frowned. "Beg your pardon?"

"Let's do it."

No, no, that's not how it works. There was a certain amount of cajoling she had to do. There were charts and projections, cost benefits, and red-tape. So much red-tape. "But don't you have to—"

John dismissed her concerns with a wave of his hand. "I'm the head children's librarian and I'm supposed to come up with ideas to advance our department. Director Wegman is already happy to work with you."

"Oh." He may have been twenty-eight minutes late, but he certainly cut through forty-five minutes of negotiation. Victoria should have been happy that he'd hold up his end. Instead, she was deflated. It didn't feel like the battle she had prepped for. She was used to committee members who agonized over the wording of a single proposal, until time ran out and other business had to be tabled. "Are you certain?"

He absently swept a light brown lock of hair behind his ear. She caught a flash of his tattooed arm and squeezed her ink pen. A fire-breathing dragon melting a Dada clock. *Strange, but beautiful artwork.* "Yep. Leave it to me and we'll have you squared away."

"Okay," she breathed. "I guess we should plan something else then."

"What kind of food do you like?" he asked, leaning forward and resting his elbows on his thighs.

The sudden movement and the question startled her. "What?"

"What kind of food do you like?" he repeated. "If we plan any more, it should be over a meal. My treat."

Victoria frowned. "No, I think we can very easily discuss plans here or at the library."

John scoffed. "Oh come on, Dr. Reese. There *is* such a thing as a free sandwich."

No there isn't. "We're getting off topic."

"I tend to do that. If you don't hold me to task, I'll veer anywhere," he said with a wink.

He actually *winked*.

"How are you the head of an entire department?" Victoria said before thinking. "How old are you?"

He blinked. "Probably older than you."

Her face warmed at his candid words. "I ask because you have a very laid-back…" she trailed off and gestured to his overall appearance. "You seem like a man in his twenties."

John gave a nod of approval. "Thank you. You have no idea how flattering it is for a thirty-eight-year-old to hear that."

Victoria felt foolish.

He didn't seem bothered though. He shrugged that off as well. "I have a loose work ethic that hasn't done me wrong yet."

She shifted in her seat again. "Mr. Donovan, if you're not serious about this project…"

"Oh, don't mistake my laid-back demeanor for my

ability to produce results. I get things done on time," he said, "and the kids seem to like my methods."

Victoria cocked her head to the side, wondering if she heard him right. "That's fine and well, but I'm not a child, Mr. Donovan."

His green eyes traced a path down her body before they met her gaze head on. "No, Dr. Reese. You're not. I can tell I'm going to have to employ other methods on you."

Sweat pricked her scalp and the space between her breasts. He was playing with her. The subject of their meeting was waiting in the background while he batted her emotions around like a child jerking a balloon by the string. Victoria was losing the upper-hand in this discussion and was desperate to get it back.

Before she could reply, John loosened the grip he had on her emotions. He pulled back on the charm and replaced it with a small measure of professionalism. "Of course, we'll want to create a template or some guidelines regarding job skills and learning goals. I'll bet you can manage the latter while I come up with duties your students can perform."

Victoria nodded silently. Of course, she could manage it.

"And when would you like to present this to your superiors?" he asked.

"Um, I have four weeks, but I'd like to finish in three so I can polish the final draft." She circled a date on her desk calendar. "Let's aim for October 28."

"Excellent. Until then, I think it would be best if you shadow me at the library. We can start in the adult section learning the catalogue, shelving, and doing intake. When I feel like you're sufficient with that, we can move to the children's section and talk more about youth read-ing programs. I'd like you to get an idea of what your students have in store."

His suggestion was outrageous. "Wouldn't it be easier to put all of that in an email?"

"Easier, yeah. But wouldn't you rather be thorough when you advertise this to students and your bosses?"

Dang it. Victoria did like to be thorough. But the idea of shadowing him presented more challenges. If she re-acted like this upon meeting him for the first time, how could she expect to spend more time with him? She couldn't imagine what it might feel like to be stuck with him, between shelves, handling books. Him towering over her with his piercing gaze, while she tried to control her breathing. She may have been behaving foolishly in this moment, but she wasn't a *blind* fool. John Donovan was a beautiful man. "When do you suggest starting?"

"If we have three weeks, let's start tomorrow. Tuesday nights are my lighter shifts. The patrons start to filter out a little after 6 p.m. Like I said, we can start where you might be more comfortable—the adult section."

Victoria wasn't imagining his double meaning. Was she? "Okay."

"Great." He stood up, as if that was his cue to end the meeting. Another move that Victoria didn't appre-ciate. Surely there was something else to cover. "Oh, one more thing."

She relaxed slightly in her chair. "Yes?"

John crossed his arms over his barrel chest. "It might be in poor taste to become a temporary library worker with your...record."

"Excuse me?"

The merriment returned to his forest green eyes. "In

my email, I mentioned your overdue book. What was it? *For the Duke's Pleasure*?"

Victoria shot up from her chair. "*For the Duke's Convenience* and I definitely returned that book."

"I hear this often," John said. "Patrons sometimes lose books in the shuffle. Sometimes a book accidentally ends up on their shelves or tucked away in a stack by their beds. It happens."

Victoria's fists clenched in embarrassment at his accusation. "Mr. Donovan, I can assure you the book is on one of your shelves."

"I can do another sweep—"

"I suggest you try that," she said, rounding her desk, heading straight for the door.

"—but you should know that your balance is outstanding."

She paused at her door, hand resting on the knob. "Outstanding by how much?" Even after checking her library account, she decided to lie in favor of plausible deniability. She turned to see him saunter towards her. John's steady approach set her already frayed nerves on edge. He didn't stop until he was toe to toe with her. Victoria stood between him and the door, struggling for air that wasn't clouded by the pleasant scent of his aftershave. *Pine or birch or something green.*

"I'm afraid you're running up the tab, Dr. Reese."

Their proximity clouded her mind and made her knees weak. Victoria leaned against the door for relief. "Am I?"

"Yes, ma'am." His voice was low gravel coming from the core of his exquisitely chiseled chest. She glanced at his denim shirt, wondering if the buttons were the snappy kind that you could wrench apart, and also if

John even owned an iron. He hadn't moved any closer, but his frenetic energy was migrating to her body causing her fingers to tremble. "I'd say you're pushing $30 in fines. It's almost criminal."

"I'm not paying that," Victoria said, trying to keep the haughtiness in her voice.

"Well then, that *would* be criminal, wouldn't it?"

"I can easily contest the charges."

"I'll bet you could. You seem like a woman who likes to contest things."

He was teasing her again. The quirk of his mouth was driving her mad. Was he flirting with her? "Good you recognize that now, Mr. Donovan. I'm also very organized."

John raised a brow in response. "I'll remember that."

"I'll see you tomorrow?" she asked, opening the door.

"Six p.m., try to be on time."

Victoria couldn't help the undignified snort that escaped her. "Really?"

John stepped over the threshold, into the hallway. "I'm going to try out punctuality and see how it fits. Formalities are good, right?"

"Yeah," she breathed.

"I'll see you then."

He walked off, leaving her with a slacked jaw. Before she could process what happened, the department secretary, Debbie, nearly walked into John as she passed by. She excused herself, sidled up to Victoria's office and the two women watched the Viking walk away. Debbie was bubbling with excitement, her red curls bouncing with every movement.

"Who is he and what did he want?" she asked in a hushed voice.

"Um…" Victoria needed a minute to put her head back together. She blinked before shifting her gaze towards Debbie. "I'm working with John, I mean, Mr. Donovan—I'm working with the library in hopes of starting an internship."

"*He's* a librarian?" Debbie whispered. Her blue eyes were huge orbs behind her glasses. "The way he walked by was like a dream. It's like he just appeared, smelling like the forest. Did you see his tattoos?"

"Yes, Deb, I saw all of it." Victoria smelled him too.

"What does he do at the library?" Debbie asked.

"He's the head of the children's department."

Debbie gasped. "You're joking."

Victoria sagged against the door frame and rolled her eyes. "That's what it says on the library website."

"He's too hot to be a children's librarian."

She smiled in spite of herself. "Jeez, Deb."

"It's true," Debbie said with a grin. "Oh, before I forget, are you going to the department meeting tomorrow? I'm ordering sandwiches for everyone."

There is no such thing as a free sandwich. "Only if you're buying."

"Great, I'll put you on the list," Debbie said. "Are you heading out soon?"

"No, I've got to stick around and finish up some emails."

The secretary hitched her purse on her shoulder, "You're the only one who stays after office hours." Her tone matched that of Paula's: concern and judgement.

"These emails won't send themselves." She closed her office door and retreated to the safety of her desk. Behind the solid tank of a desk, she could control all the tasks set before her. Except one. John Donovan had rattled her, in *her* office, with his smile and his charm. Victoria tried to return to her computer, scrolling through the dozens of emails, all waiting to be answered.

I can tell I'm going to have to employ other methods on you.

After meeting John, it would be impossible for her to keep her mind on work. She hoped that the effects of his personality wouldn't continue being a distraction in the future.

Chapter Six

John searched the cupboards for something nutritious to feed his niece. He'd lost track of time and forgot to grocery shop. His short meeting with Victoria Reese was almost enough for him to forget Becca at the library. As he ran his hand through his hair, he searched the refrigerator next. A case of beer, a head of iceberg lettuce, leftover Chinese takeout, and a fuck-ton of condiments. This wasn't good enough for a little girl. *What do kids eat? What does Victoria like to eat?*

"We should order a pizza," said a haughty voice from behind him. He checked over his shoulder to see Becca with her hands on her hips. She had changed into her pajamas and tied her hair with a silk scarf.

"Probably…" he said, turning back to the pitiful contents of the fridge. "Remind me to go to the store tomorrow."

"You need a planner," Becca said, taking a seat at the kitchen island. "Then you wouldn't forget everything all the time."

"You raise a good point, honey." John moved to the "all-purpose" drawer which housed the takeout menus and random screw drivers. When he found the menu to the local pizzeria, he brought it to Becca. "Pick what you want."

She didn't bother looking. "I'll have cheese."

He sighed. "Are you and your mom still doing this vegetarian thing?"

"Uncle Johnny, it's not just a 'vegetarian thing.' We're not contributing to the senseless murder of farm animals."

He shook his head with a chuckle. "God, it's like listening to a tiny Jessi. I'm looking forward to two full months of your stern judgement."

That pulled a grin out of her. "What was Mom like when she was my age?"

John leaned down against the counter and took a second to think about it. He and Jessi had gone to the same middle school, but rarely hung out in the same circles. They hadn't really gotten to know one another until high school. "From what I can remember of your mom, I know she always had her nose in a book," John joked. "When we got older, she was going to protests and handwriting zines with her feminist collective."

"What's a zine?"

He rolled his eyes. "It's a very indie magazine pamphlet that doesn't make any money."

"And she was just as pretty as she is now?" Becca asked.

"Sure, I'll bet she was as cute as you are now," he said, reaching out to tap her upturned nose. "You both have those big brown eyes and little noses."

Becca looked down and sighed. "Yeah right…"

John drew himself up to full height and looked down at his niece. This felt suspiciously like a landmine. "What's up?"

"Nothing."

"What did we say about that?"

She gave one of those exaggerated pre-teen shrugs. "I don't look like any of the girls at my school. I'm too tall and my hair doesn't do what theirs does. There's this awful group of girls in third period who sit in the back making fun of people and they keep calling me a giraffe. Sixth grade is stupid and I'm basically alone. Like, there are hardly any other black girls there. There are a couple, but they're older girls and I'm not cool enough to be around them. And there's this guy, Connor, he's in fifth period P.E. and every time I see him, I think I'm going to barf. He keeps saying hi and I don't know what to say."

Boom.

Where does one even start?

"First of all, let's talk about this boy," John said with a frown. He'd already spent most of his college years prying Jessi away from the lurid clutches of frat boys. He wasn't ready for round two. "You don't have to say anything to him if you don't want to. A simple 'hi' will do just fine."

Becca just glared. "Are you kidding me?"

"Do I look like I'm kidding?"

"I like him, Uncle Johnny, and I'm trying not to look like a complete idiot in front of him in P.E., which is hard to do when I'm tripping over my own giraffe legs."

"You're going to be tall like your dad and me," he tried.

"But do I have to be tall *now*?"

"Girls grow earlier than boys," John said. "And this business about not looking like other girls is silly." He knew that wasn't even scratching the surface. What

Becca was referring to was much deeper than that. She was attending a predominantly white private school and couldn't find her crowd. He could relate to an extent, but would never fully understand her anxiety.

Her expression told him as much. Before she could shut down and return to "nothing," he had to convince her that she was alright.

"What has your mom told you about fitting in?"

"That it doesn't matter."

"Well, she's right. But that doesn't change the fact that you're still feeling shitty."

Becca's eyes went round. "Uncle Johnny—"

He held up a hand. "Look, I'm not going to beat around the bush, honey. Being twelve is shitty. You just left fifth grade where you knew everyone, your mom is in Europe doing work you don't understand or care about, and your parents are divorced. Is that the long and short of it?"

She nodded.

"Okay, got it. You can't control these things. You can't go back to fifth grade, you can't bring your mom back early, and whatever is going on with your parents is their problem." He took a deep breath before continuing. "You're going to one of Farmingdale's whitest schools, but that doesn't mean you can't make friends with girls who *think* like you. There's got to be at least ten like-minded girls who can create another vegan feminist collective, right?"

Becca managed a hesitant smile. "Maybe?"

"Alright, find those girls, form a gang, and start your own zine about dismantling industrial farming."

"Okay…"

"And about not being blonde, blue eyed, and average height… You are truly beautiful as you are."

A shadow flickered across her delicate features. "I don't feel like it."

"And you're not going to feel like it for a few years," John said honestly. "Everyone who hits this age feels strange in their bodies, but it's because you're still growing, Becca."

"It's just hard, is all."

"Yes, ma'am," John agreed, walking around the kitchen island. "It's okay to admit that it's hard."

Becca's pointed chin rested on her knuckles as she watched him. "Do you need a hug?" she asked.

"Yeah, I could use one, if you're not too busy."

She threw her arms around his waist and lingered for a moment. "If it makes you feel better," she murmured against his belly.

He chuckled as he held her, remembering how small she used to be. An ankle-biter who followed him around asking a million questions about the trees, the sky, ants on the sidewalk. If he closed his eyes, he could keep her at that safe age when her life wasn't so tumultuous. When he released her and pushed her back on her barstool, he smiled down at her. "I do feel better. Thank you, honey."

"Me too," she admitted.

Crisis averted. For now.

After getting Becca to bed, entirely too late, John climbed into his own. As he plugged in his phone and set the alarm, he caught a missed email in his notifications. Curious as to who could be emailing at midnight, he took the bait.

Mr. Donovan:
I've checked my bookshelves, my nightstand, and my
"Friend of the Farmingdale Public Library" tote bag.
The book in question is not here. It appears that your
people are mistaken.
Regards,
Victoria Reese, Ph.D.
Assistant Professor of English
Pembroke University
v.reese1@pembroke.edu
Office: (309) 555-6043
Cell: (309) 555-3689

The timestamp read 11:56 p.m. Six minutes ago. John
settled against his pillows and read the message again.
Really? She thought this was a good time to contact him
about a book? It made sense, of course. When they'd
met, she was wound tighter than a Swiss-made watch.
It didn't take away from how beautiful she was. As she
held it together, he noticed small ticks that made her even
more charming. The way she quietly sucked her teeth or
cut her eyes when he said something stupid. The turn of
her neck when she slipped a braid behind her ear. The
way she bit on her lower lip...
    He knew he'd laid on the charm extra thick during
their non-meeting. He probably didn't need to, but she
was too captivating to resist. With her buttoned-up demeanor and her classy skirt suit. Patent leather nude
pumps, which managed to match her soft cinnamon skin.
High-strung and gorgeous. Not necessarily the kind he
went after, but he felt drawn to her nonetheless. Upon
shaking her hand, he'd felt it. "It" felt like nervous energy that needed to be stroked with a calm hand, kissed

away, or held gently. By the time she'd pulled away from him, John wanted to do all of those things and more.

He was about to reply to the email, but paused. He had a better idea. *Should I?* He pressed and held her cellphone number until he could copy it into his contacts. He labeled the phone number: "Sexy Prof" and began his text:

John: Your email regarding a missing book was basically the equivalent of a 'wyd.' Just wanted you to know that.

He waited for her response. *This is probably a dumb idea.* John was prone to fits of impulsiveness that usually got him into trouble. But picturing her tearing through her home, searching for a smutty paperback, made him smile in the darkness of his bedroom. She even searched her library tote bag. Of course Victoria was a Friend of the Farmingdale Public library.

Sexy Prof: New phone, who dis?

John laughed. *Okay, Dr. Reese.*

John: Mr. Donovan. I retrieved your number from your email and thought better to text you: $30 fines are not what I expected from a university professor.

Sexy Prof: Mr. Donovan, I shouldn't have to tell you about the danger of making assumptions. Either way, the book: Is. Not. Here.

John: Was it a good book at least? What I'm asking is: Was the Duke worth the trouble?

Sexy Prof: The Duke was fine.

John: A *convenient* choice?

Sexy Prof: Convenient enough at the time.

John: I encourage you to turn yourself in, Dr. Reese. Throw yourself at the mercy of library law.

Sexy Prof: NEVER!

John: Fair enough... Goodnight for now, Dr. Reese.

Sexy Prof: Mr. Donovan.

Chapter Seven

There was no such thing as a free sandwich.

The department meeting had devolved into the toxic cesspool that she imagined it would. Today's meeting did not have the pretenses of a democracy as English faculty members sat at a long boardroom table with Kenneth at the head. The sandwich Victoria picked at sat beside a copy of the spring semester schedule. With a mouthful of deli ham, she saw red as she skimmed the printout. Her usual African-American Literature was listed, as was the Post-Colonial Literature, but Composition I and Technical Writing Skills were added to her lineup. *Tech and freshman comp? Where the hell did they come from?* She glanced from her sheet to the faces of two other women in the department. Jennifer Klaus, their Children's Literature professor wore an equally confused expression. Alison Kelly, the Victorian Literature professor, was slack-jawed as she stared at Kenneth. He remained oblivious to the three women as he and three male professors, Medieval, Early American, and Creative Writing, laughed it up on the other side of the table.

"Where on earth are we getting these adjuncts?" he asked the men. "I swear, I saw one of them dressed like a student, just the other day. Wearing a political T-shirt like it was the '70s…"

Victoria frowned, hoping he wasn't bad-mouthing *her* Paula.

"I really wondered if she got a handbook from HR." Kenneth laughed, spraying bits of his sandwich at Gabe Bates, the Creative Writing professor. She doubted Gabe minded the bullets of pastrami since he was already so far up Kenneth's ass.

"Someone forgot to tell this generation to dress for the job they want, not the job they have," said the resident Medievalist, Dan Combs. "I think I know which one you're talking about, Ken. I passed her class as she was telling students 'grammar was a tool of the white supremacy.' I mean, really, Pembroke doesn't need that kind of agenda."

He and Kenneth exchanged a look that ended with an eye roll.

They *were* talking about her Paula! She was the only one in the department who would say such a thing. And although Victoria agreed with her, she certainly wouldn't voice it to her students.

"It's sad that we're reduced to gossiping about underpaid and overworked adjuncts," she said loudly. "With the way you hire them, I just assumed we needed any warm body at the front of a classroom."

The men stopped speaking to see the rest of the faculty members seething. "I'm sorry, Victoria, did you have something to add?" Kenneth asked.

Her face warmed. "I think we have more important things to discuss than how a woman dresses. Last time I checked, Pembroke didn't have a dress code policy for faculty."

"But we have a standard at this institution," said Dan. "Our students deserve to see something they can aspire to."

If that were really the case, they'd see more faculty of color.

"Victoria isn't here to teach you how to avoid another trip to HR, Dan," said Alison. "I want to know how I ended up getting switched from the university library committee to institutional assessment. Also, why am I teaching two sections of Composition II?"

"Exactly," Jennifer said as she swiped a highlighter across her paper. "I've had to teach three sections of comp for the past two years, Ken. I've had multiple requests from students to offer more Young Adult. Where are the sections?"

While the men stared at the women, Victoria quickly checked off the classes her male colleagues were teaching next semester. Dan only had two classes, both in his area of study. Gabe was responsible for Intro to Creative Writing, a Poetry Seminar, and an... Independent Study? And because Kenneth was department chair, he had several course releases, freeing him up to teach only one Shakespeare class.

She and the other women were being dumped on.

"Why am I teaching two writing classes?" Victoria chimed in.

"Since Dan is writing his book, he's asked for a release. It's only fair. One of Gabe's majors has taken all of his classes and requires an independent," Kenneth said, staring at her coldly. It was as if he'd read her thoughts and shut down every possible argument she could lob at him. "As per our conversation last week, I naturally assumed you were more interested in the *practical* ed-

ucation of our English students. What better class than
Technical Writing? You can now show them how to write
a business email."

Victoria underestimated just how petty Kenneth
could be. She'd caught him unawares at their last meeting and he'd held on to his grudge for the whole weekend. But he wasn't just punishing her, he was dragging
Jennifer and Alison into the fray. She closed her eyes
and took a breath. "Is there a reason why some of these
classes aren't going to the adjuncts?" she asked.

Kenneth gave a mirthless chuckle and glanced at his
male colleagues. "But didn't you just say they were overworked as is?" He shrugged. "It couldn't hurt to have
full-time faculty shoulder some of these responsibilities
for the next semester. Who knows? Maybe that will be
my Four-Week Initiative, cutting non-unionized con-
tingency labor. That would save money, wouldn't it?"

Victoria fell quiet. She had talked her way into that
one. The politics of hiring part-time adjuncts was a
messy problem that extended well beyond their university. No, most institutions shouldn't lean heavily on part-
time workers, especially if those same workers couldn't
have access to health care, or job security. But most institutions saved money using contingent labor. These
instructors generally needed to teach about six classes
per semester just to make ends meet. Paula was only
teaching for a little side money, but Victoria knew many
instructors who would be hurting if just one class was
taken from them. If she didn't stop talking, her mouth
was going to get them all in trouble.

"I'm not teaching this many comp classes again, Kenneth," Jennifer said with force. "You can give one of
them to an adjunct who needs it because I'm done."

Kenneth held up his hands in mock-defense. "No need to get hysterical, Jennifer..."

"I'm not hysterical," Jennifer said, jabbing a finger at her schedule. "Since you've hired me, I've barely had a chance to teach in my area of study."

"You're teaching the classes assigned to you. Next fall, we'll see about giving you YA."

And with that, their leader was finished with the debate. The women folded their arms in protest, but that was about it. Time for discourse was officially over.

"Now, if we're quite finished with that, let's move on to the next order of business. The distribution of our incoming majors..."

Victoria balled up the remainder of her sandwich and tossed it in a nearby wastebasket. "Yes, Ken. How many students have we acquired?" she asked in a dry voice.

He glared at her before shuffling through papers. "It appears we have five new prospects, all of whom would like to work with you, Dr. Reese. They've expressed interest in African American Literature."

As terrible a meeting as it was, a hopeful smile pulled at Victoria's lips. There were new converts because of *her*. And Williams couldn't take that away from her. She made a difference. "I'm glad to hear it," she said with a humble nod. "It's a great benefit for the whole department."

"Yes, well..." Kenneth trailed off with a perturbed expression. "Please remind them there are other facets of the program to explore."

"Of course," Victoria said. "I'll let them know to register for Children's Literature. Jennifer, do you still have that awesome unit on representation in picture books?"

Jennifer's lips quirked into a lopsided smile. "I sure do. Send them my way."

"And Alison," Victoria added. "I think your Victorian survey will pair nicely with my Post-Colonial Lit course."

Alison glanced between the two women before smiling. "Of course. We can give them the before and after of the British Empire."

Victoria faced Kenneth with a cheery smile. "There you go, Ken. Jennifer, Alison, and I will show the *five* new majors the ropes of the program."

Seeing the storm clouds in his face almost made up for the fact that he and his boys' club screwed her and her colleagues out of their fair share of courses. Almost.

Victoria was exhausted.

And her day was not finished. Her usual drive home was replaced with a drive to the public library. The job-shadowing with John had nestled in the back of her mind all day. More specifically, their text exchange continued to nag at her. He was perfectly professional during their short interaction, employing that same humor, so why did she feel guilty? After blowing through her house like a hurricane, searching high and low for that book, she'd collapsed in her bed and wrote the email. She didn't know what prompted her to do something like that. She wasn't normally driven to pen late-night emails. Part of her didn't want John to think he'd ruffled her feathers. The other part of her had simply wanted to talk to him.

Victoria had to admit she'd felt a thrill when he'd written her back almost immediately. When her phone vibrated on her nightstand, she'd smiled in spite of herself. *Turn yourself in, Dr. Reese.* She chuckled as she pulled her Volvo into the library parking lot. Just as John said, the cars were starting to clear out. Tuesday night would be a quiet work evening. She sat in her car for a few moments, getting her bearings. Still dressed in a black pencil skirt and white button-down shirt, Victoria hoped that she wouldn't engage in any strenuous manual labor. Based on her observations, many library workers sat behind the desk or pushed a cart of books to the stacks. Surely it wasn't that hard of a job.

Victoria grabbed her purse before leaving her car and walked to the front entrance. Inside, the building was nearly dead. An elderly man was seated in the periodicals area reading a newspaper and a teenager appeared to be doing homework at the computer stations. There was one older woman manning the checkout counter. Just as she assumed, the woman sat on a barstool reading a novel.

"Excuse me," Victoria said, making her way to the counter. "I'm here to see John Donovan."

The woman, whose nametag read "Martha Crane," set down her book and adjusted her glasses. "What's that, hon?" she asked in a loud voice. The sound pierced the silence and made Victoria jump.

"I'm looking for John Donovan," she said, leaning forward and raising her volume just slightly.

Martha frowned and turned her head. "Hon, you've got to talk into this side. My hearing aid is acting funny."

Victoria was used to librarians shushing her; not shouting at her. "I need John Donovan!" she said in a strong voice.

"And you can have him," said a familiar voice from behind her. "No need to shout...yet."

"Well there you are," said the checkout woman. "Right behind you."

Victoria closed her eyes and willed the ground to open and swallow her whole. She practiced her irritated expression before turning around. When she did face him, Victoria inhaled through her nose. She didn't know it was possible for him to look more handsome, but here they were. He was indeed more enticing than she remembered. John was dressed in a black Henley shirt and dark blue jeans. The Henley hugged his muscles in all the ways that yesterday's denim shirt couldn't. Victoria tore her eyes from his body and found that his face wasn't too much better. His sandy beard quirked from pursed lips. *Oh god, the beard...*

John's eyes appeared to be taking her in as well. Her face burned as his gaze wandered downward at an achingly slow pace, before making their way back to her face. This momentary standoff of staring made her uncomfortable. She only hoped that she didn't appear dumbstruck by his beauty. Victoria pursed her lips just to make sure her tongue wasn't in danger of wagging. An easy smile stretched across his face as he sauntered towards her. "You got my book, Dr. Reese?"

Victoria was once again startled by his ability to switch topics at a moment's notice. She did hear him correctly. *And you can have him...* She knew innuendo when she heard it. Though it had been awhile. "No, I don't, Mr. Donovan."

He sidled up to the counter, close to her, and said in a soft voice, "One way or another, I will come a-collectin', Dr. Reese."

She glanced over her shoulder at the old woman, who had returned to her book. Not even the deaf woman could save her. "I won't have anything to give you," she said in a low voice.

"Is that a fact?"

She drew a shaky breath and nodded her head.

"I'll be the judge of that," John said, dropping his gaze down to her shoes. "Are you going to be comfortable in those?"

Now we are going to talk about shoes? Again, the sudden shift. The more he gazed at her body; the more naked Victoria felt. It was as if he was discarding one article of clothing at a time before settling on her shoes. "They'll do just fine."

"I hope so, because your students will spend a lot of time on their feet," John said, straightening away from the counter, away from her. "You might want to remember that for next time."

"Next time?"

"You didn't think I only needed one night with you, did you?"

There! There it is again! Her brain was actually shouting at her. The way his voice dipped to a dark rumble, the way his lips lifted at the corner in a cocky half grin. *He's definitely flirting with you!*

Victoria ignored her brain and gaped, "Yes, I did actually."

John rubbed the side of his bearded face and frowned. "Oh no, Dr. Reese. We've got a couple more nights together before you understand the nature of the job."

All of this could have been put in an email. "Fine…"

"Great," he said with a clap of his hands. "Let's get started." John walked towards the offices behind the counter, beckoning her to follow.

"I've always wondered what was behind the counter," she said, taking note of the carts of books and computers.

"My office is just through here," he said over his shoulder. "You can leave your purse there before we get to work." His windowless office was a bit smaller than hers and plastered with reading posters and famous children's book jackets. His desk was a disaster. It was a cluttered mess of papers, books, and empty Styrofoam cups that once held coffee. "Sorry for the mess. I keep meaning to get around to a spring cleaning."

Victoria smirked. "It's autumn."

He actually appeared to be embarrassed. "So it is."

Framed photos also occupied his desk. One featured two women, one black and the other white, possibly in their sixties, drinking margaritas. The other photo was the one that caught Victoria's eye and held her attention. It was a black woman and a small girl who appeared to be her daughter. The photo was taken while the woman was mid-laugh, her dreadlocks wound in a careless bun that sat at an odd angle on her head. She and the girl were both quite beautiful. Victoria's heart dropped slightly as she glanced at John's bare ring finger. *Ex-wife?* "She's lovely," she said, gesturing to the photo.

John looked down at his desk. "Oh, Jessi? Yeah, she's great."

Is she? "Is that her daughter?" Victoria asked.

He picked up the photo and examined it thoughtfully. "Yeah, that's Becca, my niece. I took this picture when she was about six or seven. She's twelve now."

Victoria was oddly relieved, but also a little confused. "She's your niece?"

His grin crinkled the corners of his eyes. "We get that a lot. Jessi is my twin stepsister. We were the same age when my parents divorced and my dad married her mother."

She nodded. "Oh, I see."

"My dad died when we were seventeen. After that, we grew pretty close and we've been best friends ever since." He picked up the other photo with the older women. "And our mothers became best friends as well."

The relief flooded her as she nodded along, and she felt foolish for it. *There's nothing for you to be relieved about. It's none of your business anyway. His romantic attachments are none of your concern.* "That's nice," she said politely.

"Do you remember being twelve?"

The abrupt question made Victoria chuckle as she did the math in her head. "It was twenty-two years ago, so barely?"

John nodded. "Yep, it's been a cool twenty-six for me. I ask because I'm taking care of Becca for a couple of months while Jessi is abroad for her job."

"Ahh, so you're now thrust into a father role."

"Being a fun uncle only gets you so far," John admitted. "Becca is so smart and so…"

"Tempestuous?"

"Exactly."

"It's a terrible age," Victoria said. It was heartening to see another side of the man who rattled her with his charm. Underneath that façade, he was insecure about caring for a child. "They're so doubtful at that age; too caught up with what everyone thinks of them."

"I tried to tell her as much, last night. There's a tiny part of her that's still willing to listen, but I don't know… Hollingsworth Academy is beyond my control."

"It helps if she has people in her corner when she gets

home from that place," Victoria said with a grin. "Keep listening to her without too much judgement, and she might continue to talk to you."

John set the photos down on his desk and tossed a few of the empty coffee cups in a wastebasket. "Thank you. That's sound advice, Dr. Reese," he said, maneuvering around his desk. "Now let's get you in the stacks."

Just when she thought it was safe to lower her guard and talk about something else, he was switching gears again. He moved swiftly, brushing against her as he exited the office. An electric charge traveled swiftly up her arms and to her heart. With a deep breath, Victoria set down her purse and followed him.

Chapter Eight

"Are you familiar with the Dewey Decimal System?" John asked.

Victoria struggled with the stack of books balanced against her jutting hip. "Of course," she said as she stopped the top book from sliding off. He carried a stack of ten books with the ease of a seasoned cocktail waitress.

"Good, which books are located in the eight-hundreds?" he asked, watching her shift her stack around.

"Easy, literature."

"Okay, how about the four-hundreds?"

Victoria searched her mind for that area of the library. *Four-hundreds are...* "I don't know," she finally admitted.

"You're standing next to the four-hundreds," he said.

She frowned before looking at the books around her. "Languages? I'm not in this area often."

"That's fair, but your students are going to have to study all of these areas if they want to shelve correctly."

Victoria, a former straight A student, was strangely disappointed that she didn't know every square inch of the nonfiction section. "Right."

"And the books you're holding?"

She craned to check the spines of her books, tipping them to the side. "These are nine-hundreds. History, I'm assuming?"

"Yep, go ahead and shelve those while I work on biographies."

Victoria shifted the books to her other hip as she followed him towards a more secluded spot in the non-fiction area. Near the back, there were two unoccupied study rooms with the lights switched off. When she found her assigned section, she propped her books on an empty space and shook out her arms. They were already shaking under the weight. Behind her, John had already set out to do his work.

In the quiet space, Victoria was more aware of their proximity. Right behind her, John's movements were quick-paced while she lagged behind, studying the numbers. She now felt guilty about leaving books in the wrong place when she didn't want them. After she shelved a second Revolutionary War book, Victoria sensed a shift in the air. There was a warmth at her back that wasn't there before.

"I've got the Vietnam War in my pile," John said. Why did it seem like he had whispered it into her ear?

She saw the book and his extended tattooed arm wrap around her before she could react. A tiger and a Celtic cross. She took the book without replying and searched the numbers for its place. It was on the bottom shelf. Victoria crouched down, bumping against John's legs. "Sorry!"

He stepped back. "No worries."

Heart pounding as she balanced on her high heels, Victoria slipped the book in the correct place. *Is it getting hot in here?* She shook out the collar of her blouse, fanning cool air against her neck and chest. When she stood, she quickly moved to the next book. "Oh, doesn't this Roosevelt book belong in biographies?" she asked turning to hand it to him.

They bumped into each other, her book knocking into the stack he held with one arm. Books tumbled from his grasp and onto the floor.

"Sorry!" she said, stooping to gather them.

He knelt beside her. "Dr. Reese, I'm getting the sense you don't respect my books."

He was close again.

Despite the heat emanating from him, she tried to laugh. "I do respect books, Mr. Donovan." *God, he* does *smell like the forest.* Victoria tried to steady the tremor in her hands as she picked up the books.

"I have yet to see evidence of that," he said, taking four books in his massive hands. "And I think you're mistaken. This goes in the World War II section."

They stood together, Victoria weaving slightly on her feet, her back brushing against the History shelves. Her breathing had changed; her pulse quickened. John moved closer to her with Roosevelt in hand. "Does it?"

"Mm-hmm." He crowded her senses, pushing reason right out the door. As he held her gaze, he reached around her and placed the book to the left of her waist. However, his hand remained on the spine.

Victoria tried not to smell him. She tried not to tilt her head back and close her eyes. *Citrus, fresh soap, birch.* She bit her lip and willed her body to ignore his. "You'll have to excuse me," she said. "I'm new on the job."

The corner of his mouth quirked. He had not stepped away and she did not want him to. "That much is evident," he rumbled. The hand that had held Roosevelt fell on her wrist, his calloused fingers circling her with a gentleness she hadn't expected.

Victoria didn't move away. "But I'm a quick learner," she breathed.

John raised a brow. "Is that a fact?"

She licked her lips and nodded her head.

"Learning sometimes requires the student to relinquish control, Dr. Reese. You hardly seem capable of that."

She wasn't imagining his flirtatious tone or how scandalously close he stood. His hand was on her wrist, thumb stroking her riotous pulse. He was also issuing her a challenge: could she give up control? "It's been a long time since I was a student."

John smiled down at her. "Not too long, I hope."

Her brow knit in confusion. "Wait, what are we talking about?"

He blinked as he snapped his mouth shut. Soon his shoulders shook in quiet laughter and he released her wrist. The spell was broken. "Jesus Christ," he said in between louder chuckles.

Shaken from her reverie, Victoria raised her hand to her mouth and averted her eyes. She was certain that embarrassment colored her brown cheeks as she quickly returned to her neglected pile of books. "Never mind."

His laughter grew louder. "Oh, Dr. Reese…"

She faced the bookshelf and fumed. "I said never mind."

Then his laughter subsided. "Never mind?"

"I think I misunderstood this interaction."

"What did you misunderstand?"

Victoria closed her eyes and sighed. "Please."

"I asked if you were capable of being a student," he

said, keeping his tone light. "I'm pretty sure that was a simple implication."

She picked up another book and ignored him. Another Vietnam War book.

"Dr. Reese, I didn't think I had to spell it out to an academic. It kinda takes the fun out of this interaction."

Her movements stilled. "What?"

"If you want me to speak plainly, all innuendo aside, I think I was asking, in so many words…if you'd like to start a sordid affair with me."

Victoria dropped the book in her hand.

"You really have to stop abusing my books."

She spun around to find John directly behind her. His arms were crossed over his chest, the devilish smile on his face issuing another challenge. "What did you say?"

"You heard me."

Victoria's mind was awash with a million questions. "What do you mean a *sordid affair*?"

He shrugged. "It could be fun."

"But I don't have fun," she blurted out.

"Yeah, I picked up on that."

Victoria reached up and scratched the back of her scalp. She was sweating again. "I don't have time for a sordid affair."

"How long did it take you to read *For the Duke's Pleasure*?"

"*For the Duke's Convenience*," she corrected. "And I don't know, a couple of days."

"So you are capable of taking time to enjoy *something*. I'm happy to loan out my services for the professor's convenience." The laughter in his voice eased the tension in her shoulders. "She's certainly beautiful enough."

Victoria averted her gaze and blushed. "I don't think it's a good idea to mix business and pleasure," she lied.

"So being with me would be a pleasure?" he asked. "Because it's hard to tell. You're a bit thorny."

Horny, is more like it. While his frankness was a bit unsettling, the hunger in John's eyes made her feel things she hadn't felt since…well, reading *For the Duke's Convenience*. "I… I don't think, I didn't mean it like that," she stammered. "We're supposed to be working on book stuff." *Book stuff?* Victoria had lost the expansive vocabulary she was known for. John asked something of her that she hadn't ever imagined in her bookish life.

As if to press the point, he leaned forward until his mouth was at her ear and whispered. "I assure you, we can do both." Warm breath tickled her skin and sent a shiver up her neck. "But to be fair, only one would feel like work."

There was nowhere else for her to move; History was at her back and John was tantalizingly close to her front. Victoria turned her face just slightly to meet his profile. In his sandy brown beard, tiny flecks of silver hid near his temple. For a second, she wondered what it would feel like to reach up and run her finger along that spot. She didn't know what her next move would be, but she found herself not wanting to escape. "How would uh… the book part work if we're engaged in…" She searched for the words and came up miserably empty.

John pulled back slightly until they were face to face, just a mere inch or two apart. She was going to pass out if she couldn't control her own breathing. "A sordid affair?" he asked with a quirk of his lips.

Victoria nodded dumbly.

"I don't usually engage in sordid affairs," he whispered. "But I'm painfully curious about a well-organized, extremely professional woman who's so buttoned-up that she might pass out from suffocation." *So he can hear my labored breathing.* "I want to know why she's in love with a rakish duke. He is a rake, right?"

"Pretty much," she said with a shaky voice. "He's reformed by the end of the book though." He was close enough to kiss, if she wanted, but she wasn't sure if she should. She wanted to do something, anything to break up the unbearable tension that made her breasts heavy with anticipation and set her skin on fire. "He'd probably try to kiss a woman in a library before asking about a sordid affair though."

A wide grin spread over John's face. "Is that a fact?" He nodded thoughtfully before adding. "I probably should have kissed you first, huh?"

She tried to give an easy shrug. "I mean, I'm just telling you what the duke would have done…but yeah."

John straightened up to full height. "Gotcha, so I put the cart before the horse?"

"Kind of."

He nodded again. "Like I said, I'm new to sordid affairs. But I don't think I'm going to kiss you right now."

Victoria hoped she hid her disappointment well enough because the trap door beneath her heart swung open, spilling its contents downward. "No?"

He shook his head. "No, Dr. Reese. I realize my mouth ran away from me, but I can't go kissing women in the stacks. You'd have to meet me halfway."

Her heart pulled itself back up her chest as she parsed his words for meaning. "Halfway?"

"If you're interested in something remotely impulsive,

you're free to kiss me. If not, we'll go back to shelving and I'll keep my books to myself."

Impulsive? He didn't know her at all. And those who did would tell him that Victoria Reese did *nothing* on impulse. Victoria Reese always had a plan. But his choices were intriguing. He quietly gave her control of the situation even when her arousal was anything but controlled. Could she go back to shelving his books without remembering his scent? *It's a G.D. birch forest on a hot summer day.*

"Okay," she said quickly.

"Okay, what?" Wicked humor danced in his eyes.

She shut her eyes tight and closed the distance. She pressed her mouth tightly against his and clutched his rock-hard biceps in an attempt to hold on to something. His beard tickled her lips and cheeks as she blindly pushed forward. For his part, John held on to the shelves behind her, in an attempt to let her continue "meeting him halfway." Victoria pulled away, breathless from a dry kiss and feeling idiotic. "I don't know why I did that," she said, breathing hard.

John raised a brow. "Did what?"

"I just kissed you."

He gave an impolite scoff. "Hardly. I'm old enough to know that real rakish kisses involve tongue."

Victoria scoffed right back. *How dare he tell me what a rakish kiss involves.* "I don't know you like that."

"But that's the point of impulsive kissing," John said, drawing away from her. "You give way to emotion and cast aside inhibitions. Like the movies."

He did have a point. A closed-lip kiss wasn't exactly a proper ravishing, but his options threw her off-kilter. This wasn't part of tonight's plan. She had no way to prepare for such a moment. "That's fair," she said, and added, "Maybe I should try again."

"I certainly wouldn't stop you," he purred, returning to her intimate space. "Whenever you're ready."

This is bizarre...and exciting. It was a fantasy Victoria had cultivated in her mind for years; meeting a man in the stacks and making out with him until an elderly librarian cleared her throat. She just never expected to act it out in her thirties, during a charade like "let me train you in the art of shelving history books." Placing her hands on his biceps again, she leaned forward. Victoria kept her eyes open this time, staring into John's smoldering emerald gaze. "I'm ready," she whispered.

"I am too," he replied in a soft voice.

She started with a light peck against the seam of his closed lips, flicking a nervous tongue against his bottom lip. When she felt it appropriate, Victoria let her eyes fall shut and angled her face against his beard, easing her tongue past his barrier. A groan escaped his throat as he opened his mouth and allowed her entry. She raised herself on her tiptoes in an effort to reach him, possibly stand over him, and opened her mouth wider. Hanging on to his muscular arms wasn't enough for her, so her hands traveled over his shoulders and gripped the back of his neck. His tongue met with hers and slid against it slowly. So achingly slow were his movements as his hands left the shelves and fell on her hips.

Hair fell away from his bun as she dug her fingers into his scalp. Chest to chest, they stood interlocked, arms wrapped around each other. Her breasts strained against the hard muscles of his torso, pushing with insistence. He dipped his head and gently pulled her bottom lip between his teeth. Victoria wanted more and she wanted it now. She almost didn't hear the moans coming from her. She hadn't moaned like that in a long time. Waves crashed against her beach and she hadn't battened down the hatch for this incoming storm. A single kiss had wet the juncture at her thighs and sent her swaying from its pleasure. When John's mouth tore away from hers, his lips traveled down her jaw and found their way to her neck. He sucked and nibbled at the sensitive skin at her pulse. "Johnny," she breathed.

He let out a choked moan in response and licked her collarbone. "Victoria," he whispered as he nuzzled her neck. A flat tongue lathed against her hot skin before suctioning it with a satisfying pop. *That's going to leave a mark.*

"Mr. Donovan, you've got a call on line one," Martha announced on the loud speaker. "Mr. Donovan, call on line one."

Victoria's eyes sprang open and she pushed him away. "Oh my god," she said. Her questions and concerns quickly came back, shoving away pleasure and impulsivity.

John stepped back, chest heaving and his shoulder length hair disheveled, his lips stained red with her lipstick. "Sorry," he breathed.

"Nothing to be sorry for," she said, reaching upward to push her braids behind her shoulder. "I initiated that."

"Right," he said, retying his hair into a more secure bun behind his head.

Victoria wanted to reach out and yank it loose. "You have a phone call."

"Right," he repeated.

"You have lipstick on your mouth."

"Okay."

Victoria grabbed her pile of books. "And I think I should go."

John stepped in front of her quick escape. "Victoria, wait."

She held the books at her chest like a protective shield. "What?"

"If you have to leave now, please come back tomorrow night."

She shook her head. "I'm busy all week. I've got a million meetings."

"Thursday then?"

His face was flushed and his expression was hopeful. Victoria found herself wanting to keep him hopeful. *She* wanted to be hopeful even if it meant being foolish and impulsive. Their kiss was only a taste of what could be even sweeter if she allowed herself to try. She relented. "Same time?"

John released a breath. "Yes."

She reached up to his face and swiped her thumb over his lips. "Your mouth is a bit stained," she whispered.

He caught her wrist and gently bit down on the tip of her thumb. "With you," he said, speaking around it, his tongue grazed her. The jolt of electricity made a path from her hand to her breasts, and then down to her womb. Victoria stood there with a finger in his mouth until she was able to wake up from her stupor. He licked delicately, at first, only to devour her thumb, swirling his tongue around it. What was probably seconds felt like an eternity.

Wake up. Wake up. Wake up!

When her drowsy brain finally caught up to her racing heart, her eyes flew open and she pulled her hand away from his lips. "Goodnight, John, I mean Mr. Donovan." She slowly pulled away and hurried from the History section, taking care not to look over her shoulder.

"Goodnight, Dr. Reese."

Chapter Nine

After Victoria had hurried from the library, John had waited a beat before making his own exit. The phone call that had thankfully interrupted their serious make out session, was from his babysitter. Becca had started her first period and he didn't know how to manage without John's help. Luckily, it had been near the end of his shift. His drive home involved reciting a series of helpful comments for his niece. *You see, Becca, when a girl gets to a certain age, her eggs need to go somewhere...*

"Where is she?" he asked as soon as he opened his front door.

Chris Flynn, John's best friend and workout buddy, stood in the foyer with his hands in his blonde curls. In the time he'd known Chris since high school, John had never seen his friend so distraught, and Chris had already been intimately acquainted with the Farmingdale Police Department for petty theft charges when they'd met. John's father had barely tolerated Chris and his "trailer-trash" family, but John's patient mother had accepted and straightened out the stray that John kept bringing home. Becca hadn't cut off an appendage, she was just on her period. But since he and Chris were damn near brothers, his concern for Becca was akin to a nervous father. "She won't come out of her bedroom. Dude, I've been trying to talk to her through the door, but she's not hearing it."

John dropped his bag at the door and walked to the living room searching for his laptop. "Did you try Skyping Jessi?"

"No, it's like, 3 a.m. in Stockholm, right?"

Goddammit. He forgot about the time difference. "Okay. I need a plan."

"Do you have any uh…you know, products?" Chris asked.

John shot his friend a glare. "Do I look like I keep maxi pads in my house?"

Chris flung his hands up. "Shit, man, I'm just asking."

They both looked down the hallway at the guest bedroom door. "I've got to talk to her."

"Good luck with that."

John pulled his friend by the front of his shirt and walked him down the hallway. "You're not leaving me yet," he whispered.

"I'm just the babysitter," Chris hissed, shaking himself loose. "All period problems are reserved for the parent or guardian."

"Help me talk her off the ledge, man."

They stood at Becca's door staring at one another. Chris widened his blue eyes and nodded to the door. "Go ahead then."

John knocked softly. "Hey, Becca?"

They got no response aside from the increased volume of music in her room.

"What is she listening to?" John asked.

Chris rolled his eyes. "Alanis Morissette. The entire time we've been here, I've heard 'You Oughta Know' twenty times." His voice dropped to a low growl. "I feel like I'm in a fucking time machine."

John tried not to laugh as he knocked again. "Becca, honey. Please talk to me."

"Leave me alone!"

"I can't do that."

"I don't want to talk!"

Chris nudged him. "You might want to try a firmer hand," he whispered.

Firm was not a tactic he used on children. He'd dealt with his share of rowdy kids at work and knew that a softer approach was more effective. John shook his head. "She's not going to respond to that. I know I didn't."

His friend shrugged. "If you say so."

John reached into his back pocket and pulled his wallet out. "Do me a favor and go to the store. Get anything you can think of to stop this meltdown: pain reliever—the kind that puts you right to sleep—pads *and* tampons, one of those heating pads, and lots of chocolate."

"How about some booze?"

He handed Chris a wad of bills. "A bottle of Makers would be great."

"Check."

"You're saving my life, you know that?"

Chris grinned. "Better you than me, Johnny."

As Chris left for his mission, John turned to the door. "Becca, I can't help you if we don't talk about it."

"You can't help," she shouted.

"I think I can," he said.

"You don't understand."

"Honey, you're not the first girl to start her period," John said. "Open the door and we can talk about it."

"I'm not going to talk to my uncle about this!"

John cracked his neck to the side. This is not what he wanted to do tonight. Not too long ago, he'd had his hands on the delicious curves of one Professor Reese. He could almost feel her lips on his, smell her perfume… "Becca turn off the music and come to the door."

"You're not coming in here."

"Fine, I'm not coming in, but I need you to turn off Alanis and come to the door."

There was a pause. The music stopped. "What?" Her voice was muffled against the door.

John breathed as he slid down to the floor. "Take a seat and we'll talk through the door." He learned the move from his mother. They'd spent a few teary conversations talking through a door like a confessional. He heard Becca join him from the other side.

"Fine."

"Thank you," he said, leaning his head against the wooden surface. "Now can I ask you a few questions?"

Becca heaved a tired sigh. "Fine."

"First, when did it happen?"

He heard a sniffle. "During sixth period math," she muttered. "I stood when the bell rang and Kelly told me that I had it on the back of my jeans. She gave me her shirt to tie around my waist."

John nodded. "That was really nice of Kelly."

"She's cool."

"Did you go to the nurse's office?"

"Yeah."

"Why didn't you call me?"

Becca went quiet. "Because I didn't think you'd come get me."

John ran his hands down his jaw. "Honey, I'd come to get you. Every time. I might be a little late, but I'd move mountains to get you." Was this what made her so anxious and moody? Currently, the adults in her life had other things to do. Her mother was clear across the globe learning about city planning while her father... God only knew what, or who, he was doing.

Another sniffle. "I didn't want to be a bother."

He leaned his head back and closed his eyes. "Becca..." He was fighting the impulse to open the door and scoop her up, to hold her tight in his arms and hug the disappointment out of her voice. "You'll never be a bother. You're my niece, my little girl."

She said nothing.

"Did the nurse give you something at least?"

"I got a couple of crappy pads."

"Good, Chris ran to the store and he's getting everything you'll need for the next few days."

"This is so embarrassing," she moaned against the door.

"There's nothing to be embarrassed about. Chris and I know enough about this to help."

"I mean it was embarrassing at school," Becca snapped. "I had to tie a shirt around my waist for the rest of the day. Like an idiot."

He smiled. "I doubt anyone knew what was happening. The shirt around the waist is actually pretty clever."

"It's not funny."

"It *is* clever. Good thing Kelly was there to help you. What's she like?"

Becca shifted against the door. "I like her. I did like you said and asked her if she wanted to be in a girl gang. She's going to draw up a charter."

John put his hand over his mouth to hold back the

laugh. "That sounds good," he said after a beat. "She's a good writer?"

"She's getting an A in English."

"Any chance others will join the gang?"

"Kelly said that McKenna and Devon would be interested."

"Okay, that sounds like a proper gang."

"None of them have gotten their periods yet," Becca said. "Kelly thinks it's a huge deal."

"She's not completely wrong," he said carefully. "It's a milestone, but it doesn't change who you are. You're still Becca."

"I feel like someone else."

No doubt the hormones talking. "Trust me, it feels like that, but you're still Becca."

"I feel angry and sad and fat. My body hurts and I'm so tired."

"I think that's normal too. Your mom told you it was coming and what to expect, right?"

She scoffed. "Yeah, in graphic detail. I was just hoping it would happen on a weekend."

John grinned at her seriousness. "You can't plan these things, honey. But you can stay home from school tomorrow and Skype your mother. I'm sure she'll want to hear the news."

"I have to go to school," she said in a tired voice. "I'm going to meet up with Kelly, McKenna, and Devon about our charter."

"Would that make you feel better?" he asked. "Because you can stay here if you want. I don't go to work until the evening and Chris can come back by again."

"I'll be fine."

"Can I get you anything while we wait on Chris? Cup of tea?"

"You're not supposed to have caffeine when you're on your period," she said.

John didn't know that. "Right, of course. Anything else?"

"No, I can wait."

"Alright, honey. Do you need a hug?"

To his surprise, the door actually opened and his niece crawled out of her room. She had wiped her face but her brown skin was puffy and reddish from crying. Her large brown eyes were still watery, making John's chest tighten. "If you need one," she said.

"I could use one," he said, moving her curls out of his face. "Becca, one more question."

She looked up at him. "Yeah?"

"Where on earth did you learn about Alanis Morissette?"

She frowned. "From Kelly. She said that we need a feminist anthem; the older the better."

"The mid '90s is not *old*," he growled in her face.

"It's ages ago," she said.

He took her by the armpits and pulled her from the floor, lifting her high above him. "You take that back, Miss Richards."

Becca's giggles sounded like music to his ears. "Put me down, Uncle Johnny!"

"Not until you apologize," he said, jostling her.

"Okay, I'm sorry," she said through her laughter. When he set her down, she shot him an impish look. "I know I'm supposed to respect my *elders*."

"God, you're the worst," he said, ruffling her curls.

"Get some rest and try to vary up the songs a little. You ruined Chris's evening with 'You Oughta Know.'"

"Fine."

He closed the door to her room and made his way back to the living room. He checked his phone for a message from Chris and laughed when he saw:

Chris: On my way back, a hot pharmacist helped me with the period stuff. THANK YOU, BECCA!

He left Jessi a text message for her to wake up to:

John: Your little girl is a little lady now. Chris and I are handling the fallout :)

God, he could use a drink. Just when he thought he had a handle on Becca, he found he was barely scratching the surface. And then there was still the business that occurred in the library between him and Victoria. John still couldn't believe she'd kissed him. Seduction in the stacks hadn't been his objective, but sharing such a small space with her delicate flower scent, that ass in a tight skirt, drove him mad with want. There were cameras back there for that very reason. Horny teens were always getting up to shenanigans in the History section. John cursed his recklessness, but did not regret that kiss. Victoria was timid with her hands, but not with her mouth.

He also wondered what he was thinking suggesting a sordid affair. He knew that it was probably similar language used in the book she stole, but he had no idea what that would look like. John wasn't a duke, he was a Midwestern public librarian who hadn't properly seduced a woman in two years. And he was also a researcher. An idea struck him, making him run upstairs to his bedroom.

When he found his e-reader, he searched the title *For the Duke's Convenience*. John took a deep breath and purchased the book, frowning at the traditional romance cover. An Edwardian-era rake with black hair and an intense gaze appeared to be ravishing a young blonde woman with a plunging neckline. "Jesus," he muttered.

This is going to be a struggle.

Chapter Ten

"I call this meeting to order," Paula said, knocking on Victoria's coffee table.

Victoria rolled her eyes and looked between Paula and Regina. The day after the library incident, she'd let it slip to Paula in the faculty break room. Before she knew it, the text chain had begun. Paula demanded a "wine night," which prompted Regina put her sons to bed and tell her husband not to wait up. "This feels more like an intervention."

"That will come later," Regina said, pouring herself another drink. "For now, I want to know who this guy is and when you're going to fuck him."

Victoria choked on her wine. "Jeez, Reggi."

"That was the end-goal when you kissed him, right?"

"Our girl actually kissed him." Paula clapped excitedly.

Victoria groaned and buried her face in her couch cushions. "I can't believe I did that." But she had and there were no take-backs. Not that she hadn't thoroughly enjoyed the way John's arms had wrapped around her waist, pulling her flush against his body. The initial embarrassment of the kiss had worn off as she'd driven home, and had been replaced with excitement.

Regina was already on her phone, her red nails scrolling furiously. "I don't know how you didn't do it the first time you met him. This boy is fine…"

"Lemme see," Paula said craning her neck. "Good god, Vicki."

"That body is all kinds of right."

Victoria sat up. "Okay, okay, ladies," she said. "Let's calm ourselves and talk about the facts. What's our plan? I need a plan."

Regina pointed her phone at her. "It's a *fact* that this white boy has an ass that won't quit. You need any other facts?"

"I don't need to see the photos."

Paula picked up her wine glass and swirled the contents. "Because you're already well acquainted with it in real life?"

Her friends were impossible, but she was glad to have them. They'd been tight ever since their first unsure days of college, when they were still figuring things out. Regina was the bombastic ass-kicker, Paula was the dreamy writer who always landed on her feet, and Victoria kept everyone in line with an organized plan. "I need you to get serious," she said, raising a brow at Paula.

Paula put her hands up in defense. "What's the plan, Vicki?"

"Better yet?" Regina interrupted. "What's holding you back?"

Victoria shrugged. "It's not professional and it's not me. I reached out to him to start a project for the department, not to have some…sordid affair." The fear of losing herself in anything other than work was very real for her. There were too many things she needed to accomplish in her career. For four years, she'd struggled to make a new name for the Pembroke University English department. Before her, Jennifer, and Alison had started, two more men had filled their positions and the department had lacked in diversity. When Victoria had arrived, she'd been anxious to revamp their program with new courses. Over time, she had learned just how slow the wheel turned regarding university policy. It wasn't a sprint, but a marathon. And she couldn't reduce speed for a man, no matter how beautiful he was. Or how powerful his hands felt as they held the small of her back.

"Well, you can pump the breaks and go back to just working any time you want," Paula said, eyeing her. "You don't have to do anything."

"That's true, girl. What do *you* want to do?"

Victoria looked at them both and then down at her wine. "He's so attractive…"

Regina sat on the edge of her seat. "And?"

And she wanted to climb him like a tree. "And I have to think about it. What he's asking is…a little bizarre."

"So when was the last time you two spoke?" Paula asked.

"At the library."

"But that was last night," Paula said. "No emails or no texts?"

She shook her head. "I haven't had time to deal with it. And if I had to guess, he's got his hands full with his twelve-year-old niece."

"Yes," Paula said. "You said something about a sister and niece?"

"His stepsister is in Europe at the moment and he's keeping her daughter."

"Oh my god, I'm getting sexy single dad vibes." Regina giggled.

"Right, and it's another reason to not get involved," Victoria said. "I've never dated anyone with children. What if I disrupt their situation? I'm so used to following my own schedule and a little person requires a lot of time. I don't think he's even considered how complicated the logistics would be." Victoria's mind went back to how John had teased her in the history section. *Who asks such a question?* She bit her lip to keep from smiling like an idiot. "Besides, kids kind of get in the way of...fun times."

Regina rolled her eyes. "If that were the case, Pete and I would have stopped after the first one."

"You're not even a little curious to see how he gets along as a temporary dad?" asked Paula. "What if they're really cute together? You could have a peek into your future as doting parents of your own little girl."

Victoria grimaced at the idea. "Jesus, that's just a little too terrifying, don't you think? I haven't even agreed to have the sordid affair yet." If she was going to consider being the mother of John's imaginary children, she'd have to first unlearn most of what her mother taught her.

Paula didn't let up. "Oh my god, what if he could see you interacting with his niece? And he fell in love with how you two bonded..." The dreamy far-off look in her friend's eyes made Victoria frown.

"Wait, are you plotting something for your new book?" Victoria asked.

Paula looked sheepishly into her glass of wine. "Maybe? Sorry, girl."

"Okay, because I do not like the idea of auditioning for a motherhood role. If he doesn't get that my career is currently my baby, then that's a definite turnoff. I already spend enough of my life playing roles for other people. Playing mommy can't be another one."

Regina narrowed her eyes. "What does that mean?"

She sighed. "You know what I mean, playing roles, wearing masks. I have to do it at work, whenever I go home to see my mother. It's exhausting."

Paula set her glass down, her face shifting to a somber expression. "You're doing what Paul Laurence Dunbar instructed."

Victoria gave a sad smile. Another one of Paula's literary figures was correct. "'We wear the mask that grins and lies, it hides our cheeks and shades our eyes.'"

"If we're going to go there," Regina added. "Let me remind y'all that Claude McKay offered the opposite advice: 'If we must die, let it not be like hogs.'"

"Therein lies the problem," Victoria said, raising her finger in response. "Because it was DuBois who said that black folks live in a constant state of dualism. According to him, I can never be *just* Victoria Reese. I have to be someone else whenever I step foot in the hallways of Pembroke. There's no way around it."

"That's fair," Paula said. "Now that we've got the black philosophers out of the way, what are you going to do in *this* situation?"

Victoria chuckled. "Good question. I don't know yet."

"Can we keep it real for a minute?" Regina asked.

"Yes, let's."

"Kevin wasn't your last screw, was it?"

Victoria's face colored. "Reggi..."

"Keeping it Real Rules apply here," her friend said. "You know how this goes."

Their Keeping it Real Rules were set in place years ago to keep transparency between the three best friends.

Whenever one of them was in a tight spot, the other two made sure to "gather her" before she did anything stupid. Absolute honesty was needed for the problem to be solved. Victoria was a fan of the concept, but often found herself on the embarrassing end of her girlfriends' interrogations. "Kevin was the last," she admitted.

"He was a year ago," Paula gasped. "Not even a little harmless hookup?"

"The Keeping it Real Rules call for a judgement free zone," Victoria reminded her friends. "Please, cut me some slack."

"Fine, fine, fine. But Paula raises a good point. You can't keep letting your work get in the way of having, as you call it, 'fun time.' You dumped Kevin because he wanted to spend time with you. You complained that he got in the way of work."

"He didn't even meet your parents," Paula added.

Kevin hadn't been destined to meet her parents. The university IT worker was too boring for her father and not impressive enough for her mother. Katherine Reese would have pounced on his inability to spot the salad fork at a restaurant. Whenever it came to men, it was her mother, not her father, who discriminated harshly. Katherine's behavior had always confused Victoria, considering how dangerously close she was to becoming "a bookish spinster." No, she absolutely didn't want to juggle both her mother and a boyfriend. "Kevin was also terrible in bed," she said.

"What do you think John might be like in bed?"

She leaned against the couch arm and thought about it. Judging by the way his arms had felt around her body and the passion in his kiss... "I can only imagine," she flashed the ladies a grin and wink.

Regina pulled up the social media photos once more and nodded. "Yes, ma'am, I'm imagining as well."

"Alrighty then," Paula said, taking another drink. "While we're sitting here imagining, can I ask you another question? Does he seem like a safe guy?"

Victoria nodded. "He does. Even though the kiss was a little startling, I still felt like I was in control."

"If you say no to his proposition, can you keep working with him?" Regina asked. "Will it be weird?"

Victoria had thought about that. "Sure, it might be weird, but I have a choice. If I don't want to engage, I'll let him know and we'll just set boundaries. Simple as that."

Her friends exchanged a covert glance at one another. "What?"

Regina cleared her throat. "To hear you describe how magical the 'History Section Kiss' was, I feel like *simple as that* might not be the case."

"Right…" Victoria replied. She had also thought of the alternative. "If I do want to engage, I need to be careful."

"Careful is your middle name," Paula pointed out.

"I thought your full name was Victoria Reserved Reese," Regina added. "Your flirting skills are kinda dusty."

Victoria scoffed. "Who's dusty? I'm the one who made out in the History section."

The three fell out with laughter. "I've seen you work those hips, so I know you've got it in you," Paula said over Regina's giggles. "But sometimes, you do this thing when you get nervous."

"What thing?"

Regina stepped in. "What Paula's trying to say is

sometimes you get kinda snappish at men who have taken an interest in you. I'm surprised you let this one get far enough for a kiss."

Victoria sat back and thought about it. She remembered what John said about her being thorny. "You don't get to where I am by being nice."

Paula nodded. "Girl, I know that's right. But if you intend to say yes to a sordid affair, maybe you can employ some of that DuBois Duality and balance out the salty and sweet. Your resting bitch face is impressive, but do you have another expression?"

Victoria plastered a crazed grin on her face. "This better?" she asked through clenched teeth. Her girls collapsed in tipsy laughter. "What? Don't I look *happy*?"

"It's a start," Regina said through her giggles.

Once Paula and Regina had sobered up, Victoria got them out of her house and took her remaining bottle of white wine upstairs to her office. There, she set out to make a plan for the sordid affair decision. She started off using the tried and true method of listing pros and cons. On the whiteboard she had installed over the summer, she drew a large T and began scrawling two lists.

Pros:	Cons:
John is hot	I'm too busy
John is single	Temporary?
Amazing sex, maybe?	Not professional
	Could jeopardize internship
	What if colleagues found out?
	YOU DON'T KNOW HIM!
	He's responsible for a child
	Mom wouldn't approve

Victoria frowned at the last item on the cons list. *Mom wouldn't approve?* She wiped it off with the heel of her palm and took a sip of her wine. "How old are you?" she muttered. Old enough to know she didn't need to check in with her parents anymore. She tilted her head to the side as she stared at her lists. "I could just keep John to myself…"

When in doubt, say nothing to the parents.

She carried her wine glass to her desk and sat down. She could already tell the cons list was winning the battle. Fall semester was always a beast and she couldn't spare time for a fling. *Except…* She opened the calendar on her computer, which was synced with her phone. "What if…" Victoria scanned the next few weeks that she and John would be working together and began piecing together a loose schedule. She took into account every meeting, each class, and possible lunch break options. She remembered that John said his niece went to school at Hollingsworth Academy. If Victoria was seriously considering having an affair, she needed to think about the girl's feelings. No need to take her uncle, and primary caregiver, away from her. When she found the school's website, she glanced through their academic schedule, counting every conference day, half day, and school closure. Victoria jotted down her findings and added them to her calendar.

Her bottle of wine was nearly empty when she finished her plotting.

When she looked upon her work, a wave of pride swept through her. But when the wave rolled back out to sea, she was left with her initial embarrassment and anxiety. Sure, each day was planned with care, but nothing about it seemed sexy or…sordid. She had felt more joy from creating a syllabus schedule with weekly class lessons and reading lists. The calendar she stared at on her computer felt like the work of a madwoman. *Be that as it may... I've always felt better with a plan.* Best to walk into a foreign situation with a small measure of confidence, a tool to make one feel in control. Is that what she wanted at the end of the day? To feel in control? If John was serious about his offer, the only way she'd be comfortable enough to engage was to feel empowered. Excel spreadsheets made her feel empowered.

Tired, Victoria stood to leave her home office. As she turned out the light, she caught a glance of her pros/cons list and remembered what John said in the stacks. *If you're interested in something remotely impulsive...* Having interest was very different from actually doing. Fantasies were great and all, but acting on them was risky. Victoria didn't do risky. She sighed as she flicked the light off. While she wasn't normally an adventurous person, her body had definitely informed her that she was ready to take a chance. Victoria wanted to *do him*.

Chapter Eleven

Jessi's laughter rang loudly in John's ear. "I can't even picture how you and Chris managed," she said. "Two hulking dude-bros wringing their hands over maxi pads."

"We weren't wringing our hands," John insisted while looking through the mess on his desk. He was searching for a titles acquisitions list before his sister video called. Martha waited in the doorway tapping her toe.

"You got it?" she asked in a loud voice. *When is she going to get that hearing aid looked at?*

"Jess, hold on. Martha, give me a few minutes, will ya?"

"Mr. Wegman needs the Children's acquisitions by the end of the day."

"Yes, yes, I know. Budgets are due. Give me thirty minutes and I'll find them for you."

The old woman shrugged before hobbling away. "Sure thing, Donovan."

"You know damn well you can't multitask," Jessi chided him. "Let's talk when you get home."

John continued to search the papers on his desk. "No, no. I want to talk to you now. Did Becca get a chance to call you during her lunch period?"

"She could only talk for a few minutes, but oh god," Jessi sighed, "I miss my little pumpkin. She sounded so pitiful. I shouldn't have come out here."

"Jess, she's fine. She's just a little mixed-up right now."

"And I'm probably to blame for that. Still no word from Allen?"

John rubbed the side of his face. "No word."

"You know, when we last talked, I forgot to mention how the events of this summer might be affecting how he regards you."

"Just because I'm keeping his daughter doesn't mean he can't call her. Really, Jess. One punch at a church cookout and *I'm* the monster?"

His sister bit back her smile. "Not a monster…"

"You should be proud of my restraint. He knows he got off easy," John said, pulling a face. "If Becca knew what kind of asshole her father was…"

"I need you to keep him and his mistresses to yourself," Jessi said in a steely voice. "Becca doesn't need to hear it."

"Of course."

There was a pause in their conversation. John fought to push aside the anger he felt when he'd first seen his sister's tear stained face. John had wanted to punch the person who'd contributed to Jessi's pain and who better than the man who was cheating on her?

"John?"

He refocused his gaze on the papers before him, right on a spreadsheet of children's book titles. "I found my list," he muttered.

Jessi laughed at him again. "I wanted to say thank

you for doing this for Becca and me. Thank you for not making me choose."

He immediately softened. "Yeah, of course. How *is* the research going?"

"Oh, Stockholm is great! We're coming up with some exciting urban development plans. I'm collaborating with a civil engineering group from Norway. They've done brilliant things with Oslo's lower income districts. It's stuff I can bring home and implement in our downtown area. I just have to apply for the grants, of course."

John smiled. "Becca sounds just like you, so full of ideas and ready to topple the patriarchy, as she puts it."

"Our moms are responsible for some of that," Jessi said with a chuckle.

"That's true," he said, massaging the back of his neck.

"What's wrong with you?"

"Mmh?"

"You sound edgy and tense," Jessi said. "Is it work?"

"Work is fine," he said. "I'm fine."

"I know my step-twin's voice. What is it?"

Jessi was good at whittling things out of him so he decided to skip the runaround. "It's a woman."

His sister tried to keep the laughter from her voice. "A woman, you say?"

"It's not a big deal."

"A woman doesn't make you sound like that," Jessi said. "She must be interesting."

Interesting wasn't the word. "Sure."

"Are you planning to stay mum about her?"

"I think that would be for the best."

"So I need to send in a scout to do some spying? Don't worry, I'll get a full report from your niece."

"I wouldn't worry about it."

His sister tilted her head to the side and gazed at him with narrowed eyes. "Look, if the lady in question becomes a bigger deal, you're free to explore that. Our mothers would love the opportunity to jump in and take care of my pumpkin."

He rolled his eyes even though he was thankful for her words. The last thing he wanted to convey was his inability to take care of his niece. "I'm not that hard up for a date," he said. "I'm not going to leave your daughter at the mall."

She chuckled. "Please don't think you'd be the first person to lose a child in a mall. But seriously, I left her with you because you're more than capable. And regardless of her current attitude, you're her favorite person. Have a little single dad fun on the side."

John's mouth twisted in mock-disgust. "I don't know what you think 'single dad fun' looks like, but I'll take your advice under consideration."

"Can you at least tell me what she looks like?"

"I'm not getting into it."

"Ugh, you're no fun," Jessi pouted.

"I hate to let you go, Jess…"

"Yeah, yeah. I get the picture."

"I love you, sis. Stay safe."

"Love you too. Give Becca a kiss for me."

He hung up and checked the time. Victoria would be here soon. John snatched up the spreadsheet and carried it to the checkout counter. "Here you are, Martha."

"Didn't think you'd find it in that mess," she said without looking up from her book.

John raised a brow. "Well I did."

"You need to let maintenance in there and clean."

He pressed his lips together in a thin line. "Yep."

"I don't know how you can get any work done."

"Right," John ignored her and pressed on. "Martha, if a woman comes in asking for me, could you be a dear and direct her to my disaster-zone office?"

"Same gal from the other night?" Martha asked with a ghostly smile. She glanced up from her novel for the first time. "Yeah, sure. I'll send her your way."

Martha Radcliff was a tough old bird who wasn't rattled by anything that came her way. Whether it was a belligerent homeless man, a "can I speak to your manager" haircut, or Mr. Wegman's erratic demands, Martha remained unfazed. Rather than argue with her, John turned on his heel and walked back to his office. He was on edge alright.

He threw himself in his chair and swiveled away from his desk, facing the bookshelves behind him. Usually, a good book could steady his frantic thoughts. If he could lose himself in someone else's story, his knee bouncing would cease, his fingers wouldn't worry a random thread on his shirt.

John's father had believed his lack of focus was based on lack of willpower and thought organized sports were the solution. If John focused on the game that would somehow translate to him concentrating on other aspects of his life. Whether he held a football or basketball, John had still floundered in school, anxious about his academic standing. He'd liked making John Sr. proud, but it hadn't helped his day-to-day struggles. Luckily, his mother had recognized his ADD early enough to intervene with quiet activities. One of her unorthodox attempts included filling his bedroom closet with blankets and pillows. Believing that the small space would help him, she told him to sit quietly and meditate in the dark. It had been a frustrating exercise since he'd still struggled to turn his mind off. She eventually moved a lamp into his closet and told him to try reading. *That* actually worked. After an hour of sitting in his closet reading Tolkien, surrounded by the quiet and coziness, he was able to steady his thoughts and do productive things like his homework.

Unfortunately, ADD often contributed to his inability to sleep. And today was no different as he was running on half a night's sleep. He was still getting used to Becca's early schedule and made the mistake of reading until 4 a.m. He was halfway through the duke saga and was pleasantly surprised that he didn't hate it. The main character was a saucy governess with plenty of cheeky quips and a bosom that would not stop heaving. The duke in question was one of those noblemen who wasn't averse to working, but his dark past made him difficult to love. By the time John had forced himself to put the book down, the two characters had run off to Scotland for a quickie marriage to save the governess's virtue, or something like that.

If John was honest, he'd say the duke was a bit of a dick and the governess could probably do better. But he understood that wasn't the point of the story. Women apparently loved the fantasy aspect of grand balls, carriage rides, and powerful wealthy men to protect them. Did Victoria like those things? Did she want him to take charge and force her into a Vegas marriage to protect her honor? He shook his head. Of course not. She was a self-possessed woman who valued her job enough to put up with his antics. Victoria was coming into this partnership with her university in mind. But that kiss... It would be difficult to complete any task without being re-

minded of her soft lips pressed against his. Or the scratch
of her fingernails against his scalp as she undid his bun.

The soft knock at his door made his heart jump into
his throat. As John swiveled in his office chair, he tried
to keep his pulse in check. Victoria stood there, purse
in hand, hesitant to cross the threshold. She wore something similar to the outfit from Tuesday night: a heather
gray pencil skirt that settled just above her knees and
a light pink button-down blouse. Her pale pink pumps
were crossed at the ankle as she leaned against the door
frame. The fact that she looked more like a librarian
than he, aroused him immensely. "Hello," she said in
a bright voice.

He cleared his throat and stood. "Dr. Reese," he said,
gesturing for her to take a seat. "Thank you for coming."
As soon as he said it, he cringed inwardly at the wording.

Victoria didn't appear to notice as she sat down at
his desk. She gave a cursory glance at the mess that still
covered its surface before flashing a smile. Something
about the smile felt a little forced, but John tried his best
to ignore it. "Of course."

When he sat down, he shuffled a few papers around,
making space for nothing in particular. He just wanted to
appear in control of the clutter. "About the other night..."
he started.

"Before we get to that, can I tell you something?" she
asked, but didn't give him time to respond. She dropped
her purse on the floor and leaned forward, resting her
elbows on her knees. "I got into an email battle with
someone from Admissions, who wants me to join the
Diversity and Inclusion Taskforce. Which at Pembroke
means all the faculty of color get photographed several
times so we can be featured on the website. The most

that this taskforce will do is make me and one other brown professor, Dr. Reddy, work hard to create some kind of projected goals document that will ultimately be ignored."

Boom.

John was about to open his mouth to reply, but she went on.

"And it's not that I don't want to improve Pembroke's 'diversity problem,'" she said with air-quotes. "It's just that this work always ends up on a few people's backs. I tried this when I was first hired on. Back then, I didn't know how the hidden cost of invisible labor worked. How they take your desires and twist them around like you're asking too much to have more women of color alongside you. You end up having to give and give just to fix their mistakes. Four years ago, I was young and gung-ho about making Pembroke woke A-F. Oh my god, I sound like our students. Does your niece say things like that? Jesus, this woman wouldn't take no for an answer either. She just kept hitting reply and coming back with a new reason why I should pile more stuff on my plate. Finally, I just told her 'Laurie, please eff-off.' But of course, I was way more polite than that because Laurie's feelings would have been hurt and I would have been the *aggressor*. But I ended the email with 'Best,' so surely, she'll know how pissed I am…" She ended her speech with a smart shrug.

"Whew chile" was a phrase that he'd often heard his stepmother, Sandra, use and he had never quite understood how appropriate those words were until now. On the one hand, John did not know what words could be offered to let Victoria know he felt bad about the situation with Laurie from Admissions. On the other hand,

he was pleased that she felt comfortable enough to share this with him. He would take the same approach he had with Becca: sympathetic but candid. "Your labor is important," he finally said. "And you did good by rejecting this woman. Someone once told me that 'no is a sentence too.' You shouldn't have to explain yourself to the Lauries of the world."

Victoria's brow creased slightly, as if she were thinking about his words. "Yeah," she murmured, more to herself than to him. "Yeah, you're right. No is a sentence too. But this is a daily occurrence. Pembroke's team player cult mentality makes it difficult to say no."

John nodded as he leaned forward. "But will the cult pay your therapy bills?"

"Visits to a therapist are included in my health care benefits," she said with a dismissive shrug.

John dipped his head to hide his grin. "How about this: Is Pembroke University going to pay for your inevitable mental breakdown?"

Victoria's eyes flew to his as she let out a shocked laugh. "I guess not."

"What are you currently doing to alleviate the stress?" John asked.

"Wine?" she said with a mirthless chuckle. "I'm trying not to get in the habit, but when I get home, I feel so…angry. I go to bed angry and then I wake up ready to start the whole thing over. I feel like I'm in this enraged cycle of wanting to explode or sleep. If I don't get some kind of release soon…" she trailed off, meeting his gaze.

John was hesitant to pick up where she left off. Thoughts of how they left their last meeting danced around his mind. If she was in need of a release, he could certainly make good on his offer.

"Which brings me to the other night," Victoria finished.

He exhaled slightly. "Right."

"When you first suggested a sordid affair, I think I was shocked by the ridiculousness of it."

John straightened up in his chair and scoffed. "I don't know about—"

"But then I thought about it as I sent my fourth email to Laurie: 'what if I had a way to get my release?'"

As he rubbed his hands against the denim of his thighs, he followed Victoria's train of thought as best he could. It appeared that she was thinking aloud, plotting as she went along. "Okay?"

"Maybe the sordid affair is the ticket," she said, returning to the beaming, albeit manic smile. "Last night, I talked to my friends about it and they were really supportive. I made a pros and cons chart and then I made a tentative schedule for each week. If I planned it correctly, this thing might work."

When he caught up to her, John stilled his movements. "I'm sorry?"

Victoria continued. "My friends and I talked, and I realized that I'm in desperate need of…fun. And you could be the person to supply that kind of…fun."

John sat back in his chair and regarded her quietly. She still wore a strange smile which didn't quite fit her face. "Is that a fact?" he finally asked.

Her vigorous nodding shook glossy black braids framing her oval face. "Yes. I thought we could lay out some ground rules for how this might work efficiently. You know, so it doesn't interrupt our work together."

He rubbed a hand over his mouth and narrowed his eyes at her. *What?* While he fully expected things to be

awkward between them, he didn't realize that Victoria
would treat this so…businesslike. He didn't know he
was already a topic of conversation amongst her friends.
God, there's a pros and cons list? "Efficiently," he murmured.

"I know that doesn't sound steamy," she said quickly.
"But try to understand that I can't let too many extra-
neous activities interfere with my work. Fall semester
tends to be a stressful one for me."

He didn't know it was possible for a woman to talk
about sex without actually referring to it. Sensing his
confusion, Victoria slipped her purse from her shoulder
and went through it. When she revealed a day planner,
John sighed and closed his eyes. "Jesus…"

"I've planned out our affair for the next three weeks,"
she said, slapping the book down before him. Pride lit
her face as she pointed at the days marked in pink highlighter. "How organized is that?"

John let his gaze wander over the many pink mark-
ings before asking, "What part of sordid did you not understand, Dr. Reese?"

Victoria's brow furrowed. "I know what sordid
means. But there's no reason why an affair can't be orderly too."

Orderly was a tall order for John's regular life. His
attraction to Victoria was a chaotic swirl of debris in a
tornado. Order was impossible when he stared too long
into her sable-brown eyes. And he sure as hell struggled to order his dick to stop stirring when he stared at
her full red lips. Especially when the top lip was a perfect cupid's bow while the bottom stayed in a perpetual
pout. John finally dragged his gaze away from her face

and down to the planner. "You have me scheduled for one o'clock tomorrow. What's happening tomorrow?"

"That's where you come in," she replied. "You can figure out the fun stuff."

John blew out an exasperated laugh. He didn't even know which issue to tackle first. There was her aversion to saying the words "sex" or "sexual" and then there was her manic desire to etch their sexual encounters in stone. "You want me to drop what I'm doing to seek you out and sexually pleasure you?"

Her russet-brown cheeks flushed under his perplexed gaze. "Well, when you say it like that, it sounds silly. What I'm suggesting is order." She glanced back at the mess on his desk. "It looks like a little order in your life might not be a terrible idea."

John ignored her little jab. "No, Dr. Reese, it's not silly to want to have sex with someone. The part I'm struggling with is this." He gestured to the day planner. "When I said a sordid affair, I had something else in mind. What? I'm not entirely sure, but this is a bit much."

She rolled her eyes. "I did all of this with your niece in mind."

"Please explain."

"You're taking care of a child and I don't want to get in the way of that. So I looked up her school times and any holidays before I planned for us."

It was weird, but extremely considerate of her. John couldn't help the grin that spread across his face. He buried his head in his hands and chuckled. "You are something else, Dr. Reese."

"So you'll accept my terms?" she asked.

He peeked at her through his fingers. "That depends."

She narrowed her eyes at him, her curiosity properly piqued. "On what?"

"That we try it your way for only one week. I'm pretty sure I can convince you that this is unsustainable. You can't schedule fucking."

A soft gasp escaped her lips. "Do you have to be so crude, Mr. Donovan?"

John shrugged. "But you can't," he said. "If we're going to start dating, there has to be some spontaneity."

Victoria cocked her head to the side. "But we're not dating, we're having an affair. And a fairly short one at that."

Her words punched him in the gut. He masked his disappointment and cleared his throat. "Maybe I don't understand your terms."

"When you suggested this, I assumed you only wanted something quick and physical. I thought this would be more interesting if we skipped all the awkward first date stuff."

John clenched his jaw. He was well aware that he suggested the affair, but the thought of Victoria dismissing him as a *quick and physical* man who wanted to skip wooing her, offended him. "Have you ever done anything like this before?"

"No," she admitted. "But there's something exhilarating about jumping straight to the dessert. Based on our kiss, I think we have chemistry, right? I'm attracted to you and I'm certain you find me attractive."

She wasn't wrong there. "Of course I find you attractive. You're a gorgeous woman who I wouldn't hesitate to…" he trailed off, looking at his desk. "But I'm not like these books. I'm not a cock to lend out for a few weeks."

Victoria flinched. "I've offended you."

"No, no," he said, glancing back to the planner. "You're just being efficient."

"I knew it," she sighed. "When I drew this up last night, there was a part of me that wondered how crazy I would sound."

Her smile had dropped as she admitted her nighttime plotting, and John had a desperate desire to bring it back. From what little John knew of her, Victoria had a personality that made it difficult to give in to her own impulses. He found himself not wanting to disappoint her.

"I commend your boldness," he offered as he looked down at his papers. He tried to move them around again to avoid her eyes. This agreement was quite different from John's usual romantic pursuits. He actually liked eating his dinner before getting to dessert. Things like funny text messages, meeting up at a coffeehouse, making pasta for a lady were all in his Rolodex of moves. He liked making a connection with a woman.

When he'd created another pile of papers he smoothed down his shirt and reassessed the situation. She wasn't asking for him to seduce her. Apparently, they were past that point, which *was* flattering. She was demanding that he compartmentalize his feelings for four weeks and then abruptly end an "affair." They could skip the formalities of courtship, have illicit meet ups, and go their separate ways. Someone like his friend, Chris, would jump at the chance to have a fuck-buddy like Victoria. A smart, sexy woman, who just wanted him for his body? It could be an entertaining proposition. "Do you have any more terms?"

Victoria nibbled her bottom lip before answering. "In our allotted time together, I'm up for almost anything,"

John almost did a double take. *Just so there isn't any confusion...* "Please expand."

"Do I have to?"

John leaned forward, resting his elbows on his desk. "While you were plotting out our schedule, you didn't bother to think about your desires?"

"I was hoping you'd surprise me?" She gave a nervous cough as she shifted in her seat and crossed her legs.

He shook his head. "So you want a structured, well-planned passionate affair? Is this oxymoron more or less what the duke would agree to?"

She appeared to think about it. "The duke had some questionable ideas regarding consent that I think we should avoid."

"I imagine that goes with the time period."

"Right."

"And what else?"

Her face reddened again.

"I can't agree to what I don't have full understanding of, Dr. Reese," John said. He found himself already enamored by her demure demeanor. It appeared almost anything could make her blush. He wondered what brushing his fingers along the inside of her thigh would do. "Tell me what's on your lists of wants."

She appeared to think about it. "Alright... I've never done it in a public place. I wouldn't mind that."

"Noted." He was already plotting.

"I've never done phone stuff either."

John licked his lips. "You mean phone sex?"

Victoria nodded.

"Nor have I," he admitted, his eyes darting to her lips. "But I now find myself motivated to try it."

"I'm not a fan of anything too rough," she said in a stronger voice. "Like choking or spanking."

John felt his own face redden. "Got it," he said with a cough. "So a softer approach then?"

"But not too soft," she added quickly.

Her list was making him a little hot under the collar. Beneath his desk, he adjusted his jeans and gave another cough. "Right, not too soft," he repeated in a husky whisper. "Anything else?"

"I prefer condoms, but I am on the pill—" she paused, "—so, if one of us forgets while we're, you know, in a public place or whatever, it won't be a crisis."

That was also good to know. "That can be arranged," he said with a decisive nod. "That it?"

"Yep."

"Okay."

She flashed him a bright smile. "So, you'll do it?"

John paused, making a little pros and cons list of his own.

Cons: Victoria was intense, a tight ball of nerves, and a taskmistress whose withering looks could shrink the balls of a lesser man. Following her schedule would probably cause him more stress than he needed.

Pros: He liked the idea of coaxing that tight ball of nerves into a more relaxed state. She was a gorgeous Pembroke girl whose withering looks certainly turned *him* on. And, upon closer observation, her sex schedule managed to work around his own.

Lastly, with all this talk about release, John felt like he was deserving of that as well. He wanted a little freedom from his many responsibilities at the library. And as much as he loved her, John would soon need a break from Becca. "Lay out those terms one more time?"

Victoria rolled her eyes with a sigh. "Three weeks of rigidly scheduled passion."

"One week," he corrected. "Of rigidly scheduled passion. The following week, we'll do it my way."

"Wait—"

"I assure you, it will be just as fun as your plan."

"Deal," she said in a resigned tone.

"Good," he said with a quick nod. He wasn't positive that this was a good plan, but he did appreciate an interesting challenge. Though he couldn't put his finger on it, there was something about Victoria that made him sit up and take intense interest. She was captivating, witty, gorgeous, and not someone who he could keep his mind off of. Sure, he'd follow her arbitrary timeframe, but he was now dedicated to keeping things interesting. After all, she was down to have *fun* in public. "When do I start?"

"Tomorrow at one," she said with a grin. "I'll email the spreadsheet to you using my personal email account. We'll have to do all Sordid Affair-related emails on personal accounts."

She's thought of everything. "And tonight we'll just continue working like this isn't a thing?"

"Exactly."

John stood and moved around his desk towards her. "In that case, come join me in the Children's Department so I can read Halloween books to the kids."

Her mouth fell open. "Now?"

He leaned down and took her by the chin. "It's in the job description, Dr. Reese. Or did you forget why we were meeting tonight?"

Chapter Twelve

Victoria marveled over John's performance with the children of the reading hour. The patience he took to speak to those who had questions or who blurted out their own observations, was fascinating to watch. Only an hour ago, they were negotiating the terms of their sordid affair. John sat before her and the children, a giant man on a tiny stool, acting out the silly voices of each character and showing each page to his audience. He was almost a defanged and gentler version of the man she'd kissed in the stacks. Victoria blushed at the memory. *Jesus, I am not compartmentalizing well...*

John's broad shoulders shook with laughter as a towheaded boy of five revealed that his older sister must have been a witch because of her nasty attitude. He countered lightly with a diplomatic answer. "Sometimes witches get cranky when they don't want to be bothered." He tipped his head with a curious smile. "But other times, they're very sweet and they love their little brothers, right?"

"I guess," said the little boy kneeling on the carpet. He had been a squirmy child the entire time John read. Victoria couldn't help but notice him because he kept bumping into other children. "So my sister is a good witch?"

John shrugged. "It sounds like it. You have to remember that witches are just like you and me. They love and laugh and cry, but there's a small difference..."

"What?" the children shouted. Now all of them were interested in the existence of witches. Victoria cringed inwardly. This was definitely not a yarn she would spin for kids. She didn't have the talent to talk to small children, let alone tell them lies. Everything her parents had told her as a child was direct and forthright. The mystery of Santa Claus had been cleared up when she was nine and asked her mother how their family would be found if they moved to another base. Katherine had cut a glance to Archie, who looked visibly perplexed by the question, before breaking it all the way down for young Victoria.

Victoria glanced at the few mothers who hung out, she noticed their overall lack of concern. Either they were flipping through their magazines or on their phones.

John put down his book, *Ten Little Ghosts*, and leaned closer to his captive audience. With his forearms resting on his thighs, tattoos in full view, he explained his little theory. "It's magic, of course. Witches don't like to talk about it because they don't want people to treat them different."

"What kind of magic do they have, Mr. John?" a young girl asked. Victoria frowned. He was really digging himself deep, but he didn't seem fazed at all.

"Oh, well, let's see..." He pursed his lips and gave them a serious look. "Witches are really good with animals, they know what animals need and take great care of them."

"Is that why they have cats?" the squirmy boy asked.

"Yes, now does anyone here have a cat?" John asked.

A few children raised their hands. "I do! I do!" some shouted.

"That's wonderful news," he said, nodding with approval. "And do you take good care of them?"

A chorus of ardent yeses were shouted.

"I don't mean just petting them and playing with them," John said with playful gravity. "I mean, do you help your mommies and daddies feed them and change out their litter?"

A less enthusiastic affirmation was mumbled.

"Well I think we probably need to do a better job, don't you think?"

"Yeah," said the cat owners.

"And I'm also talking to you all who have dogs? Are you guys scooping the poop?"

The crowd dissolved into giggles and "eewws."

"It's one of the best ways to get your witch magic," he said with a shrug.

One shy little girl in the back of the group, twisted her blonde curls around her fist and raised her hand.

"Yes, honey?"

Her face crumpled up as she struggled to articulate her anxiety. "But what if you have a rabbit. Can you be magic then?"

John crossed his arms over his chest and frowned. "I didn't know that any of you had pet rabbits... This changes everything."

The girl's expression was stricken with fear. The other children looked between her and John, waiting for judgement.

"My dear, what is your name?"

"Katie," she said in a small voice.

Victoria's brows knit in worry. This Katie seemed extremely anxious at the thought of talking more than was necessary. Her face turned red and her fist continued to twist her hair. Even the mothers managed to look up from their magazines and phones to gaze upon the interaction. "Katie, my dear, could you come up here and talk to us about your rabbit?"

Katie was surprised. She hesitated, but picked herself up from the floor and walked through the group of children to meet John. He promptly picked her up by the armpits and plopped her on his knee. Katie loosened the grip on her hair as she looked up at John's face. "What do you want to know?" she asked in a small voice.

"First, could you tell everyone what your rabbit's name is?"

"Her name is Coco."

John nodded, thoroughly impressed. "Boys and girls, I forgot to tell you how important and magical rabbits are."

A murmur ran through the group and Katie's eyes widened into two shiny blue orbs. "They are?"

He glanced down at her with a sage expression. "Oh yeah. You see, bunnies are so quiet you wouldn't know how magical they are. They don't bark and they don't meow, because they're trying to find new ways to cast spells."

"What kind of spells?" Katie asked in a hushed voice.

"They have the power to run really fast. Does your Coco run fast?"

She nodded her head. "She does!"

"That's what I thought. Is she a really good hider?"

"Yes!"

A woman who sat near Victoria chuckled quietly. Her

own blonde curls were pulled back into a ponytail and her blue eyes crinkled with a warm smile. She turned to Victoria and whispered, "She never talks like this."

Victoria shared her smile. "She must really love her bunny."

"Last year, we got Coco for Katie's anxiety," the woman explained. "I think it's been working for her self-esteem."

Victoria nodded as she felt her heart bloom. When she glanced back at John and the girl, she couldn't stop grinning at the two of them.

"Now, Katie, do you take good care of Coco?"

"I do."

"Does everyone want to know how you're supposed to take care of a magic bunny?"

Hands shot up following a chorus of "I do, I do." John nudged Katie. "Go ahead, Katie."

The little girl sat up straight and addressed the group of children with her expert opinion. "You have to change their water every day and give them fresh hay to eat."

John nodded. "It's probably magic grass, huh?"

"Yeah, and you have to give them vegetables too. And I help Mommy change out her litter box so it doesn't stink."

"Do you give Coco carrots?" another little girl asked.

"Sometimes, but Mommy says that carrots are really sweet and you can't give too many."

Ooohs and ahhhs ran through the group as Katie educated them. Victoria glanced over at Katie's mother, who was quietly wiping her eyes and trying to busy herself. The pride she had for her daughter's effort spread to the other mothers who watched with affection.

"Okay, you little ghosts and goblins, Halloween is

coming soon and I need you to keep an eye out for the witches in your neighborhood," John said as he set Katie down. She returned to the floor beside his leg. "They're very nice folks."

"But don't they turn you into toads?" asked the squirmy boy who had managed to end up near the other side of the room.

"Oh no, nothing like that. Those are just rumors for us regular humans. No, witches help out with their chores, they take care of animals, they share with their friends, and they go to bed on time." He paused to furrow his brow at the children. "Wait a minute…"

The kids looked among themselves with sneaky grins. The realization was dawning on them.

"I think we've got a group of young witches here!" John cried. "How did I not see it before?"

The kids squealed with excited laughter as he stood up and placed his books on a nearby shelf.

"I can't wait to see what kind of magic you come up with," he told them. "But for now, it's time for you to go home."

"One more book, Mr. John," cried a voice from the group.

He shook his head. "Nope, I can only read you two books tonight. You all have to eat dinner and go to bed soon."

Eventually the crowd dispersed as mothers gathered coats and their own children. Victoria stood and made her way to John. "You had me a little nervous there," she said.

John peered down at her with a grin. "Oh?"

"Your taxonomy of witches had me on the edge of my seat."

"A little Halloween magic can't be bad. They're at the age where everything is still mysterious."

Katie's mother approached them while her daughter explained the details of Coco's magic to a small crowd of children. "Mr. John," she started. "Thank you for what you did this evening."

John's face softened. "Of course, how long has Katie dealt with anxiety issues?"

The mother nodded. "For the past two years. We've taken her to a pediatrician who specializes in ADD and anxiety, and we're working on a plan to help her."

"I'm assuming Coco is a big help?"

"A tremendous help," she said. "It's interesting how powerful one anxious bunny can feel when she's taking care of another. You telling her that Coco is magical might rub off on her as well." She glanced over her shoulder at her daughter, who was still holding court. "Before, she would never have asked you that question. And she certainly wouldn't be talking to the other children like that."

Victoria found herself grinning at the girl. "She's quite the authority on rabbits. She looks like she has the makings of a professor."

"I know." The mother chuckled. "It's wonderful to see her shining."

"Send me an email and I can suggest some helpful books for you and Katie," John said, offering a business card from his wallet. "I have experience with this and I can relay some tricks I've used."

"That would be wonderful," Katie's mother said, taking the card. "Thank you for being understanding."

"It's no problem."

"Now I've got to pry my child from her adoring fans."
She laughed.

When the woman wandered off to collect her daughter, Victoria turned to John. "When we first met, you said you had a hard time staying on subject. Did you mean that you have ADD?"

His green eyes smiled. "In that situation, I had a difficult time keeping my mind on business. It wasn't my ADD though."

She averted her eyes to make sure they were out of earshot of the children. "Right. I didn't realize," she said, suddenly remembering how she teased him about his messy desk. "I'm sorry."

"Why are you sorry?"

Victoria flinched, immediately feeling awkward and foolish. "I didn't mean *sorry* sorry. Like it's a pity you have ADD or anything like that. I have plenty of students who need accommodations and they perform just as well as my other students." As her face warmed, Victoria realized she was rambling like an idiot. "Jeez, if you don't want to talk about it, you certainly don't have to."

John gave a good-natured chuckle as he led her downstairs. "I don't mind talking about it. It's not something I'm ashamed of."

"Of course not," she said, quickly. "Do you mind me asking, how long have you known you...had it?" From behind him, she cringed at her inability to find a better way to ask.

"I'm pretty sure I've had it since I was a kid, my mother did the best she could to come up with ways to help me concentrate. But I wasn't formally diagnosed until I got to graduate school."

As impressive as that was, Victoria did feel for a student who struggled without the right tools. She wondered if she had students in her own class who needed help but didn't know how to ask for it. As they made their way back downstairs, she asked, "When you realized what it was, did it upset you? Or was it a relief?"

When they entered his office, John shut the door behind him. "A bit of both. I had a concrete answer for what was different about me and that made me feel better. On the other hand, I realized I'd have to work harder than most to complete the same tasks."

Victoria didn't want to say something patronizing like "well good for you!" but the teacher in her was accustomed to giving people encouraging overtures. She didn't need to do that with John. He was a man, not one of the students. He was self-possessed and had a swagger that showed. Contrary to what she believed upon meeting him, he knew how to do his job. She'd seen that firsthand. "A person can go a whole lifetime without making those kinds of observations about themselves," she said.

The corner of his lips quirked into a small grin. "Is that a fact?"

She leaned against the edge of his desk and watched him stuff his hands into his jeans. He was wearing another Henley shirt, this one gray and just as tight fitting as the last. The atmosphere in his small office shifted. An electric current ran between them as she tried to hold herself together. "Oh yes. You seem to know yourself really well."

John shrugged his broad shoulders. "It's all trial and error, Dr. Reese."

He also had the ability to make Victoria forget everything with every unsteady breath she took. When he said he would employ other methods on her, did they involve a piercing green gaze that made her knees shake and skin heat? In an effort to stay on topic, she replied, "Well, I have to say that the work you do with children is admirable, Mr. Donovan. I'm confident that my students are going to learn a lot from you."

He stepped away from the door and crossed the room in two easy strides. "I don't want to talk about the children, Dr. Reese."

His quick movements caught her unprepared with the crushing kiss he issued. As his lips pressed against hers, she gave a surprised moan. John's tongue ran along the seam of her mouth and eased past her lips, licking as he went. Victoria's hands instinctively went for his head, shoving her fingers through his loosely tied hair. Sliding his arms around her waist, he pulled her close into his body. She closed her eyes and tilted her head against his insistent tongue, losing herself like a sail boat in his wild seas.

When he broke away, he gazed down at her through hooded eyes, panting from the exertion. "I'm sorry that wasn't scheduled."

Victoria reached upward and touched her swollen lips. "No, it wasn't," she murmured. She wouldn't complain though. It was a kiss that knocked the wind out of her and left her dizzy. She was satisfied with her original idea of hammering out the details, but she certainly didn't mind this either. Before she could ask for more, he broke the spell.

John ran his fingers along her spine and smiled. "I'm afraid I have to get home and relieve my friend of his babysitting duties."

"Of course." She stood straight and took a breath. "How is Becca?"

He moved away from her and began gathering papers from his desk. "Oh, she'll live. The poor girl had a period meltdown the other day."

Victoria hissed. "Oh no. Stain on the back of the pants?"

He chuckled as he packed his bag. "How did you guess?"

"It's happened to all of us."

John led her from his office and turned out the light. "God knows I wouldn't go back to that age for anything. How did we manage it?"

"You talk like a man who thinks the stress is long over. It gets worse," she said. "I mean, don't tell her that."

John's faced creased with a wide grin before he laughed. "I won't. But I need to convince you that there are blessings that come with our age."

"Mmh."

"I'll go over our schedule tonight."

"You will?" she asked as she followed him to the library entrance.

"I will," he said. "And by the week's end, I'll convince you that you don't need it."

"Order, Mr. Donovan. We need order in our lives."

She caught the grin he tried to hide as he opened the door for her. In the nearly empty parking lot, he turned to face her. "You have enough order in your life. I'm here to bring a little disorder. I think you'll prefer that much more."

He was challenging her and she didn't know how to respond. She simply liked feeling in control. Time management was the security blanket that ensured she wouldn't be swept away by her feelings. Whenever she looked into John's eyes, she knew there was a danger in getting lost in his chaos.

In her undergraduate days, she'd had a devastating crush on a classmate in her Creative Writing class. As she had fallen in love with Phil, her grades had taken a dive as well. She had volunteered to read his short stories and offer him critiques, while she wrote saccharine-sweet poetry about him. After they broke up, it had taken everything in her power to get back in the game and save her final exam grades. The problem was that she hadn't had a plan back then, but she had one now. "I'll see you tomorrow, Mr. Donovan."

He nodded. "When we kissed in the History section, you called me Johnny. Do you remember that?"

She shook her head even though she did. It was a slip-up she wanted to avoid speaking about altogether.

"Well you did," he said, backing away from her. As he walked to his pickup truck, he called over his shoulder. "I wouldn't mind hearing it more during our scheduled meetups."

Dang it.

Chapter Thirteen

By 12:30, Victoria had already taught two classes, shoved the last student conference out the door, and had quickly checked in with the writing center workers. As usual, she was productive and anxious. Today, the source of her anxiety was not work-related, but John-related. Last night, she had been bold enough to send him an email, detailing where to meet and how much time they had. It had taken her nearly an hour to pen a paragraph-long message, that basically said: "I'll be waiting in my office, come get me." The thrill of clicking send was enough to make her giggle in her home office. If she only had one week to have her version of a sordid affair, Victoria wanted to get started. She now sat behind her desk wondering what to do with herself. When her phone buzzed, she swiftly grabbed for it. It was a text from John.

Mr. Donovan: What's the naughtiest thing you've ever done?

Okay, we're starting. Victoria settled in her chair and thought of interesting things to reply. She enjoyed writing, but she didn't know that she'd also be a fan of sexting. She was ready to engage.

Victoria: Let's see… ALLEGEDLY stealing a library book.

She waited for a moment, a smile playing on her lips.

Mr. Donovan: I wouldn't put it past you, Dr. R. When the Duke was in your possession, did you at least treat him right?

Victoria: I may have dog-eared a few pages.

Mr. Donovan: My god, you're a monster. Could I make you an offer?

Victoria: Go ahead.

Mr. Donovan: In the future, could I slip my bookmark between your pages?

Victoria: That doesn't sound quite as naughty.

Mr. Donovan: You haven't used my bookmark. It's big enough to take care of any book.

Victoria paused to take a breath as she tried to figure out her next witty response. Her phone vibrated again. Paula was calling her. She groaned and answered. "What?"

"Damn, girl. What did I do?"

She sighed. "I'm sorry. I'm actually in the middle of something."

"A meeting?"

"Not exactly," Victoria hesitated. "I'm texting someone."

"Reggi and I are downtown about to grab some lunch. I was going to ask if you wanted to join, but apparently you're texting someone?"

"Is it the librarian?" Reggi's voice asked in the background. Victoria rolled her eyes.

"Reggi wants to know if you're too busy with the librarian to have lunch with your friends."

"Yes," she admitted. "I'm in the middle of sexting with him and you guys are seriously interrupting my response time."

"Oh shit!" Reggi said.

Paula lowered her voice. "Do you need any help? I write romance for a living, you know?"

That doesn't sound like a bad idea. Victoria pushed aside the thought. "I'm going to have to let you guys go."

"Report back to us," Reggi shouted.

"Maybe," Victoria said as she hung up. When she returned to John, she hadn't come up with anything witty so she typed the next best thing.

Victoria: Do you have condoms?

When the three dots lit up her screen, and then disappeared, Victoria closed her eyes and cursed her bluntness. Asking about condoms, though prudent, was not sexy and didn't belong in a sexting exchange.

Three dots reappeared.

Mr. Donovan: No. But that's not what I had in mind. Do you read poetry, Dr. R?

Victoria frowned and bit her thumbnail. *Poetry?*

Victoria: Of course...

Mr. Donovan: Do you like Eliot?

Victoria: I think The Waste Land is a bit overrated.

Mr. Donovan: Perhaps. I was thinking of The Love Song of J. Alfred Prufrock

Victoria: ??

Mr. Donovan: "Do I dare to eat a peach?"

Victoria, growing dizzy, released the breath she held. John was simply too clever for her to keep up with. He was going to arrive at her office any moment and she already found herself sweating over him. She waggled the collar of her shirt in an attempt to get air to her armpits.

"A man has never quoted Modernist poetry to me," she whispered to her empty office.

Good lord, what was she going to do with him? Better yet, what was he planning to do with her? Based on that text message, she had an idea. Eliot may have been writing about the malaise and hopelessness of World War I, but John Donovan was referring to a totally different peach.

Before she had too much longer to think about it, a commanding knock at her door made her jump in her chair. She glanced at her watch, saw he was fifteen minutes early, and grinned.

"Come in," she called out.

John stepped inside and closed the door behind him. Time slowed down soon after that. Victoria was suddenly conscious of her own breathing, the grooves in the leather armrests, and her trembling fingers. John leaned against the door and quietly regarded her before speaking. She was pinned beneath his intense stare, unable to open her mouth for a simple greeting. He came dressed different from what she was used to. He wore dark gray slacks and a black button-down shirt with the collar undone by two buttons. Hooked on his arm was a camelhair coat. He was handsome in his jeans and tight-fitting Henley shirt, but this new Sophisticated John took her breath away. As he folded his arms across his chest, a broad smile stretched over his face. "Dr. Reese."

"Mr. Donovan," she breathed. "Thank you for coming."

He pushed away from the door and approached her desk. "Don't thank me yet." He slung his coat over the spare chair and took a seat on the edge of her desk, on her right.

Victoria swallowed. "Right."

She watched as he rolled up his sleeves to the elbow, revealing muscular forearms; one was covered in sandy brown hair, the other covered in tattoos that she still wanted to examine. Both arms were meant for lifting books and women. His physique, while long and lean, appeared powerful enough for bareknuckle boxing. He lounged gracefully against her desk as if he had all day to stare into her eyes. But he didn't have all day. They were scheduled to part ways in an hour. Since she didn't know what he would do, or how many times he'd do it, Victoria thought it safe to schedule an hour. "I didn't get a reply from you," he said in a silky voice. A wicked smile touched his lips as a satisfied glimmer lit his forest-green eyes.

Panic rioted throughout her entire body while she clenched her thighs. Sexual magnetism radiated from his body, threatening to render her powerless. "I couldn't think of anything smart to say," she admitted. *When in doubt, just be honest.*

John slowly stood from the desk and took one step towards her. She sat completely still as he reached out and stroked her cheek. His gaze was as soft as his caress. "I find it hard to believe that this mouth didn't have anything smart to say." A huskiness lingered in his voice causing Victoria to tremble under his touch. John's thumb rested against her bottom lip, stroking the curve with an aching slowness that relaxed the muscles in her shoulders. "Claire the governess always has a clever retort in her arsenal."

"You're reading the book?" she asked as his fingers trailed down her jaw towards her neck. "Why?"

"I'm a man who does his research. And this research was especially worthwhile." He leaned over her, close enough for her to sneak a peek of chest hair through the small V of his shirt collar, and adjusted the lever of her office chair. Victoria shot up a few inches, closer to his face. She fought to keep her eyes open and remain upright in her chair, but the scent of forest knocked her senseless. His hand, at her neck, gently pushed her against the soft leather back. With his hands planted on her armrests, he leaned forward and brushed against her lips while he spoke. "The duke proved he was a skilled lover, but I noticed there were certain things missing from his repertoire."

"Like what?" She was desperate to know what the

duke was lacking. Even more desperate to know what John would bring to the table.

"I could tell you," he breathed. "But could I just show you?"

Victoria's breasts tingled against the silky fabric of her blouse. A hot ache vibrated between her thighs, making them clench involuntarily. Her cheeks flushed when she felt the warm slickness wetting her panties. She gave a jerky nod. "Yes," she whispered.

John's tongue traced the soft fullness of her bottom lip, taking it gently between his own lips and tugging. His kiss was a slow and drugging one that sent new spirals of ecstasy through her body. Victoria was tentative in her response, testing the waters with a lick and nip, while her hands raised to meet his jaw and neck. While John's tongue made a long and languid exploration of her mouth, she tried to savor every second. Under her hands, she felt the slow rhythmic movement of his jaw as he plied her lips with each deep thrust of his tongue.

Victoria would have happily drowned in his sinful kiss, had he not left her lips and slowly trailed down her jaw. John angled around to her ear, taking her lobe between his teeth. She let out a muted gasp at the surprise sharpness that mingled with pleasure. When he released her earlobe, he gave it a gentle lick before moving down her neck. While his mouth was busy, John's hand moved to the buttons of her shirt, undoing a few before running his fingers down the curve of her breast. "Can you stay quiet, Victoria?" he asked, his mouth at the hollow of her collarbone.

Him calling her Victoria made her face flush with excitement. Her heart hammered in her ears with every swipe of his tongue along her burning skin. His ques-

tion made no sense. If he continued like this, she could
make no guarantees. "Maybe?" she said in a shaky voice.

John pulled away long enough to flash her a devilish
smile. "Maybe?" he asked before returning to her racing pulse. He sucked long and hard at her skin, releasing
with a satisfying *pop*. When he pulled away again, he
crouched before her on the balls of his feet. She gazed
down at him, still trying to catch her breath. "I ask, because I'm about to do something that might make you
scream in pleasure. And I'd like to remind you that other
professors are just right next door. So, can you stay quiet,
Victoria?"

She smiled in spite of herself. "What are you going
to do… Johnny?"

John narrowed his eyes and smirked. "I'm going to
do what I promised on the phone." He moved his hands
from the chair's armrests to her thighs. She was thankful she wore another skirt today; a skirt would offer
easy access. He slid his hands down to her bare knees
and settled on his own before her, like a man praying
at an altar. "Let me know when you want me to stop."

Victoria nodded. She didn't want him to stop.

He pushed her knees apart as far as her skirt would
allow and sat back on his heels. "I never told you about
the depraved things I thought about while you shelved
my books," he said while studying her thighs.

"No," she whispered, trying to quell her fluttering
heart.

His large pale hands were a contrast against her
brown legs. They gripped her, pinning her down in a
soft possessive way that made her feel safe and restless
at the same time. "You were bent over trying to find

the right place to put a Tim O'Brien book. I tried not to stare, but you looked so delicious."

Victoria had never heard herself described as *delicious*.

"Your ass and these thighs were straining against the fabric of your skirt." He pushed her skirt the rest of the way until it stopped just short of her pelvis. "You had no idea what you were doing, but my God, you were turning me on."

"I've never had to shelve books before."

"That much was evident," he said with a chuckle. He ran the back of his fingers along the inside of one of her thighs, leaving goosebumps in his wake. She shivered at the sensation that ran up her body and to the back of her head. She let her heavy eyelids close momentarily as she soaked in the pleasurable caress of his hands. "But I'm not interested in your ability to shelve books."

"Of course not."

He kissed the inside of one thigh. "How did you feel while we were so close to one another? Me, right behind you, watching you?"

With her eyes still closed, she recounted the shudder she'd felt when he handed her a book. His hand wrapped around her waist to place FDR in his appropriate spot. She stood there, wrapped in the warmth emanating from his body. She was intoxicated by the same woodsy cologne that night, feeling the walls close around her. She wanted to succumb to his quiet lure. "I wanted you," she replied.

"Do you want me now, Victoria?"

She opened her eyes and gazed upon the man who kneeled between her thighs. The look in his startling green eyes probed her to her very soul. They seemed to ask permission for the next step. She gave him a tremulous smile. "Yes."

John gently kissed her thigh, tonguing the soft flesh as he went. She watched in fascination as he closed his eyes and breathed deeply, moving higher and higher. His tongue made whorls around her skin, etching his mark on her, making her knees shake. He reached his fingers under her skirt and grasped the edges of her panties. He gave her one last look of confirmation before he tugged them downward, down her knees and past her ankles. He took the lacy black undergarments and stuffed them in the back pocket of his trousers and continued with his mission. "Shall I part my hair behind?" he said, softly reciting Eliot, his hot breath brushing her most intimate parts. Another kiss, much further along her thigh. "Do I dare to eat a peach, Victoria?"

It wasn't a question, so much as it was a declarative, and she bit her lip to prevent the low moan mounting in the back of her throat. She breathed deeply and opened her legs revealing the entrance to her feminine center. Victoria closed her eyes and tilted her head back to receive him. His tongue said everything that his words could not. Her deep breathing soon became quick pants as the tip of his tongue parted her folds and flicked against her sensitive clit. Upon the first intimate contact with his mouth, she squeezed her eyes shut and arched away from her chair, meeting him halfway.

He gripped her closer to his face, pulling her hips forward and working his tongue past her inner lips, laving the hot flesh at her center. The careful ministrations he gave drove her so delirious she rocked her hips to match the rhythm of his mouth. She wanted to moan so badly, wanted to express the full pleasure she was receiving at John's hands—no, mouth. Victoria was on the verge of tears. Her hands found the top of his head, shoving her fingers though his ponytail, pulling him closer. His tongue swiped up and down, over her opening and over her clit, at a feverish speed. His beard offered a different, even more beautiful pleasure as it scratched against her thighs. Victoria panted through each wave of sensation and resisted the urge to cry out and close her thighs around his head.

But when he took one hand away from her hips and slipped a finger inside her, she lurched forward and bit her lips. A long finger curved along her walls, stroking at the same pace as his tongue, pushing her towards the edge. "Johnny," her hoarse whisper broke the silence. "Oh god…"

John didn't stop at her interjection. In fact, he took that as instruction to move faster and added another finger to the equation. His tongue worked a figure-8 and wouldn't finish until he got the signal. His two fingers filled and stretched her, making her beg for more. Her wordless imploring for a release took the form of soft moans and gasps that shook her body. When she opened her eyes and looked down at John, she gasped at the sight.

A dressed-up man licked and sucked her like she was the last woman on earth, like her body offered the last drink of water. It was enough to knock her off the edge. One hand clutched an armrest while the other grasped the back of his head, as she lost her mind in her office chair. Around his fingers, her walls spasmed and jerked. Victoria's thighs squeezed together as she hunched over and hissed her orgasm as quietly as she could. Tears sprang to her eyes as her body quaked to the last licks John gave her.

When it was over, she collapsed backward in her chair, releasing him and relaxing her legs. Her breath came in halted gasps that shook her entire body. She stared at the white expanse of the office ceiling before she could bring herself to look him in the eye. The reality of being on her college campus, in her office, and with people walking the hallways, was exhilarating. Only when John's lips left her and he cleared his throat, did she feel it polite to look down. When she did, her breath hitched in her throat. John removed his fingers and sat back on his heels. With his eyes locked on hers, he grinned and licked his fingers. He finally stood, pulled her underwear from his back pocket and wiped his face before making his way back to the guest chair that sat before her desk.

With her mind dazed and her body still radiating with pleasure, Victoria watched him as he wiped his hands on her lacy black panties and stuff them in the pocket of his coat. "Dr. Reese," he said, giving her a perfunctory nod. His gesture was almost funny. If her legs weren't still shaking and her breath still shallow, she would have laughed. Victoria took it as a signal to straighten up in her chair and pull her skirt down. Apparently, she was not going to get her underwear back.

As she swiveled to face him, she willed her knees to stop jiggling. "Mr. Donovan." She was again left speechless. There was nothing witty to retort after what he did for her.

"I hope that was to your liking," John said. His mouth curved at the corners as his gaze swept over her body.

"Yes," she said. *Of course it was.* She still felt the

sensation of his scruffy cheeks against the insides of her thighs. Victoria was certain she'd feel his beard tickle her for the rest of the day. "Thank you for that."

"I'm sorry I got here so quickly," he said, glancing at his wristwatch. "I was trying for punctuality this time."

"No apologies necessary."

His gaze locked on her. "I couldn't help myself. Just knowing you were waiting on me was enough to put the pedal to the metal."

Victoria grinned at the phrase. "No need to speed on my behalf."

"If you could see yourself right now, you'd say otherwise," he said as his eyes twinkled with mischief.

"Thank you." Her voice was shakier than she would have liked. Her eyes left his face and widened when they fell to his astride legs. The bulge straining against the flat front of his trousers stood proudly, distracting her from forming her next sentence. "Your um…"

John followed her eyeline and glanced down at himself. "Completely natural," he said with a chuckle. "He'll go away…eventually."

Her sudden curiosity made her sit up straight in her chair. "He doesn't have to," she said, sneaking another glance at the bulge. "I don't want him to feel left out."

John licked his lips as his fingers clenched around the armrest of his chair. She couldn't help but notice the way his nostrils flared as he stared at her. "That's very kind of you."

Kind, but also a little selfish. She wanted to see what was making such a big impression against his pants. Better yet, she wanted to *handle* it. "It's nothing," she breathed. "I just want to make sure you were…" She didn't know how to finish that sentence without sounding like an idiot. *Also satisfied?*

"Of course," John said, standing from his chair. He took up his coat and returned to her desk. "I know what you're trying to say and I certainly appreciate the offer, Dr. Reese. But we're going to have to put it on hold for now."

Victoria's eyes widened. "You're leaving?" What she wanted to say was that they had at least forty-five minutes left, but she held her tongue. The agreement that she issued him already looked transactional, making him stay the entire hour would make him sound like a gigolo. *Oh god, what if he thinks I think he's a gigolo?*

As John planted his hands on her desk and leaned down, he flashed her a wolfish grin, as if he were reading her thoughts. "Lord knows I hate to eat and run... but I forgot I had a meeting with the library community outreach program." Inches away from her face, he lowered his voice to a gentle purr. "Otherwise, I would stay here and bend you over this desk."

Victoria inhaled sharply, but found herself leaning forward to meet him. Her gaze was fixed on his mouth. "Are you sure you don't have time to do that?"

He angled his face to the side of her cheek. "I don't have the kind of time you deserve," he whispered. His hot breath brushed the shell of her ear, sending a shiver down to the base of her neck. She wanted to lean into his lips, but forced herself to keep herself upright. "Too bad you wanted to skip straight to the dessert."

Victoria's eyes flew open from their drowsy state. "What?"

John pecked her on the cheek before straightening away. "I'll see you tonight for actual work?"

She gasped as if someone tossed a bucket of cold water in her face. Of course, they had another job shadow meeting that evening. But she couldn't imagine going to the library for…work. But he had a busy day and she had plenty more things to cross off her list before 6 p.m. Victoria was resigned to let him go. "Right."

"I can see you forgot about our project," he said with a chuckle. "Don't let me be the only one following your schedule."

Victoria slumped in her seat as she watched him walk to the door. "I know the schedule," she said. She forced herself not to check her calendar for their next *fun* meeting. She'd do that once he left. "Thank you for coming to this meeting. I hope your next one is just as eventful."

John chuckled as he opened the door. "I can guarantee you, honey, it won't."

When he quietly closed the door behind him, Victoria waited two minutes before she shot her fist in the air for a victory punch. First day of Sordid Affair was a resounding success. Short but thrilling. Victoria wanted to get out of her chair and follow up with an end-zone dance, but thought it more prudent to check herself over first. The mirror she kept in her office showed what she felt: a dewy glow in her cheeks, smudged lipstick, and a partially unbuttoned blouse. She couldn't shake the goofy grin or the tremor in her thighs, as she refastened her top.

A little midday dessert wasn't half-bad.

Chapter Fourteen

John hadn't realized how quickly Becca would work at creating her gang of twelve-year-old feminists. But Becca was her mother's daughter, and the gang was formed in swift order. When John picked her up from school on Friday, she declared that their patron saint, Alanis Morissette, had decreed that women need a space to themselves to create art and take control of their destinies. Of course, that meant his home would have to be available for such a space. John was also required to find these creative women snacks and drinks. Because who can create on an empty stomach?

The last girl to arrive to Becca's Saturday night sleepover was McKenna. The freckle-faced girl showed up with her mother, who was hesitant to let her daughter cross the threshold.

"Becca!" McKenna screeched, running past him and into the living room where festivities were already in progress. The collective was complete and John girded his loins for the rest of the night.

McKenna's mother, Mrs. Townsend, hovered at the door, looking from him to the group of girls who were digging into a gluten-free cheese pizza. "And you're Becca's…uncle?" she asked, looking him up and down.

"I am," he said, holding out his hand. John watched as she stole a peak at his tattooed arm and tentatively reached out to give him a weak shake. "Becca's living with me while her mother's in Sweden."

Mrs. Townsend pulled her hand back and crossed her arms over her chest. "McKenna needs to take her allergy medication before she goes to bed."

"That can be arranged."

"McKenna doesn't eat dairy," she countered.

"Becca gave me a list of each girl's dietary restrictions," John said. "I found McKenna some organic chicken nuggets."

"McKenna doesn't watch scary movies," Mrs. Townsend said, moving rook to bishop.

John nodded. "I've already changed the parental settings on all devices in my home," he lied. He knew censorship was horseshit in a world where every child had the internet in the palm of her hand.

Mrs. Townsend was running out of moves. She glanced around John, at the children and pursed her lips. "Are you CPR trained?"

"Renewed my certificate last year, ma'am."

"Well…" The flustered woman shrugged her shoulders in a helpless way that made John feel less defensive. She leaned forward and whispered. "This is McKenna's first sleepover and I'm just…"

John nodded again. "I know you're worried and that's natural," he said. In his line of work, he'd had plenty of time to observe how parents interacted with independent children. Some held on tight and moved aside all obstacles, while others kicked back and relaxed. Mrs. Townsend was in the former category, armed with a bottle of allergy medicine. "I deal with kids all the time at the library and I can say that you're leaving McKenna with a group of really nice girls. I'm here in the background ready to jump into action if anyone needs me, but tonight is about them…writing feminist manifestos or dabbling in witchcraft."

The woman's tight expression softened as she snorted a laugh. "Oh god, you're right." She took a deep breath and straightened her shoulders with a resolute nod. "Okay. Thank you for saying that. I mean, that's what we did. Playing Bloody Mary and making prank calls didn't kill us."

"Of course not," John said, patting her on the shoulder. "She'll be fine."

It was enough to assure McKenna's mother as she finally forced herself from John's doorstep and returned to her car. John shut the door and breathed a sigh of relief. When he turned his attention to the girls, he was met with a disappointing reality; girls could be just as messy and loud as boys. John's sparsely decorated living room was filled with pillows and blankets, while drink cups were being strewn around the floor and coffee table. Quinoa chips were spilling out of their bag and the no-trans-fat granola cookies found their way onto the floor. The packet of paper plates and napkins were still in their plastic wrap, ignored in favor of each girl simply *holding* a slice of oil-slicked pizza.

And the sheer noise…

John's expensive speaker system, used only for AM Gold hits of the '70s, was now attached to someone's phone. Backstreet Boys were being piped through at a volume John wasn't comfortable with. Though none of them were alive in the '90s, each girl was singing at the top of her lungs about wanting it that way. *How the hell?*

When they weren't singing, they were shouting declarations at one another.

"I love Howie," screamed the blonde one. *Kelly?*

"No, Brian was cuter!" said McKenna. *Good luck, girls, they're all married with children now.*

"Becca, do you have Adele?"

"Duh!"

"I want to listen to Taylor Swift," cried a fourth girl. Maybe she was Devon.

John's home, his bachelor pad, was being torn apart right before his eyes. One girl was fine, four girls were more than any single person could handle. As he surveyed the destruction, he wondered what to object to first.

"Ladies," John said, raising his voice above the fray. "Maybe we could lower the music a little?"

"But we're singing," Becca said.

"That's fair," he said, walking over to his stereo system and turning the knob down two clicks. "But if you turn the volume down, you might actually be able to hear each other when you talk."

Becca rolled her eyes.

"I brought makeup!" Devon shouted, and proceeded to spread a bag full of cosmetics on the coffee table.

The living room exploded into varying pitches of "Makeovers!"

Ooh, what are the rules on makeup? John quickly retreated to the kitchen where it was quieter, and immediately began texting his sister. Damn the Swedish time difference.

John: Jess, I need your help. Is Becca allowed to wear makeup? The girls are breaking it out.

Sis:...??

John rolled his eyes. Her three dots appeared on his screen before the next message appeared.

Sis: It's fine, lol. You have soap.

John: What about the other girls? Should their parents know?

Sis: :D :D :D

John: I'm serious!

Sis: Me too. It's a bonding thing, totally normal. Just make them wash their faces before they go to bed.

John: Fine...

Sis: You're fucking hilarious...

John: *middle finger emoji*

Sis: LOVE YOU TOO, LOL!!!

John was slightly relieved, but hesitant to return to the living room. The girls ran that territory now. Perhaps if he retired to his bedroom, he could hear himself think. Surely, no one would set anything on fire this evening. He'd make himself come down in a couple hours to check on them. Maybe they'd tire themselves out and send themselves to bed? As John crept back into the living room, three girls were swarming Kelly, smearing all kinds of garish colors on her face.

"How does it look?" she asked.

"Hold still so I don't poke your eye," McKenna said.

"Let's not injure eyeballs," John said in a loud voice. He considered staying downstairs just to make certain there would be no makeover-related injuries.

"We're not," the girls said in unison.

"What are you doing?" Kelly asked.

"I'm giving you a nighttime eye," Becca said. "I've seen my mom do it all the time. It's totally easy."

"Hold still, Kelly!"

John cringed as he stood off to the side. *For the love of god, Kelly, please stay still.* When they were finished with her, she looked into a mirror and declared she needed a purple lipstick. The girls sifted through the loose makeup until someone found the closest shade, something call "Sinful Lilac." John rolled his eyes. Kelly applied it…liberally, smacked her lips and examined her face again.

"Perfect," she squealed. The other girls cheered and high-fived while Kelly took a selfie. Then the girl turned around and called out to John. "Mr. Donovan, what do you think?"

Four pairs of eyes zeroed in on him, daring him to say anything unfavorable. John raised a brow and rubbed a hand over his mouth before answering. "Kelly, you look…colorful."

The girl flashed a beaming smile. "I know!"

"Omigod, you guys," Becca said. John noticed how many of them started their declarations, observations, and questions with this phrase. "You know what we should do?" His niece leaned over to whisper in McKenna's ear, causing the girl to giggle behind her hand.

"Omigod that would be hilarious!"

The children were still whispering to each other as John started to make his getaway. He just had to make the stairwell and he'd be home free.

"Oh, Uncle Johnny…" Becca called out in a singsong voice. His hand was on the banister. "We think you should have a makeover."

John grimaced. "I don't think I can pull it off with this beard," he said with a low growl.

"We can decorate your beard," said the helpful Devon, holding up a bag of flower barrettes.

"Omigod, you guys," Kelly said. "We can paint his nails!"

He locked eyes with his niece, whose brown cheeks were red with laughter or rouge, and then at the mess in his home. Her dark brown eyes shined with joy instead of hurt and John was thankful for that. Tonight, she was with friends and not worried about bullies, her body, or her father. If this made her happy, John would man up and get his nails painted. He pulled away from the banister and marched to the scaffold. "No glitter polish!"

As much as he'd tried to put her at ease, Mrs. Townsend came to John's house, at 6 a.m., to retrieve her child. The other girls had parents who didn't mind sleeping in on a Sunday. By noon, the last of the friends had been shuttled away, leaving him and Becca alone once again. Luckily, he had an ace up his sleeve: His stepmother, Sandra. She'd been clamoring for some granddaughter time and was on call when John needed Becca to vacate the house. With his niece prepped and out the door, John was in the clear. The kids were gone and he was now on his way to adult time.

Last night, he'd received an email from Victoria regarding today's meeting. He tapped his hands against his steering wheel as he pressed on the accelerator. His destination was Pembroke's campus, but not the professor's office. Apparently, she had other plans, all of which were detailed in her email. *Park at Moulton Student Center and walk towards Felmley Hall...*

John smiled as he remembered Victoria's hurt-bunny expression when he announced his departure. He did have a meeting with community outreach, but it gave him a little satisfaction to let her dangle. Today, she had his undivided attention and he looked forward to having hers as well. He may have left her office laughing, but the walk back to his truck had definitely been an uncomfortable one. Their one-sided hookup was amazing enough though. He'd never gone down on a woman in her place of work. *Tick that one off the list.* The memory of Victoria's thighs clasped around his head had been seared into his brain and her taste... He licked his lips as he recalled each tongue-swipe against her tiny bundle of nerves.

"Loosened that right up, didn't ya, Johnny," he said with a chuckle.

Every sharp breath, shuddering gasp, and low moan reminded him that under her buttoned-up façade, Victoria was a hungry woman. She needed a release alright. When he pulled his truck into the Moulton Student Center parking lot, and walked towards his destination, he noticed how quiet the campus was on a Sunday. At 2 p.m., it was nearly a ghost town. John hitched his shoulders against the autumn winds and marched through the quad until he spotted a large glass building in the distance.

They were meeting at the university greenhouse.

He shook his head and wished he knew what this Pembroke girl was thinking. Maybe she got this fantasy from her paperback romance. After all, dark dalliances in the garden was something the duke specialized in. The rake had scandalized more than one maiden in his manor's labyrinths. John was nearly finished with the book and could see why some women would be titillated by a dark, broken man who needed to be fixed. However, something told him Victoria didn't have the patience for fixing. If he had to guess, his lover wanted something bigger: unbridled passion…in a university greenhouse.

When he approached the entrance, he looked around and saw a young woman jogging on the other side of the quad. John had to assume they were fairly isolated as he opened the door and stepped through. Humid heat hit him in the face, banishing any of the outdoor chill that had snuck past his jacket collar. Hundreds of species of plants covered every inch of the building. Much of the greenery hung from the ceiling or was contained to a dozen tables, positioned in two neat rows. The center aisle was clear enough for observation and maintenance. Some of the plants on the periphery of the greenhouse were large potters containing fruit trees and rose bushes. Bamboo stalks and trellises of ivy lined the walls but there were no signs of his wallflower. He wondered if he'd find her at the venus flytraps…

"Victoria?"

"Back here, John." Her voice was muffled, squashed by the thickness of the building's atmosphere. John loosened the buttons of his jacket and shook out his collar as he moved through the center aisle. The building made an L-shape where the orange trees grew, and opened into a large atrium where he found Victoria sitting on a bench. Legs crossed and wearing another cute blouse-skirt ensemble. Her braids were wound into a large bun at the top of her head and her skin was already flushed.

Once his eyes landed on her, John slowed his pace and grinned. His heart did a little jig when he saw her crossed thighs tighten. The skirts she kept wearing drove him insane. Her voluptuous thighs filled and strained against the fabric like a warning. John's fingers itched to handle every dangerous curve with care. A tremulous smile lit her face when they locked eyes. She reached downward, absently smoothing her toned calf muscle and asked, "Did you find it okay?"

Her movement, unconscious or not, made his pulse race. "I did," he said, shrugging out of his jacket and hanging it above a salmon-pink hydrangea bush. "Have you been waiting long?"

She shook her head. "I got here a few minutes ago," she answered.

John looked around. "Nothing but the quiet and the flowers?"

Victoria stood and approached him. "If you're worried about privacy," she said with a bashful grin. "I know for a fact that the horticulture students only do maintenance work on Mondays."

Fuck privacy. John was well aware of the risk he took every time he met with Professor Reese. John had a difficult time keeping his hands to himself wherever and whenever they met. Even now, he was unsure what to do with them. "I trust in your planning," he said. "Now tell me the significance of the greenhouse."

She sidled up to him and leaned against a table of white African violets. In her heels, she still stood several inches shorter than him, even with her back straight and breasts pushed out. Above the warm musky scent of the flowers, John could still pick up her familiar perfume of orange blossoms and vanilla. Victoria was a flower nestled amid a thick rainforest, waiting for him to inhale her. "I come here when I need to get away from the florescent lights of the office. Being around the plants takes me somewhere else." She gave a self-conscious shrug. "It's a calming place."

"Calming?"

A smile tugged at the side of her mouth as she ducked her head. "It can be."

"What's your favorite plant?" he asked, stepping around her. "Show me what you like to look at."

Victoria's brow creased slightly as she looked up at him. "You want to see my favorite plant?"

As exhausted and horny as John was, he wanted this one thing from her. It was some semblance of normalcy in a still very weird arrangement. They weren't going to fuck until Victoria engaged in some Midwestern niceties. "Yes, please. What blossom attracts you? I already know what mine is."

She grinned and flushed under his gaze. With her hands on her hips, she glanced around the atrium. "I usually breeze through the first room to sit back here," she said, walking around the table of violets. "I like to check in on these guys."

John followed her to a group of tall pink and yellow orchids. Their label read Orchids of Tanzania. "These are lovely," he said, as he stood behind her. Reaching around her shoulder, he ran a finger down the drooped flute until he reached the opened blossom. Each petal was a shock of taffy-pink, dotted with black freckles, and lemon-yellow patches near its center. "Why are they your favorite?" John asked, his voice dropping an octave right above her ear.

Her head bowed towards the flowers, in an almost-reverent motion. He could imagine her eyes closed as she inhaled the blossoms' heavy perfume. "The petals are wild and…dynamic," she murmured. "They feel like exciting flowers."

John contemplated her meaning as she leaned closer for inspection.

"Did you paint your nails?" she asked, twisting around to meet his gaze. A smile played on her lips as she waited for an answer.

Jesus… John glanced at the hand that still stroked the velvet petal before her. Dark purple nail polish covered each fingernail. It was the only color in Devon's makeup bag that appealed to him. "I hosted a slumber party last night and the girls got to me," he admitted.

Victoria bit back her laughter. "That might be the cutest thing I've heard today."

"The day is still young," he said, fighting the urge to slip his hands into his pockets. "I'm sure you'll find something else."

"I wouldn't count on it," she said, turning back to the orchid. "Your nails rival the beauty of this mysterious plant."

John would take the compliment. "What is it about the Tanzanian orchid that feels exciting, Victoria?"

Her hand began stroking the same delicate petal, brushing against his fingers in the process. She inhaled deeply and relaxed her shoulders. "I imagine where it came from. I don't know much about Tanzania, but I know it has the Serengeti Plains and beautiful wildlife. These flowers were a part of that."

John was lured by the soft lilt of her breathy voice as she murmured about far-off lands and found their fingers intertwined. "It's a far cry from little old Farmingdale, isn't it?" he whispered against the back of her neck. Her skin was warm to the touch and damp with a light sheen of perspiration. John kissed the spot just below her hairline and felt her shiver under his lips.

Victoria's head fell to the side as she sighed, "Yes."

He wrapped an arm around her waist and pulled her against his chest. Her hand left his and clutched the table in front of her. "I haven't had a decent night's sleep in days, Victoria," he said, tracing a path of kisses to the exposed side of her neck. "But I hope to god I can dream of you tonight. You with these flowers, in this heat."

Both of John's hands roamed her body: one at the first button of her blouse, while the other reached down to the hem of her skirt. He licked and nipped at the delicate curve of her ear as he fumbled blindly at her buttons. As her bottom pressed against his groin, John lost what sense he walked into the greenhouse with. All blood was flowing downward and need was overriding dexterity. Victoria sensed this and pulled his hand from her breast to her hip. "I've got it," she breathed. She made quick work of unbuttoning the herringbone blouse, while he hitched her gray skirt over her ass.

"Thank you," he said, pulling at the sides of her panties. He dragged them down her legs and waited for her to step out of them.

Victoria spun around and immediately snatched the undergarment from him. "These are staying with me this time," she said with a playful grin. Her eyes glittered with amusement as she wound her panties around her wrist.

A low growl crept up his throat as he jerked her hips to him. "That's not fair."

"Surely this makes up for them." She continued to undo the buttons of her blouse, revealing the edges of her lacy black bra. With a couple of tugs, she pulled her shirt out of the waist of her skirt and became the first to get topless. John soon joined her by wrenching his own long-sleeve T-shirt over his head and tossing it on a nearby table.

"Watch out for the geraniums, John," she scolded.

"I don't give a fuck about the geraniums, Victoria," he said. "I only care about my orchid."

Her face flushed from the valley of her breasts right up to her cheeks. She forgot the shirt and focused her attention on his belt buckle, feeling bold enough to pull it apart herself. Her nimble fingers set upon the button and fly of his jeans, bumping against his hard-on that strained for her touch. John hissed and closed his eyes when she found what she was looking for, and backed her against the table behind her. "You have no idea how badly I need this," he whispered as he slipped the thin bra straps down her soft shoulders.

"The sleepover was that bad?" she asked, shoving his pants to his thighs.

"It was four girls who would not stop talking." John reached around and unhooked her bra. He tossed it at the geraniums and marveled at her breasts. Ample wasn't the word. John had large hands and palming even one was a beautiful challenge. He tested the weight and gently massaged while covering her mouth with his. He moved around her quiet moans, teasing her bottom lip with his teeth. "How does that feel?"

She jerked her head up and down in reply.

Not wanting the other breast to feel left out, John's other hand joined in on the kneading. Her nipples, dark brown stiffened peaks, were begging for his attention as well. As his kiss deepened, he lifted her onto the table beside the orchids. She didn't break away, even as she made room, shoving away several pots. Her legs wrapped about his thighs, drawing him closer, desperately holding him against her. Their tongues sparred with wet and plunging thrusts, a fiery dance that competed against the heat of the greenhouse. John feared that Victoria's kisses were a powerful toxin, sweet and deliciously drugging. Behind those belladonna-dark eyes lay a trap that he was more than willing to fall into. The desire to taste her kisses consumed him. She was going to ruin him for any other woman.

And then she reached into his briefs.

John squeezed his eyes shut, broke his kiss with a ragged gasp, and pressed his forehead to hers. Her grip was like her handshake: firm and confident. When she pulled along his rigid length, Victoria ran her thumb along the tip, wiping away the drops of fluid. John's breath caught in his throat as he watched her bring her finger to her lips and suck.

"I wanted to do that last time, but you had to run to a meeting," she said with a throaty purr.

Goddamn... "I was a fool," he said, nearly doubling over as she returned to his cock. John wasn't going to let her work alone. He licked the tips of his fingers and applied them directly to the already moist folds between her thighs. Victoria's eyes widened at his touch. It was the same surprised expression that had lit her face when his tongue first touched her. He relished the way her full lips made an "o" and her brows drew upward in the middle. As his fingers rubbed tight circles around her entrance, he knew she was ripe enough to unravel in his arms.

They touched each other while breathing short shallow pants in the humid air. As she massaged his hot, silky column of flesh, John kept his pace quick and his pressure consistent. Even as her hips squirmed against his hand, Victoria managed to maintain eye contact. Her eyes darkened with dilated pupils, staring defiantly back at him, until her body hitched. "Johnny," she pleaded.

She was on edge and her grip on his cock was slipping. His name was on her lips, begging for release, and he sped up his pace. John moved over her, swallowing each plaintive moan that escaped her mouth. His hand stayed between them, working feverishly as their kiss intensified. Her hands left his shaft and seized the back of his head. John loved it when she went right for his hair. He imagined that he had grown it out just for her to rake her fingers through it. *No sense in leaving my hair in a bun when I meet with her.*

"J-Johnny…" Victoria whispered, breaking away from his lips.

"Ride it, honey."

"I'm—I'm—" Her eyes squeezed shut as her hands tightened on the back of his neck. "Oh god." He felt primal pleasure sweep through her body as she clenched around him. Her thighs shook as she arched against his chest. The skin-to-skin heat building between them sent of jolt of electricity to John's heart. Victoria wrapped her arms around his shoulders and hugged him tightly as she rode a warm wave of bliss. "Johnny," she sighed. The sound was so sweet to his ears, he took her by the thighs and lifted her from the table, raising her to his eye-level.

"Did you come?" he asked, panting against her cheek.

Victoria nuzzled his neck, planting light kisses around his excited pulse. "Of course, I did," she breathed heavily.

He carried her to the nearby wooden bench. "Would you like to come again?"

She chuckled in his ear. "Of course, I would."

Good to hear. John laid her on the narrow bench and straddled her body as she hitched her skirt higher. He grabbed one of the condoms from his back pocket before shoving his jeans and briefs lower. A devilish grin spread across Victoria's face when he exposed himself further.

"Hello again," she said to the stiff rod being covered with latex.

"He's excited to be here," John said as he lowered himself over her. The bench didn't offer much room for him to maneuver, but he would navigate the space as best as he could. With one hand planted beside her head, he propped himself up in a one-armed pushup.

"I'm excited to have him," Victoria quipped.

He had to hold back his laughter and leveled his erection between her thighs. Her aroused satiny flesh was indeed ready to accept him. As he sank into her lush, wet sheath, John gritted his teeth and breathed through every push until he filled her to the hilt. With no more jokes in her quiver, Victoria's mouth fell open and her back arched away from the bench.

"Ooh, okay," she squeaked, grabbing onto his wrist beside her head.

John paused to analyze her face; her russet-brown

complexion had gone red again. "I can go any speed you'd like."

"Yes, please."

He laughed that time. "What?"

Her eyes flew open. "Just go," she said. "Fast and hard."

John withdrew slightly and plunged hard, knocking her so hard that her breasts bounced up. She held on to the bench and his wrist as he drove into her, each stroke as delicious and hot as the last. The sensations that wrapped tight around his cock propelled him to the precipice. In that moment, John was in an incredible aware and focused headspace. It was as if a singular goal was branded in his mind. Caress, stroke, thrust, squeeze. There was nothing else but him and Victoria. Beautiful and brilliant Victoria, nestled deep in a rainforest, waiting on him to inhale her essence.

His free hand traced the lines of her body, starting with her long elegant neck, over the ridge of her collar bone. He paused his journey only to cup the sweet fullness of her breast, teasing and pinching her sensitive nipple between his thumb and forefinger. She gasped at the pain before moaning in delight. With another powerful thrust, he dipped down and took the erect tip in his mouth and sucked, lashing his tongue like a healing balm. Victoria's hand came around his head and held him there. She arched her back and rocked her hips in time with his pace. "Please..." her voice came in trembling whisper. "More."

John would give her more.

He raised himself, switched arms, and gave her other breast the same careful attention. He delighted in her response to his every touch. It seemed as though her body was specially molded for his hands and mouth. He savored every sigh, every crease of her brow, every squeeze of her hand. The primitive idea that Victoria could be made only for him to pleasure, pushed him over the edge. She was his. She belonged to him. Victoria was his flower.

"Victoria," he gasped.

As if she could sense he was on the brink, she reached downward and touched herself. Her fingers were on the same bundle of tight nerves he'd caressed only moments earlier. She opened her eyes and her dark stare seared into his soul as he impaled her. Bold and challenging. He kept his eyes locked on hers in an attempt to let her catch up. If he watched her pleasure herself, he would certainly explode. When her tight walls spasmed around him, he felt safe enough to grip her by the waist and fuck her fast and rough. Her pants became moans, and then staccato-like screams. She slapped her own hand over her mouth as tears streamed down her temples. "Oh…my…god," she said, her muffled shouts captured by her fingers.

John wasn't faring any better. He felt a combustion rising in him like the hottest fire, clouding his brain. Electricity seemed to arc through him as a burning tide raged between their joined bodies. A savage growl choked him as he lurched forward, clutching Victoria's hip tightly. He gave himself over to the rolling wave of sensations. Stars bursting behind the dark veil of his eyelids, the sound of his heart pounding in his ears, his lover's quivering damp thighs… John felt and saw it all. He fell into her arms, burying himself in her hold and hesitant to break their connection. He wanted to stay there, inside her, for the rest of his life. John belonged to her now. Victoria traced gentle circles along his back with her fingertips, sending another shudder through his body. "Am I too heavy?" he asked, breathing harshly against her cheek. With his eyes closed, he could feel her smile next to his mouth.

"You're fine," she whispered. "I like this weight. I feel…safe."

It made John sigh to hear that. *She feels safe.* But eventually, he needed to release her. He couldn't bear the thought of his hard weight suffocating her feminine softness. Slowly, he lifted himself, pulling out of her. She moved her legs aside to allow him space to sit. As Victoria unwound the panties wrapped around her wrist, John chuckled to himself.

"What?" she asked, slipping her legs through them. He watched her pull them up her thighs until they hid her beautiful juncture.

"Oh nothing," he said with a disappointed sigh.

She flashed him a cheeky grin. "You don't need these to fuel your imagination for the rest of the day."

He removed the condom and tied it off before tossing it into a nearby trashcan. "I suppose I don't… But I was hoping to give the pair under my pillow a buddy."

This made her burst into laughter. John smiled as he hitched up and fastened his pants. "You have a really goofy laugh," he told her. "It's kind of a raspy hyuk, hyuk."

"It's not," she protested through the chuckles. She went back to the table of geraniums and found her bra. As she hooked herself into the garment, she leaned over to inspect the flowers.

"But I like it," John said, standing from the bench and stretching his tired arms. He didn't think he could last so long in a one-armed horizontal position. "It's a laugh of honest joy."

"I think your laugh sounds hearty." Victoria tossed him his shirt and began searching for her own. She plucked it from the concrete and shook it out before draping it around her shoulders. "Like a Viking."

As he slipping his shirt over his head, he began to chuckle.

"See? There it is," she said, planting her fists on her hips and standing legs astride. "Ho ho ho!"

Seeing this lighter side of Victoria, made John's insides light and warm. While she continued to do a terrible imitation of Eric the Red, he walked over to her and slid his arms around her waist. "I don't sound like that," he said in a low voice, pulling her close.

"And you do the menacing growl too," she said as she tickled his beard. "Ho ho ho, I drink mead."

Why would she want this to end in three weeks?

"I must take a shield-maiden for a wife," Victoria continued.

John raised a brow. "Do I?"

She stopped talking to purse her lips. Another creeping blush settled in her cheeks. "What do you have planned for today?" she asked with a clumsiness he was used to.

To save her pride, he didn't miss a beat. "I've got a child-free day, so I'm going to the gym." He knelt his head to kiss her cheek. "Then I'll probably pillage a nearby town and bathe my broadsword with the blood of Christians. You?"

Her wide smile, with its one dimple, returned. "I actually came to campus to grade papers. I have twenty-three left."

"Well then, I should probably let you get to it." He said the words but made no moves to release her.

Victoria worked around his arms, buttoning her blouse and stuffing the hem back into the waist of her skirt. "Just to be safe, I should leave first and then you can exit after a few minutes."

Even though it was Sunday, she still worried. John took a deep breath. "Sure."

She smoothed her skirt down and patted her braided bun, making certain that every skinny plait was in place. "How do I look?"

He buried the animal inside his chest; the one who was *really* doing all of the growling. It ordered him to never let her go. John ignored it and swallowed before answering her. "Beautiful."

"Thank you, John," she said, planting her hands on his chest and standing on her tiptoes. She kissed his lips, softly and sweetly, the warmth of her breath fanning across his face. "And thank you for doing this."

He pulled his own reins and stopped himself from sipping any more of her nectar. "It's my pleasure," he whispered.

As she settled back on her heels, her chin dipped until all he could see was the fluttering fringe of her lashes. "I mean it. I don't know how many men—" her voice caught in her throat.

Taking her by the chin, John tilted her face upward. "—would promise you a sordid affair?"

Her dark gaze flitted from his eyes to his mouth. He could tell the wheels were turning in her head as she regarded him. "Right…that."

He didn't get it exactly right though, did he? Something else hung in the air; something on the tip of her tongue. "Thank you," she said for a final time before stepping away. "I'll see you tomorrow?"

"Sure." John watched her walk around the corner. When the door in the other room closed, he realized how empty and lonely this glass building was. Earlier Victoria had mentioned the greenhouse's calming effect. He doubted she could come back to this place without a vivid reminder of their passionate union. A few moments passed before John pulled on his jacket and made his exit. The cold October winds shocked him back to reality and forced him to continue his comparatively ordinary day.

Chapter Fifteen

Victoria glanced at her notes while she scribbled a portion of her lesson on the whiteboard. "Okay," she said in a loud voice. "Now let's talk about Frederick Douglass's Narrative and its rhetorical prowess compared to... Harriet Beecher Stowe's *Uncle Tom's Cabin*." Once she finished writing, she turned around and faced her students. Some of them furiously flipped through their textbooks, evidence they may not have read the night before. "Both of them are trying to address something, they're trying to fix a huge social problem. Tell me what Douglass has that Stowe doesn't?"

Several hands flew up.

"Hannah?"

The young woman near the back of the classroom referred to her notebook before answering. "One obvious thing that separates them is Douglass's firsthand knowledge. He was a slave on a plantation and he witnessed the horrors."

"Exactly," Victoria said, jabbing her marker in the young woman's direction. "We have a primary source of information that's incredibly candid and, at points, gruesome. Someone tell me about Douglass's writing style that drives his point home."

"The events are shocking," said a young man near the door. "But they're really detailed. Like, he's cataloging the facts in a really clinical way."

Victoria nodded.

"It's like even though it happened to him, he has to take a step back and write it objectively," said another student.

"You're both right," Victoria replied, stepping away from the podium. She strolled down the center aisle of her class and addressed her students. "These horrors are catalogued, as Jeremy pointed out, in a way that would shock us. But as a writer, imagine sitting down to list all of the tragedy in your life... How do you do it? Is there a way to shut off part of your brain to write, or what?"

Hannah jumped back in with her opinion. "I don't know if you're shutting off part of your brain. I don't think anyone can do that and write what Douglass has written." The young woman searched for the words. "He knew what he was doing, because this feels like enough pathos to draw a reader in, but he backs it up with his logos."

Victoria smiled. *Bingo.* "So you're saying he's playing a delicate balancing act?"

Hannah nodded. "Right."

"Does he have to?" asked the girl who sat beside Hannah. "Stowe got to write sentimental stuff that made people cry. Why couldn't Douglass go full pathos?"

Victoria absolutely loved it when her students asked *each other* the questions that mattered. "Good question, Nina. Why does Douglass hold back?"

One of her black students, Izzy, a few rows back, joined the discussion. "Because Douglass was also trying to be an activist. If he went full pathos, he wouldn't be taken seriously. He had to be careful if he wanted to convince white Northerners to care about what wasn't in their own backyard."

Victoria could have cried after hearing Izzy's eloquence. "She's right. Douglass, who presumed that his father was his master, had to sneak to another plantation to see his own mother. He witnessed cruel beatings, experienced conditions of squalor, and saw how Christianity was perverted to justify slavery. He had to mind his rhetorical p's and q's before bringing this information to white Northerners."

As Victoria spoke, students took notes. She paused to allow them time before adding, "But let's not discount Stowe's writing because she's a white woman. She had the same audience, didn't she? Her novel pulled at the heartstrings of white *women* of the North. This is a demographic who was buying and reading more novels, much to the chagrin of their counterparts. Sentimentality was an incredibly powerful rhetorical device. Which portions of *Uncle Tom's Cabin* reached out to her target audience?"

Before anyone could answer, the classroom door swung open. In walked her only other black student, Braden. Victoria glanced at her watch. He was forty-five minutes late. Braden ambled slowly to the empty seat near the front and sat down. He kept his backpack and coat on, and his earbuds in.

Victoria took a deep breath and tried to keep her momentum, but she absolutely abhorred tardiness. *Ignore it and continue.* "Harriet Beecher Stowe's audience. White women of the North. How did she reach them?"

The momentum was gone.

Everyone knew Braden's track record of lateness. He

varied from day to day, but always managed to miss most of the discussion. The class wasn't that large, so his entrances were always noted. Interestingly enough, his lack of in-class participation didn't show in his papers or midterm exam. Braden was getting a B+ in her class and somehow it made Victoria furious.

Finally, a student saved her from her stewing. Nina raised her hand before stating, "I think her chapter about the elderly woman and her son, Albert, being separated was awful. Aunt Hagar couldn't convince Mr. Haley to buy them together."

"And then after that, on the boat," added another student, Jeremy. "The woman, Lucy, didn't know that she and her baby were sold to Mr. Haley. And then the asshole turned around and sold her baby off to someone else."

Victoria nodded. "Exactly, Stowe uses this entire chapter to address the dangers of motherhood for female slaves. Motherhood is temporary and cannot be promised. At any point, the human being *you* created can be wrenched away from you. That kind of pain can be felt by any woman regardless of race, don't you think?

"Stowe doesn't just stop at telling these stories," Victoria continued. "She includes an important conversation on the boat that shouldn't escape your notice. Remember the group of white women who debate slavery? One woman is clearly upset by the practice, while another one counters with what?"

Pages flip to that spot in the textbook. As she waited for her students to find it, she snuck a glance at Braden, who propped his head against his fist and appeared quite bored by the discussion.

Izzy found the passage and called out: "'O, there's a

great deal to be said on both sides of the subject… I've been south, and I must say I think the negroes are better off than they would be free.'"

Victoria's gaze flew back to her students. "Yes, Izzy. And the woman asks her to imagine if her own children were taken from her. This forced the reader to ask themselves the terrible question: What if it *were* my children? And when that wasn't enough, Stowe actually breaks the fourth wall and addresses her audience directly. Upon learning of her and her child's fate, Lucy becomes desperate and tosses herself overboard. She'd rather choose death over another plantation. Stowe takes the time to inform the reader that the trader isn't surprised because 'as we said before; he was used to a great many things that *you* are not used to.' The reader has no choice to take part in his dark world, because in many ways, they're already a part of it in real life."

The students scribbled that into their notes. Not Braden though. Braden sat there unmoved by Harriet Beecher Stowe's words regarding motherhood.

"Braden, take out your earbuds," Victoria said in a sharp voice.

The young man sat up and heaved a sigh before pulling the earbuds away from his head. He wrapped them around his neck and continued to stare into space.

"Stowe's sudden shift to second person, to address her audience is a literary device called apostrophe," she said as she made her way back to the whiteboard. She wrote the word in large block letters and put an asterisk beside it. "The guilt a reader should feel should be counted as pathos. Stowe employs it regularly while Douglass lets the facts, or logos, do most of the heavy lifting."

When she turned around, she was met with a raised

hand from the front row. A young man beside Braden asked, "So Douglass was relying on logos rather than pathos?"

"He did both," she corrected. "But he used his writing style in such a way that made the events more like a catalogue of atrocities. He took great effort to list each overseer on his plantation, but all of the descriptions are still vivid enough for the reader to feel something."

Satisfied with her answer, the young man wrote the information in his notebook.

"I'm going to cut it short today," Victoria announced, which began the immediate shuffle of papers and books. "Because I want to use the next class to cover the Negro spirituals. We're going to listen to a few before breaking into smaller groups to analyze the lyrics."

As students packed up and filed out of the classroom, Victoria spied Braden trying to be among the first to leave. Which was pretty easy since he hadn't unloaded his belongings or taken off his outerwear.

"Braden, why don't you hang back," she called after him.

The young man stopped short and lifted his face to the ceiling for another loud sigh. He made an about-face and returned to the front of the classroom. She waited for the class to empty before gearing herself up for another lecture.

"You were forty-five minutes late to a fifty-five-minute lecture," she started. "Do I have to remind you that participation is part of your grade?"

He shrugged. "So I was late." His slouch and lack of eye contact made her grit her teeth. It wasn't bad enough that he was late, but his apathy was insulting. Had he been one of her father's enlisted privates, Braden would have been quarterdecked faster than he could give another shrug.

"But it's a daily occurrence," Victoria said in a voice edged with iron. "I don't know what makes it so difficult to get to my class, but you need to get it together and hop to it. Because the next time you arrive late, I will ask you to leave and mark you absent. Enough absences, and I'll have to dock your grade by a full letter. I only use five letters and you're already down to four."

The young man sucked in his cheeks and rolled his eyes. "I get A's on my papers."

She breathed through her nose, knowing full well her nostrils were probably flaring. "You earn A's because you're smart. But *smart* isn't all that's required in my classroom. The rest is showing up and talking to your classmates. If you think skating by on *smart* alone is cute, keep it up and see how far it gets you in the real world." The words felt frighteningly familiar as she said them, but she was already riled up.

Braden finally looked her in the eye only to say, "Man... I thought you were one of the cool ones. Like, there aren't that many of *us* and I thought you'd be down."

Cool ones? What on earth does that mean? "Excuse me?"

"Why are you stressing?" he asked. "I read your stuff; I write your papers. Why do I need to come here and talk about this depressing shit?"

If she had ever taken that tone with her parents, or even ended that statement without a "sir" or "ma'am," she would have expected a swift punishment of forty-four sit-ups in two minutes. "No, Braden, there *aren't* many of *us* at this university. And because of that I can't slack on my job because you want to slack on yours. My job is to push you to push yourself. Because when you eventually leave these walls, you will still have to prove yourself to *them*." She pointed a finger to the classroom wall to emphasize her point. "I'm going to tell you what my mother told me when I was your age. 'You've got two strikes against you: You're black and you're a woman. That means you have to work twice as hard to get the same amount of recognition as your white colleagues.' The reality is harsh and the strikes exist. If me telling you this doesn't make me *down enough*, then be disappointed. Just make sure you show up disappointed and *on time*."

Braden stared at her.

Victoria's heart was pounding by the end of her sermon. She'd evoked her mother's words and immediately felt conflicted. Yes, they were true and had been meant to prepare her for adulthood, but they were often said in place of encouraging words. *Work harder because your best is just the start.* She closed her eyes and exhaled. "Look, I'm not scolding you for the fun of it. You're an excellent writer. You make insightful observations, and you express yourself like a graduate student. But you must come to class and you must come correct. I've given you warnings in the past; this is the last one. Show up."

"Fine."

She'd take a *fine*. "Thank you."

"Do I have to talk about everything though? Some of this stuff seriously bums me out."

Victoria tried not to sound exasperated. "Not everything about African American Lit is going to be sunshine and rainbows, but it's an important part of this nation's history. Why did you sign up for the class?"

He shrugged again. "Because it's an easy A."

Her jaw clenched. "You don't have to talk about everything we read about, but I need to hear your voice at some point." It would be different if he had anxiety issues that prevented him from taking center stage. Victoria actually had those students, and she set aside time during her office hours for them to discuss the course content. Those students came prepared to talk directly to her instead of the full class. Braden just wanted a pass to avoid discussing *depressing shit.*

"Fine."

This was as far as she would get with him. He knew what was expected of him and now it was on him to prove he understood. She'd find out next class.

"Carry on," she said, dismissing him with a wave of her hand. He turned on his heel and slouched out of her classroom without another word.

What did she expect him to say? *Thank you for harping on me, it's really great to be talked down to!* Victoria gathered her things and tried to calm her nerves. She wondered if she had crossed a line by being so blunt with him. It was one thing to lay down the law, but she shouldn't have said he had a "strike" against him. Everything she'd said could be misconstrued as harsh and unflinching. She had basically called the boy lazy and uncaring. She'd added the words of encouragement only because she realized her misstep. Who knew if Braden would come back to her class? And if he did, would he harbor some kind of resentment towards her?

Victoria recalled his words. *I thought you were one of the cool ones...* It angered her that *because* they shared the same skin color, she was seen as someone to offer favors. Would he say such a thing to a black male professor? As soon as the words had come out of his mouth, Victoria had reverted back to her natural state: Defensive. She had to prove her authority to colleagues like Ken, but there were rare moments when she had to defend her right to be in the front of the classroom to children whose parents paid their tuition.

On the flipside, she still had the strong desire to save every black student who passed the threshold of her classroom. They were rare, but the few who made it scrimped and scraped every last penny to get to Pembroke, and their peers knew it. Any other professor would not have thought twice about marking Braden late or absent. His B+ average would have slid away from his lax grip. No one else would have told him how hard work was the only way to make it out of this place. She *had* to tell him the truth. *Always have a plan... Work hard because your best is just the start.* If it *was* the truth, why did it hurt to repeat her mother's words?

There was a lump in Victoria's throat that wouldn't budge because she knew she had crossed a line. She couldn't save every student, she just had to do her job. Teach, grade, and nothing more. She wasn't a counselor or a psychiatrist. She blew out a harsh breath. *You can't be everything to everybody, Victoria.*

Victoria had decided to skip the weekly Graduate Research Symposium after class and had returned to her office for a breather. She still had a few papers to grade and rather than give her interaction with Braden any more thought, she'd thrown herself into those. She had finished marking up one paper when her phone trilled with a Katherine Reese ringtone. Her body immediately tensed as she considered ignoring it. No, it was their weekly call. If she missed it, she'd never hear the end of it.

Victoria steeled herself before pressing the answer button. "Ma'am."

"Did you read the article I sent you?" Katherine asked, pushing straight through.

"Huh?"

"Beg your pardon," her mother corrected. "*Huh*, is used by low-rent people who don't have proper command of the English language."

Victoria squeezed her eyes shut and fought the urge to remind her mother that she was in fact an English professor who understood how the rigid class structures of grammar subjugated the underprivileged. "Which article are you referring to?"

"The one I posted on your Facebook," Katherine said impatiently.

"Mother, I don't exactly have time to be on Facebook right now," she said, wedging the phone between her cheek and shoulder. She minimized a student paper and got on the internet. Victoria wasn't quite sure if she even remembered her login information. "Could you just tell me what the article was about?"

"Scientists are saying that female fertility *isn't* on the strict clock they once thought it was on. Apparently, women in their fifties can still have healthy births. I think they referenced Janet Jackson's latest pregnancy..."

Victoria stopped listening after that. Her mother posted an article about fertility on her public wall? She logged in incorrectly twice before she had access to her Facebook page. *G.D. it!* There it was, plain as day, in black and white: a link to the article with the additional comment, "YOU STILL HAVE TIME (winky-face emoji) BUT DON'T PUSH IT!!!" Friends had already reacted with likes. The first comment was from her grandmother: "I had your mother at 37."

"…we all know that her *first* child was by that De-Barge boy. That girl would be about your age actually. Anyway, she did it and god only knows how. She probably did the IVF treatments like Brenda's daughter did. But the point is, your ovaries might have a fighting chance. Isn't that exciting news?"

Victoria didn't know where to start. First, there was the validity of her mother's science news sources. If there was one issue she constantly lectured her students on, it was "check your sources." Second, her mother put her on blast in front of the whole world. She maintained a carefully curated social media presence for work-purposes. She immediately clicked on her privacy settings and adjusted who could send her future posts. "Please, please, do not send me articles like this," Victoria said as she deleted the post. "I don't need everyone knowing my business."

Her mother scoffed. "The fact that you don't have children isn't what I could call *business*, Victoria. Everyone already knows you're childless."

She swallowed hard, trying not to reveal her anger. "I feel like we've had this conversation before and I don't have anything new to add to it."

"But don't you want children?" Katherine asked. "They bring so much joy to your life."

"If that's the case, why did you stop after me?" Victoria asked. "You could be bothering one of my siblings about grandbabies instead."

"Oh, your mother is *bothering* you?" she said. "I hadn't realized concern for my only child was considered a *bother*. I didn't have any more children because your birth was complicated enough. I nearly *died*, Victoria."

She had heard her origin story more than once and had no interest in going down that road. "I understand, ma'am. Childbirth is still very dangerous and I'm lucky to be here. And I didn't mean to say that you were… bothering me."

The unmistakable Kathrine Reese sniffle emerged. "I try not to be a bother, but if I don't check on you, who will? You give and give to your children and they turn around and let you know they don't need you anymore. It's a thankless job, you know?"

"Yes, ma'am."

"And you'll understand that when you eventually become a mother. Everything you slave for, everything you give, gets distilled down to two words: *a bother*."

Victoria ran a hand over her mouth and suppressed a groan. Arguments like this one escalated because she made an attempt to stand up for herself. Katherine Reese knew how to take one tiny piece of her daughter's argument and turn it back on her. Even though Victoria had taught rhetoric for nearly a decade, she was still unarmed against her mother. If they had a closer relationship that wasn't based on constant criticism, Victoria would have called her mother right after class and asked for advice regarding Braden.

She could have told her mother how the students sometimes felt like her children. It wasn't right or fair, but as a female educator, it was expected that she would nurture her students while she taught them. Unbeknownst to Katherine, Victoria often came home from a job feeling exhausted by playing mom to young people who weren't hers. And sometimes she messed up and treated them like her own, right to their faces.

But this phone call wasn't for those purposes.

"I'm sorry, Mom," she said in her most contrite voice. If she apologized now, she could save herself from the rest of this lecture. "You're not being a bother. I totally understand where you're coming from."

"I'm not trying to scold you for the fun of it," Katherine said still sniffling. "I just worry sometimes, that's all."

Victoria closed her eyes. She didn't know it, but her mother had repeated the same thing she had said to Braden. Or had Victoria repeated from her mother? She wasn't certain, but she felt terrible all over again. "I know, but there's nothing to worry about," she said. "Even though it's stressful, I really do enjoy my work."

Her mother sighed. "Oh Victoria—"

"So, what do you and Dad have planned this evening?" she asked, swiftly changing the subject.

Her mother didn't miss a beat to talk about herself. "Your father has some card game with the boys," she said dismissively. "I'm joining the ladies of the event planning committee. We're getting ready for your uncle Jeffrey's retirement celebration. I had to convince Brenda that embossed invitations are really the only way to go. She insisted everyone would be happy with emails, but I think it's just plain vulgar. For heaven sake, the man lost one of his *fingers* in The Gulf War."

"That's true," Victoria intoned as she scrolled through her Facebook newsfeed.

"I told her, 'Jeffrey didn't sacrifice his blood on the battlefield so that we could settle for email invitations.'

And that shut her right up. The other ladies agreed with me and I went right ahead and ordered 80 cardstock invitations with gold-embossed script. Tonight, we're reviewing The Drake's catered offerings. Do you think salmon canapés are old-fashioned?"

"Huh?"

"Beg your pardon," Katherine corrected. "I think we should have something with salmon as an hors d'oeuvre. I don't think we can swing a full entrée, since the invitations bit into the budget, but there are the vegetarians, aren't there…"

If Victoria had to guess, she would say her mother had her party planning binder perched on her lap while she spoke. Katherine's questions weren't meant to be answered; Victoria was only a sounding board for her thinking aloud. "There probably will be vegetarians," she murmured, typing "John Donovan" into the Facebook search bar.

"But not enough to waste salmon-entrée-money on," her mother said in a breezy voice. "I think we should stick with the sirloin and chicken. Everyone eats chicken. I read somewhere that chickens are the most consumed animal in the world."

As she scrolled through John's photos, she didn't bother telling her mother that vegetarian wasn't the same thing as pescatarian. Her beautiful librarian filled her screen and captured her focus.

"What we really need to do is to decide on the cake," her mother continued. "You know what? I need to let you go because I think I remember hearing something about a new black-owned bakery somewhere downtown. I'll have to Google them. Let's talk later?"

"Yes, ma'am."

Katherine hung up.

Victoria put down her phone and willed her body to relax. As she went through each photo of John, her mind drifted back to their last tryst. Images of them fogging up an already humid greenhouse with their passionate lovemaking appeared. She opened her day planner, seeking out their next rendezvous. Tomorrow.

Thank god.

Chapter Sixteen

"Seems like you've got something on your mind, Dr. Reese."

Victoria was in the middle of jabbing a box cutter through cardboard when John's voice hummed like a faraway echo. The steady rhythm of unpacking picture books, counting, and marking numbers was a comforting way to take her mind off what bothered her. When John had told her they were going to the library basement to take inventory of a new shipment of children's books, she'd been strangely relieved. What may have been considered boring by most, actually calmed Victoria. She hadn't thought about her mother once.

"Dr. Reese?"

Victoria head jerked around to see John sitting on the floor with a pile of books. He was staring at her. "Beg your pardon?"

His mouth quirked into a lopsided grin. "Pardoned."

"Did you say something?"

He shook his head. "You looked like you were in deep thought, that's all. You got something on your mind?"

Quite the opposite. She had zoned out a while ago, completely focused on her task. "Nope."

"It's just that you're very quiet," he said.

"The job is pretty simple," she said, ripping open her box. "You count the books, make sure they match the packing list, mark correct on the invoice…then put the invoice in that pile. I could do this all day."

His low rumble of laughter made her look up from her work.

"What?"

John pulled himself from the floor, dusted off his khakis, and walked towards her work station. Victoria's space held a pristine collection of books, perfectly stacked and arranged in straight rows. She was rather proud of the work she was doing. Once her boxes were emptied, she had planned to put the books in alphabetical order on a nearby cart. She was really looking forward to that part. That's why it made her nervous when John approached her work station. His makeshift corner of the basement looked hazardous. His piles of books were balanced in precarious positions, small to large, threatening to topple over. "Oh nothing," he said, running his large hands over her work. "I thought we would talk about tonight."

"I'd like that very much." Victoria watched as he moved one book out of place, before moving to the next stack. He picked up a picture book, looked it over, and placed it in the wrong pile. "Ooh, you know what? I'll handle this bit and you can handle your situation." She straightened her stack and moved one of the books just a smidge, putting it right back in its place.

His deep Viking laughter grew louder. "Dr. Reese, you're being nitpicky."

"No, I'm just—please don't touch that," Victoria said, shielding the books with her body. "Mr. Donovan, you're messing things up."

Having placed herself between him and her work, Victoria found herself much closer to him. She bumped into the solid wall of his muscular chest as she straightened up what he had moved. "No one in the history of library work has enjoyed this task as much as you do. That disturbs me." He lifted the thick curtain of her box braids away from her shoulder to expose her worried face.

"Whatever the job is," she said, turning to face him, "I like to do it *right.*"

"Right? Or Perfectly?" he countered. He stood over her, one hand on his hip and the other on her stack of *Eloise in Moscow*. It was difficult to argue with a man whose expression was a mixture of mirth and lust. John's pine-green eyes twinkled as he stared down at her. She couldn't tell if he was teasing her or if he wanted to kiss her. Victoria found herself okay with both. Perhaps she was being a little too protective of her collection of children's literature.

"You got me," she sighed. "I like perfection if it's possible."

"As do I," he said, leaning forward. "I'm looking at her right now."

"I don't know about that, Mr. Donovan." *What an odd compliment.* She felt anything but perfect in that moment, dressed in jeans, a *Golden Girls* T-shirt Reggi got for all of them, and sneakers. She'd slowly let herself wear comfortable clothes around John since he was taking this library work seriously. Perfect was a word boyfriends used. And John was anything but that. Still, she was a little curious about his declaration. "How so?"

John's smirk widened into a wolfish grin. "You're an intelligent, beautiful woman with a dirty little secret," he said, brushing against her lips. He kissed the corner of her mouth, sending an involuntary tremor of arousal to the pit of her belly.

Victoria's eyelids fell shut as she weaved in her sneakers. "I am? I do?"

"You're a sex kitten with OCD."

Her eyes flew open to see John pull away from her and cross his arms over his chest. "What?"

"You're a perfect mess," he said with a shrug.

Laughter bubbled up in her chest and escaped in the same raspy chuckle John had described just a couple days ago. "Shut up," she said, playfully pushing his shoulder and then immediately straightening the pile of *Eloise* books.

"See!" John exclaimed through his laughter.

"There's nothing wrong with a little order," she giggled as she blocked his advances. "No, stop ruining them, John!"

He began mixing up her stacks on purpose, putting *The Stinky Cheese Man* on the *Fancy Nancy* pile, and shuffling the paperback *Berenstain Bears*. "There, now it's perfect."

Victoria threw up her hands. "Fine, you win. They're all out of order and now it's going to be a chore to shelve them. I was trying to get them ready for the next person and you've just made it harder for them."

"The next person to shelve them is me. And I don't care," John said, pulling her to him with his powerful arms. Trapped in his hug, she had no choice but to leave the mess and stand still. Even though she was irritated, the warmth of his embrace was so male, so comforting. "Don't pout, Dr. Reese. It's cute as hell, but I want to talk to you."

"I'm not pouting," she said, avoiding his laughing eyes.

"You are. So much so, that I want to suck on that bottom lip that's stuck out."

This made her laugh again. Victoria still couldn't keep up with him. Between his flirty quips and his stolen kisses, she was always in a state of heightened arousal. "What do you want to discuss, Mr. Donovan?" she asked in a mock-serious tone.

He hugged her closer to his unyielding body, her softness pressed tight against his hardness. *Speaking of hardness...* The unmistakable poke of something below the waist caught her attention and warmed her face. "I want to discuss that," he said in a low voice.

Her breath caught in her throat.

"Tonight is the last night of *your* schedule. The next time we see each other, I'm going to take you out on an actual date. Lunch or coffee or something inane, and we're going to have first-date banter."

"We're already pretty good at banter," she pointed out.

"I'm going to ask you about your childhood pets, we're going to hold hands at some point, and I'm going to drop you off at your doorstep hoping for a kiss."

The list he made was laughable. The things they had already done were salacious enough to make Victoria blush at certain points of her day. John wanted to date her. The idea of dating him made her heart pound. Dating meant...trying. And that was added work she didn't need. Their trysts were fun and dangerous. She didn't have to try or perform. "So, I guess we need to make tonight *really* fun..."

"I'm sure that can be arranged, Dr. Reese." He dipped his head and gave her a kiss that was surprisingly gentle.

The soft touch of his lips a delicious sensation that made her release a sweet sigh. Victoria melted under his tender touch, finding it difficult to keep herself upright. It was alright though, his embrace was solid and affirming, like a haven for her tired soul to fall into. When John finally pulled away, she was left wanting and unfulfilled. There had been a dreamy intimacy to their kiss that was unlike so many others. Victoria's disappointment must have shadowed her face, because John gathered her against his chest and stroked the length of her spine. "You wear your emotions so openly, Dr. Reese."

Something about this interaction puzzled Victoria. John had made an abrupt shift from teasing her about her orderly personality to hugging and kissing her in an intimate, *loving* fashion. Victoria wasn't accustomed to being held like this. Like something precious, threatening to crack, if not treated with absolute care. "I hadn't realized," she said. The lure of his voice, his warm caress, the smell of his woodsy cologne, was enough to put her in a catatonic state. Was a simple hug really all it took to calm her rabbit-heart?

Only when he released her was Victoria shaken from her quiet reverie. John made another unexpected move by asking her, "Now, where would you like to have 'fun'? There's my office, which is right behind the checkout desk. Martha's hearing aid is still messed up, but I can't guarantee the patrons won't hear us. As you can see, the basement's pretty quiet, but I can tell you're wildly uncomfortable about messing up your…system," he said, gesturing to her workstation.

Victoria couldn't control her burst of laughter. "Thank you for understanding," she said. "Do you have a whiskey locker we can use?"

A sandy-brown eyebrow arched as he stared at her. "Excuse me?"

She looked around the basement space. "It's a closet where all the cleaning supplies are kept. Is that one?" She pointed to the door labeled "Maintenance."

"A whiskey locker?"

She took him by the hand and pulled him towards the closet. "It's what my dad calls it."

"Will I learn more about this at a later date?" John asked as he flicked the light on and checked the dimensions of the small space.

Victoria entered first and moved aside the Caution: Wet Floor signs. "You will," she said with a grin. "But first, I'd like to have one last night of covert fun."

John closed the door behind him. "I can give you that, honey. I can *fun* you real good until my shift is over." Under the dim yellow light of the single bulb, he looked bold and dangerous. He was dressed in a tight black T-shirt. Its sleeves stretched and held on for dear life around his biceps, while the expanse of his wide chest rose and fell with every deep, measured breath. John reached into the back pocket of his slim-fit khakis and pulled out a trusty condom.

Victoria let out a dizzying breath as he approached her. Her stomach contracted and a rush of heat flooded her entire body. Wet-hot desire pooled between her thighs as she awaited his touch. Something came over her as she appraised his beautiful body. She could never tire of staring at his thick, sinewy thighs wrapped in tight khakis, or the way his stomach was tanned and taut with a ladder of firm ab muscles. Victoria eyed the glint of the condom wrapper and shook her head. "We don't need that right now," she said in a suffocated whisper.

John paused right before her. His green eyes darkened as they flitted to her waist, and he shot her an irresistibly devastating grin. "Dr. Reese, would you like me to—"

"No, not tonight, although you do that *extremely* well." Before he could ask any more questions, she closed the distance between them and rested her hands on his belt buckle. She tried to steady her shaking fingers as she slowly unraveled the leather at his waist. When she got to the button and zipper of his pants, she felt slightly more confident. Victoria looked up to see John watching her, realization dawning in his eyes as she leisurely pushed his waistband over the tight curve of his ass.

"Are you sure you want to do that?" he asked, huskiness lingering in his tone.

"Absolutely," she said, pressing her hands to his bare hips and sliding them to the tops of his thighs. His muscles jerked in response as she caressed his hot skin. John's heavy cock stirred and stood, presenting itself in its full glory. Victoria backed John against a shelf of cleaning supplies and gaze up at him. "If it's okay with you…" she asked, licking her lips.

"Jesus Christ, yes." His voice rasped out in a strained affirmative.

She knelt down to the floor and held him in place. When she was face-to-face with his iron-hard organ, Victoria almost second-guessed her bold action. The proud erection stood beautifully; its girth and long shaft a pleasant memory of the pleasure she received on Sunday. She was hardly an expert at giving blow jobs— it had been years since she'd even tried—but Victoria wanted to give to him what he so selflessly gave her. John was such a generous lover, careful to pleasure nearly every part of her body and intuitive enough to know when she wanted more. She wanted him to feel that same pleasure.

As she took him in her hands, she heard him take a sharp breath. "Victoria..." he murmured, placing one gentle hand on her cheek. The velvety hot hardness of his cock jerked under her delicate touch. She ran her fingers along the sides tracing the pulsing veins, to the dark thatch of pubic hair at its root. When she leaned forward and gave the smooth tip a tentative lick, she glanced up at John, who had closed his eyes and rested a hand on his chest. She could tell he was fighting to keep his breathing in check, alternating between shallow pants and low drags of air. She held on to his narrow hips and gave it another try. As she wrapped her lips around him, she did what came naturally. *No need to overthink it.*

Above her, John pulled his shirt off and tossed it somewhere behind her. As he angled his hips forward to receive her mouth, Victoria pulled his pants down further, delighting in running her fingers along the springy hair of his thighs. Her other hand held his girth in place, as her tongue slid and caressed as much as she could manage. His soft moans and harsh pants made her quicken her pace. Victoria was surprised that the sounds of his pleasure turned her on so much. As she sucked and massaged him with her lips, she had the urge to touch herself. She waited a few seconds before pulling her mouth away and used her fist to stroke the slickness on his cock. "Do you mind?" she asked, pulling at her belt and loosening her jeans.

John glanced down, his brow creased and his lips drawn tight. "By all means," he said in a hoarse gasp.

She grinned as he completely lost control to the sensations that rocked through him. She returned her lips to his shaft and sucked vigorously. "Good god, honey," John breathed, resting his hand on the back of her head. He didn't push her to take more, instead, he ran his fingers through her braids to massage the back of her neck. Each groan and shudder he gave thrilled her to the center of her wet sex. She worked her fingers in her pants fast and hard, even more excited by their brazen act. Victoria was so absorbed by her motions and his taste that she didn't notice that John had wound her braids around his fist. "Come up for air, baby."

"Mmh?" She intoned, her mouth still full.

John's dark green eyes glittered above her as he gently pulled her away from his cock. It popped from her mouth and flipped upward.

"Was I not doing it right?" she panted.

He gave a dark chuckle as he lowered himself before her. "No, darling, you did it right." He pulled out the condom and ripped it open with his teeth. "You do it entirely too right for me to last."

"But—"

"No buts," he said in a firm tone as he sat flat on the floor and slid the latex down his shaft. "I'm not going to finish without you."

Victoria heaved a disappointed sigh.

"Don't pout, Dr. Reese," John said, pulling her pants to her knees. "I told you what I'd do to that bottom lip."

She grinned as she stood and slipped her shoes off. Her pants followed. "You promise?"

John reached up and gave her a swift smack on her bottom in response. "Don't test me, honey."

Victoria lowered herself onto him, not able to recall

a time in her life when she'd felt this free or daring. She didn't want it to end. The next time they met, things would surely change. *Date.* It would be another role for her to play, another mask to wear. She tried to push the strange anxieties of Thursday from her mind as he sank inside her. *Enjoy this moment, Victoria. Enjoy this wild, reckless moment with him.*

Chapter Seventeen

A Thursday lunch date is nothing to be nervous about.
But as John charted the familiar path towards Victoria's office, the pit in his stomach said something entirely different. *Where do you take a woman like Victoria for lunch? How do you even make lunch sordid? What will she think of my beat-up truck with the door you really have to slam for the lock to catch?* As he traversed the hallway with its dark reddish-brown wood flooring—probably something fancy like mahogany—his hands sweat under the potted orchid he carried. He found the plant at a downtown florist and had bought it immediately. Now, it weighed him down with its symbolism. What if she thought the gesture was corny? What if she didn't want a visual reminder of greenhouse sex in her office? He banished the thought when he recalled their "whiskey locker" sex. They'd shared something magical in the dark, cramped space of the library basement. He really thought Victoria was loosening up and coming into her own when she knelt before him.

John needed to forget that saucy memory as well if he wanted to appear presentable at her place of work. When he came upon Victoria's door, he shifted the orchid to one hand and knocked.

He waited and there was no answer.

He knocked again and jiggled the door knob. It was locked. Disappointment settled in his belly. *Maybe she forgot*, said the nagging doubt. *No, Victoria doesn't forget. She plans.*

"You looking for Vicki?" asked a female voice from behind him.

John spun around and found a woman poking her head into the hallway. She wore a fashionably cropped afro with a pen stuck behind her ear. Large gold hoop earrings swung against her neck as she regarded him with a raised brow. "I am," he said, walking towards her. "Do you know where I can find Dr. Reese?"

The woman stepped out into the hallway where he could see her better. She was dressed in a black turtle neck, blue jeans that were ripped at the knees, and bright pink Doc Martin boots. "I might," she said with a sly grin. "Who's asking?"

"John Donovan," he said, sticking his hand out for a shake.

Realization lit her hazel-brown eyes as she took his hand. "Ahh, okay. You're the Viking…"

He knew his face was turning red by the second, but he pushed past it, pretending everything about that statement was completely normal. "And you're a friend of, uh, Victoria's?"

She nodded with a wide grin. "I'm Paula, and Vicki's probably still in her classroom. Her Post-Colonial Lit class is really popular; those kids usually stick around to talk about the readings."

"Gotcha."

Paula crossed her arms over her chest. "She's just down the hall, and to the left, in room 155."

John smiled, hoping he didn't appear too desperate to see her. "Thank you," he said, his heart kicking into a full gallop. "It was nice to meet you, Paula."

She retreated to her office with the same knowing grin. "You too, Mr. Donovan."

He took a deep breath and headed in the general direction Paula had pointed out, following the room numbers as he walked. *So that is one of the friends who probably knows all about me.* He hoped he made a decent enough impression, since women *did* talk. He stopped outside of the open door of room 155 and peeked in.

Her friend hadn't been lying when she said the class was popular. Five or six students surrounded Victoria's podium as she tried gathering her things. One young woman was jabbering excitedly about something… John leaned against the door frame to eavesdrop on the scene.

"So, do you think I can write ten pages based only on Irie Jones's trip to the salon? I want to talk about a biracial girl's hair journey through a Marxist lens."

Victoria nodded. "Of course, you could write ten pages, Izzy. Irie would make for an excellent character analysis. She's trying to navigate two worlds in a London that claims racial diversity, but falls short."

The young woman was practically mooning over her professor's words. "Do you think Zadie Smith based Irie Jones on herself?"

"It's hard to say. Maybe, maybe not?" Victoria shrugged. "When you do analysis work, it's really tempting to put the focus on the author, but we have to avoid that. You must take the text at face value, as a stand-alone textual artifact. Unless Smith says 'this is me on the page,' you have to treat Irie with objectivity."

Izzy scribbled something in her notebook. While

other students clamored for face time, he noticed how Victoria hitched her satchel on her shoulder and glanced past the small group. Her gaze landed on him, standing in the doorway with a potted plant in his hands, and her eyes widened. He flashed her a smile and watched her expression turn from surprise to mild embarrassment. She returned his smile, but he saw the fleeting emotion and it stabbed him in the chest. John stepped away from the door and back into the corridor. He could hear her tell the remaining students to email her any questions. When she finally made it to the hallway, Victoria flashed him another smile. This one, John noted, didn't feel as carefree as the one he'd grown accustom to. This one felt…off.

"Mr. Donovan," she said in a breathy voice. As her small band of groupies left the classroom, she took him by the arm and guided him back towards her office. "I'm sorry I'm late getting out of class."

John peered down at her. "It's not a problem," he said coolly, allowing himself to be led by the elbow. "I hope I didn't interrupt your students."

She shook her head. "They're great kids, but if I let them, they'd add an extra hour to the class."

"Where's the fire, Dr. Reese?" he asked, trying to match her pace. She may have been shorter than him, but her little legs carried her quickly.

She slowed down once they neared her office door. "Oh god, I'm sorry," she said with another embarrassed expression. "I don't know why I did that." Her hands shook as she unlocked her office.

He followed her inside and watched her scurry around her desk, putting her things away. Something was wrong;

Nervous Victoria was back. It was their first meeting all over again. "What's wrong, darling?"

She paused to look up at him, actually *seeing* him for the first time. "Is that for me?" she asked in a warm voice.

He'd actually forgotten he held the potted orchid. "Yeah, I thought you might like something to brighten your office. It's no Tanzanian Orchid, but the florist assured me it was just as hard to take care of."

John exhaled as she giggled and finally approached him. She took the plant and gingerly stroked its full petals before hugging it to her chest. "This is beautiful, John," she said in a soft voice. "And so thoughtful of you."

To his surprise, she raised herself on her tiptoes and kissed his lips. Her soft hand rested on his chest as she balanced herself against him. John wrapped an arm around her waist and kissed her back. "You're welcome."

"I don't think I greeted you correctly," she admitted, her warm breath fluttering against his cheek. "I think I just got nervous about my students assuming... I don't know what they would assume. I'm sorry."

John felt the tension from her body melt away the longer he held her. "I certainly wasn't expecting a kiss on sight," he murmured, looking for a way to kiss her again. "I understand that you have to be professional."

Her lips tugged into a tremulous smile. "I'm glad you're here."

"Are you hungry?" he asked, not wanting to let her go. Every lush curve conformed to his body, reminding him that she was made for his hands.

She waggled her eyebrows in a lascivious manner.

"For food," John added quickly.

They shared an intimate laughter that lightened his

heart. *Okay, things are fine*. They just had to find their footing and things would be as carefree as they had been last week. "I'm famished," she said. "I had a lot of coffee before class and now I'm coming down."

John released her. "Put the plant down and put your jacket on, I'm taking you downtown."

Victoria carried her orchid to her desk and took a moment to pick a place for it to sit. "I'll have to read up on how to take care of her," she said, placing it on one corner before changing her mind, and moving it to the other side of her desk. "My mom is the one with the green thumb."

He watched her move it one more time, closer to her computer. "Is that a fact?"

"Oh yeah, my mom can bring anything back from the brink. When she's not planning military events, she spends a lot of time with her gardening society," she explained, planting her hands on her hips. "Should I put this near the window?"

"I honestly don't know," John said, holding back his laughter.

"I like the way it looks here," she twisted the pot so the blossom faced her. "But I wonder if it needs a lot of sunlight."

"The Tanzanian Orchids didn't appear to be quite as exposed…as we were," he said with a chuckle.

She shot him a cross look before she rolled her eyes. "Okay, funny guy. Let's go on this first date."

John opened the door as she scooped up her jacket. "After you, Dr. Reese."

They took John's pickup downtown and parked on the street, in the heart of Farmingdale's Restaurant Row.

Mid-October swirled the leaves with a light wind and hid the sun behind dreary gray clouds, but John felt a bright radiance from the passenger's side. Victoria sat with her hands on her lap and knees pressed together. She was the perfect picture of primness. As he turned the ignition off and sat back in his seat, John reached out and set his hand on her thigh.

"Are you hungry?"

She looked down at his hand and then to him, before smiling. "I am."

John squeezed her thigh. After their week of unfettered access to one another's bodies, John was finding it difficult to keep his hands off her. Even while he drove, he'd resisted the urge to run his fingers along her jawline, down the length of her slender neck. *Jesus...* "I was going to take you to Bordeaux, but you tell me where you'd like to eat."

Her lips parted and a pink tongue darted to the corner of her mouth. John swallowed the impulse to lean over and lick the same spot. *First date manners, John.* "That sounds great," she said in an airy voice. "I haven't had a chance to go there."

Their conversation was too light for the heavy sexual tension crowding the small cab of his truck. Victoria's eyes caught his and flickered with renewed interest. Her nut-brown skin flushed slightly, causing John to tighten his grip on the steering wheel. "Victoria..."

"No, I know," she said, shaking her head. "I'm having a hard time thinking too. I feel very distracted right now."

Welcome to my world. John removed his hand from her thigh and leaned back to his side of the cab. "That settles it," he said, unclipping his seatbelt. "We're going to ignore this palpable lust and pretend to enjoy ourselves in a crowded restaurant."

Her laughter came out in a snort. "Yes, okay."

John got out and trotted around to her side as she opened her door. He took her by the hand and eased her down. They held hands while he closed her door, hesitant to release one another. He pulled her closer to his chest and dipped his head. "In the meantime, do you mind if I kiss you?" he asked.

Her face tilted upward. There was mischief in her eyes. "You're so polite."

"No harm in asking," he murmured against her lips. Her eyelashes fluttered against his cheeks as her soft curves molded to the contours of his lean body. Their bodies, like their lips, fit one another perfectly, keeping a quiet, barely imperceptible rhythm that John felt with every heartbeat. Victoria's tongue moved against his in a delicate dance and when she felt comfortable enough, she reached upward and rested her fingertips against his jaw. John liked her fingers there, he liked them anywhere on his person. At last, when he remembered they were on the street, he parted a few inches from her.

"That was nice," she breathed as she opened her eyes.

The corner of John's mouth quirked. "You almost sound shy about it."

Victoria gave a tiny shrug. "I'm not used to this kind of public attention," she said, lowering her voice to a near-whisper.

He leaned closer. "I think I've already proven that I'm happy to give you any kind of attention you need."

She gave a tiny nod.

"And that I'll drop whatever I'm doing to give it to you."

Heat flared in her cheeks as she gave another nod. "Yes, you've proven that," she said with a grin.

"Ms. Reese?" said a man's voice from behind them. John straightened up and turned around to see an older gentleman wearing a tweed jacket and ratty scarf. His white hair flew in different directions as his gray eyes narrowed on them both. Victoria's body stiffen against his and her hand pulled away from his grasp.

"Kenneth," she said in a tight voice. "Hello."

"Catching a bit of lunch?" he asked, peering from her to John. He let his gaze wander up and down before returning to Victoria.

"My...associate and I were taking a break from work," she said in a hurried voice.

The man extended his hand towards John. "Your associate?"

John was confused as well. *I couldn't even get "friend" status?* "The name's John Donovan," he said, taking Kenneth's gloved hand. "Head of the Children's Department at the Farmingdale Public Library."

Kenneth engaged in a quiet squeezing competition during their handshake, and lost. "Interesting," he said, pulling away. "Working with children? How admirable."

Admirable. When Victoria had said the same word to describe his story hour, John had felt pride in his work. When this man uttered the term, snide disdain hung in the air like a dark cloud.

"Dr. Williams is the English Department's Shakespeare scholar," Victoria said to John. "And the Chair."

"Mmh." John didn't care for the man. Kenneth reminded him of an old professor in his graduate studies who balked when John admitted that he'd never read Macbeth. For ten straight minutes, Professor Whitlock had lectured him about how "woefully" unprepared he was for his Literary Criticism course. John had sat there, amongst his peers, stone-faced and waiting for the rant to end. He had very nearly dropped the course, but that would have given Dr. Whitlock too much satisfaction.

"And John does wonderful work with children's literacy," Victoria added in a bright voice.

Kenneth Williams echoed the same terse "Mmh," before adding, "And what are you two working on?"

"Dr. Reese and I are teaming up to create an internship for your students," John said in a business-like tone. "We're just nailing down the details over lunch." Judging by Victoria's tense demeanor, mentioning their lunch date would be a terrible idea.

Williams looked to Victoria and arched a white brow. "Is this for your Four-Week Initiative?"

Victoria gave a rigid smile. "It is."

"As I pointed out during our last meeting, we don't even have a Library Sciences program at Pembroke, Ms. Reese." The old man's tone dripped with sarcasm. "Our students go on to pursue actual literary careers."

John cleared his throat and bridled the irritation in his voice. "Victoria, I thought you were a doctor," he said, staring directly at Kenneth. "Our friend keeps referring to you as *Ms.* Reese."

Kenneth appeared positively apoplectic by John's intrusion, his red-mottled face pulled tight with a perturbed expression. Had he expected John to just stand there and let him talk to his lady that way? The old professor suffered from an elitist outlook on the world. That's where guys like John came in. He was there to gently remind folks like Ken that *no* was a sentence.

"Thank you for the reminder, Mr. Donovan," Victoria said in a calm voice.

"My apologies, Victoria," Kenneth ground out through a clenched jaw.

"Also," John added, suddenly feeling himself. "Are you saying libraries don't aid in a student's actual literary career?"

"With all due respect." Williams sighed wearily, as if John's contribution to the conversation were a pesky interference. "While a degree in Library Science is *practical*, and sometimes even necessary, the vast majority of Pembroke's English students tend to be accepted in more prestigious graduate programs."

Oh really? John clenched his fists. "With all due respect—"

"Dr. Williams, I'm sure I can meet with you later to discuss our work," Victoria interrupted. "But still I'm confident that my idea will benefit all of our students. Especially those in Children's Literature and the Early Childhood Education."

Williams regarded her with a smug expression. "Yes, well, I suspect I'll have a chance to look at your findings at another Curriculum and Policy Committee meeting. Good day to you both." And with that, the old man took his leave, ambling in the general direction of the university.

John didn't unclench his jaw until Victoria touched his arms. When he glanced down at her, she wore a pained expression. "I'm sorry," she said quietly.

"For which part?"

Victoria hesitated, blinking her confusion. "That's just Ken, I'm afraid. He's even rude to the university librarians. I've heard the complaints."

He couldn't help his rueful grin. "He's even rude to the university librarians… So little old me from the kiddie department should expect it?"

She frowned. "That's not what I meant. He's just a jackass who likes to throw his weight around. Hell, he's been my nemesis since I took this job."

John narrowed his gaze on her and tilted his head. "But you're a professor, same as he."

Victoria exhaled. "Not exactly. I'm an assistant professor while he's been an associate for thirty years. He's still my boss and one of the people who will sit on my tenure review. That man, and a handful of other men, hold my career in their hands."

John took a deep breath and held it for a second. His irritation was threatening to ruin the special moment they'd shared before Dr. Williams's interruption. But dammit, he *was* irritated. She'd called him an associate. What did that even mean? He couldn't decide if it was because she was simply awkward or if she was embarrassed to acknowledge him. Surely, the old man saw them huddled together in an intimate manner. He had certainly looked John over in an attempt to size him up. *An associate?* "Look, I understand that academia is toxic. Despite my 'practical' education, I remember it being a cesspool of gatekeepers who kept the marginalized away. But you're just as accomplished as that asshole."

Victoria's brows scrunched together. "Yes, but be that as it may, I still have to work with the old guard in order to make any progress." She worried her thumbnail between her teeth. "In fact, he's right. I still need to get his committee's approval."

John sighed. "Fine. Do what you think is necessary."

"What's wrong?" she asked.

He shrugged and said the one thing he reprimanded Becca for. "Nothing."

She shot him a disbelieving look. "Nothing?"

He tried to remain passive as he shook his head. "Nope." His phone vibrated against his chest and he pulled it from his jacket. It was a local phone number that he didn't recognize, so he reluctantly answered it. "Hello?"

"Mr. Donovan, Becca Richards's guardian?" asked a woman.

"This is he?"

"I'm the principal of Hollingsworth Academy and I have Becca in my office."

"What's wrong?" he asked.

"Becca was in an incident with another student. Both students are fine, just a little rattled."

"What kind of incident?" John's mind and heart began to race with terrible images of an injured or traumatized Becca.

"Let's just say that Becca got into a scuffle with another female student. No one is injured, per se."

"She got into a fight?" John demanded. Victoria's eyes were on him with piercing intensity. "Is she okay? Is she hurt?"

"No one is injured," the principle repeated. "I'd appreciate it if you would come to the school so we could discuss the next step of this conflict."

"Yes, fine," John said in a terse voice and hung up. He faced Victoria with a resigned expression. "I'm sorry to do this to you, but Becca…"

"Let's go," she said, hitching her purse on her shoulder. She moved to open the passenger's side of the pickup.

He watched her, bewildered by her swift movements. "I'm taking you back to your office, right?"

"No," Victoria said as she climbed into her seat. "We're going to the school. You need to see about this now."

"But this…" John paused. He was close to saying this wasn't part of their first-date plans. "You don't have to do this. I can drop you off at your office and get her."

"Hollingsworth is just a couple blocks away. Let's go see what's wrong." Victoria slammed her door shut.

John took a deep breath and made his way around the front of his truck to the driver's side. When he sat behind the wheel, he snuck a covert glance at Victoria, who sat staring straight on with a determined look on her face. His irritation was replaced by a sense of relief. She didn't have to do this, but she was accompanying him to something he had no preparation for. John was thankful.

Chapter Eighteen

Principal Karen Schmidt, who looked to be Victoria's age, glanced at her before addressing John. She lowered her voice. "This is really a matter for Becca's parent or guardian."

Victoria stood behind John, holding her jacket, memories of middle school anxiety creeping back into her adult existence. Hollingsworth Academy appeared to be the junior version of Pembroke: moneyed and lacking in melanin. The small lockers and the cool girls were no longer ghosts of her past, but actual frights that surrounded her. "I'm a friend of the family," she said, taking a step forward. "I'd like to be present while you talk about a young black girl's next step in disciplinary matters."

Her words made the principal take notice. The woman tucked her long blond hair behind her ears and swallowed. "If that's alright with Mr. Donovan."

John, clearly growing impatient with the preamble, growled, "Of course she stays. Can I just see my niece please?"

Principal Schmidt walked them into her office, where young Becca sat in a chair off to the side of her desk. The girl was holding herself and bent over at the waist.

She stared at the floor, refusing to look up at her uncle who walked through the door.

Two chairs sat before the principal's desk, Victoria let John sit closer to his niece and watched the scene unfold. Principal Karen Schmidt took a seat behind her desk and tried her best to interact with everyone in the room. "Becca, your uncle is here."

Becca finally looked up, her large brown eyes watery and red. She looked from John to Victoria and said, "Is she my lawyer?"

John scoffed. "What?"

"I know I'm in trouble, but I didn't think it was that big of a deal."

"She's my *friend*, honey," he said with an exasperated tone. "Can someone please explain what's going on here?"

Victoria and Becca locked eyes and stared at one another for a long time. Victoria saw herself in the girl and her heart broke. She remembered sitting in a principal's office feeling misunderstood. She also picked up on Becca's suspicious gaze. The girl wanted to know who she was and what connection she shared with her uncle. Victoria couldn't believe she was here, but when she'd caught the stricken expression on John's face, she'd known that she couldn't leave him alone. Seeing about a child in distress was far more important than a lunch date.

Principal Schmidt cleared her throat and recounted the events. "Becca and her friends were engaged in a conflict with another group of girls. It occurred during the lunch hour and everyone involved has had a visit with me. I've called all parents and I'm conducting meetings with everyone to see if we can reach a resolution."

"Can you tell me what the conflict was about?" John asked impatiently.

"Becca," Principal Schmidt gestured.

The girl shrugged her narrow shoulders. "Basically Jenny, Megan, and Bridgette were doing what they always do. They were making fun of me and Kelly and we tried to ignore them, but they wouldn't shut up. So McKenna and Devon joined us and we all told them off together."

"Four against three," Principal Schmidt said with pursed lips.

"The odds aren't as much an issue as the pattern of behavior exhibited by Jenny, Megan, and Bridgette," Victoria said. "If they have a habit of bullying, shouldn't that be looked into?"

Everyone in the room shifted in their seats to look at her. Hope shined in Becca's eyes, John raised a brow, and the principal frowned. "Dr. Reese is right," John said. "Becca has come to me with these concerns regarding a girl who's been calling her names. Is this the same girl?" he asked his niece.

Becca nodded.

"Well there you go," John said with a righteous tone. "What does this girl's parents have to say?"

"Jenny and her parents were concerned that Becca behaved with aggression in response to playful children's banter," the principal said blandly. "I'm wondering if they're correct."

Victoria sighed loudly. "Really? *Becca* behaved with aggression? What are you really trying to say? To hear you tell it, Becca just pummeled this girl without provocation?"

"Ms...."

"Dr. Reese," Victoria finished. "I think you need to take a closer look at these accounts. I'm sure that when you do, you'll find a young lady who is just defending herself against your garden variety bully. How do you expect a child to behave when they've been badgered?"

Principal Schmidt gaped at her, mouth wide open and eyes blinking. "Excuse me?"

"What Dr. Reese is saying," John interjected, "is that you're telling one side of the story. You can't expect me to sit here and believe that my niece wasn't goaded into a fight. Was it actually a fight?" He directed the question to Becca.

"I shoved her," Becca admitted.

"And Jenny fell in the cafeteria," Principal Schmidt finished.

"And did she touch you first?" John pressed.

Becca shook her head, her gaze falling back to the floor again.

"Well then it wasn't your job to put your hands on her," John said. "But I assure you, Principal Schmidt, my niece wouldn't act unless provoked. You can look through her records and see for yourself. Becca has never been in a fight."

Karen Schmidt gave a curt nod. "Of course, Mr. Donovan, we take a student's history into account. But you should know that we have zero-tolerance for violence on our campus. All of the girls will have to be reprimanded."

"And what will this punishment look like?" Victoria said, her body tense and ready for a fight on this girl's behalf. Becca, like all little black girls stuck in these junior Pembrokes, needed a sponsor and she was fully prepared to stand with John. "Because I should let you know, one educator to another, harsh punishment for the victim of bullying can only serve to crush a student's spirit. Especially if they're already a marginalized student."

Karen appeared to hold her breath as she stared Victoria down. "Becca will have a week's work of after-school detention with the rest of the girls who were involved. Admittedly, by the time a cafeteria worker could intervene, it had turned into a brawl."

"Making it difficult to know who exactly started it," John said.

"Perhaps." Principal Schmidt said in a tired voice. "*Everyone* will start their detention period on Monday and it will end next Friday. Mr. Donovan, you can pick Becca up from school at 4 p.m. instead of the usual dismissal time."

"Is anything going to happen to Jenny and her friends?" Becca cried. "They were the ones who started it."

John shot her a glare. "Becca."

Her watery eyes shot it right back. "What?"

He sighed and returned his attention to the principal. "Mrs. Schmidt, the problem between these girls is definitely not over. Does your zero-tolerance policy extend to cases of bullying?"

"Of course," the principal said, tucking her hair behind her ear. "All of the girls will engage in a truth and reconciliation exercise during their detention sessions. We practice more holistic methods of discipline in matters like this."

Victoria loosened her shoulders slightly. Although she recited the policy like any other school administrator, Principal Schmidt's idea wasn't terrible. Perhaps forced apologies in a group setting would help the girls understand their different perspectives. John heaved another tired sigh and stood to shake the woman's hand. "Thank you for your time, Principal Schmidt. Becca will be present for all detention sessions next week."

Becca had heard enough as well. She folded her arms over her chest and flung herself out of her chair, storming out of the office. While she waited in the hallway, Victoria took the time to address the principal. "Thank you for allowing me to sit in on this meeting," she said.

The woman looked between her and John. "Right. Any idea when Becca's mother will be back from Sweden?"

"In about two months," John said in a tired voice.

Principal Schmidt nodded. "I see. Have you considered letting Becca meet with a counselor? Acting out in school is sometimes a sign of sudden upheaval in a child's home-life. As I understand it, her parents recently divorced?"

Victoria didn't like the woman's tone, but chose to keep her mouth shut. She'd already overstepped her welcome as it was. Apparently there was upheaval in the Donovan Clan that she wasn't aware of. "Yes, they have," John said.

"And could this contribute to Becca's aggressive attitude?"

Victoria bit her tongue, close to excusing herself from the room altogether. This scene reminded her of the two years she'd been stuck in Beaufort, South Carolina. She'd been, yet again, the new kid in a sea of white faces who were more or less indifferent about her sudden appearance. Those who weren't indifferent had made her tenure at Pinewood Elementary a nightmare. Defending herself against their taunts had earned her a couple trips to the principal's office. As small as Victoria had been, she'd still understood what *aggressive* really meant and how grossly inaccurate it was.

"There's no evidence of my niece having an aggressive attitude," John said with thin-lipped irritation. "What we're dealing with is a bunch of pre-adolescent girls acting out their insecurities in petty ways. Sometimes that takes the form of a cafeteria brawl or name calling in the classroom. As I said, Becca will be present in every detention session next week. Is there anything else?"

Victoria's gaze flew to his face when he was finished, thoroughly impressed by his swift and just response. He accepted Becca's punishment because he had to, but he wasn't going to let this woman brow beat him or speak ill of his niece. *If only my parents had done the same for me...* His sense of fairness was just as attractive as his sexy swagger.

The principal arched a brow and paused for a beat before shaking her head. "No, Mr. Donovan, that will be all. Thank you for coming."

"Of course." John snatched his coat up and exited the office. Victoria quickly followed. Once in the hallway, they met with a sullen Becca who dragged her backpack on the floor. Her uncle overtook her and strode towards the front entrance. "Pick up the pace, Becca."

Victoria trailed behind the girl, recognizing the slump in her shoulders. She remembered feeling that resignation after coming home from a long hard day of school. When they eventually made it to the parking lot. He opened the door for them to get in. Becca slid inside, acting as the small bit of real world separating John and Victoria.

"Becca, when I said I'd move mountains to get to you, I didn't mean this," John said as he started the ignition.

"I didn't mean to get into a fight," she said.

"If you're not looking to get into a fight, you certainly don't throw the first punch."

"I didn't punch her," Becca protested. "I don't even know how."

John shot her a glare as he maneuvered them out of the parking lot. "Well, according to your principal, shoving is just as bad."

"It wasn't my fault," Becca said. "I only pushed her to shut her up. And then her girls stepped to me and then my girls stepped to them."

Victoria hid her grin behind her hand as she looked out the passenger's window.

"Jesus Christ, I don't send you to school so you can have standoffs with the Sharks," he muttered.

"I don't know what that means."

"I'm going to take Dr. Reese back to the university and when we get home, you're going to Skype your mother and tell her what happened."

From Victoria's perspective, John's approach to children waffled between tender to quick-tempered impatience. She got the feeling that Becca wasn't used to seeing her uncle act as a hard-edged disciplinarian. Victoria sat in the truck as an interloper on a very awkward family scene, unable to say anything helpful.

Unfortunately, Becca picked up on that and sprang. "Who are you?" she asked, staring at Victoria.

She did the only thing she knew how to do and held

out her hand to shake. "I'm Victoria Reese, I work with your uncle John."

Becca cautiously took her hand and shook it. "Nice to meet you."

"I'm sorry you had a bad day at school," Victoria said.

"Yeah, well, they're happening more and more," the girl muttered. "Thanks for saying what you did back there. I don't think the principal likes me."

"The principal is trying to do her job," John said. "When a fight breaks out, she has to call everyone's parents."

"Yeah, but she made it sound like I did everything."

"Honestly, John," Victoria said. "Her tone did suggest that Becca was solely responsible. Some of her language was coded in an offensive way."

John sighed when he stopped at a traffic light. "Yeah, I heard it," he said.

Moved by the girl's gratitude, Victoria patted the girl's leg. "Becca, honey? What did this girl say that made you so angry?"

Becca dipped her head and sniffed. "The same thing she always says. She called me a frizzy haired giraffe."

Without thinking, Victoria wrapped her free arm around a girl she barely knew and squeezed her tight. Becca didn't resist the hug, but leaned into it. She looked over her head and exchanged a glance with John, who watched them with curiosity. "Jenny sounds like a real… you know."

"Yeah, I know."

"I had a bully like her when I was a kid," Victoria said, rubbing Becca's arm.

She sniffed. "What did you do?"

Hesitating, Victoria cast another glance at the other adult in the truck.

John kept his eyes on traffic and smirked. "Yes, Dr. Reese, what did you do?"

"Well," she started. "Her name was Kiki and she was hell-bent on making my life miserable while we rode the bus. She and her little girlfriends were always terrorizing me and my friend Suzie and one day, I just snapped."

"You snapped?" John asked rounding a corner.

"I punched her in the face." Victoria closed her eyes. This was certainly not something to tell a kid who had a full week of detention ahead of her.

Becca looked up at her with wide-eyed wonder. "Really?"

"Yes, but it was wrong," she added.

John snuck another look at her, trying to temper his grin. "I wouldn't have guessed it by looking at you, Dr. Reese."

"You punched her in the face?"

Victoria blushed. "Yes, but it was wrong," she repeated.

"Did you get in trouble?"

"Definitely." Victoria remembered her suspension vividly. Her mother had been aghast by the news and had fretted about what to tell the women of her charity circle. *My own daughter is out here brawling like a common guttersnipe.* Her father's reaction had been entirely different. The strapping Marine who treated her like his son, had wanted Victoria to reenact the events, showing him how her fist had connected with Kiki's jaw. The argument between her parents that evening reverberated off the walls of her girlhood bedroom and in her mind now. The memories made her realize how much she was projecting on Becca. Victoria probably hadn't needed to say anything in the principal's office. But she'd recalled how her own mother refused to defend her and felt the same wave of shame and disappointment. "Anyway, I was lucky I didn't seriously injure Kiki. It could have been worse than a suspension for me. And I didn't feel good about hurting her," Victoria said. "I never felt good about using my fists like that."

"Hmm," was all John contributed.

"It felt good to push Jenny," Becca said. "For a second. And then I felt really scared. Like I didn't know what to do next. Before I could stop them, my friends jumped in and it was a mess."

"Do you feel sorry you did it?" Victoria asked in a gentle voice.

"I do. I just wish she would leave me alone, you know?"

"I think when you and the rest of the girls are stuck in a room with one another and have to talk about your feelings, things might change. You never know what's happening in Jenny's life that makes her act like a…you know. People who are happy with their lives don't tend to be mean for the sake of being mean."

She caught John in her periphery, quietly nodding along to her words.

Becca wiped her eyes. "Maybe you're right. I really don't want to hate her."

"That's because you're a good kid, honey," John said as he pulled into the Stevenson Hall parking lot. "You just have to learn how to use your words."

When he pulled to a stop, Becca straightened away from Victoria. "Thanks for listening," she said.

Victoria gazed into the girl's large and nervous brown

eyes, startlingly similar to her own at that age. The twinge of pain and embarrassment she felt in that moment rendered her silent, so she quietly nodded. Meeting John's niece was like looking into a mirror of the past. The encounter made her heart pound and palms sweat. As she slid her seatbelt off, she smiled at Becca. "Of course," she finally said.

"See you later, Victoria," Becca said with a smile. It was a real smile that lit up her glum face and made Victoria want to cry.

"Let me walk you to the building," John said, climbing out of his side.

As they walked away from the truck, cold air hit Victoria in the face, relieving her flushed skin. "I'm sorry for telling her that story," she said to John. "I just didn't know what else to say."

John chuckled. "Better she hear about your fight than my many bloody noses and cracked ribs."

"Well, it's probably not ladylike for her to hear about it."

"I'm much less concerned about Becca being ladylike than I am her confidence," he said. "And I assure you that my sister feels the same."

She took a deep breath and finally looked him in the eye. "Good luck with everything."

"Listen, I'm sorry," he said.

"For what?"

He dropped his gaze to his shoes. "I feel like something between us is off."

Strangely, Victoria felt it too. For the first time in their sordid affair, things seemed different. She'd feared this would happen. They had introduced the "real world" into their playful game and life with John was becoming complicated. She could have accepted his original offer to be dropped off on campus before he retrieved his niece, but her need to help him had felt more pressing than her need to leave. That need wasn't sordid; it was potentially messy. *Like, relationship messy.* "I know that we had something scheduled for tomorrow, but it's Saturday and that time should probably be spent with Becca. She needs you right now."

John peered at her for a moment before giving a jerky nod. "Yeah, okay."

Even though she suggested it, she was secretly hoping he'd say no. That her goodwill offer would be ignored and they'd make it work anyway. But this was probably for the best. Victoria hid her disappointment behind a quavering smile and held out her hand.

John's face flickered with emotion. "What are you doing?"

"I figured a handshake was better in front of your twelve-year-old niece," she said.

He reached out and held her hand in his. They tried to shake with professionalism, but Victoria couldn't muster the effort. She not only wanted him to hold her hand, but to hold her. "Call me when you're ready for our next appointment," he said in a husky voice.

She slowly pulled her hand from his grasp. "I will."

"Good."

Chapter Nineteen

After a Skype conference with his sister and niece, it had been decided that Becca would be better suited with a confidence-boosting activity on the weekends. With Jessi's permission, John had signed Becca up for kiddie kickboxing lessons at Chris's gym. He knew what it was like to be a frustrated kid with no outlet. Becca could punch her way to a Zen-like serenity instead of shoving schoolgirls. After making arrangements with Chris, he checked his phone for any missed messages from Victoria. Nothing.

There were still no messages the following morning. It had been hell getting Becca out of bed, but they made it just in time for her first class. As he watched his niece do sit ups through a viewing window with other parents, he felt a rough clap on his shoulder. "She looks good, Uncle Johnny," Chris said.

"She's not exactly a fighter," John said.

"That's what the classes are for. Come on, man, let's fire off a couple of rounds with the bag."

John kept his eyes on Becca as the kids lined up for more calisthenics. "Yeah, sure," he murmured. "Dante's going to take it easy on her, right? I don't want her to get hurt."

Chris chuckled. "Aww, fatherhood looks cute on you. Don't worry about her; Dante's great with kids."

He was reluctant to leave the window and follow his friend to the boxing area of the gym, but he forced himself to back away. Hiring Dante last summer to start the kickboxing classes was the best business decision his friend could have made. News of the kid-friendly and women-only classes had spread throughout town, making Flynn Fitness the busiest gym in Farmingdale. John was proud of his buddy's business savvy, considering what kind of mess he was when they were kids.

As they stood with a heavy bag hanging between them, John still saw the goofy kid he'd grown up with, just a bit taller and more muscular. Chris swept his blonde curls out of his face and flashed him the same good humored grin. "Boxing gloves or sparring gloves?" he asked.

John pulled off his hoody and tossed it on a nearby bench. "Sparring," he said.

Chris tossed him a pair and held the bag while John slipped them on. "It's been a minute since you've rocked the bag so we'll start with a two-minute circuit."

John focused on the bag before him, drowning out Chris's voice. He laid into the bag with a speed and force that set him drifting into another place. The strength of his jabs and crosses knocked the bag and Chris back a few inches, catching his friend off guard. John's quiet fury was punctuated with a few well-timed uppercuts and knee thrusts, battering the heavy bag and causing him to break a sweat. His mind was on Victoria and how poorly things had gone yesterday. He'd initially thought he held his own while matching wit with her asshole boss, but after a fitful night's sleep, he now wondered if he'd sounded like an idiot in front of both of them. Victoria was a crazy smart woman who said things like "textual artifacts," who had a small legion of young scholars who followed her around for her literary advice. After being out of school for a decade, how could John fit into the world of elbow-patch academics?

Before he was aware of it, two minutes had turned into five.

"Okay, break." Chris called him out of his trance.

He dropped his arms and broke his intense stare on the bag. His breath was racing as blood pounded in his ears. "Shit," he whispered.

"Shit's right," his friend said with a low whistle. "You okay?"

John tried to catch his breath. "Yeah."

"Right," Chris said stepping from behind the bag. "I know you well enough to say only two things calm you down when you're stressed: fighting and reading. What's got you battering my gym equipment?"

"Give me a minute," John panted. They sat side by side on a bench as John waited for his resting heartbeat to lower.

"Men at our age have to pace ourselves, Johnny."

"Fuck you, I'm in my thirties."

Chris laughed outright. "And somehow knocking on forty's door. Seriously, dude, What's up with you? You look more stressed out than usual."

John glanced at his friend. "If I tell you, will you promise not to bro-out?"

"Okay?"

"I met someone," John said. "And I don't know what to call what we're doing."

"Hooking up?"

He shrugged. "No, I don't think it is."

"Situationship?"

"I don't know." John struggled to find the words. "I think she's... God, I don't know."

"Start from the beginning," Chris said, employing a trick he'd learned from John's mother.

John breathed deeply and relayed the events that led Victoria and him to part ways yesterday, leaving out the necessary bits. When he'd finished, he felt his face redden and managed to avoid eye contact with Chris. "I feel like a dumb kid again. Does she like me? Or does she *like* like me?"

Chris gave one of his good-natured chuckles. "She sounds...interesting, I'll say that."

"I should call her, right?"

"I don't know about that," Chris said. "She made the schedule."

"What if I want more than the schedule?" John asked. "I've only known her for a week and I want to be with her every day. I think about her before I go to sleep; I wake up with her on my mind."

"Jesus, I need to meet this Victoria," Chris said under his breath. "I don't think I've heard you this sprung since Patricia Mayweather in our junior year of college. When she dumped you, you were a real bummer to be around."

John rolled his eyes. "This isn't a Mayweather situation."

"No, it sounds worse actually."

"I got to date Patty for a full year at least," John reminded him. "I've got a couple weeks with Dr. Reese."

"Weird. Was there anything in particular that pissed you off yesterday? Like, what made you two leave stuff so awkward?"

John thought back to their ruined lunch date. "What if I'm not good enough for her?"

"Fuck that," Chris said. "She wouldn't have bothered

if you weren't good enough for her. Do you know how many women ask about you after you leave a session? Man, I'm getting tired of cleaning up after you."

John looked at his friend and grinned in spite of himself. "Cleaning up after me?"

"Yeah, I have to distract them with a tiny white lie."

"How tiny?"

"I tell them you're dating someone so they can redirect their attention to me," he said. "So I need you to start dating someone ASAP."

John ran his hand down his beard and laughed. "God, you're terrible."

"You have no idea," Chris said with a devilish grin. "But when they find out you have a brain under those muscles and tattoos, and that you read to children for a living, women lose their collective shit. As a simple small business owner, it's hard to compete with."

"Okay, so I'm good enough to be with a Pembroke girl?"

"Yes, and she's not a Pembroke girl. We're not kids anymore," Chris reminded him. "She's a Pembroke *woman* who likes your books."

"Sure, but she makes me a little anxious."

"That's because she's a challenge. And to be honest, you haven't had one of those in a while. Who was the last woman you dated? Blair? God, she was pretty simple to figure out."

"Yep, I imagine that's why it lasted just three months."

"And that was a couple years ago," Chris said. "You've been working and hanging out with me all that time."

There was truth in his friend's words. He'd been coasting for the past two years, keeping a simple routine of work, exercise, and visiting family. But in the last week, two tornados had entered his life, knocking things off-kilter. Becca's schooling and coming-of-age drama was colliding with Victoria's project and proposed affair schedule. It was usually during these times of heightened stress, John's inability to concentrate became a problem. When he tried to balance too many things, something always fell. It was another frustrating reminder that he had to work twice as hard as the average person to complete the same task.

"Have you talked to Jessi about her?" Chris asked.

"I normally would, but I don't want her to think I'm more distracted than usual. She's expecting a fairly intact child by the time she gets back."

"I'm just saying, it might help to have a woman's opinion. By the way, Jessi's divorce is final right?"

John raised a brow as he stared down Chris. His friend, a known serial monogamist, was always itching to find his next ex-girlfriend. Even though he'd known Jessi as long as he had John, the idea of his best friend sniffing around his sister made John clench the bench beneath him. *Better that than Chris's neck.* "Choose your next words wisely."

Chris abruptly stood and walked behind the heavy bag, the swagger in his walk matching his lopsided grin. "You think she's ready to start dating yet?"

"Chris..."

"I'm sorry, I'm back to your dude-bro friend."

"I'm ready for the next circuit," John said, standing up.

Chris laughed. "Just pace yourself, old man Donovan."

"Oh man, that was so fun," Becca said, practically skipping down Main Street. "I got to practice fight this kid named Patrick and I kicked him in the balls!"

John furrowed his brow. "I know that feels like something you'd want to brag about, but let's refrain from shouting it on the city sidewalks."

"Dante said that I've the perfect legs for kickboxing," she said in a rushed voice. "He said I've got reach."

They were on their way to The Coffee Hound to celebrate her first class with one of those frappe monstrosities. Hearing her jabber on about fighting in a sanctioned manner made John proud of her even if she was now a terror to the boys in her class. He was also relieved to think about something other than Victoria. "My sweetie is going to be known for her reach."

"Plus, I'm already more flexible than most of the class. I can kick over my head. Ooh, look at that dress!"

John laughed as Becca stopped at a storefront window and examined a pink cocktail dress. He could relate to her shiny-object distraction. "That's pretty cute," he said, casting it a brief glance.

"Hey, that's your friend, Victoria," Becca said.

John stopped dead in his tracks.

"What?" He peered into the store window, trying to hide behind the pink dressed mannequin. He watched a voluptuous woman in a small black dress saunter towards the window, hands on her waist, full hips swaying with every step. He recognized those hips immediately. It was Victoria alright, and that dress... Her cleavage was ample, much more than he was used to seeing in those prim professor blouses.

"Yeah, that's her." Becca, hopped up on post-workout endorphins, whizzed past her uncle and entered the store. She didn't have time to hear him hiss, "Becca, no!"

Chapter Twenty

"Paula, you're day-drunk on white wine," Victoria said, squeezing into the black minidress that she'd found on the sales floor. "I'm not listening to you."

Paula, who was in the next dressing room stall, made a sound that may have been teeth sucking. "First of all, bitch, when housewives do it on TV, no one says boo. Second of all, I'm not the one who gave that boy a schedule."

"Girl," Reggi sounded off in the stall on the other side of Victoria. "And then you've got the nerve to *not* follow the damn schedule. Aren't you supposed to be with him right now?"

"I panicked," Victoria huffed as she pulled the zipper up her side. "I started doubting everything once we ran into Dr. Williams. He acted like an asshole and John gave it right back to him." Even though the whole confrontation had made her break out into a cold sweat, she was thrilled John had come to her defense. Hadn't she already told Kenneth how she felt about being called *Ms. Reese*? It had been so satisfying seeing her boss look flustered by John's clever retorts. "I can't imagine how he'd react to my mother, the queen of criticism. Thinking about those two squaring off makes me sick."

"Katherine be might critical as hell, but you're too grown for her to be a cock-block," Reggi said with a scoff. "Besides, I'd like to sit ringside for that introduction. You need a guy like John in your corner."

It was easy for her friend to think about the long-term relationship that Victoria was actively ignoring. Even if Katherine did approve of John, she'd still pester her about her future. *When will you get married? We'll spare no expense with the invitations. Uncle Jeffrey didn't lose a finger in the Gulf so you could serve him salmon.* Their weekly phone calls would become a daily occurrence. "Anyway, now Dr. Williams is running loose probably telling everyone I'm cavorting with a children's librarian in order to complete my Four-Week Initiative."

"He wouldn't be completely wrong," Paula said. "But I see what you're saying. When I met him on campus, I totally understood why you'd want to cavort. He's a gentleman who brings women potted plants."

"Potted plants?" Regina asked.

"He brought me an orchid plant," Victoria explained. "It was a beautiful gesture." *And a naughty private joke.* A smile touched her lips every time she glanced at it.

"Aww, that's really cute."

Victoria returned to the issue at hand. "And then there was this thing with his niece, Becca. The situation at her school felt so familiar and painfully awkward. I remember being helpless when I was her age, not knowing where I fit in or who to ally with. By the time he drove me back to the school, it all felt too messy."

"Okay, that's a long list of excuses," Paula said. Victoria could almost hear her roll her eyes. "But that's life; it's messy and complicated. Romance is no different."

"Day-drunk Paula is right," Regina added. "While I

commend you for trying to stay neat and in control, romance isn't like ticking boxes on a sushi menu."

The comparison wasn't unfair. "Maybe you're both right," she said as she checked herself out in the mirror. "I think I'm shocked by how quickly I got used to the idea of a fun, flirty affair. It was so…liberating. Like I was rebelling against something."

"And the first time he started talking about 'first dates,' you freaked out," Paula said above the sound of swishing fabric. "Are you afraid of commitment?"

"I like John," Victoria said, staring at her reflection. "God, this sounds so stupid. I think I *like* like him, so yeah, I'm afraid of a ton of things."

She was met with silence. For once her friends had nothing to say?

"This one's a little too low-cut for my taste," she said, changing the subject.

"Let's see it," Regina said.

She tried to hitch the neckline upward before pulling back the curtain. "What do you think? Too much?"

Regina cocked her head and narrowed her eyes. "I think you could go lower actually." She went ahead and adjusted the neckline herself.

"Hey, wait—"

"Aw hush, you don't get to have these titties and not show them off every once in a while."

"Reggi!"

Penny, the boutique owner, and a statuesque black woman with a giant sandy colored afro and leather leggings, walked over. They had been loud enough for her to listen to their dressing room discussion. With her hands on her hips, she pursed her lips and appraised the dress on Victoria. "She's right, that one is actually classified as a 'freakum dress.' And you're filling it out perfectly," she said with a smile. "I think you should try on some shoes for the full effect."

"Aaaayyyeee," Paula called from her stall. "Get it, girl."

A bashful smile spread across Victoria's face as she checked herself out in the three-way mirrors. "Yeah?" The little black dress hugged her hips, snatched her waist, and outlined her full bust before settling on her shoulders. She wound her braids into a neat bun at the top of her head and looked at the lines of her neck and curves of her shoulders. *Not bad at all.*

"Well, you got legs for days, so yeah," Reggi said.

Paula whipped back the curtain to reveal her own dress. It was an A-line emerald green cocktail number that stopped above her knees. The boat neck bodice and three-quarter sleeves sparkled while the skirt was fluffy taffeta. The dress complemented her full figure so beautifully, Victoria actually squealed. "Paula, you look like a sexy black June Cleaver."

They collapsed against one another in laughter as Penny strolled back with a simple pair of black velvet pumps. "Try these on," she instructed as she knelt down and held them in place.

Victoria slipped her feet into the shoes and smoothed down the front of her dress. "Okay," she said, admiring herself in the mirrors. "This might be okay."

"She's not used to anything but work clothes," Reggi told the store owner. "So this right here, is literally blowing her mind."

"Calm down," Victoria said, still staring at herself. "I like it, but where does a Pembroke professor wear a 'freakum dress'?"

Penny shrugged. "It sounds like you need to wear it just the one time with the children's librarian."

The store went silent as Victoria's eyes widened.

"I know that's right. Okay?" Her friends shouted in unison as they exchanged high-fives with the woman.

Victoria released the breath she held and chuckled. "As the proprietor of this store, I'm swearing you to secrecy," she said.

The woman placed her hand on her chest. "I promise."

"Since she *likes* likes him," Regina said with a cheeky grin and wink, "She should probably buy this dress?"

Penny smiled. "It couldn't hurt."

"Now please walk the runway," Paula goaded. "Do your hip thing."

Victoria did as she was told and walked the clear space of store, working her hips as she went. As the women whooped it up, she grinned. She couldn't ask for better hype-women than her friends. But when she saw Becca's familiar face in the storefront window, she stopped in her tracks. Next to her, was her uncle Johnny, who stopped short and did a double take. He tried to hide behind one of the mannequins, but she saw him. Before she could back up and return to the protection of her friends, Becca burst through the front door. "Dang it."

Becca came streaking inside, face flushed and sweaty and curls all askew. "Victoria?"

She froze with an awkward grin plastered on her face. "Becca, what are you up to?" She glanced at the window where John had already disappeared.

"I just got out of kickboxing class," the young girl panted. "I'm really good at it."

"Oh wow…"

Becca took a moment to look her over. "That dress is awesome."

"Thank you?" Victoria said as she tried to bury her panic. *G.D. it!* John was going to follow Becca inside and they'd have to talk and she hadn't solved any of the problems regarding their weird relationship. She could feel herself spiraling and couldn't stop the free fall.

The door opened and John entered the safe space of women trying on dresses. Victoria felt exposed in more ways than one. She wasn't wearing the armor of her buttoned-up work attire. They weren't meeting for an illicit hookup; they were out in the open with her friends and his niece looking on in curiosity. Her sexy catwalk was over and she stood awkwardly while he approached Becca, laying a hand on her shoulder.

"Mr. Donovan," she breathed.

His eyes took a slow tour down her body before returning to her hot face. "Dr. Reese." Her stomach dropped and her breasts tingled when he licked his lips and his nostrils flared. He and Becca were both dressed in workout clothes, but John's gray sweatpants caught her attention. There was a definite outline against the front of his pants that she tried not to focus on. His sandy hair was slicked flat with sweat as if he had also exerted himself that afternoon.

"John, it's nice to see you again," Paula said, racing towards the clusterfuck. She sidled up to Victoria while Reggi found herself on her other side. Even Penny made an appearance. Four thirsty women against a man and child. Victoria held her breath and hoped for the best.

"I'm Regina Crawford, banker and one of Vicki's closest friends."

The store owner edged in and said, "I'm responsible for her dress."

A flicker of amusement lit John's face as he regarded each woman who crowded around Victoria. "Ladies," he said, tilting his head. "It's lovely to meet you."

"Charmed," Regina said.

"I'm John Donovan and this is my niece, Becca," he replied.

"We know," Regina said. Victoria shot a glare that her friend ignored. "Victoria told us about the project you're working on."

John's eyes flitted back to hers before he blushed His eyes dropped to her cleavage once again. "Yeah, well. I'm hoping that I can help her as best as I can."

"Oh, I'm sure you will," Regina said in a demur voice. She looked down at Becca who watched the entire exchange with a bemused grin. "Baby girl, your hair is doing the most right now."

Becca grinned. "I was kickboxing," she said with pride.

The mother in Regina couldn't help herself, and she gathered the child away from John's grasp. "That doesn't mean you still can't look cute. Lord have mercy, look at these curls."

Without Becca as his shield, John stood alone and looked sheepishly at the ground. "We got a late start this morning," he explained. "I didn't have time to help her in the hair department."

Victoria shook her head. "You don't have to explain," she said in a low voice.

Regina wouldn't stop. "You got this baby out here looking bedraggled."

"Reggi…" Victoria said through her teeth. She knew

what her friends were trying to pull and it was thoroughly embarrassing.

"Let me fix what's going on here while you two chat about your little project," Regina said leading Becca to the dressing room area. Paula and Penny picked up on what Regina was putting down and joined her, leaving Victoria alone with John. The two stood before one another uncertain of what to say.

"Honestly," John started. "If we weren't late, I would have helped her do something with her hair. I'm not completely inept."

Victoria tried to suppress her grin. "They're not concerned about Becca's hair in the least," she said in a quiet voice. "They're preying on your insecurities as a white dude while they push us together."

John gave a nod of recognition. "Gotcha. And why would they do that?"

"Because my friends are messy."

"Right," he said, biting his lip. "My best friend, Chris, might be as messy."

Victoria ducked her head to hide her smile. In truth, she was happy to see him. She felt terrible for evading him since yesterday evening. Throughout the night, she'd considered texting him, but decided against it. Instead, she had opted to hang out with the girls to discuss yesterday's events. She went to sleep thinking about John and woke up thinking about him. Victoria sighed before explaining herself. "I just wanted to spend time with my friends today. I was hoping to call you before seeing you."

"It's fine," he said. "You were right. Today was a good day for me to spend time with Becca. As she said, she's taken up kickboxing. Apparently, it's life-changing."

She glanced back at the group of women crooning around Becca and smiled. "I'm glad to hear it."

"You look gorgeous," he said, changing the subject. "That dress is amazing."

When Victoria turned back to meet his intense gaze, her face heated up. "Thank you."

"I know that I'm supposed to wait on you to call me, but I feel like acting impulsively," he said. "Would you like to come by my house tomorrow? Becca is staying over at her friend Kelly's house and the girl's dad is going to take them to school on Monday. I think they're still hammering out the details for their feminist manifesto."

Every doubt she had just shared with her friends, was quickly banished by his invitation. *Eff the consequences and be with this man!* "Yes," she said quickly. "I'll come to you."

"Good," he said with a determined nod. "I'll leave the 'fun' planning to you."

"Okay," she breathed. "I'm sorry with how we left things yesterday. I think I just got nervous."

"Dr. Reese, you never need to feel nervous around me." John stepped closer towards her, his green eyes sparkled. "I thought I already proved that you can feel other things."

Victoria's breasts heaved against the tight neckline of her dress, constraining her breath. "Right," she said.

"I've thought about us in your office, in the greenhouse, inside of a closet," he whispered in a low purr, "and I can't shake your taste, your scent, or the feeling of your beautiful lips wrapped around my cock."

She stood there in a dress and a pair of shoes that weren't hers, trembling under his steady gaze, feeling naked and vulnerable. The soft huskiness of his voice, paired with the rawness of his words, made her panties damp with desire. "John," she whispered.

He shook his head. "No," he said with a quirk of his mouth. "Not now, my dear. I'll be your Johnny tomorrow."

Victoria nodded her head silently. *Tomorrow.*

"Becca, honey, we need to head out," he called, keeping his gaze locked on Victoria.

"Do we have to?" Becca answered from somewhere in the back of the store.

"Yes, ma'am."

Becca trotted to the front of the store, meeting up with her uncle. Her curls were gathered in a tighter, neater bun at the top of her head. "See you later, Victoria," she said with a sunny smile.

"I'll see you later, sweetie."

John threw an arm around the girl and guided her towards the door. "Dr. Reese."

"Mr. Donovan."

When they left, she let out the breath she held and shook out her arms. Anxiety and nerves coursed through her body, shaking her to her very core. "Oh my god," she whispered. "Oh my god."

"Girl…"

"Bitch…"

"Okay…"

The women surrounded her with knowing looks, tongues wagging like thirsty wolves. "I know," she breathed. "I didn't sound like an idiot, did I?"

"I couldn't tell," Regina said. "You two had your heads together talking so low."

Penny leaned against her counter and crossed her arms. "He looked like he was going to eat you up."

"It was probably the dress," Victoria said. Her knees were still shaking after their interaction and she couldn't wipe the wide grin from her face. She returned to the three-way mirror and gave herself another look. *Dang it, I look good.*

Penny gave a throaty chuckle. "I wish my dresses could take the credit, but eighty percent of that exchange was you."

"The Facebook pictures don't do his body justice," Paula said. "He really does look like a Viking dressed in sweats."

"Right?" Victoria asked excitedly. "I've seen him in jeans, dress slacks, but the sweatpants might be a game changer."

Regina's jaw fell. "I've never heard you say anything sexual about a dude, much less openly objectify one… How big is it?"

She shook her head. "A lady doesn't kiss and tell."

"Suck and tell, you mean?" Paula asked.

Victoria burst into laughter. "Okay then, suck and tell."

Wide-eyed and visibly shook, Regina clutched her heart and rolled her eyes upward. "Jesus Christ, Vicki. You have to tell us everything."

Maybe she didn't need the dress to catch John's attention, but wearing it made her feel sexy enough to let her hair down in front of her friends. Today, she didn't feel like Prim Victoria, too polite to talk about sex with the girls. This new Victoria was just a little more reckless and exciting. "Where to start..." she mused at her reflection.

"Preferably at the beginning," Paula said. "Let me get a pen. This could end up in my next book."

Chapter Twenty-One

Victoria woke up on Sunday morning, feeling excited and nervous about her first real date with John. As she pulled into his driveway, she examined the bungalows that lined the quiet suburban cul-de-sac. While many of them were already decorated for Halloween, John's home was not. He didn't even have a festive autumn wreath on the front door. The only evidence that John was in a fall mood were the dead leaves he'd forgotten to sweep from his porch. Victoria chewed on her lip as she parked her car, wondering if he wasn't a fan of Halloween. What if her planned activities weren't interesting enough? *Get out of your head, Victoria!* John wasn't the kind of person who nitpicked over her work.

As she made her way to the front door, she pulled her red checkered flannel shirt down her waist and ran her tongue over her teeth. Her nerves were getting the best of her, making her second-guess her appearance. After yesterday's freakum dress—that she had definitely bought—she wondered if jeans and a comfy flannel would make an impression. *Get out of your head, Victoria!* He'd liked her well enough when she wore a *Golden Girls* T-shirt to the library. She flung her braids over her shoulder, took a deep breath, and knocked on his door. After a minute, the door swung open to reveal John dressed in a nearly identical outfit.

Victoria laughed as soon as they exchanged looks. John broke into a grin. "What?" he asked.

"Twinsies," she said, gesturing between the two of them. "You look like a sexy lumberjack."

"As do you," he said, holding his hand out. "Come in."

She took his hand and crossed the threshold, shocked to find a neat and tidy home. In fact, it looked barely lived in with its distinct absence of accents, wall hangings, or rugs to cover the hardwood floors. In the living room, there was a sectional, one plush easy chair, a glass coffee table, and a television.

John caught her sweeping appraisal of his home. "I have to keep it like this," he said. "It makes things easier to clean."

"That's smart," she said with a nod. "Is that why you're the only one on the block not celebrating Halloween?"

He chuckled. "If I put up decorations, they'd stay up until Christmas. I try to cut clutter in certain parts of my life."

"Of course. That makes sense," Victoria said as she reached out and touched his arm. "I was just hoping you didn't hate Halloween or something."

"Who could hate Halloween? It gets everyone pumped for the other holidays," he said with a grin. "It's the gateway drug of holidays."

She couldn't help but laugh at his analogy. "Maybe you're right."

"Should I give you the tour?" he asked. "That's what people do, right? It's the only reason to buy a house."

Victoria glanced at her watch. "I'd like to take the tour later, but we have to get going."

John's brow creased in confusion. "You just got here."

"I know, but I planned the whole day and if we don't leave now, we're going to be late to the first thing." To prevent him from asking too many more questions, she stood on her tiptoes and gave him a quick kiss on the lips.

He held her in place, wrapping his strong arms around her waist. "You mean I got a kid out of the house and I can't even have sex with you upon arrival?"

Victoria lowered her lashes. "Not now, I'm afraid."

A low growl rose from his chest. "Then what good is a teen girl sleepover?"

With her body pressed against his, she was starting to reconsider her original plan in favor of a house tour if it meant starting with his bedroom. "It sounds like you're still stuck on last week's sordid affair. We're trying it your way, remember?"

"Perhaps we can do both? Now?" John asked in a low voice before swooping down for another kiss. She melted under his lips and let out an involuntary moan as he tilted her head back for more. Before she could lose her head, Victoria planted her hands on his broad chest and gently pushed him back.

"That's very tempting," she breathed. "But you're the one who promised hand-holding and first-date banter."

She tried not to laugh at John's pitiful expression. "Fine," he said. "I'll go."

"I see you've picked up a few things from Becca."

"It usually works when she does it," John said, pulling a zip up hoodie from a coatrack. "I see it doesn't work on everyone."

* * *

When they pulled up to Smith's Apple Orchard, Victoria cut the ignition and looked at John. "Ta-da."

He surveyed the bustling crowd and smiled. "Ta-da, indeed."

"I thought we'd have a fall-themed outing today." As she tried to read his expression, she added. "If you don't like it, we can do something else." It had been a long time since Victoria had been in charge of planning a date and she hoped she wasn't too rusty.

"No, no, I've always wanted to come here," he said, taking her hand. "I've skipped it in the past because it never felt like a place for single men to wander."

Joy and relief surged through her as she flashed him a beaming smile. "Well, you're not single today and I've got a list of things for us to do," she said, pulling out her phone. "We have to buy some pumpkins, and then hit up the corn maze, see the petting zoo…"

John took her phone from her. "I'm going to hold on to this while we explore the orchard. We don't need a list to have fun."

"But I don't want to miss anything," Victoria protested.

He placed the phone in his pants pocket. "And I keep telling you that we don't need a plan."

"Alright," she said with a resigned sigh. "Please don't let me forget to stop by the barnyard petting zoo, they have goats this year."

He chuckled as he tweaked her nose. "We will see the goats, woman."

They exited the car and made their way to the entrance. Along the way, John slipped his hand into hers and tugged her closer to his side. She looked up at him to see him watching children running around, dodging those who slowly strolled. Their excited shrieks of laughter made him grin. Victoria liked the way the corners of his eyes crinkled when he smiled. She also liked the way he held her hand with a protective squeeze, like she was actually his girlfriend. For a moment, she let her mind wander to her and John actually dating. It was a tempting idea to have something more stable than what they currently had.

Their first stop was the barnyard petting zoo. Upon seeing the animals, Victoria pulled away from John's grasp and ran to the first goat. "Look at him," she squealed.

John doubled over with laughter. "You're serious about these goats," he said.

"I wanted to be a farmer when I was a kid," she said, stroking the gray and black goat's nose.

"Did you really?" John's tone was incredulous. "I can't picture it."

"Oh yeah, I was convinced I'd have chickens and goats and some cows."

"What did you want to grow?"

She shrugged. "Corn, maybe? The crop wasn't as important as the animals. I wasn't allowed to have any pets when I was a kid because my mom didn't want to deal with the mess. I must have thought if I were a farmer, I could have a collection of animals and no one could say anything about it," Memories of her farm schematics made her chuckle. She remembered visiting her local library and asking for books on livestock and animal husbandry.

John dug for something in his pocket. When he retrieved a quarter, he fed it into a machine that dispensed feed for the goats. "Here, hold out your hand." Victoria tried to contain her excitement as she collected a handful of feed from John. "You look like you're going to lose your mind," he said with a chuckle.

"This is the best," she said, watching her new goat friend nibble at her hand. When he was done, the goat licked her fingers with a rough tongue before pulling away to join the others. Victoria wiped her hands on her jacket and glanced to John who was watching her with amusement in his eyes. "Actually, this may have been a date meant for me more than you."

"Anything that makes you smile like that is a good date to me," he said. "They've got rabbits too, if you're interested."

"We might need to remember the teachings of the little girl from your reading group before we interact with the bunnies."

John winced. "Damn, you just reminded me that I still need to email her mother."

"And that's why you make lists," Victoria said, biting back a grin.

"Lists are for work," he said as he took her hand again. "Not for *fun times* as you like to call them."

They walked around the goat pen and into a barn where the rest of the animals were. Near the entrance, there was a large rabbit hutch managed by a teenage boy who wore a Smith's Apple Orchard sweatshirt. He held one of the bunnies in the crook of his arm and let children pet its ears. "You have to be quiet around him," he told the kids. "And use a soft touch." The young man fielded all their questions while keeping a secure hold on the animal.

"So when did you make the transition from farmer to professor?" John asked, watching the rabbit showing.

Victoria made a face. "Around Becca's age, I guess." She didn't really have to guess. It was right after that school bus fight with Kiki that the tide had shifted. "My mother got tired of my tomboy antics and made me behave like a lady. But I used to do a lot of fun stuff with my granddad and my father."

"A tomboy?" John said with a raised brow. "I still can't picture it."

"I was a military brat," she explained. "My dad is a Marine and I don't think he knew what to do with a daughter. It was a weird tug of war between my parents. Everywhere we moved, my mother made sure to hook up with local officers' wives and plan charity events or galas. That was her thing. I don't know, maybe the farm fantasy was a way for me to put down roots?"

"Okay, now the 'whiskey locker' makes sense," John said with a smirk. "Outside of going to school in Chicago, I've spent my entire life here."

"That's where my family eventually ended up after my dad retired. I went to school at the University of Chicago, you?"

"DePaul."

She nodded. "Do you ever feel like going somewhere else?"

John seemed to think about his answer. "My sister's trip to Sweden reminded me that I want to visit more of the world." He stroked his chin and narrowed his gaze on the rabbit demonstration before them. "I guess if the opportunity ever arose, I'd try something new. But for now, I like my job and I like Farmingdale."

"Did you know that, outside of school, this is the longest I've ever spent in one location?"

"Really? How long have you been here?"

Victoria counted the years in her mind. "A little over four years."

"And we're just meeting…" he mused. "I can't imagine walking past you in a grocery store and not seeing you."

"It may have happened," she said with a smile. Victoria couldn't imagine what rock she had lived under before meeting John. He was so large and vibrant that a chance meeting should have taken place much sooner.

"When was the last time you were at the library, before we met?"

She searched her memory. "I don't know. It's been a long time."

"Possibly not since January?"

Her gaze flew to his face. "Yes, probably. Why would you say that?"

John couldn't hide the mirth in his eyes. "*For the Duke's Convenience* was the last thing you checked out. Fines are ten cents per day and ten months of fines adds to about thirty dollars."

Victoria bit back a grin and crossed her arms. "If I buy the book for eight dollars and gift it to the library, will you take me off the wanted posters?"

"Absolutely not." His green eyes danced with merriment. "It's out of print anyway. You managed to steal a very old paperback."

She opened her mouth to say something sassy but was cut off by the young man. "Did you guys want to pet the rabbit?" Victoria looked around to find they were alone, the group of children having long left in favor of something else.

John had already stepped up to the teenager. "Of course. Do you mind if I hold him?"

"If you're careful," the teen warned. "He's a Dutch, so he's kind of feisty."

The handoff was a little rocky as the little guy left the warmth of one arm to the massive hands of another. John scooped its bottom and kicking legs with one hand while the other held its upper body. The small Dutch settled down once John held him to his chest. "He's not too feisty," John said in a soft voice.

Her ovaries nearly exploded as she watched John cradle the black and white Dutch to his chest like it was an infant. The rabbit nuzzled its nose against his neck, his little tongue darting around licking John's skin. "He's giving you tiny kisses," she said, trying to bury a squeal.

"It tickles," he said with a low chuckle.

"I need a picture of this."

"Your phone is in my pocket," he reminded her. She slowly approached him, taking care not to disturb the rabbit, and felt the outside of his pants. "Watch it, Dr. Reese," he whispered with a wink.

"You watch it, Mr. Donovan," she said under her breath. She slipped her hand in his pocket, brushing her fingers against his rock hard thigh. When she had snapped enough photos, she began petting the rabbit herself. "He's so soft," she murmured, pressing her face against its fur, inhaling the scent of woodchips and hay.

"You want to take him home with you?" John asked, peering down at her. "He could be a good way to start your farm. They can't pull a plow but they poop a lot."

"Tempting," she admitted. "But this little guy should stay with his brothers and sisters."

Eventually John transferred the rabbit back to the capable teen and they exited the barn hand in hand. Victoria's breath appeared before her face in the brisk autumn air. "Maybe we should get some hot cider," she said, stuffing her free hand in her jacket pocket.

"Before we tackle the other items on your list?"

"Yes."

"Excellent."

"Are you having a nice time?" Victoria asked, enjoying the firm grasp of his hand in hers and the warmth of his body. John looked so handsome with his sandy blonde hair bound in a ponytail, and his Brawny Man outfit, she found it difficult to stop staring at him. He was a perfect fit for their environment, easygoing and confident with himself. For a second, Victoria hoped that by extension, she was a perfect fit *for him*.

John pulled her close and planted an affectionate kiss on her cheek. "Anytime I'm with you, I'm having a nice time," he said with an easy smile.

Chapter Twenty-Two

When Victoria brought them to the next leg of their journey, John debated how to tell her that this was a terrible idea. They were quickly approaching the entrance of McLean's Haunted Warehouse, a Farmingdale attraction that he hadn't visited since he was in high school. Sixteen-year-old John had liked the idea of impressing Kimberly Yates, but had left her near a bloody corpse midway through as he'd dashed towards the exit. Thirty-eight-year-old John was secure enough in his masculinity to admit that this wasn't his idea of fun. As soon as he'd set eyes upon the cardboard zombie cutouts, his heart rate had accelerated.

Before he could voice his concerns, Victoria paused beside him. "Are you okay?"

He took a deep breath and nodded vigorously. "Yeah, sure. I'm cool," he lied.

She narrowed her eyes and smiled. "Are you sure?" She held up their joined hands. "Because your grip just got tighter and sweatier."

"I don't do haunted houses," John admitted. He glanced at the entrance again, reminded of the breakneck speed he'd run when Kimberly had screamed. "When I was a teenager, I got scared and left a girl in there."

"That happens," she said in a serious voice, no trace of irony or humor. "But you're an adult now. You're also a lot braver than I am."

He scoffed even though her observation made him straighten up. "How do you figure?"

The warmth in her smile matched her voice. "You're a man who takes chances. I like that about you, John. I think I take more chances when I'm with you."

He was momentarily speechless in his surprise. John had no idea that Victoria regarded him in that way. "Is that a fact?"

"Besides I don't think it will be as terrifying as you remember. I hate to say it, but these are a bunch of theater majors hamming it up and competing for the limelight," Victoria said easily. "You remember the theater kids from high school, right?"

He did. They were an exuberant crowd. John rubbed his sweaty palms against his jeans and scanned the ticket line. "A little thrill isn't a bad thing, I guess."

"A little thrill is a *great* thing." She laughed. "I love scary stuff. Halloween frights are my favorite."

While John enjoyed learning about the woman who originally wanted him for his body, he was nervous about what this knowledge would do to his heart. The first part of their date had been delightful. They drank hot cider, picked out two pumpkins, and wandered around the corn maze. In the car, she had kept mum about the second activity as she'd stuffed herself full of kettle corn. He'd been expecting a low-key, relaxing dinner or a movie. John could have easily seen a movie with her; instead he was going to have a heart attack. "I don't do well with crazy shit jumping out at me," he warned. "I make it a point to never watch horror movies either."

Victoria leaned against his chest and rubbed his shoulders. "If you don't want to do this, we can always go home," she said, giving him an out. And he probably would have taken it if her breasts weren't pressed against him while she loosened the tight muscles of his neck.

"Mmh," he groaned at the pleasurable pressure from her hands. "You'll hold my hand?" he asked, letting his eyes fall shut.

"Of course, I will," she chuckled. "You're not leaving me in there like your little girlfriend."

A smile spread across his face. "Kimberly Yates was really pissed."

"What was all that Halloween magic you talked about with your kids?" she asked applying that same pressure to his deltoid muscles. John was very close to agreeing to a number of dangerous activities, if she kept touching him like this.

"I was talking about lighthearted spooky magic, as in Charlie Brown's *Great Pumpkin.*"

Victoria ended her massage by cupping his face and stroking his beard. "I can be your blanket, Linus," she teased. "You can hold on to me for dear life all you want."

For the first time since they arrived to the haunted warehouse, John's pulse slowed its rapid pounding and his breathing returned to normal. "You promise?" he asked as he held her flannel covered hips. She felt warm and alive, even in the chilled autumn air. A steady anchor for him to hold on to.

She nodded as she ran her thumb along his jaw. "I do."

John blew out a sigh. "Alright then, let's get this over with."

He could tell she was trying to hide her excitement

as she took him by the arm and pulled him forward. John could keep his shit together for a few minutes if it meant Victoria could have fun. At the ticket counter, a large heavyset man collected money and distributed tickets. He took his role seriously, dressed as a ghoulish butcher with blood splatter on his dingy white apron. A real cleaver sat on the counter, covered in matted blood and hair. A realistic touch that made John sick.

"What's this year's theme?" Victoria asked the man as she slapped down her cash.

"Zombies," he said in a menacing voice. "Also, half of the proceeds are going to Farmingdale's no-kill animal shelter."

Victoria turned to John, her eyes shining. "Isn't that nice?"

He rolled his eyes and said nothing.

"Can you please explain to my friend the basic rules of your haunted warehouse?" she asked the bloody butcher.

The man dropped his menacing voice and switched to a thick Chicago accent. "Sure. It's advised that pregnant women, folks who suffer from epilepsy, or those who have pacemakers not participate in the walk-through. If that doesn't apply to you, just follow the marked path and you won't get lost. If you have a hard time seeing in front of you, you're allowed to use your cellphone, but we don't allow photography. It kinda ruins the surprise for future guests. Lastly, the zombies are instructed not to touch participants. Don't worry, sir, an actor is not going to reach out and grab you."

"See? That's all there is to it," Victoria said with an encouraging tone.

"Hardly," John said under his breath.

"Oh, come on," she said, pulling his arm. "You're going to have fun."

"At best, I'm going to look very wimpy in front of you. At worst? I might throw up in front of you."

"You're not going to throw up," she said as they stood at the precipice of a darkened entrance. From somewhere inside there was a loud crash, followed by terrified screams that pierced the evening air. His heart thudded in his chest.

"Before we go in there," John said, gripping her hand. "Tell me why you're attracted to this."

Victoria looked at him, eyes wide with anticipation and a broad grin. Her perky nose and the cute dimple on her left cheek eased his fear, just slightly. If John could remember this face, he might make it through this horrifying walk. "Because none of this is real," she said. "It's all pretend. I never take chances in the real world, because it could all go wrong. But here, where the zombies are actors, I can feel the exhilaration of danger and come out safe on the other side." She squeezed his sweaty palm. "And you will too."

He nodded. "Okay."

John let her lead him, all the while hoping to make it to other side sooner than later.

Her laughter should have annoyed John, but he found himself joining in on the roasting that she was determined to give him. Victoria sat at his kitchen island drinking wine, while he chopped tomatoes for pasta sauce. "The way you used me as a human shield to get through that abandoned bus," she cackled, tears already forming in her eyes. "But then that girl zombie jumped out from behind you..."

John smiled to himself as he returned to the refrigerator for parsley. "That's right," he said, closing the door. "I used my date as a human shield."

She wiped her eyes. "Oh my god, the look on your face when the guy pressed himself against the quarantine fence." She started laughing again. "The sheer panic!"

"They were getting dangerously close to touching us," John said. "I was told there would be no touching."

"I'm sorry, John," Victoria said, attempting to be somber for a second. But once she met his gaze, she fell apart all over again, nearly sliding off her barstool. "I just remembered the guy on the hospital gurney," she howled.

John laid his knife on the counter and planted his fists on his hips. "Now how exactly am I supposed to redeem myself after that debacle?" he asked. "How can I possibly come out looking like a man?"

She wiped her face and took a sip of her wine. "Johnny, if you were sitting from where I am, looking at you, you wouldn't have to ask such a question."

He raised a brow. Were they already in "Johnny" territory? As he studied her face, he noted the pinkish tint in her brown cheeks. John had reason to believe that Victoria was a little intoxicated. "Is that a fact?" he asked nonchalantly.

She nodded. "You're very manly," she said. "Being afraid doesn't make you any less of a man, it makes you more human."

He went back to chopping. "So you didn't mind my excessive shouting during the tour?"

"The girlish screams, you mean?"

He chuckled. "There was nothing girlish about them. They were throaty masculine shouts of anger."

"I thought it was sexy," she said sweetly. "Masculine posturing has never been a turn-on for me. It's all a performance that gets old and tired."

"I'm glad you think so," he said, transferring the chopped tomatoes to a bowl. "Are there any performances that personally tire *you* out?"

She sighed, propping her head against her fist. "Oh, working at Pembroke is a constant performance. This semester especially."

"Tell me about it," John urged. He'd been slyly wheedling information out of her for most of the afternoon and evening. So far, he'd learned about her parents, who were still married and living in Chicago, her education and what drove her towards studying literature, and her hidden wild streak that drove him to senseless frights. In the car ride home, she'd made a point to distract him from the horrors of the haunted warehouse by making him talk about his life. John had shared a lot of information about his family, ADD, and his career, and found Victoria to be an engaging listener.

"I guess Pembroke has this aura," she said, making a wide motion with her arms, "that's old-money, WASP, and conservative. I still feel like I need to prove that I belong there. And you'd think I'd get the hang of it, after moving around so much, but I still feel like the new kid trying to find a place to sit in the cafeteria. You know what I mean?"

John nodded as he started on another tomato. "Kind of," he said. "I haven't had to be the new kid too often, but the 'fake-it-till-you-make-it' nonsense from graduate school still lingers."

"Exactly! And I feel like I'm faking it. I just want to know when I'm going to make it. I'm thirty-four and I'm an assistant professor, which qualifies as "making it" in academia, but I still have to do so much extra work to be seen. It doesn't matter that I ran the same race, jumped the same hurdles as the assholes in my department, and I still have to put up with their shit."

Her rare curse word made him glanced up from his chopping to see her take another drink. "What do you mean?"

"Oh, it's nothing," she said with a sad smile.

"Go on," he said. "I'm not going to tell your department that you feel inadequate."

She shrugged. "I've talked to my girlfriends about this a million times. When you're a woman trying to be yourself in these institutions that don't want you, that didn't ask for you to pull up a seat at the table... You get angry, and you want to lash out. But you don't, because being angry comes with a whole host of implications. You end up getting called aggressive or hysterical by a man who hasn't had to worry about job security since the '70s."

"Hmm."

"I don't know if any of that makes sense," she said in an apologetic tone.

John transferred more chopped tomato to his bowl before wiping his hands on the towel on his shoulder. "You're actually making perfect sense," he said as he ducked down to retrieve a skillet.

Victoria frowned. "Yeah?"

"Oh yeah," he said, placing the skillet on the stove. "My sister, Jessi, has said the same thing for years. She's a civil engineer and it's a regular boy's club wherever she works. She never has the opportunity to be angry in public. She saves it for me actually. We usually hit the gym and beat the ever-living shit out of a punching bag."

"Does it help her?" Victoria asked sitting up.

John turned on the heat and drizzled the pan with olive oil. "It's hard to say," he admitted. "She still has to show up to work the next day. She still has to put on the mask. I don't know if it's a performance you can really drop." He watched the flame lick the bottom of the skillet, waiting on her to say something.

"It *is* a mask," she murmured.

John now understood why their confrontation with Kenneth had rattled her so. She'd remained silent in the face of the old professor's criticism because her job was on the line. Realizing that made him feel sad for her and angrier at her boss. "But you wear it well," he said, looking up at her, "because you have to. In Jessi's case, she's a ball-buster who some men would call a bitch. Your mask might be wrapped in rules and regulations. If you can keep order and control all situations, you might keep the mask from slipping. But I'll bet it tires you out, right?"

"I'm exhausted."

"Then I'll tell you what I tell my sister. You have to remember why you do the work you do. What are you bringing to the field that wasn't there? How are you changing the world? Whose life have you touched with your work?" When the heat was high enough, John dumped a small bowl of garlic and shallots to the skillet and stirred them.

She smiled. "Maybe you're right."

"I don't claim to know the answers," he said honestly. "I just know that when Jessi calls me about a new project that she's starting, I hear the excitement in her voice and I know she belongs where she is. She might feel like she's faking it, but I know different."

Victoria's smile grew wider. "That's really beautiful," she said in a soft voice.

John turned down the heat. "Now tell me what you bring to your work that wasn't there before."

Victoria appeared to think about it. "I don't know," she said.

"Tell me."

She ducked her head to hide her bashful grin. He caught it, though, and held on to it. John found himself collecting her smiles as though they were currency. "I guess, when I first started to teach at Pembroke. There was this young man, around eighteen, who stayed after class on the last day of the semester. He wanted to thank me for teaching him how to read better. He went to a high school where his learning needs were ignored and he appreciated the time I took to break down the poems I made the class read. He looked so sincere when he said thank you…" She looked up from her glass of wine. "I guess I hold on to that moment when I feel shitty."

John paused in his stirring to look at her. Victoria's eyes shined brightly with the memory and possibly the wine. "There you go," he said softly. "You're not faking it, Victoria."

She nodded. "Thank you, Johnny."

He tried to not let the small gesture make his heart bloom. He cleared his throat. "Talking about these things usually helps," he said in a perfunctory tone as he dumped the tomatoes into the skillet.

"Well, I don't think I talk about it like that often," she said.

"I'm going to let this simmer for a while," he said,

tossing his towel on the counter. "You want me to top you off?" He gestured to her wine glass.

She shook her head. "I think I'm already tipsy."

John left the kitchen and moved towards the living room. "You want to move to the couch while we wait on the sauce?"

Victoria slid off her barstool and joined him. When she sat down, he followed, giving her a respectful distance on the couch. He couldn't stand the silence, so he turned on the television and put on the Dave Matthews Band station, setting it on low volume. She leaned against the cushions and tucked her legs under her. "This is awkward," she murmured.

He didn't have to ask what she meant. They'd just finished their first real date after a week of carefree hookups. She was in his home now; he was making her pasta. It was almost laughable how "normal" they were trying to behave, instead of doing what was most natural, like ripping each other's clothes off. "It doesn't have to be," he tried. "We don't have to do anything but sit here and talk."

She shifted in her seat. "Thank you," she said. "But I don't want to do that."

John met her gaze and took a deep breath. Victoria stared at him, heady desire in her eyes. With some of her braids shrouding half her face, she looked downright wicked. "What would you like to do?"

A small ghost of a smile played on her lips. "I'd hate to be blunt," she said. "Because that takes the fun out of it."

She'd had quite a bit of wine, so John wanted to make certain anyway. "What would you like to do, my dear?" he repeated.

Victoria didn't reply. Instead, she left her side of the couch to stand before him. John watched quietly as she stepped between his spread legs and undid the first couple of buttons on her flannel shirt, revealing the top of a black lace bra and gentle curve of her breasts. John breathed through his nose as Victoria slowly ran her hands down to her waist. When her hands stopped she flashed him a wanton smile. "Would you like me to take this off or would you?"

She was issuing him a challenge. "What would you like?" he asked.

"I'd like you to take it off."

John rubbed his trembling hands along the tops of his tense thighs as if this was the first time he had undressed Victoria. Every muscle in his body was tense, ready to spring. He held his emotions at bay and concentrated on her body. One moment at a time. However, it didn't stop his blood from rushing away from his head, straight to his cock. "Come here," he said in a voice he could hardly recognize. A primal hoarseness surged from his chest, cloaked in the desperate desire to hold her soft body in his arms.

Slowly, Victoria came to him, lowering herself to straddle his pelvis. On her knees, she lifted herself slightly so that she stared down at him. Her braids made a curtain around his face as he gazed up at her. "Is this okay?" she whispered above him.

"Yes." His hands found her thighs, squeezed their thickness, and slid up to her hips. John pulled her downward against his growing erection and released a sigh. Her softness pressed against his hardness, creating a delicious sensation. He groaned under her weight and closed his eyes as Victoria ground her hips in a circle.

John arched away from the couch, lifting his hips to make contact with hers. He breathed through her gentle rocking, pushing and pulling her by the waist. When she set her own pace, he dragged his hands past her stomach, and settled on her full breasts. Even encased in flannel, he still felt her stiff peaks pressing against her bra, waiting to be released. He ran his fingers along the surface of her exposed skin. It was warm to the touch. A thin sheen of dewy perspiration coated her neck and the valley between her breasts. Blindly, he fell upon her buttons and undid them one at a time. Cock straining against his jeans, Victoria's slow grinding became an uncomfortable pleasure. When John finally opened his eyes, he sighed.

Light filtered from the kitchen, casting a glow on his dark living room and illuminating Victoria's face. Her eyelids were heavy as she locked eyes with him. She bit her bottom lip as she clung to his shoulders. Braids swayed against her face, covering the crease of her brow as she continued to swivel on top of him. Now exposed, she shrugged out of her sleeves and tossed the top on the floor. John cupped her ample cleavage, slipping his fingers under the barrier her bra created. When he brushed against her stiff nipples, she exhaled sharply and squeezed her eyes shut. "Johnny," she breathed.

He groaned at the sound of his name as he quickly slipped the bra straps down her shoulders. He unhooked the front clasp, releasing her bosom. John fanned his fingers across her small dusky nipples and squeezed her flesh in his large hands. Victoria curled her back and folded her body against his arms. Her hands slid from his shoulders to his chest and neck, digging her nails into his skin. When she let her head fall back, her mouth fell open and her eyes closed. Her sharp pants kept the same pace as her grinding, "Please," she gasped. "More…"

While John enjoyed having a near-naked woman dry-hump his stiff erection, he wanted to give her more. Whatever she asked for, he would give it to her. He left her breasts and started undoing the buttons on his own shirt, determined to keep up with her.

Holding her ass to keep her steady on his lap, he took off his flannel. Victoria wrenched his undershirt over his head and tossed it over the couch. John pulled her against his naked torso and covered her mouth with his, delivering a shuddering kiss. She returned it with reckless abandon, sending new spirals of ecstasy through him. Their tongues circled and sparred, sliding against each other. Victoria kissed him with a hunger that belied his previous apprehensions. He moaned against her lips and kissed her deeper, plunging his tongue further. When she broke away, Victoria gasped for air, her chest heaving against his.

"I want…" Her voice was strained.

"What, darling?" he whispered, his lips brushing her neck. "What do you want?"

She was near tears with want. Her fingers fisted in his hair pulling him closer to her. "I want to drop the mask. I want you to *see me*."

John's breath caught in his throat. Before, sex with Victoria felt almost like a game. A fun list of positions and locations to share passionate moments before they had to return to their previously scheduled lives. Now, as he listened to her breathy request, he knew he was getting a different Victoria. He could see her as clearly as he could he feel her pounding heart.

She wants more.

Chapter Twenty-Three

As soon as Victoria said the words, she knew they were the truth.

John had listened to her fears and told her it was okay. That she was okay. As she straddled his lap, she searched his gaze with clear eyes. This beautiful man wanted more than her schedule, more than her rigid guidelines. He wanted her. And she desperately wanted to give herself to him tonight.

"Hold on, darling." He picked her up, fitting her legs around his waist, and carried her to the stairwell. She wrapped her arms around his neck and stared into his eyes as he took her upstairs to his room. The décor inside the master bedroom was just as stark as the rest of his home. Only necessary furniture filled his space, the king-sized bed the focal point. In the darkness, he gently set her on the foot of his bed and turned on the small nightstand light. A soft yellow light brightened the room, casting a shadow of his body against the wall opposite her. The sound of a drawer opening, packages crinkling and ripping, sent a ripple through her belly. Already wet and aching from the impromptu lap dance downstairs, Victoria wanted to see John naked and wearing only a condom.

She reached down and began working on her belt buckle in preparation.

"No," he said, appearing at her side. "I want to do that."

He held a shining condom packet between his teeth as he unbuckled his belt. Her hands froze as she watched him. His muscular chest was a sight to behold, something she could never get used to staring at. His pecks jerked while he slid his belt off and dropped it to the floor. Ripples of never-ending abs coursed down his torso, stopping at the flat smooth surface just at his waistband. Sandy brown hair peppered his chest in a fan and tapered into a single line, pointing in the direction she wanted to go.

He unzipped and shoved his jeans down his thighs, the imprint of his cock pressing against his underwear, inviting Victoria to reach out and touch it. She sat on her hands in anticipation while he stepped out of his pants and kicked them away. Down to his snug gray boxer-briefs, John stepped before her where they could properly appraise one another. Her topless, and him, nearly naked. Through the thin layer of his briefs, he gripped his length and stroked himself gingerly as he stared down at her. "Are you capable of relinquishing control tonight?" he asked through gritted teeth, the condom still in his mouth.

He'd asked her something similar when they were in the library stacks. Up until now, she had been in control of their interactions. John had been so accommodating to her schedule and it made her confident enough for this exact moment. "I can," she said in a halted voice.

"Do you trust me?" he asked, removing the condom and tossing it on her lap.

Victoria nodded.

John hooked his thumbs in the waistband of his briefs and slowly pulled downward. Her heart pounded in her ears as desire pooled in her panties. Her clit throbbed against the pressure of her jeans. She pressed her knees together, holding the condom between her thighs. "You told me that it had been a while since you were a student."

She gave another wordless jerky nod.

When he finally revealed his iron-hard cock, Victoria swallowed. She was already acquainted with the throbbing organ, but tonight was different. John was calling the shots and she was going to let him. Victoria took a deep breath and watched his penis jerk upward when he took a step closer. She was inches from it. "Do you trust me, Victoria?"

She had a difficult time tearing her eyes from his cock and meeting his gaze.

"Victoria," he repeated.

She looked up to see his glittering green eyes peering at her. "Yes."

"Put the condom on," he commanded with a voice edged in steel. "Slowly."

Victoria quickly ripped open the package. Her hands shook as she pressed the latex up to his mushroom tip and rolled it along his hot shaft. She breathed through her nose, intoxicated by the forest musky scent of his body. As she handled him, she was reminded of how bold she had been in the cleaning closet of the library. John's cock radiated such heat and masculinity, it was a challenge for her not to do more than simply slip a condom along its shaft. Nothing more.

Once she was finished, her hands lingered until John

gently pushed her to her back, and stood between her thighs. He ran his fingers down her breasts, over her nipples, leaving fire in their wake. She inhaled and closed her eyes. He traced a path down her belly until he stopped at her belt buckle to flick it apart. She heard the zip and tilted her hips so he could shove the fabric down her thighs. She didn't open her eyes until her jeans left her ankles. John had taken her clothes and tossed them on the floor.

Victoria was completely bare.

Cool air hit her throbbing pussy, now slick with her liquid. She shivered and her thighs quaked while John leaned over her, his body casting a shadow in the room. "Do you want me inside of you?" he asked, climbing onto the foot of the bed.

"Yes."

"Tell me," he said.

"I want you inside of me." Feeling his rigid length brush against her thigh was enough for her to tell him anything. She would recite anything if it meant he would enter her. "Now."

John bowed his head to kiss her shoulder, then the top of her breast, his tongue caressed her nipple. As he gathered the puckered flesh in his mouth, he grasped her other breast and kneaded her until she moaned and squirmed beneath him. "Are you wet for me?" he asked after leaving her nipple with a satisfying pop.

She arched her back in response and spread her legs under him.

"If I touch you right now," he said, trailing his hand down her belly. "Will you be dripping wet, Victoria?"

She was positive. When he touched her, his fingers slid easily past her folds, brushing against her sensitive nub, lighting a fire in her chest. Arching her back away from the bed, she gasped. "Yes."

"I missed this pussy," he whispered against her ribs. "One day without it was too much."

His fingers were like magic; working spells against her clit. Victoria bit her lip as the small pulses vibrated from her womb. "Johnny," she choked out, bucking against his hand. This was just as beautiful as their scheduled sex sessions, only now, she felt free to shout and cry at will. And his hands were willing her to be her loudest.

"Do you want more, baby?"

With her eyes squeezed shut, Victoria nodded. "Please."

He took away his hand, leaving her bereft and empty. She gently eased a shaky breath from her lungs and opened her eyes to see he had lifted himself over her until his body imprisoned her. With powerful thighs between hers, he stroked himself while watching her squirm under his piercing stare. "Do you want this?"

More than anything.

The corners of Victoria's lips curled as she thrust upward. "Okay," he said with a wicked smirk. Leaning over her, John braced himself on his arms, planted on either side of her head. When he rested the tip of his cock against her warm wet entrance, Victoria tightened her thighs around his narrow hips and raised her own. "Slow down, sweetheart," he crooned in her ear.

"No," she said with a breathy laugh, her breasts pressing against his tickling chest hair. "I want you inside me now."

John chuckled as he slid his length along her hot swollen flesh, sending a jolt through her core. "Can you take this cock?" he asked.

Running her hands along the corded muscles of his back, she arched her back again. "Only one way to find out," she whispered.

When he entered her, Victoria inhaled sharply and dug her nails into his skin. Each time John penetrated her was a delightful new surprise that she relished in. She wrapped her legs around him tighter and rode the sensation of him sliding against her tight walls. Every inch of him moved slowly, filling her to the hilt, until the pleasure forced him onto his forearms. He leaned into her, nostrils flaring, muscles taut. "Oh, Jesus…" he exhaled.

She wanted to continue the sexy banter with him, but the lump in her throat prevented her from speaking. Electricity buzzed between them, she felt it between her thighs, in her belly, and in her breasts. The gentle friction of his bare chest excited her nipples in a way she hadn't expected. He filled her with every satisfying thrust of his hips, driving into her with a groan that seemed to kill him. Victoria arched her back away from the bed to meet him, to match his pace, to take more of him. She needed to feel all of him. As her hands fluttered over every muscle of his taut body, she wrapped her legs around his narrow hips.

"Oh God." John abruptly halted his strokes, pulled out of her, and untangled himself from her legs.

When she felt the sudden shift, Victoria opened her eyes with a start. "What?"

"I'm about to lose it, darling," he said through labored breathing. His chest heaved with exertion. "You're so perfect, but I can't come yet."

She was confused when he heaved her from the mattress and sat before her. Her eyes were on his cock, sitting straight up. "What?"

"Sit on it and ride me, baby," he said, placing his long legs on either side of her.

Victoria didn't need to be told twice. Climbing on his lap for the second time that evening, she lowered herself on to him, slowly sheathing his length. He let out a long shuddered breath and closed his eyes as her walls clung to him. Now sitting and facing him, Victoria controlled the pace, raising and lowering herself against him. John held her back with one hand and grabbed her breast with the other. Victoria hung off his broad shoulders and bounced like her life depended on it, all the while keeping her eyes on his. His green eyes darkened as they locked gazes, staring hard into hers. She loved seeing the redness in his face as he breathed through every stroke. She watched the way his nostrils flared and his brows furrowed in concentration. She was doing this to him. Knowing that she was in control of this moment was enough to send a rapturous wave of bliss to crash against her shores. Her forehead pressed against his as her muscles spasm and jerked. She pulled John's bare chest to her breasts and cried out in pleasure. His large hands left her breasts and pushed her ass downward to take every last inch of him.

"Oh baby," he whispered in her ear. Sweat covered their bodies as he laid her back against the softness of his mattress. Victoria's body went limp with the force of her orgasm, but she didn't want him to leave her body. Still inside her, John leaned over her and slowly rocked against her body. "There's nothing more beautiful than this."

The gentle and languorous strokes made her body re-awakened with want. He worked slowly, with patience, drawing his own pleasure with caution. While he moved above her, Victoria combed the hair that escaped his ponytail with her fingers. She ran her hands down the expanse of his chest, fanning her fingers along his nipples. Feeling brave, she pinched them both and watched him hiss. His response made her walls flutter against his sliding cock. She obviously aroused him as much as he did her and that knowledge made her raise her hips to meet his. She wanted to see his release; she wanted to know what complete loss of control looked like. He lifted her by the hips and set her torso on an incline, driving himself into her with a singular force that sent her close to another orgasm. John held her in place and pumped frantically until he threw his head back and shouted. His body seized as his hands tightened on her hips. Cords stood out on his neck as he moaned through the downpour of fiery sensations.

After a moment, he loosened his grip on her and opened his eyes. When he looked down at her, Victoria's breath caught in her throat. John was a wild man. His hair hung over his drawn face, his eyes sparkled like a wildfire. "It's never felt like that before," he said in a hoarse voice, exhausted from the workout.

"No, it hasn't," she admitted, letting her eyes drift shut. This was more intense and they were more connected.

He lowered himself against her body and held her close. John buried his nose against her neck and breathed deeply. "Victoria," he said in a hushed voice.

She let her eyes drift closed and settled against his

weight, treasuring the feeling of him still filling her. "Yes?"

"If I get to do that for one more week, I could die a happy man."

Victoria chuckled. "I don't want you dying on my account."

John lifted his head. "Did you come again?"

"Don't worry, you wore me out," she said with closed eyes.

"Look at me."

When she opened her eyes, a lump formed in her throat. He appeared to be quite sincere with his question. "John, it's not—"

"I don't want to half-ass lovemaking with you, darling," he said with a furrowed brow. "Seeing your face when you let loose is my favorite thing."

She let out a halted laugh. "I don't think you have to worry about that. I came twice."

"But you'll be honest with me if you don't?" His eyes searched her gaze with a keen interest.

"Of course," she said, taking ahold of his face.

"Because I'll do it again and again," he said as he slid out of her. He leaned down to take her nipple between his lips. With the flick of his tongue, Victoria inhaled sharply. "I'll find new and inventive ways to satisfy you."

He wasn't concerned if she experienced an orgasm the first time. Instead, he worried the second or third. Victoria grinned in spite of herself. He was positively over the top and she found herself wanting more. "Do you know how you could satisfy me again?"

John laid a tender kiss in the valley between her breasts. "Anything, my dear."

"Could you finish making dinner?"

Chapter Twenty-Four

John awoke with the delicious curve of Victoria's ass pressed against his morning wood and sighed with contentment. A Pembroke girl was in his bed after blowing his mind the night before. Her warmth filled his bed and his heart. He couldn't help the smile that stretched across his face as she shifted against him. John lifted his head to see her eyes closed, thick lashes downcast, and her breathing light and steady. Under the covers, he ran his hand along the lines of her silhouette until it stopped at the flair of her bare hip. It amazed him how soft her skin felt in his palms, like warm silk fluttering in a light breeze. His wish was fulfilled; John was free to run his hands over her at a leisurely pace, interrupted by nothing. A soft sigh escaped her lips as he found her breasts. When she shifted her bottom again, she brushed against his hot club, sending a shiver down John's spine.

"Victoria," he whispered in her ear.

"Mmh."

"Are you awake?" he asked rubbing a thumb across her nipple. Her back arched in response, pressing her bottom closer towards him.

A sultry groan came from her. "I am…"

John kissed her bare shoulder. "Me too."

With her eyes still closed, she chuckled. "The book-mark is also awake," she said in a low voice.

"He is."

"What does he want?"

John grinned. "He wants to curl up with a cozy book."

This got an outright laugh from her. "He feels insistent on that."

Actually, he was in pain. Throbbing against the cleft of her ass drove John mad with desire. Seeing her braids pinned up in a messy bun did something to him as well. Her mask had slipped. John was seeing Victoria as she was: a wanton sex goddess without a schedule or rules. "Can he come in and sit a spell?"

"You're mixing up your metaphors, Johnny."

"You know what I mean."

Ding Dong.

Their bodies tensed at the sound of the doorbell downstairs. "Who the hell is that?" John asked, flinging the covers off him.

"Are you expecting anyone?" Victoria lifted her head as he walked around the bed towards the window.

John cracked a venetian blind and spied his front yard. "Fuck."

"What? Who is it?"

A yellow 1960s Volkswagen Beetle with a rusted bumper was parked in his driveway, behind Victoria's car. "It's Margaret and Sandra," he said in a flat voice.

"Who?"

John turned to face Victoria, his erection long gone. "My moms."

Her jaw dropped as she clutched a sheet to her chest. "What do we do? Should I hide? Should I go out the back?"

He shook his head as he searched the bedroom for clothes. Anything would do. "No, no, you're not going anywhere. I'll try to make this quick."

Victoria left the solace of his bed searching for her own clothes. "I left my overnight bag downstairs."

"Jesus." He rifled through his chest of drawers and tossed her a black T-shirt. "Try that on."

She caught it with one hand and yanked it over her head. "Pants?"

He found her an old pair of plaid pajama pants. "These?"

"They'll have to do." Victoria tried to keep the panic from her voice as she grabbed her discarded panties from the floor. John found a similar outfit for himself and hoped they didn't smell like sex. After a moment, they quickly appraised each other.

"Twinsies," he said.

"Not now!" she snapped.

"Right."

He took off downstairs, two steps at a time, skipping the last three. Sandra and Margaret peered inside. "Mom…Mom. Hi. What are you guys doing here?"

Margaret Pierce narrowed her hazel eyes at her son and his heaving chest. Sandra Donovan raised a brow at the stirring behind John. Victoria stood off to the side hugging herself, probably trying to keep her bra-less breasts in check. Her overnight bag sat at John's feet. "We brought food for you and Becca," Sandra said slowly, pushing a foil-covered casserole dish at him.

"But it looks like we've interrupted something," Margaret intoned, a bowl of cookies in her hands.

"Becca isn't here," John said, still standing in the doorway. His mind was a scramble of possible excuses to get his mothers to leave so he could get back to Victoria. But the curious expressions the women wore told him that nothing would stop them from finding out more. "She's at school."

"We figured as much," his mother said in a dry voice. "Are you going to let us in or what?"

He girded his loins as he stepped back and opened the door wider. "Come in, ladies. I'll put on a pot of coffee."

The corner of Sandra's lips quirked. "We could probably use it, honey."

As the women entered his home, John took their coats and hung them. Victoria stood at the bottom of the stairwell, still having not said a word. He took the cookies and casserole, gearing up to make introductions, but his mother quickly jumped in.

"I'm Johnny's mother, Margaret Pierce, and this is his stepmother, Sandy," she said in a warm but perfunctory voice. "And you are…"

Victoria quickly extended her hand. "Dr. Victoria Reese, ma'am."

Margaret smiled. "Margaret is fine, dear."

"Sorry," she said while giving a firm shake. "Margaret."

"A doctor," Sandra murmured. "Where'd you find yourself a doctor, kiddo?"

He tried to dismiss Sandra's innocent comment as he rubbed the back of his neck, but it still stung a little. Rather than focusing on his feelings, he glanced at the one person who would feel most out of place. Victoria's mask had reappeared in an instant. John couldn't blame her one bit. No one wants to visit with two mothers the morning after the debauchery they got up to. Especially the debauchery he'd been hoping to get up to just a few moments ago. "Why don't you guys just take a seat in the living room while Victoria and I whip up some coffee," he suggested, guiding Victoria away from the impending interrogation. John steered the free food and his lover to the kitchen before anyone could object.

With their backs to the women, Johnny shoved the food in the refrigerator while Victoria busied herself with his coffeemaker. Her hands shook as she rinsed out the glass pot. "Take a breath, baby," Johnny whispered.

"This is not in the plan," she said under her breath. She splashed the water into the sink before filling it up. "Where do you keep the coffee?"

"The cabinet to your right." He moved around her to retrieve several mugs and spoons. "They're not going to pounce on you."

"I've been having sex with their boy." Victoria found the coffee. "Filters?"

He reached around her and pulled the filters from a higher shelf. "They don't know that."

"Do these look like my pajamas?" she asked gesturing to the oversized shirt that hung off her body. "I might as well be dressed like Tom Cruise in *Risky Business*."

John chuckled at the thought.

"It's not funny," she hissed. Victoria shoveled spoonful after spoonful of coffee grounds into the machine, until John steadied her hands.

"That's a bit too much," he said, taking the spoon from her.

"I don't make coffee."

"Then why are you making coffee?"

"Because I don't know what else to do," she said. "Do you have any light carpentry you need me to work on while they're here?"

"Kiddo, you have creamer, right?" Sandra called from the living room.

John emptied half of the filter back into the canister. "Yep," he said. "You want sugar?"

"If you got it."

"What's our plan?" Victoria asked, gazing at him with frantic eyes. "We need to go back in there with a plan."

He met her pleading stare with a furrowed brow. "There is no plan, honey."

"G.D. it."

"What was that?"

"Goddammit," she said in a low voice.

Once he got the coffee brewing, John edged closer to her and kept his head low. "All you need to do is act normal and pleasant, my love. Let me handle the rest."

Her head snapped up. "What did you call me?"

John pursed his lips. *Right.* "I didn't mean..."

"Honey, bring me one of those cookies while you're at it," Margaret called.

"Will do," he shouted.

"I can't do this right now," she said in a shaky voice.

"Don't panic," he whispered, glancing at the coffee pot. It was only a third of the way full. "I didn't mean to call you that, I just— It slipped. Like a pet name."

Victoria didn't reply. Instead, she went through his cabinets for a plate and set it on the counter before moving around him to the refrigerator. She dug through the bowl of cookies and set two fistfuls on the plate. She tore off several paper towels and began folding them into neat squares. John was losing her to the spiral in her own head.

"We'll talk about it later," he said. "For now, you don't

have to worry about my moms. They're not judgmental at all. They love liberated professional women."

"Stop talking, John," she said, folding her last napkin. "It's making me more nervous."

He stopped talking. When the coffee pot was halfway full, he pulled it out and filled two mugs before shoving it back under the drip.

"I'll carry the cookies and cream if you get the coffee," she said.

"Thank you," he said softly.

She caught him staring at her. "I'm really sorry, John, but I'm going to flounder in there. I just want you to know before it happens. I'm not good with my own mother and I would never be caught in this situation with her."

"But you have nothing to worry about." He tried to make her believe his words, but her expression remained stricken with anxiety. There wasn't anything left to do but to push her into the lion's den and hope his mothers could behave themselves until they left. Once alone, John would probably need to ease her anxiety again. He couldn't believe he called her *my love*. In the quest to comfort her, the words had actually slipped from his lips. John had to convince her that he didn't mean it. After he convinced himself.

Chapter Twenty-Five

Victoria didn't have time to dissect John's meaning when he'd called her "my love." Instead, she carefully wandered back to the living room where John's two mothers sat. Both of them chatted comfortably on the couch, while Victoria gripped a plate of Halloween cookies in one hand, a small pitcher of cream in the other. She nearly dropped both when she saw what was neatly stacked on the coffee table ahead of them. Victoria stopped short in front of John, who carried hot coffee behind her.

One pile was her folded flannel shirt and bra.

The other pile was John's flannel and undershirt.

Dang it.

Silently, she set the plate of cookies beside the clothes, taking care not to touch them. Victoria didn't want to claim ownership of the lacy black bra that was folded at the middle, it's straps gently placed in the hollow of the cups. She also took care to not look at the women as she made her way to the easy chair at their side.

"Thank you, dear," Sandra said with a gentle smile.

John spotted the clothes immediately after she had and calmly placed their coffee cups beside the cookies. He shot both of the women a piercing glare before joining Victoria at the easy chair. As he lowered himself to perch on one plush chair arm, he cleared his throat. "No need to fold my laundry anymore, Mom."

Victoria kept her eyes in her lap.

The women's laughter tinkled with good humor. "Oh, Johnny, go ahead and wipe the scowl off your face," Margaret chided. "We know very well what the morning after looks like."

"Mother."

"Victoria," Sandra interrupted. "What do you do for a living?"

She had no choice but to participate in this conversation while her discarded clothes just sat there taunting her. Victoria looked up and tried to smile. "I teach at Pembroke University, in their English department."

"Impressive," the women said in unison. They both went for their coffee at the same time and settled against the couch.

"Thank you," she breathed.

"Victoria and I are working on an internship together," John said. "We're hoping it will be a successful partnership between the library and university."

"Is that a fact?" Margaret asked in a sardonic tone that matched her son's. "It looks like a pretty good partnership already."

Victoria shifted in her seat. "We've been seeing each other for a few days," she admitted. As she addressed the women, she watched her tone and kept their relationship as vague as possible. Only last night had Victoria declared how she wanted to drop her mask and get real with John. In the cold light of morning, in front of his mothers, she wondered if she may have spoken too soon.

Margaret's face broke into a grin. "Oh, you don't have

to explain anything to us, dear. I just like teasing Johnny to get a rise out of him."

Victoria exhaled as John slid an arm around her shoulders and gave a gentle squeeze. "This is my mom's idea of humor," he said with a wry grin.

In truth, Victoria had expected a couple of women who mirrored her mother's excessive prudishness. Instead, they were easygoing and jovial to their boy. She saw the resemblance between Sandra and the daughter in John's office photo. They shared the same large soulful brown eyes which seemed to be filled with laughter. Despite the woman's age, not very many lines creased her mahogany face. Sandra kept her hair short, pressed and curled, like most black women would at her age. Victoria imagined her making weekly visits at her local beauty parlor. John's mother, Margaret, took a relaxed approach to her appearance, wearing an oversized gray sweater and flowing pants. John must have taken after his father because the woman's fiery red hair and tawny eyes were a far cry from her Viking son's looks. Her smile was playful as she looked from Victoria to John.

Regardless of how charming both the women were, Victoria had not exaggerated when she said she'd never find herself in this situation with her own mother. Katherine Reese could not stand joking, public displays of affection, or ladies behaving like anything other than ladies. Victoria's face heated as her mind burned with the memory of what she and John had done on the couch. Sandra sat there, politely sipping her coffee in the same spot where she'd dry-humped her stepson. *Jesus.*

"Victoria," Sandra said, leaning forward taking the black bra by the straps. To Victoria's horror, the woman caressed the satin fabric with her thumbs. "Where did you find this? Maggie and I were going to do some shopping today and I had a mind to pick up some new brassieres."

Victoria choked on her own spit as she watched Sandra fondle her underthings.

"Oh dear, is she okay?" Margaret asked sitting up.

"Fine," she rasped through the coughing. "I got it at Victoria's Secret."

Admitting that was perhaps the single most embarrassing thing she ever done in her life. Beside her, John's body shook with quiet laughter. "Of course," he said in a low voice.

Margaret peered closely at the garment. "Trish, down at the church, said that Victoria's Secret doesn't go over double-D. Sandy, you're at least a triple-D, aren't you?"

Victoria wanted to cover her eyes when Sandra held the bra by the straps. "I haven't been measured in a few years. This one looks like a C cup." She looked from the bra to Victoria's chest as if to confirm her breast size.

"Well, we need to go to Dillard's first to get you measured," Margaret said. "Shelly still works in the afternoons, doesn't she?"

"Once you get to be our age, you're just looking for something that fits whatever gravity pulled down," Sandra continued, nudging her friend in the ribs. "But it would be nice to treat myself to something fancier."

"The girls don't know how good they've got it," Margaret said as she set down her coffee. She too, took up the bra and marveled over its craftsmanship. "I like the little lacy bits here. It doesn't scratch you, honey?" she asked Victoria.

She pressed her lips together tightly and shook her head. "Mm-mm."

"Well that's good," Margaret said, folding the underwear and placing it back on the coffee table. "I can't stand the itchiness. I've gone and just cut all of the tags out of my shirts these days."

"How will you know how to wash your clothes?" John asked with a chuckle.

His mother dismissed him with a tut and a wave of her hand. "When you've been washing clothes as long as I have, you just know. I don't need a tag telling me what temperature to use."

Victoria didn't know whether to laugh or cry or both. She simply sat there, hugged next to John's hip waiting for all of it to be over.

"So Johnny," Sandra said. "I've heard my grandbaby is fighting?"

John went stiff. "Not exactly."

"Jessi gave me the lowdown," Sandra said, returning to her coffee. "I'm assuming you've taken care of things?"

"Yes, ma'am," John said in a grave tone. "Jess and I talked to her and she knows what she did was wrong."

"Well did the girl deserve a good pop in the mouth?" Margaret asked innocently.

Victoria's eyes widened, not expecting something so brash coming from someone's grandmother. It turned out that Becca had a tribe standing behind her, offering more support than she remembered receiving from her own mother.

"Mom, no one got popped in the mouth."

Margaret frowned. "Everyone knows that's the best way to stop a bully."

Sandra nodded. "I'm inclined to agree with your mother: Don't start none; won't be none."

The two ladies clinked ceramic mugs with their shared sentiment, causing Victoria to laugh outright. These two geriatric gals were charming indeed. "I'm sorry," she said with her hand over her mouth.

"And it's obvious that the good doctor also agrees," Sandra said, tipping her mug towards her.

"Victoria was in a fist fight when she was Becca's age," John said with a laugh.

Her gaze flew to his sparkling green eyes. "John."

"What? You were."

"Ladies, I don't want you to think—"

Margaret held up a hand. "You need to stop there, young lady. You're not here to prove a damn thing to two old biddies like us. Relax yourself and poke a little fun."

"She's right, you know?" Sandra said, biting into a Halloween cookie. "You've already impressed us by putting up with our shenanigans. Lord knows John's used to it."

Victoria forced herself to relax. After all, they were giving her permission to. She took another deep breath and smiled. "Thank you."

"Now that we've established that Becca runs these streets," Sandra said with a smile. "Are you two dating? Because we haven't seen John with a woman in at least two years. That, or he's not bringing them around us anymore."

She glanced at John who looked mildly embarrassed. "I…uh, I don't know if we're dating? I mean, we're supposed to be working on this project and I hadn't really… I guess what I'm trying to say is—"

John stopped her. "Victoria and I have been seeing each other for about a week. I would have introduced her to you on the first date, but I thought that might be rushing things."

His tone made his mother roll her eyes. "Okay, I can see we're being intrusive."

"Now that she's met you," he continued. "I should probably propose to her tomorrow? Maybe set the wedding for a week from now?"

Sandra chuckled into her coffee mug. "See what I mean?" she asked Victoria. "We joke and meddle in young people's lives."

Victoria relaxed her shoulders again. She was thankful that John's smart mouth had saved her from rambling about the nature of their relationship. She was also thankful that they were so understanding and lighthearted about the situation. "Sometimes you have to laugh," she murmured.

"Ladies, was there a purpose to your visit today?" John asked, swiftly changing the subject.

"We wanted to make sure that Becca wasn't starving," Margaret said. "And we wanted to offer up our babysitting services. I heard that Chris is watching her while you are at work."

"I'm not turning down free childcare services," John said. "But with her after-school detention all week, you'd have to pick her up at 4 p.m."

Sandra chuckled. "I never thought I'd hear about Becca staying after school for detention."

"She regrets what she did," Victoria said. "We're hoping that whatever truth and reconciliation meeting the principal sets up, might help the situation."

Sandra and Margaret looked at her. "Oh really?"

Her face warmed. She hadn't meant to include herself in Becca's matters. "Well, John…"

"Victoria went with me to the school to collect Becca."

Sandra shook her head with a sad smile. "You two have swooped in to help her while Jessi is away and Allen hasn't called once. I don't understand that man."

Margaret scoffed. "The coward isn't going to show his face in Farmingdale after what he did to Jess."

"And after how this one responded," Sandra gestured to John with a laugh.

"Didn't you just say that's how you deal with a bully?" John asked. "I popped him in the mouth." The women fell out with laughter, while Victoria grew confused. John gave her a sheepish smile and hugged her closer.

"John punched Allen in the face at a church picnic," Margaret explained. "When we found out Allen was sleeping around, he still had the nerve to show up un-invited."

"It wasn't my proudest moment," John said. "But luckily, Becca wasn't present to see me battering her dad."

"You're a good brother," Victoria said, laying a hand on his knee.

"Yeah, well, the Donovan clan managed to horrify the parishioners and priest."

"It's wasn't the first time a Catholic church has seen a fight at a picnic and it won't be the last." Margaret chuckled. "And yes, he's a good brother. You'll have to meet Jessi when she gets back from Sweden."

The way his mother threw out the suggestion made Victoria blush again. She was expecting her to stick around, meet more members of the family, and possi-bly attend holiday dinners. Little did they know; she'd only planned a three-week sordid affair. In that moment, Victoria realized she was in a pickle. Continuing a relationship with John was tempting and very attractive, but she hadn't bothered to make an exhaustive pros and cons lists for this situation. "Of course," she said, keeping her voice light.

"I think it's time we got out of these kids' way," Sandra said, taking her purse and a cookie. As she eased herself off the couch, she smiled at Victoria. "I have a feeling we've meddled enough for one day."

John stood to join her. "Are you sure? You guys don't want to stick around and show her some baby pictures?"

"Har har," Margaret said. "We've got shopping to do anyway."

As they walked to the door, the women surrounded Victoria, petting her and stroking her hair. "I hope you have a lovely day," Sandra said.

"Yes, do let us know if Johnny misbehaves or keeps you from your work," Margaret added.

Victoria smiled warmly at the two. "Oh, thank you. It was nice to meet you," she said. And even though the circumstances were odd, she did like John's maternal figures. She could see how being raised around so many loving women could make an impact on him. He must have grown up feeling supported, able to take risks without the constant fear of admonishment. "Good luck with your shopping trip."

John kissed them both, and all but pushed them out the door before closing it. He rested his back against the door and sighed. "I'm sorry about that," he said, eyeing her closely. "Are you ready to cancel our sordid affair?"

Victoria crossed her arms over her chest. "Between their showing up and examining my underwear, which we foolishly left on the floor, this is not shaping up to be a sordid affair."

He shrugged his broad shoulders. "Understandable."

"But they are truly lovely women."

"They are," he said, leaving the door. He wrapped his arms around her and drew her close to his body. "And they are meddlesome. Especially when they get a whiff of a new woman."

She looked up. "It's been two years?"

"Very nearly," John said. "I haven't been looking too hard. I've kind of been waiting on her to fall into my lap."

"That's not very ambitious," Victoria said.

"And yet here you are."

She felt a strange twinge in her heart. He spoke as if they were "meant to be" in a romantic sense. She'd only briefly entertained the idea while they were on their date yesterday and then put it out of her mind. "John…"

"Don't," he said in a soft voice. "Don't think about it too hard, don't outline this feeling."

Easier said than done.

"We've got about two hours before you have to go to work. How would you like to spend the rest of our sordid affair time?"

Victoria's pursed lips spread into a grin. "Two hours?"

John ran his hands down her spine until they settled on her ass. "Two hours. I can feed you and for the rest of the time…"

"You'll feed me?"

"The Donovan Inn offers a complimentary breakfast and room service. Emphasis on the service."

Victoria tilted her head back to receive a kiss from

him. After the near heart attack his mothers offered, she was ready to return to the warmth and comfort of his arms. Tucked away in his muscular grasp, Victoria felt safe. She had a day at the office ahead of her, but moments like this made her believe she could face it.

Chapter Twenty-Six

"You met his mothers…plural?" Paula asked as she stirred her coffee.

Victoria hovered over the break room microwave, watching her Tupperware of leftovers spin under the orange light. "Apparently his mom and his stepmom are best friends who bonded over his father's death."

"So how did that go?" her friend asked, taking a sip from her mug. "Were they nice?"

"Oh, they were awesome," Victoria said. "They're kind and funny and incredibly excited to welcome me as a new daughter-in-law."

Paula's eyes widened. "Ooh, I can see where this is going."

She nodded and checked on her lasagna. Cold in the center, fried at the edges. "You have no idea how nice it was to meet ladies my mom's age, who didn't judge or didn't tell me to sit up straighter." Victoria jabbed at her dinner with a plastic fork before shoving it back into the oven.

"But it's antithetical to your previously planned affair, which is now in its second week?"

"Exactly," Victoria said, slamming the door. "I have

another week to figure things out and I hate feeling like this."

"Like what exactly?" Paula asked as she leaned against the counter.

Victoria let out an exasperated sigh. "'Does he like me? Are we going steady?' Honestly, I feel like a teenager."

Paula gave a throaty chuckle over her coffee and rolled her eyes. "I think he *does* like you and you *are* going steady. I also think once your week is up, you'll still be going steady."

"Maybe? Anyway, tell me about your love life. I've been holding you and Reggi hostage with my woes."

"I'm glad you asked," Paula said with a grin. "I've got a date with a member of the Farmingdale Fire Brigade on Thursday."

"Ooh, do tell…" Victoria waggled her eyebrows. "What's his name and how did you meet?"

Paula's eyes fell shut as she sighed. "His name is Tomas Piña and our meet-cute was at The Coffee Hound. We were reaching for the same low-cal sweetener and there were sparks."

Paula's romance writing is basically her real life. "Nice." She nodded with approval. "Is he going to be able to extinguish your fire?"

"I'm waiting to see what that hose can do."

Victoria let out a guffaw. "Okay, now," she said through her laughter. "So, that was brilliant."

"That's what I get paid for," she said, inspecting her nails with her raised brow. "Actually, I gotta get to class and get paid for this job too."

"Today's lesson?"

"Visual rhetoric," Paula said, pointing to her "This is

What a Feminist Looks Like" T-shirt. "We're covering political statement and fashion."

"Sounds mighty progressive," said a familiar voice near the doorway. Kenneth Williams was crashing their little break room party with his smug grin.

Victoria suppressed a groan and turned back to the microwave. She would rather eat cold lasagna than spend another second with her boss. "Hello, Kenneth," she muttered.

Paula, however, was completely unfazed by the interruption. "Progressive or just a basic reality?" she asked, blowing the steam from her coffee.

Kenneth retrieved a carton of creamer from the refrigerator. "So long as your students grasp the basic understanding of writing," he said in an airy voice. "I'm getting concerned about the amount of kids who come to my class, unable to string together a sentence."

"Oof, that's rough," Paula said, matching his nonchalant tone. "But an easy fix. I'm sure you can slip a sentence diagraming lesson in between Othello and Hamlet readings. I've got some worksheets if you need help."

With her back to Williams, Victoria let a giggle slip. If throwing shade was a sport, then her friend knocked it out of the park. She admired Paula's quick tongue and verbal sparring skills.

As Kenneth prepared his cup of coffee, he stared between the two of them. "Well don't let me stop you from doing your job, Ms..."

Paula smiled sweetly. "Paula is fine." She turned to Victoria. "I'll see you later to continue our discussion."

Victoria held her hot container and grinned. "Colliding combustible elements?"

"Exactly," she said with a wink. As she walked past

Kenneth, she gave him a friendly wave. "Have a good one, *Mr.* Williams."

Kenneth's lips puckered in annoyance as Paula sashayed out the door. He turned his attention and ire on Victoria. "Dr. Reese, could I have a quick word with you?"

"What's on your mind?" Victoria asked, setting her lunch on the counter. She braced herself for a snarky exchange when all she wanted to do was enjoy her crunchy lasagna in peace.

"Your Four-Week Initiative proposal," he said coolly. Arrogance dripped from his words as his cold gray eyes regarded her. "Specifically, the man you're working for."

Though her heart was beating fast, she faced him head on and crossed her arms over her chest. "John Donovan."

"Right, that man. I perceived something amiss when I saw you last Friday. I do hope I'm not misinterpreting the nature of your relationship…"

Don't get angry. Hide your shade behind a smile. Be like Paula. "What do you think you perceived, Kenneth?" If he was going to bring this silliness to her doorstep, she was going to make him say it in plain language.

Kenneth shrugged carelessly as he smoothed down his tie. "I don't wish to tell tales out of school, but it appeared that you two were discussing more than internships."

Victoria's jaw clenched. "Did it?"

"I hope this little *tendre* for the librarian doesn't cloud your judgement. As academics, we require a certain amount of objectivity when it comes to presenting our findings. By the way, how are your internship findings?"

The mother-effing gall of this man… A quiet storm of

fury built in Victoria's chest. Rage radiated to each limb of her body and pulsed like magma right below her skin. "Kenneth, I find this line of questioning entirely too inappropriate," she said through her teeth. "My *tendres*, as you call them, are none of your business and have no bearing on my work at Pembroke University. Would you ask a male colleague these questions?"

"Of course I would. The quality of work any colleague produces is my concern," he said in faux-dismay. "Oh dear, I've hit a nerve, haven't I?"

Breathe, Victoria. "I assure you, I'm reacting out of curiosity," she replied, picking up her lunch. Standing here one moment more was out of the question. "I'm simply curious how my business suddenly became yours." She shoved herself away from the counter and attempted to leave the room.

Kenneth called after her; his voice heavy with sarcasm. "I'm only asking that you polish that proposal when you present it to President Kowalski. We wouldn't want you embarrassing the department."

Victoria stopped at the exit, keeping her back to him. "You should probably put that same energy into your own Four-Week Initiative," she said. Her fingers gripped her Tupperware with force as she bit out the next sentence. "You don't want to be known as the professor who rested on his laurels after getting tenure thirty years ago."

She didn't wait around for his next clever retort. Her heels clacked loudly against the floor as she marched away.

Victoria made herself eat lunch even though she had long lost her appetite. As she jabbed at her floppy lasagna, she fumed over Kenneth's accusations. She knew this would happen. One slipup, in public, and she would have to pay for it. The tone of his voice suggested that she was doing something horrific, like interfering with a student. She and John were two consenting adults who just so happened to work with one another. It wasn't like they were two professors fraternizing at the same institution. Yet even as Victoria reasoned through every argument against her, the same niggling thoughts crept up and settled into her brain.

But isn't this your chickens come home to roost? You were worried about appearing professional before you embarked on a sordid affair...now look at you.

She shoved her lunch away and sat back in her chair. "G.D. it," she muttered, sick to her stomach.

When the Katherine Reese ringtone chimed, Victoria repeated her sentiment in a louder voice. She snatched up her phone and answered in a harsh voice. "Yes, Mom?"

"Adjust your tone," her mother said.

Victoria bristled at the command. "What can I do for you?" she asked.

"The question is what can you do for yourself. I did some recon work on your potential boyfriend and you're going to like my intel."

Her heart dropped. "What?"

"Matthew, the divorced lawyer!" Katherine said excitedly. "Linda was telling me about his airtight prenup agreement with his ex-wife."

For a moment, she'd thought her mother was referring to John. She blew out an exhale and prepared herself for another on-phone battle with her mother. "Why do I care about this man's prenup agreement?"

"Because he's leaving his marriage with most of his

assets," said her mother. "Archie, please turn that down, I'm trying to talk to Victoria."

The background noise of the television lowered as her mother returned her attention to the conversation. "I think she only gets a onetime settlement and that's all."

"That's not making him sound great," Victoria said.

"Well it makes him sound rich," Katherine said. "And I don't know how that isn't great. You'll find out for yourself at the retirement gala."

Victoria's spirits sank to her queasy stomach. She had forgotten all about Uncle Jeffrey's retirement ceremony. As she quickly checked her desk calendar, she thought of excuses to get out of attending. She was meeting John? *No, that's not an excuse, Mom is going to ask for details.* "Ooh, that's this Friday, isn't it? I think I'm going to be busy, ma'am."

"Busy with what?"

"Uh, there's a team-building exercise for my department," she lied. While the English Department functioned under Kenneth Williams's rule, there was no such thing as a *team*, but her mother didn't know that.

"Team-building?" Katherine scoffed. "You've been teaching there for four years. I'd say you're already a team player. You're coming to the ceremony, little lady."

"But I didn't get an embossed invitation," she snapped in irritation. Her mother's problem with boundaries was driving her nuts. "How will I possibly get past security?"

"Don't sass me, Victoria," her mother said. Victoria could hear her mother pull away from the phone to shout: "Archie, come tell your hardheaded daughter about what it means to be reliable."

There was a pause in the conversation where her parents could be heard arguing with one another. "Katherine, will you leave the girl alone?"

"She gave her word and now she's going to embarrass me in front of our guests."

"They're Jeffrey's guests."

"*I'm* throwing the celebration!"

"Good god, just give it here."

She waited for the transfer of the phone to hear her father sigh loudly. "What's going on, Vicki."

"Mom's not respecting my boundaries," she said in a whiny voice. She knew she sounded like a child tattling to her father.

"Did you promise to attend this event?" Archie asked patiently.

Yes, but that was before I started sleeping with John.
"Yes, sir."

"And what do we say about starting the mission?"

Victoria massaged the bridge of her nose. "We finish the mission."

"Now if you gave your word, you need to go ahead and stick to it, don't you think?"

"But—"

"Help me out, honey," her father said in soothing tones. "Your mother had her heart set on you being here."

"Can you tell her I'm really busy?" Victoria tried. "Just tell her I'll get the next one?"

"Too busy to see your own parents?" said her mother, on another line.

"Katherine, get off the line," Archie barked.

"I will not! Are we such terrible parents that our own daughter is too busy to see us?"

"You're not terrible parents," Victoria said, switching her attention to her eavesdropping mother. "Why do you always go there?"

"How can I not go there?"

"Katherine!"

"It's really unfair that anytime I disagree with you, my loyalty comes into question."

Her mother gasped. "Archie, are you going to let her speak to me like that?"

"I'm not fixing to sit here and argue with you two about loyalty or whatever the hell else you've got cooking up," said her father. "I was minding my business, watching *Lethal Weapon*, not bothering anyone."

Victoria rolled her eyes. Her father always took the easy way out, even when he knew his wife was being unreasonable. To Archie, women's arguments were strictly women's arguments. There was no need for him to interrupt affairs that weren't any of his business.

"Now will I see you at the ceremony or not?"

She dropped her head against the surface of her desk before answering. "Fine," she mumbled. "I'll be there."

"Good," her father said. The click in the line meant that he had left the conversation in favor of Murtaugh and Riggs.

"Well now that that's settled," her mother said huffily. "Get here early and bring a pretty dress."

"Yes, ma'am..."

The second click signified that Victoria had lost the battle.

Her phone rang again and she wanted to throw it against the wall. But it was John, and Victoria had to hope that he didn't want anything from her. She was done doing favors for the day and it was only 2 p.m.

"Hello," she said.

"Dr. Reese," he purred in her ear. A jolt of electricity traveled down her neck and into her chest as she gripped her phone.

"Hi," she breathed.

"I'm just checking in," he said. "We've had radio silence since yesterday and I hope you were okay."

Something bloomed within her chest that prevented her from speaking. As Victoria sat in her office, she suddenly felt isolated. She wanted to see him.

"Dr. Reese?"

She blinked back tears. "Yeah, I'm here."

His voice dropped to a softer tone. "How are you feeling?"

Victoria brushed her sleeve across her eyes. "I'm not having a good day," she admitted.

"Would you like me to come to you?" he asked.

"No," she said quietly. "I'm just... I feel very alone right now. I'm glad you called." She told the truth and felt okay. She wasn't in the habit of doing that.

"Is it work?"

"That's part of the problem."

"Do you know where Flynn Fitness is?" he asked. "It's downtown across the street from the old theater."

"Sure, next to the post office."

"Meet me there in an hour and we'll go a couple rounds on the heavy bag. You sound like you need to punch something."

Chapter Twenty-Seven

"She's coming here?" Chris asked with a raised brow. He sat on a locker-room bench as John changed into a tank top and sweatpants.

"I invited her to come down and let off a little steam," John said, tying his hair up.

Chris laughed. "Okay."

John ignored the joke that his friend was dying to make. When he'd heard Victoria's voice on the phone, he wanted to help her immediately. From the sniffles on the other line, it was evident that she had been crying. "I'd like you to behave yourself while she's here," he said. "Could you do that?"

"What do you imagine me doing that would offend her?" Chris asked with mock-dismay.

John caught his gaze and held it. "Just don't dude-bro out in front of her."

"I'm hurt. Seriously hurt."

"Now that I know you clean up after me, I'm keeping an eye on you," John said, biting back a grin. "Victoria is mine."

"Possessive already?" Chris asked as he stood. When they left the locker room, Victoria was already waiting by the front desk, a duffel bag hanging off her shoulder.

She was dressed in a black tank top and leggings and her braids were tightly bound in a high ponytail at the top of her head. "Now I see it."

John saw it too. Saying that a woman was his wasn't usually his style, but something about Victoria made him want to snap his jaws at his own best friend. Chris, who was just as handsome, and perhaps more charming, couldn't be seen as an alternative this evening.

"Maybe I can help you two with sparring later?" Chris asked.

John narrowed in on his tongue-wagging and shot him a glare. "I'll let you know if your services are needed."

"Please do," he said as they drew closer to her.

When Victoria spotted them, she flashed a nervous smile and waved. "Hi there," she said, shifting from one foot to the other. "I don't know if I need to sign in or where I should put my bag."

"Allow me," Chris said, taking her bag. "I'll keep this in my office."

John watched her face redden as Chris slipped the strap from her shoulder. "Thank you," she murmured. He was used to seeing his friend's effect on women, just not the one he was infatuated with. Chris wasn't a real threat, but John couldn't help feeling a little territorial.

"Dr. Reese, this is my best friend, Chris Flynn," he said.

"And the owner of this fine establishment," Chris said, holding out a hand.

"Pleasure to meet you," she said with a warm smile.

"Pleasure is all mine," he said, holding her hand for a little longer than John preferred. As John fought the urge to roll his eyes, he placed a hand on Victoria's back and guided her through the gym.

"Let's get you stretched out."

Victoria looked between the two men. "I've never had two trainers before."

Over her head, Chris winked at John. *Jesus Christ, he's insufferable.* "And I'm afraid you won't," John said. "I'm sure Chris has clients to see after."

"I actually don't," he chimed in. "Let me drop this off, make my rounds, and I'll supervise you two. John's not exactly a fitness professional."

"He's not?" Victoria said with a grin.

"No ma'am," Chris said. "He's more of an apprentice. I'll let him get you set up, but I should probably chaperone…for insurance purposes." He left them to go to his office, just as John's jaw unclenched.

Victoria looked up at him with a secretive smile. *God, she's too cute in her workout gear.* "I'm guessing he's this attentive to all his female clients?" she asked, planting her fists on her hips.

John took a breath as he caught a glimpse of her breasts. Only yesterday, she was writhing under him in his bed, his lips on her nipples as he drove into her. He wanted her back in bed where *he* could be attentive to her every need. "Chris has always been a ham," he said. "And now that he's met you, I can expect him to be messy."

"I can take it." The dimple at the side of her mouth creased when she twisted her lips. "I'll bet he's no messier than the day I've had," she said, walking away.

He followed her, eyes locked on her ass. John wanted to thank the designer who created the thin fabric that molded her curves so beautifully. "Do you want to talk about it?" he asked.

Victoria shook her head, braids swinging across her

back and bare shoulders. "Not right now," she said. "I'd like to use my fists for once."

"You wanna drop the mask and free the beast?"

She turned on her heel and flashed him a grin. "Exactly."

Jesus Christ, she's done this before.

John held on to the heavy bag for dear life as Victoria pummeled the fuck out of it. Hooks, jabs, uppercuts, and swift knees knocked him off his feet as she focused her concentrated hatred on the inanimate object. She picked up the pace when Rage Against the Machine's "Maggie's Farm" came on. She mouthed the words under her breath as she wheeled off a flawless roundhouse kick, hitting the side of the bag. John avoided her as best as he could while holding the bag still. When she returned to punching, she kept pace with the song, alternating between ducking and strikes. Victoria Reese was *not* going to work on someone's farm. If John wanted to remain unharmed, he'd have to figure out who was oppressing her.

"Time," he called out.

As if she were a sleeper agent, Victoria paused midswing. Her eyes cleared as she looked from the bag to him. Chest heaving and dripping from sweat, she dropped her arm. "That felt amazing," she panted.

"Did it?" Chris asked. "You attacked the bag like it owed you money."

"Oh, I could go again," she said, running her arm across her forehead. "That was a warm up."

John exchanged looks with his friend. "Maybe I don't need to supervise," Chris said. "Looks like Dr. Reese has it under control."

"Maybe you can stick around," John said. "For my safety."

"He'll be fine," Victoria said to Chris as she took off her gloves. "It's time for a spar, Mr. Donovan."

"You heard her, Mr. Donovan," Chris said as he backed away with a grin. "It's time for a spar."

Left to themselves, John was hesitant to move away from the heavy bag and expose himself. "Would you like to talk about your day yet?"

She shook her head. "Nope, not yet."

"Before we move to the mats, can I ask you something?"

Victoria took a long swig from her water bottle. "Sure."

"Where did you learn to fight like that? As far as I know, you punched a girl in grade school and felt terrible about it. You didn't say you were a paid assassin."

Victoria laughed. "My dad taught me. He's a Marine, remember?"

"What on earth did he teach you?"

"Marines martial arts, MCMAPS," she said. "They borrowed from all kinds of fighting styles: judo, wrestling, Muay Thai, Taekwondo…"

"… Krav Maga," John finished. He'd heard of this from Dante, the kickboxing instructor. Maybe Victoria should have been teaching his niece.

"You've heard of it?"

John was nervous. "I have. It's kind of lethal."

"Of course it is, it's the military," she scoffed. "I'll go easy on you."

He hoped so. As they walked to an empty kickboxing studio, John closed the door behind him. If he was going to get his ass kicked, there was no sense in letting everyone know about it. "And how did that square with your mother?"

"It didn't," she said as she lifted her foot to her butt and tugged on it. "It wasn't ladylike."

It's sexy as hell though.

"I used to practice a lot more when I got to college; it was a great stress reliever during finals," she continued. "But I took a break when I got to Farmingdale."

Hopefully, that meant she was rusty. "I'm more of a kickboxer-grappler," John said. "I don't think I have the agility for high-flying kicks, Dr. Reese."

Victoria shook out her arms and cocked her neck before crouching and raising her fist in a defensive pose. "That's fine. It's a little impractical in a real fight."

And for some reason, that didn't make John feel better. He was equal parts terrified and aroused to spar with a well-trained fighter who had buried academic rage all day. It was a dangerous endeavor, but he was up for the challenge. Between a sordid affair and getting his ass kicked, John was game. "Just so you know, I don't have much experience fighting women."

"Then this is going to be fun."

"I was afraid you'd say that," he said, raising his fists to his face. John hunched his shoulders and crouched to her height as he slowly approached her. He would not make the mistake of underestimating the little lady even if he did have a few inches on her. "How do you want to do this?"

"We try to avoid face strikes," she said, her eyes darting to his pelvis. "And uh…sensitive parts."

John nodded. "Good, good, that's a good start."

"Otherwise, you're a pretty strong guy," Victoria said. "I think we'll be fine."

He didn't know what that meant, but didn't have time to think about it when her foot shot out and swept his legs. John was on the mat in a matter of seconds. Victoria straddled him and gave him a fake strike to the face. "What just happened?" he asked as he lay on his back.

She stuck out her hand. "I swept you."

"I don't even know you," he said, avoiding her help.

With her hand still extended, she said, "I want to thank you for asking me to do this, Mr. Donovan. You have no idea how much I needed a release."

He suddenly remembered the quiet joke that Chris didn't tell. Apparently, "letting off a little steam" didn't necessarily mean *sex* to Victoria. He took her hand and let her haul him up from the mat. Once upright, John was hypervigilant of his limbs. At any moment, he could end up on his back again. At thirty-eight, he couldn't afford too many dives.

John sized up her defenses and found them impenetrable, as usual. Victoria was light on her feet and kept her fists at eye-level, like a professional fighter. "It sounds like we might be evenly matched, Dr. Reese," he said.

Her mouth quirked as she cracked her neck. "If you think so, Mr. Donovan." She threw a jab that he side-stepped.

"I'm not a fool," he said, protecting his face. "You're a lot faster, but I've got a longer reach."

"I'm aware," she said as she narrowly avoided his fist. Victoria ducked and spun her leg in a long circular sweep in an attempt to take him off his feet again. But he'd learned his lesson the first time and hopped from the floor in time. When she rose from the ground, John plowed into her, planting a leg behind hers and took her to the mat.

"Are you?" he said, now on top of her. "You're on your back, Dr. Reese."

"Not for long," she said, shifting her hips to the side. Before he knew what was happening, John was in an arm bar that extended past the point of comfortable. Victoria's legs wrapped around him like a vice.

"Jesus Christ," he panted. *This is hot.*

"You can tap out anytime, Mr. Donovan," she said as she clutched his hand against her breasts. "I don't want to break anything you'll want to use tonight."

I think I love her.

John tapped his other hand against the calf draped across his chest. "I give," he said.

When she released him, Victoria flipped over and onto her feet in seconds. She extended her hand again in a smug fashion that made John smile. "Are you ready?" she asked.

He loved seeing her like this. Victoria was a woman in control and if he was the punching bag for the night, he was happy to do it. Her confidence and power was sexy as fuck. "I thought you said you were going to go easy on me."

She wiggled her fingers in front of him. "I'm surprised you don't have more in your arsenal, Mr. Donovan. It shouldn't take a little professor like me to get the best of you."

"This is the second time my manhood is being bruised," John said, taking her hand. When he was back on his feet, he began thinking about his next move. She favored the left jab but he noticed she kept her trunk relatively open for attack. "You have to remember that I don't want to hurt you, Dr. Reese."

Victoria shrugged. "I don't even know if that's possible."

He'd been in enough fights to know arrogance when he saw it. She was comfortable enough to trash talk, which could distract even the best fighter. "I'd feel bad if I did hurt you though," he tried.

"Says a man who's been on his back twice in five minutes. If you want to take a rest, you don't need me to send you to the mat," she said with laughter in her eyes. "Just let me know when you want to—"

John cut her off with a quick strike to the belly and placed the same foot behind her. Once the air had been knocked out of her, she fell to the floor. He covered her quickly and pressed a powerful forearm against her chest. "What was that?"

Victoria's eyes widened as she sucked air through her lungs. "Dang it."

"Are you hurt?" John asked, refusing to move his arm.

She shook her head against the mat. "Only my pride," she said with a chuckle.

"Good, now do you want to talk about it?"

She shook her head again. The look in her eyes said as much. Victoria was prepared to bury her feelings and that didn't sit well with him.

"Are you ready to tap out?"

She laughed outright. "Of course not."

John was puzzled by her response. "I've got at least forty pounds of muscle on you, Dr. Reese," he said as he straddled her chest. "You're not getting out of this."

"And I've been in tighter spots. This is nothing."

"I don't see you doing anything," John said.

And that was the problem.

He'd relaxed his grip on her and hadn't noticed how Victoria raised her hips against the mat. While pinned beneath him, she managed to bring her legs to his shoulders and clamp ankles around his neck. Pulling him backwards, she used her free arms to pry his grip from her chest. John was on his back again as Victoria squirmed away. It was a floor match now and while he was caught unaware, he knew he was better on the mat. John righted himself and grabbed her by the leg as she tried to get away.

"Nope," he said, dragging her back to him. "You're not going anywhere."

Victoria swung one leg around his chest and latched onto his arm, trapping him in another arm bar. He swore he was actually trying, but she'd managed to catch him in the same move.

"Jesus, woman. How?"

Victoria's braids swung low to the ground as she pulled his arm away from his body and locked it between her thighs. "I haven't done this in a while, but it's like riding a bike," she said with a grin.

On his back for a third time, his arms extended, he looked into her shining face. She was perspiring heavily, but proud of her handiwork. He had to admit to himself that Victoria was much stronger and craftier than he could have bargained for. John told himself to remember this moment for the future. She'd have him in a similar position, with her body or her words, and he'd need to remember that she was not a delicate flower. Victoria could handle a little rough and tumble. As unorthodox as it was, this was her version of dropping her mask.

"Have you had enough?" she asked.

Never.

From this position, his only option was to cheat his way out of the arm bar. While his hand was trapped in her grasp, he unclenched his fist and gently squeezed her breast. The gasp that escape from her lips was one of shock. She loosened her grip just enough for him to wrench his arm away and shift his torso from her reach.

Victoria scrambled for her next move as John's wrestling training kicked in. He flipped over and took her by the back of the neck, forcing her against his chest in a rear naked choke. With his long legs wrapped across her hips, Victoria's arms flailed outward. She was a trapped turtle on her back with no hope of escape. John took care not to apply pressure to her throat, but his bicep wasn't going to leave her upper chest. He'd learned his lesson three times already.

"You're a cheat," she said. "And dare I say, a deviant."

"I'm a pragmatist," John breathed in her ear. "I'm a lot better on the ground than I am on my feet."

She squirmed in his grasp, testing the weaknesses of his hold, and found nothing. "After two arm bars, I'm glad to see it."

The pleasant pressure of her ass against his groin wasn't a normal part of his grappling sessions. He'd rolled around the ground with Chris for years without any underlying eroticism. Now that he had the professor on her back, in a public place, the fear of growing hard was real. "Ready to talk?"

With nowhere to go, she sagged against him. "My boss confronted me about you today."

"Ahh, I see," John said through the curtain of her braids. He shook one out of his mouth and took a breath. "What did he say?"

Victoria wiggled her shoulder against his chest, still

looking for a way to get out. "He basically accused me of sleeping my way to the top," she sighed. "I mean he didn't say it like that, but he suggested that I'd embarrass the department with shoddy work."

"Victoria Reese doesn't do shoddy work," he grunted. "Besides, our relationship is none of his business. The fact that he even brought it up was inappropriate."

"He'll try to sabotage me."

John heard the doubt creep into her voice. She was retreating into her day planner brain where professionalism and schedules reigned supreme. If Victoria didn't stop this tired self-flagellation, she was in danger of sabotaging *herself.* "Look," he said, tightening his grip on her chest. "We've worked on this long enough for you to bring the president a finished product. Just skip ahead in the chain of command."

She planted her bare feet on the mat and pushed her hips upward, a vain attempt to pull away from his locked legs. "I could do that," she grunted. "But I'm already doing a shitty job of tiptoeing around Kenneth. The man ultimately determines my future and I'm a constant thorn in his side."

"No man determines your future," John said forcefully. He knew *he* certainly couldn't. Even though she was stuck in his grip, Victoria still held all the cards when it came to his heart. "You've got good ideas. You don't need his permission to voice them."

Victoria raised one of her free hands and touched the side of his face. "John."

His chest tightened at the sound his own name. She knew when to say it and what inflection to use. The way it rolled off her tongue made him want to release her and kiss her anxiety away. "It's true."

She gave a light and breathy laugh as she blindly held his cheek. "I wish I had your confidence around my mother."

Behind them, the door opened and Chris cleared his throat. "Looks like the doctor is in a pickle."

"I'm not," she called out. "It's just going to take me a minute to get out of this."

John craned his neck towards the doorway. "It's going to take her more than a minute."

Chris walked in and quietly assessed the situation. "Well, I'm not surprise she got you on the floor," he addressed John. "She's a lot faster than you."

"Exactly," Victoria said in a strained breath. "I took him down almost immediately."

Chris crouched down. "I saw. You got him in a lock a couple of times. What happened?"

"He cheated," she muttered.

John rolled his eyes as Chris nodded. "Sounds about right."

"Mr. Donovan ran out of cards and behaved like a cad," Victoria said.

His friend's gaze slid over to his. "You can't underestimate a desperate man," he said with a smirk. He raised himself to full height and looked down at their embrace. "I'll let you in on a secret, Dr. Reese. Johnny's ticklish."

"Chris…"

His boyhood friend betrayed him with a chuckle. "Nothing a little belly tickle won't fix."

Before she could reach downward, John quickly released her and wriggled out from under her. "Okay, okay!"

"I win," Victoria shouted with glee.

"Point to Dr. Reese," Chris said with an extended arm in her direction.

"This cad is done for the night," John said through labored breath. "I don't have anymore."

The three of them sat on the floor, John and Victoria taking a breather while Chris lounged lazily. "So what's this about your mom?" John asked.

Victoria wiped her brow and sighed. "My parents are throwing a blowout retirement reception for a fellow Marine this weekend. My mom called to remind me about it this evening. I don't want to go."

"So, are you going?" John asked.

Victoria nodded as she stretched her arm. "Yes, it's a long and complicated dance we've had since I was a girl."

He exchanged a glance with Chris, who raised his brow in response. They understood long and complicated feelings regarding parents. John Sr. had been a complicated man who had become more of an enigma when he'd married Sandy. John hadn't gotten to know him any better before his father died of a sudden heart attack. When the anger had set in, it had been a struggle to separate that anger from the grief. Jessi had helped him with some of that, but he'd made mistakes along the way. If he could save Victoria from half of that...

"You need any company when you go home?" Chris asked.

Victoria gave a mirthless laugh. "I need a full platoon when it comes to Katherine Reese. When she's in 'gala-mode,' she's relentless."

His friend gave a flippant shrug. "John should go with you. He's a terrible fighter, but great with parents."

They both stared at Chris who smiled between the

two of them. Chris appeared proud of himself for putting her in the awkward position of asking. John had just enough energy to throttle the fool. He had managed to pin him down with one idiotic suggestion. Galas in Chicago? John was a downstate guy who worked with books. But any excuse to be with Victoria was almost enough to grin and bear her overbearing mother. He just didn't know if she wanted him.

"I don't think she'd want a guy like me at a fancy party," John said. "I don't want to frighten your mom."

Victoria caught his gaze and twisted her mouth. "You'd be busy with Becca anyway."

"I can stay at your place," Chris offered. "I'll take her to kickboxing class on Saturday and drop her off at your mom's place afterwards."

John shot him a glare. He caught the fact that she hadn't corrected him and it gnawed at his belly. "It sounds like it might be a family affair."

She shrugged uncomfortably. "Kind of? It's going to be a pretty large celebration at the Drake Hotel."

"Ooh, The Drake?" Chris whistled. "I'm sure Johnny can clean up for The Drake."

He didn't need his friend to meddle like this. It was painfully obvious that Victoria wasn't making any overtures about him accompanying her to the military ball. In fact, she was the first to stand and stretch her arms. "I'm going to grab some water," she said with a fake smile. "In fact, I kinda need to head out soon."

From the floor, John tried to behave nonchalantly. "Sure. I'll see you tomorrow for our appointment?"

"Of course," she said as she backed away. "It was nice to meet you, Chris."

"I hope to see more of you, Dr. Reese," he said with

a sly grin. "Your things are in my office." She gave a breathless laugh as she shook her head and exited the room. Once they were alone Chris let out a sigh. "Now I get it."

"You asshole," John said through gritted teeth. "I wasn't planning to force myself on her little trip."

"Yeah, I noticed. And it's a crying shame too. You're exactly the kind of dude who could impress her parents."

"Did you see those moves?" John asked. "The man who taught her that would gut me if he knew I was banging his daughter."

"I saw everything, man. Dr. Reese, as you keep calling her, is a fine woman and complicated as all get out, but she's into you," Chris said in an even voice. "I'm trying to do what any good wingman does: set you up for a spike."

And he'd missed completely. "It's too soon to take that step."

"Are you guys still in some kind of situationship?"

"Maybe?" John was still learning new facets of her personality and every discovery was fascinating. It didn't add up to a real relationship though. After a week of fooling around and one date, Victoria didn't seem terribly interested in dropping the rigorous schedule of their sordid affair. *But dammit, attending a ball with a handsome man seems like her style.*

John could be her duke.

Chapter Twenty-Eight

After such a vigorous workout, Victoria expected a restful night's sleep. But she was nowhere near tired. Her mind was a super highway of rushing thoughts keeping her eyes open in the darkness of her bedroom. Between school stuff, Mom stuff, and John stuff, she didn't know which to tackle first. School drama she could handle when she saw John tomorrow as their scheduled appointment was actually work-related. Victoria had hoped they could come together to compare notes on their proposal so she could begin editing the first draft. She had to trust what John had said when he had her pinned on her back that evening. She needed to skip the middle man, Kenneth, and have enough confidence to approach the president anyway.

Victoria shifted in bed as she remembered the vulnerable position he'd put her body in. Pressed against his hard chest, staring at the gym's ceiling, while his legs wrapped around her. John held her in place with a sturdy arm across her breasts and breathed hot against her ear. Victoria could almost feel it while she was in bed. As she exhaled a long breath, she whipped the covers off her and switched on her bedside light. If she couldn't sleep, she would do some light reading to pass the time. There was no sense in watching a dark ceiling. She went through the pile of books on her nightstand and settled on a contemporary title that she recently picked up from Antonia Harper. It wasn't her usual historical romance purchase, but Paula recommended it for its lack of p-words.

She flipped to the last dog-eared page and picked up where she left off. "Okay, rough kissing in the back streets of Bangkok, here we go…"

Victoria read the same sentence three times before her eyes left the page and she stared out into space. John was in her head and refused to vacate. His sweaty body moving over her, holding her still, keeping her safe. Strong arms wrapped around her, pressing her close. Even the way he playfully squeezed her breast lingered in Victoria's mind. Her nipples stiffened with the thought. She remembered being slightly embarrassed that his friend, Chris, had walked in on their intimate grappling session. *He was good-looking too…* Not quite as serious as John, but he was similarly built with lean muscles and a broad chest. Victoria pitied the women who encountered the two of them at a nightclub. She found herself sweating at the sight of both of them. But as cute as Chris was, he was not her chief concern. She wanted John and she wanted him now. Victoria glanced at the clock on her nightstand and groaned. *One in the morning?*

The book in her hands wasn't going to help the urge that currently plagued her. She set it down and picked up her phone. *Is it too much to call at this hour?* She scrolled through her contacts until she found "Mr. Donovan." Victoria realized she'd left him hanging without addressing Chris's suggestion regarding her weekend trip. Honestly, she was desperate for someone to act as a buffer between her and her mother, not to mention some random divorced lawyer. But it was a pretty big ask of John. While he may have been good with parents, her mother was a whole other animal. Her father, Archie Reese, was a laid-back guy who could pal around with any prospective boyfriend. Katherine, on the other hand, would interrogate John into submission. It would be more painful than getting caught in one of her arm bars. After meeting his maternal figures, she'd determined that her own mother would send him fleeing in an instant.

Boyfriend? That was the other problem: they weren't in a relationship. If questioned by her mother, Victoria wouldn't even know what to say. Certainly not the truth. *I'm banging this hot male librarian and our plans are a lot more haphazard than I'd hoped.* Victoria needed to keep these separate plates spinning on their own separate sticks. There was no need to muddle her life with John meeting, and possibly getting his head bit off by her harridan mother. Her thumb slipped and pressed John's name. Or maybe it didn't slip. Perhaps she wanted to call him on purpose. Rather than dwell on which one it was, she listened for several rings. *Please pick up.* And then what? What was she prepared to talk to him about if he picked up the phone?

"Hello, Dr. Reese," said a gravelly voice.

"John, hi."

He hesitated before replying. "Hm. Formal or informal call?"

Victoria sank against her pillows and closed her eyes. "Informal. I didn't wake you up, did I?"

"Nope, I was going to read for a while. What can I do for you, Victoria?"

Yes, what can he do for me?

"Um… I couldn't get to sleep and I wanted to talk to you."

He paused again.

"John, are you still there?" She was now worried that she had made a mistake.

"Oh yeah, I'm here, darling." His voice took on a different tone, something lower and warmer. "What would you like to talk about?"

Jesus…

"I was thinking about our time at the gym and I wanted to thank you for the workout." She shifted again, trying to choose her words. "You were really…virile tonight."

She heard a dark and low chuckle and bit her lip in embarrassment. There was definitely a better way to describe him. This was one of those instances where she needed her friend's assistance. Paula wrote this stuff for a living. *Note to self: download a Paula e-book tomorrow.* "Virile, huh?"

"Mm-hmm."

"You didn't mind being caught in my hold, Victoria?"

On a competitive level, yes, she definitely minded. She'd been close to winning that fight. On another, more erotic level, she wanted more. "No," she said. "I liked it."

"Would you like a rematch?" His soothing voice probed further.

"Very much," she said.

"What are you wearing right now?"

In the soft glow of her bedroom light, Victoria looked down at herself. She was in the same outfit she wore nightly; an oversized T-shirt from the college bookstore and panties. "T-shirt and underwear," she admitted.

"Mmh, I can work with that," John murmured, huskiness lingering in his voice. "It's going to come off anyway."

Victoria's heart skipped a beat. They were doing exactly what she wanted. The anticipation made her breath shudder against the phone. "What are you wearing?" she asked timidly.

"Boxer briefs," he replied.

She closed her eyes. "What color?"

"They're black with gray pin-stripes."

"Oh."

"Put me on speakerphone, darling. You're going to want to free up your hands."

She struggled to figure out the function with her shaking hands, like she'd never handled a smartphone in her life. "Okay."

"Can you hear me okay?"

"Yes," she said in a halted voice. "I can."

"Good, turn out the light and lay back in bed, I'm going to send you to sleep, darling."

Victoria did as he said and grinned in the darkness. For some reason, the darkness helped her slip into the mood. His voice lay beside her, calming and warm against her ear. "How are you going to do that?" she teased.

John ignored her. "I should have pinned you from behind tonight."

"I don't think that's very practical," she said.

"Nonetheless, can you imagine what would have happened if we weren't careful?"

"Yes," she breathed. "I did."

"What did you imagine, Victoria?"

She remembered the thoughts that had flown through

her as she was attached to his body. "I thought you were going to get hard."

"It almost happened," John admitted. "Do you know what I was imagining?"

"What?"

"I wanted to flip you over and slip those tight leggings down the curve of your ass. You were sweaty, but I was hoping your panties would be wet too."

They probably were. Victoria reached down to touch herself for confirmation. The dampness between her thighs wet her fingertips. "Was I?"

"Yes, I reached around the front of your body and cupped you there. You jumped a little and moaned. I think you were surprised. Can you feel me pressed against your back, Victoria? I'm hard and I want to be inside of you."

On her side, she nodded her head, forgetting that he wasn't there to see her.

"You let out this low groan and push against me. You think you're ready, but you're not. You think you're warmed up, but you're not there yet, honey."

Victoria's lips curled at the corner as she slipped her panties down her legs and kicked them off the bed. "No?"

"Not yet," John said. "I make you wait because I love to see the blush creep up from your breasts, up your neck, until it hits your cheeks. It's a very soft pink against your brown skin, did you know that? You're like a tea kettle that's heating up and I want to make you blow."

There was already a change in her breathing, as she ran her hands over her belly and hips. John said all the things she needed to hear in that moment. His voice was a low rumble from his chest and he spoke with a deliberate slowness that made her ache all over.

"Before I can do anything else, I need to get that tank top off you. I pull it from your waist and slip it over your head. Your braids slap against the mat and I can see that thin Victoria's Secret bra straining against the weight of your breasts."

Victoria held back her laughter at the mention of her bra. She had worn a very secure sports bra that night and it would have been an impossible struggle to shrug out of in her sweaty state. She tried to ignore that John was still a man who fantasized about lacy underwear and got back into the mood.

"Your breathing is heavy," he continued. "You keep panting my name and begging me to hurry before someone sees us. But I remind you that I don't need—"

"—a plan," she interrupted while taking off her T-shirt. Her breasts, now exposed to the cool air of her bedroom, were still warm from the blush John described.

"Exactly," he purred. "I take my time unhooking your bra and let it fall to the floor. When I kneel over you with my cock pressed to your ass, I make a trail of kisses along your spine. Does my beard scratch your skin?"

"Uh-huh," Victoria said as she ran her hands down her neck, picking up on the heat of her skin. She fanned her fingers over the tops of her breasts, brushing across stiff nipples.

Her luxurious sigh must have been audible on his side because he said, "Tell me what it feels like, baby."

Victoria's breasts rose and fell with every breath she took. "It feels like the time your beard was between my thighs. You kissed my thighs and rubbed your cheek against my skin."

The rich timbre of his voice followed her hands down her body as she pinched and squeezed her own breasts. "Would you like my beard down there again?"

"Yes," she sighed. "Please."

"I thought you'd never ask," he said in a low chuckle. "I push your shoulders down to the mat and raise your hips upward. You're dripping wet, Victoria, and I'm thirsty."

With one hand on her breast, she let the other one snake downward. As she parted her thighs, she waited on him to continue.

"My love, you're the last ice cream cone on a hot summer day. The more I lick, the faster you melt, and the more of you I want. I kneel behind you and lick your clit and then your lips. I flick one while lapping the other. Have you ever had ice cream drip down your hand, darling?"

Oh god, I have. Her fingers worked her swollen flesh as his words scandalized her ears.

"You try to lick everywhere so you don't make a mess," he said. "But I want you to make a mess, my love. I want it to drip down your legs and stain the mat. I want you to come against my mouth. Does my beard tickle?"

Victoria bit her lip, stifling a moan. "Yes," she said in a ragged voice.

"Does something else tickle?" he asked.

The building pressure in her womb would make her weep if she didn't finish. "Yes."

"Let me hear how it feels, Victoria. You can be as loud as you want."

She nodded again. "Okay…"

"I think it's time for me to pull away for a moment.

When I do, you look over your shoulder with those big brown eyes, and give me a frown. Don't worry."

"What are you going to do?" she panted, rubbing herself.

"I slide down my waistband and take out my cock. When you see it, you lick your lips and raise yourself from the mat. You want me inside of you now, don't you?"

Victoria let out a soft moan as she raised her hips from the bed. "Yes."

"Yes, what?" he teased.

"Yes, Johnny. I want you now."

"Anything for you, honey. You're ready to receive me and as I slide inside of you, I can feel every twitch and jump of your walls. It's like you're pulling me in. How fast do you want me to go, baby? Do you want it nice and slow or rough and fast?"

Jesus Christ... "Rough and fast," she whispered in a tight voice.

"Good," he said. "Because I want to fuck you until you scream my name. I want your breasts to bounce and I want you to back into me for more. I need your hands to slip against the mat as I drive into you. Can you keep up, Victoria?"

"Yes," she said loudly. "Please."

"Please, what?"

"Please...do it...harder, Johnny." She was so close to the edge, she was dangling by a thread.

"I don't know if you want it that hard, Victoria." The wicked humor in his voice made tears stand out on her lashes.

"I do," she panted.

"Good girl. I want you to take all of my cock, right up

to the hilt. In and out, Victoria, in and out. I kneel over you and cover your naked back as you slip away from me. I cup your breasts as they rock back and forth. I'm so close to losing myself inside of you, I don't know if I can stop myself."

"Don't stop," she hissed. Victoria arched her hips in an effort to use two fingers on herself. The thread was so close to snapping, she gritted her teeth and continued to stroke herself.

"I'm not going to stop," John said. "Not until you collapse in a heap. I'm going to keep thrusting deep and hard until the room smells like sex. Until you cry out and—"

The explosion in her brain rocked her body with violent tremors as she fell over the edge. "Johnny," she cried. The room was dark, but behind her eyelids, she saw stars. Victoria choked on a sob as her muscles shook under the pressure of her orgasm. His words, so filthy and so precise, made her come with such force. It took her several moments before she had the energy to pick up the phone. "Hello?" She spoke in a broken whisper.

"Hello, my dear."

Lying naked in her bed and fully satiated, Victoria still missed the heat of John's body. She was tired like he promised, but she wanted to wrap her legs around him and hold him close.

She sighed. "Thank you."

"Of course. Do you think you can sleep now?"

"I'd sleep better with you," Victoria admitted. She found it slightly easier to tell John the truth at times. Though she was used to keeping most of her feelings to herself, he pulled something out of her.

"I know I would too," he said softly. "Can you wait for me tomorrow?"

"Maybe," she said.

"If you need to touch yourself when you think about me, please do. But know that I'll always be there to offer assistance...eventually."

Victoria smiled in the darkness of her room as she curled up to her phone. "You will?"

"Always."

Chapter Twenty-Nine

"Are you being good for your uncle?" Jessi asked, peering from John's laptop. Even while she was thousands of miles away, his sister still managed a convincing stern face. But it didn't last long as she and Becca immediately engaged in a funny face competition. John sat behind Becca, glancing up from his paperwork, and occasionally crossed his eyes or stuck out his tongue.

Becca rolled her eyes. "I'm always good."

"I'm having a tough time getting her out of bed and ready for school these days," John said while sorting manila folders. He only had a few minutes before Victoria arrived to the library and he wanted to get his office looking halfway decent for a change. After he'd picked up Becca, he had brought her to the library for a chance to do her homework and talk to her mother at an appropriate hour.

Jessi was back to stern mom in an instant. "Why is that, Becca?"

John answered for her. "It's because she doesn't go to bed until two in the morning."

After his phone call with Victoria, he'd gone to the kitchen for a glass of water only to hear Becca giggling with her friends on an early morning skype session. He'd stood on the other side of her door, listening to them talk about boys until it grew too unbearable. Connor or Kaden or whoever the fuck had gorgeous dimples. For a feminist collective, their debates certainly didn't pass the Bechdel Test.

"I can't go to sleep," Becca whined.

"Honey, you understand cause and effect, right?" his sister asked. "School is never going to start later so you need to adjust yourself to get better results. Go to bed earlier or you're going to be a mess like your uncle."

John glanced up. "What happened to a united front, Jess?"

"What time did *you* go to bed last night?"

His face warmed from her accusation. His sister or niece had no idea what he engaged in last night, but even he had to blush from the brazenness of it all. John had never gotten a woman off over the phone and discovered he was actually pretty good at it. He cleared his throat. "I'm not the one on trial here."

"Children pattern their behavior after the adults in their lives," Jessi said in a tone John had always hated.

"Becca has a mind of her own," he said as he stuffed random papers into a folder and shoved it in his drawer. The system he'd created was falling apart the more he talked to Jessi and now he wanted to toss all of his mess into a drawer. "It's not like she's going to pick up my coke habit."

"Ha, ha…"

"Mom, how long until you get back?" Becca asked, ignoring the bickering siblings.

"I'll come home in about eight weeks, sweetie. Just in time for the holidays."

"You're sure?" Becca pressed. "Because you're missing Halloween and we always celebrate Halloween together."

Jessi forced a smile. "I know, honey. Mama's just got to finish up a project here and I'll be back before you know it. Uncle Johnny will take you trick-or-treating."

"I will," John said, rubbing her arm.

"He won't dress up," she said.

Jessi directed her gaze at her brother. "He won't?"

"I'm putting 'find a costume' at the top of my list," he assured them both.

His sister flashed a brighter smile. "Well there you go."

Becca rolled her eyes, a constant habit of hers. "I guess..."

"Becca, could you be a dear and let me talk to your uncle for a minute? I'll call you again before I go to bed."

"Sure." She backed away from the computer and slowly left his office.

"Do your homework at the checkout desk where Martha can see you," John called after her.

"Do I have to?"

"Don't sass, Becca!" Jessi shouted from the computer.

As his niece exited his office, he looked down at his sister. "Don't sass? Where did you pull that one from?"

"Just wait until you have one. You're going to sound like your mom in no time."

"Why do I need a private conference with you?" John said, giving up on the stacks of paper. He shoved them all in the bottom draw and faced Jessi head on. "Am I in trouble too?"

"It depends. What's this about a woman at your place?"

John frowned. "Sandy told you?"

"Maggie told me," Jessi said. "Well, actually Mom told me later that night. According to them, she was there in the morning wearing *your* pajamas."

John pressed his lips together and stared at her. "And?"

"So you wanna talk about it?" She wiggled her eyebrows. "Mom said she's a *darling*."

He scratched the side of his beard. "Honestly, I would have talked to you about this much sooner than our mothers, but I was caught off guard that morning."

"It sounded embarrassing as fuck," Jessi whispered. "They seemed excited more than anything. They think you're going to marry her."

"I may have made a joke about that."

"So…is she the one?"

He shrugged. "I can't say just yet. I just know that I like being around her. She's…a fucking mystery."

"Oh god, you've got that far-off look in your eyes."

John's eyes cut back to the screen to see Jessi grinning at him. "I just keeping learning new things about her. Victoria has surprises and I find myself wanting to discover them all."

His sister clasped her hands together and stuck out her bottom lip. "That is the sweetest thing I've ever heard…"

"I'm just picking up on a little hesitance on her end," John said and proceeded to repeat the same story he'd told Chris. Jessi listened carefully, nibbling on her lip as she nodded along.

When he finished, she rubbed the space under her bottom lip, something she'd done since they were young. It was her "thinking" gesture that always produced helpful advice. "Okay, I see what's going on here."

John raised a brow. "Do you? Please enlighten me."

"She's a little uptight and high-strung, but you're going to get that from an academic. It just comes with the territory. They're not all squares though, and she sounds like one of the cool ones. Now, when you add the mom issues, you've got a storm on your hands. And as sweet as you are, you know you can't compete with that."

"I was hoping you wouldn't say that," John said, resting his chin on his knuckles.

"All is not lost though," she said quickly. "She just needs you to be there when things get nasty between her and her mom, and her boss for that matter. But she doesn't sound like the kind of person who's going to dump all of her problems on others either."

"So I need to anticipate?"

"And listen, and read between the lines. I think you should ask about this Chicago trip again."

John felt queasy from her recommendation. He didn't want to force his presence on her if she didn't request it. "What about Becca?"

Jessi frowned. "I appreciate you looking after your niece, but you're not the only caregiver she has. It takes a village, Johnny. Between you, the moms, and Chris— By the way, how is Chris?"

"What?"

"What's Chris up to?" Jessi asked wearing an innocent expression. "I was just wondering."

"He's being Chris, dude-bro Chris," John said, narrowing his eyes at his sister. "Why the hell are you asking?"

She waved off his concern. "Nothing, don't worry about it. All I'm saying is: you're free to pursue a cute lady. That's what family is for."

He settled down and decided to tuck that little nugget

away for another time. He was picking up a vibe between his sister and best friend that he didn't have time to investigate at the moment. "I just prefer to be asked is all."

"And that's why you're a perfect gentleman. But she might have left you hanging because she likes the orderly situation she created. Family drama on this side, boyfriend on the other side. But a little chaos never hurt anyone," she said with a grin.

Since they had moved on to his *tamer* version of a sordid affair, meeting her parents seemed as normal as it could get. Fucking, dating, meeting her mom and dad. Sure, the order wasn't to her liking, but he was intent on getting to know her. Why not go to the source of her neurosis? If last night's phone call was any indication, Victoria was losing control of the plot anyway. He'd held on to her voice and nursed its whimpering cadence when she'd said "I'd sleep better with you." John's heart swelled as much as his cock when he heard those words.

"There's another far-off look," Jessi said, interrupting his thoughts. "Your concentration has always been an issue, but this Victoria is making you worse."

Her laughing eyes were a welcome sight even if he was struggling with love woes. He missed his sister, a friend he could always depend on for support when his mind was scattered. "I'm seeing her tonight," he said. "She should show up any minute. Maybe I can nudge then?"

"You think she might be down for a Skype meeting?"

"Nope."

Jessi stuck out her tongue. "I go to Sweden and miss everything, huh?"

"Just about," he said. "I hate to do this…"

"But you've got to go," she said. "Yeah, I get the picture."

"Love you, sis."

"Love you, bro."

When he'd closed the window, he shut his laptop and formed a steeple with his fingers. He had lied to his sister, John wasn't going to nudge anyone. If Victoria could meet him halfway with her attempts to have fun in bed or over the phone, she could meet him halfway on this. John tried to ignore his pride, but he couldn't help but feel principled about it. If she really wanted him to go to Chicago with her, she would have said something instead of escaping from the gym.

A soft knock at the door pulled him out of his thoughts. Victoria stood in the entrance, not dressed in her usual teaching outfit, but in a Pembroke University sweatshirt and jeans. On her feet were a pair of red Converse sneakers. Her braids were gathered in a sloppy bun, perched atop her head, much like how she woke up in his bed. In this relaxed state, she was still gorgeous. Victoria tipped her head and smiled. "Hey there," she said in a soft voice.

John stood immediately. "Hey, Dr. Reese. You look like a student."

She wrinkled her nose as she crossed the threshold. "Ugh, after the day I had, I don't want to hear that," she said, taking a seat before his desk.

Remembering Jessi's words, John circled his desk before sitting on the edge in front of her. *Listen and read between the lines. Anticipate everything.*

"I hate today," she said, slumping in her chair. "It started with my 8 o'clock class where only three students bothered with last night's reading. Those three carried their classmates for an entire hour and fifteen minutes. Now I have to start making reading quizzes to scare the rest of them straight. If that weren't enough, I've got to handle a lacrosse player's helicopter parents who are concerned about his attendance. And since he's on academic probation and waived his rights to privacy, I actually have to interact with his parents. The graduate students are losing their minds over this insane federal tax change that now taxes their stipends like it's income, which it is most certainly not. I mean Jesus, as if graduate students aren't already neurotic. I had to talk two different girls off the ledge."

Boom.

John took it all in and remained silent.

"So after all of that, I went home and changed into something more comfortable." Victoria exhaled a humorless laugh. "But that's an average day around Pembroke. I should be able to handle it on my own."

He reached out and took her by the hand and knelt beside her. "You could," he said. "But you don't have to today."

She gave a sad smile and brushed the backs of her fingers across his face. "Thank you for saying that, John. But I'm just venting. Not everything can be remedied with your skilled hands or tongue."

"I have skillful ears too." He tried not to close his eyes in response to her soft touch. "Let's just start at the beginning with your students. While I don't have any teaching experience, I can say that you can't reach everyone. Focus on those who want to be there, those who are having trouble, and let the rest go, okay?"

Victoria nodded. "Sure."

"You have no reason to feel anxiety around the parents of a lacrosse player. Use your pull to join forces with his coach. If he can't play anymore, I guarantee you he'll get his shit together."

She raised a brow as her gaze slid away from his. "True. I suppose that could work."

"There you go," John said, satisfied with his efforts. "Everything is manageable."

But something shifted in Victoria's expression that made him doubt his words. She cleared her throat and sat up in her chair. "Do you have a final draft of the duties you'd like to give me?"

Still balanced on the balls of his feet, John froze. There was a definite shift in the air. His lover had quickly made the switch to Professional Victoria, a throwback to their first meeting. He stared at her as he slowly straightened up to his full height. "Sure," he said.

"Great," she said with a smile that wasn't hers. "That would make me happy."

That would make her happy? John returned to his side of the desk and sifted through the remaining papers. He hadn't exactly finished his cleaning task before she'd arrived and his office didn't look any better than the other times she'd visited. As John flipped through the papers, he frowned. "Now where is that paper?" he murmured under his breath.

It wasn't in his multiple stacks so he checked the drawer where he last stuffed folders in. While balancing unorganized folders on his lap, John went through sheets of paper. Invoices, order forms, budgets, book lists, random reviews. No paper regarding the library internship existed in the mess. "Wait, let me check my bag," he said. Victoria remained silent, watching him with disappointment, he was sure that's what her eyes read. He got up and crossed the room to his coat rack and dug around the compartments of his satchel. Just a couple of picture books, a notepad, and a half-empty Gatorade bottle that he should probably throw away.

"You can't find it?" Victoria asked twisting in her seat.

He scratched his head. "It's definitely here."

"Do you need help?" she asked. "I can check those papers again."

He shook his head and moved back to the desk to check the mail tray. There was a stack of letters he still needed to open, more invoices to sort through, but no internship document. John let out a frustrated breath. "I could have sworn…" He trailed off before returning to the loose papers in his drawer. His search was now less focused and slightly more frantic. "I worked on it yesterday when Becca and I got home. I printed it out in my office."

"Did you?" Victoria asked, skepticism colored her voice.

"Yes," he said with a scowl.

"And do you remember where you put it after you printed it off?"

John retraced his memory. "I made a snack for Becca before her grandmother came by to pick her up. You called while I was on my way to the gym. I swung by to pick up Becca and we went home where I returned to the document. It had a couple of spelling errors that I wanted to correct…"

"So, did you?"

"I did and then I printed it out again, but Becca needed help with her math homework, so I left the office for that." By the time he'd finished with that, John assumed that his day was more or less over. It was around midnight when he settled down to read a book. And then Victoria called him. John's eyes darted upward to see her chewing on her lip. Realization dawned on her face as she read his thoughts.

"So it's still at your home."

"Most likely."

"Your home computer isn't connected to this computer?" she asked, gesturing to his desk. "By the cloud or something?"

He shook his head.

"You didn't email it to yourself?"

"We wouldn't be having this discussion if I had," he said in a curt tone.

Victoria rolled her eyes up to the ceiling. "I tell my students to always email papers to themselves. There are word processors that you can save in the cloud and access anywhere."

John rubbed his knuckles against the side of his face. He was starting to get a little hot. Her tone was patronizing as hell. "I know how the internet works, Victoria."

"So you were just unorganized? You didn't have a plan?"

John didn't answer her right away because he crossed the room to close his office door. When he turned around, Victoria was staring at him. "Let's try a different approach," he said, crossing his arms over his chest. "I made a mistake because I was busy with other things. Some of those things involved normal errands and responsibilities, while other things were more *fun*."

Her face turned a faint shade of pink.

"I don't regret being busy with the more fun things.

But you have to cut me some slack, Victoria. A good deal of my evening was spent with you and I simply forgot."

Victoria's lips pressed into a thin line as she watched him return to his desk. "Okay…"

John couldn't get a read on her one-word reply. "Okay?"

"I'm sorry for distracting you."

He dragged in a ragged breath before saying, "I'm not asking for an apology. I'm just asking for a little patience."

"No, you're right," she said, waving him away. "I should have stuck to the schedule. We weren't supposed to meet up yesterday and I definitely wasn't supposed to call you for…fun at one in the morning. I set the plan and I didn't follow it," she finished with a resolute nod.

"Where do you get these ideas?" John asked, his temper quickly running away from him.

"They aren't ideas," she said defensively. "They're the truth. If I promised you order, I should be able to hold up my promise."

This is maddening.

"I didn't even want your plan, Victoria," he said, clenching his chair's armrests. "I wasn't interested in four weeks of highly-orchestrated romance."

Her mouth fell open as her eyes widened. "What does that mean?"

He failed to see where her confusion came from. John thought he'd made it clear when she first sashayed into his office with a day planner that he couldn't plan fucking. He wanted something more with her. Slowly but surely, Victoria was beginning to open up to him, expressing herself and letting her librarian bun down. But the shift between last night and right now was difficult to keep up with. She was putting the mask back in place and being deliberately obtuse. "I want more from you."

Victoria took a deep breath and rubbed at the space between her brows. "I don't know if I can give that to you."

"So, four weeks is enough for you?"

"I don't know. I feel like you're putting me on the spot right now and I don't have a—"

"—a plan?" John interrupted. "You didn't come prepared to a conversation about commitment?"

She shot him a glare. "No, I didn't. I came here today to talk about work. We're talking about the original reason for our being together: the internship."

"Victoria, I don't give three flying fucks about the internship. God knows I can email it to you tonight and everything will work out," John said as he stood. As he walked around the desk, he fought to keep his tone in check. When he got to her chair, she sat up straighter and narrowed her eyes at him. "The work will get done because it always gets done. I'm more worried about getting involved with a woman who only wants me when it's convenient for her. You've got me acting like the governess from that damn book."

Victoria shot up from her chair and faced him straight on. "If you felt that way, you should have said something much earlier, John."

They stood in direct opposition to one another, separated by anger and confusion. "I should have. But that's difficult when I just want to be with you. When I am with you, I try to ignore how silly this whole thing is and I enjoy *you*."

"And I enjoy you," she said in exasperation. "But I have too many things on my plate. I have a suffocating mother who insists on summoning me for parties, while my boss continually questions my competence. And then there's you…" she trailed off with a furious shake of her head. "You distract me from my path. You're handsome and smell like a manly forest and you fill my thoughts all the G.D. time. And no other man has made this impact on my life. There, is that what you wanted to hear?"

I mean, it is flattering. Any man would love to hear how he's turned a woman's life upside down with his manly forest scent. If he weren't so damn frustrated with her, he would have laughed and given her a kiss. But what she just admitted also gave him pause. "Are you saying this is *your* problem? You're pushing your anxiety on me, which is easy to do because I'm the one with ADD. You may assume my life is in disarray, but I at least know how to keep it halfway balanced. Can you say the same?"

Her chest was heaving in anger. "You've forced me and it's failing."

He moved forward just slightly, his chest nearly meeting hers. "So asking you to relax is a bad thing?"

Victoria stepped back and took a breath. "John, stop."

John ignored her and took another step forward. "Stop what?"

Her shoulders slumped in resignation as she peered up at him. Her soft brown eyes rolled upward before settling on his mouth. "I want to kiss you right now."

"And you're free to, honey. I told you, a long time ago, that you could have me. All of me. Can I have the same?"

Loops of tangled braids swung from her bun as she shook her head. "This is becoming a problem."

"You're thinking about this too hard," he said, reaching out to palm her cheek. John's heart thudded in his chest as she moved away from his touch. "How could this be a problem?"

Victoria didn't answer right away. She dropped her eyes and stared at the floor before shrugging. "I wasn't thinking when we were in the stacks that night. Maybe I didn't consider all of the risks."

He wanted to say that falling for someone was always risky. People fell all the time without consideration or plans, and they dealt with the consequences after they stood and brushed themselves off. How could she not see that they were falling *together*? How could she not understand that falling wasn't the same as failing? "But that's a relationship," John eventually murmured.

"And I might not be ready for one," she said.

She's slipping away.

"We're already in one, Victoria."

Upon hearing this, she backed away from him and wiped her hands on her jeans. She was looking for a way out. The frantic look in her eyes read frightened prey animal. "I uh… I need to leave," she breathed.

"You don't have to," John said.

"I have to keep things straight," she said in a shaky voice. "And I can't do that when I'm with you."

It crushed him to hear those words leave her mouth, but he knew they were true. He couldn't malign her for telling the truth. "Please…"

Victoria quickly walked to the door. "Let's talk about this later," she said briskly. With her back turned, he heard the sniffle and saw the discreet move to wipe her face. "I'll call you later."

When she left his office, she closed the door with a barely audible click. It was emblematic of her character. Despite a sudden rush of emotions threatening to crush her, she chose to remain quiet. He could admire her stoicism to a certain point, but now seemed to be an idiotic time for her to run away from her feelings, from him. John let her go for her own self-preservation, but regretted hearing the softness of the door closing. It wasn't a bang, but a pitiful whimper. So much for the nudge…

Chapter Thirty

Dear Professor Reese:
Attached, is a full description of Student Librarian duties.
John Donovan

Simple and perfunctory, just the way Victoria usually liked it. But the pain in her stomach told her otherwise. He'd given her what she wanted, but he was clearly very angry. She reread the short message several times, noting the shift from "Dr. Reese" to "Professor Reese." Even that small change was a sucker punch to the gut. There was no warmth in this message, only business.

"Girl, you look like death warmed over in Tupperware."

Victoria looked up from her computer screen to find Paula standing in the doorway of her office. Between the two of them, Paula appeared to be the one who got better sleep last night. Today's T-shirt was a tribute to Blanche Deveraux. Another editing pencil was tucked in her afro, right above her ear. Effortless cuteness was Paula's brand. Victoria, on the other hand, was certain she looked how she felt: exhausted. "What do you want, Paula?"

Her friend's brow shot up in confusion. "Okay, what's your problem?"

Victoria yawned into her fist. "I couldn't sleep until, I don't know, four in the morning. I woke up late and didn't have time to wait in line for coffee, so I'm running on empty."

Paula crossed her arms over her chest and leaned against the door jam. "You've been running on empty for a decade."

"Let's skip the judgement today," Victoria said. "I need positive energy only."

"Alright then, I'm positive that you're digging your own grave, kiddo. And with every shovelful, you become even more gleefully delusional. How's that?"

Victoria let her head fall against her desk with a groan. If she had even an ounce of Paula's confidence or a crumb of her bombastic attitude, she'd be making fearless decisions all over the place. "Keepin' It Real Rules?"

"Exactly. You're juggling the wrong balls."

She snorted against the surface of her desk. "Never mind the other ones," she muttered. "I've effectively dismissed those."

"Things didn't work out with Sweatpants Viking?"

Victoria shook her head. "I don't think they did."

The quiet pause made Victoria lift her head. She expected Paula to wear the "told ya so" expression she was known for, but found sympathy instead. Paula finally stepped inside, closing the door behind her. "Are you okay?"

She shook her head again, a lump forming in her throat. Victoria was forced to swallow it down because there was no time to deal with feelings. Not at Pembroke.

"Do you want to talk about it?"

"Not really," Victoria whispered. She rubbed the space between her brows and grimaced. The sudden lack of coffee was bringing on withdrawal symptoms, yet another wrinkle in her day.

"When you do want to talk about it, we can have another wine night with Reggi," Paula said as she ran her fingers through Victoria's braids. Paula only mothered her when she was heading straight for a meltdown. The last semester of their master's program had been so terrible that, more than once, Victoria had found herself in Paula's arms, breathing through a panic attack.

Perhaps this is not a good sign.

"Do you want to look through Instagram hairstyles to calm you down?" Paula asked. "You like looking at natural hair tutorials."

Victoria nodded. "Yes, please."

As Paula scrolled through afro puff, cornrows, and beautiful lace-fronts, she felt her heart rate slow. Victoria relaxed her shoulders and let her mind wander. Not surprising, she drifted back to John and the scene she had escaped. She'd hurt him. She had seen as much in his eyes, the way he'd frowned in confusion. He had reached out for her and she had swiftly moved away. She'd fled.

Becca had been at the checkout counter as she left John's office. Victoria had hid her dread as the girl greeted her with excitement. Becca had actually hopped off her stool and hugged Victoria at the waist. It had taken Zen-level concentration to not cry in front of the girl, she rubbed her back and asked her about school instead. While Becca chattered on, Victoria bit the inside of her cheek and prayed that John would stay in his office. She was more concerned about Becca's feelings at that moment. The young girl had already seen strife in the adult relationships around her, there was no need to add to the drama.

When she was able to pull herself away, she'd hurried to the parking lot, glancing over her shoulder the entire way. Victoria hadn't known what to expect. John had never objected to anything she wanted and him following her to her car had been a slim possibility. She'd said they would talk about it later and he had respected her wishes. *You G.D. idiot.*

One of the sliding images on Paula's phone caught her eye and made her sit up in her chair. "Wait, stop!"

"What's wrong?"

Victoria took Paula's phone and scrolled back to the black power fist set against a red, green, and black background. "Dang it." The picture was a reminder of one more thing she'd forgotten because of John.

"Girl, what?" Paula asked.

Victoria stood and searched for a spare notebook and pen. "I forgot that today is the first meeting of the Black Student Union," she said in a panicked voice. She glanced at her watch and found another disappointment. "It starts in ten minutes."

"We have a Black Student Union?"

"For the first time, if I can get over to the Student Union building. Jesus, I can't believe I forgot. Paula, I'm sorry but I gotta go, the kids need me."

"Go then, just be careful running around in those heels. Can't dig a grave on broken ankles…"

Victoria literally didn't have time for her friend's sass. "Okay, bye!"

She didn't get far out of her building before running into Kenneth Williams and his sycophant group of PhD students.

"Ms. Reese," he said with a startled chuckle. "Where's the fire?"

"I'm sorry, Mr. Williams," she said through a clenched jaw. Since he refused to address her by title in front of his students, she'd have to return the favor. "I'm on my way to a meeting."

His mustache quirked with a smug grin. "With the children's librarian?"

Victoria ran her tongue over her teeth and forced a pleasant smile. "I'm meeting with the Black Student Union."

His students looked at one another and then to him as if they required guidance from the old man. As if they were privy to this conversation. "We don't have a Black Student Union," Williams said with suspicion.

"We do now, and I'm running late to their first meeting."

"Are you their advisor then?"

She sighed. "Well let's see, the two other black full-time faculty members already have enough on their plates, so that leaves the one black professor of the English department." Victoria rolled the idea around in her head. "And according to the students, no other professor wanted to take the helm even though it only requires signing forms for expenses."

The PhD students coughed and shuffled their feet in response. Williams raised a silver brow as he stuffed his hands in his pockets. "Very good of you," he said in a terse voice.

"I'd love to stay and continue this engaging dialogue regarding diversity in higher education, but the students need me," Victoria said with a sweet smile. "You remember what it was like catering to undergraduate students, right Kenneth?"

She moved around his small pack of lackies and raced down the hallway until she exited the building. After a short and almost dignified jog to the Student Union building, in her skirt and heels, Victoria made it just in time. Nearly forty students packed the small room. Victoria was equal parts thrilled and saddened at the thought of so many black students in one space. On one hand, they were finally a collective, on the other hand, it was disgraceful how desperate they were to form a safe space.

Her literature student, Maya, had asked her to act as a faculty advisor back in August. When Victoria had said yes, she'd promptly pushed it out of her mind. She thought that Maya would simply forget and move on. But the plucky sophomore was more serious than Victoria presumed. She'd recognized Pembroke's problem right away and had set about fixing it.

"Dr. Reese," Maya cried from the front of the room. She was a petite young woman who wore a black blazer over her Black Lives Matter T-shirt, her hair styled in a curly neon green mohawk with jagged lightning bolts shaved on either side. Had Maya been Victoria's age, she could have been a part of The Write Bitches group. "Over here!"

Victoria squeezed past the students who were relegated to standing room only and made it to the front.

To her shock, Maya flashed a beaming smile and hugged her tightly. "Omigod, thank you for coming to the first meeting."

When she was released, Victoria let out a surprised laugh. "Of course."

As more students filed into the room, she grew increasingly concerned about the small space they inhabited. The students didn't seem bothered though; they shifted and made room for newcomers. One student maneuvered himself inside the room in his wheelchair and the kids made sure he had a spot in the front.

"Should we get started?" Maya asked the room.

A resounding yes, filled the room, causing Victoria's heart to swell. They were excited to be there and she was honored to stand before them. "Hello, everyone," Victoria started. "I'm Dr. Reese from the English department. I've had some of you as students, I'm sure. As your faculty advisor, my presence here will be minimal. This is your group and I'm just here to sign the necessary forms."

"Thank you for taking a chance on us," said a boy from the center of the room. "Me and Maya asked, like, four profs and they said they were too busy."

Instead of feeling slighted by the young man's remark, Victoria felt disappointed by her institution. "I'm sorry that you felt you were stalled, but I think you're in business now."

"It feels like we're working hard to be seen around here and no one wants to help," said another male student. "There's a Quidditch team with a history professor and it's not a big deal, but I told some people that we're starting a Black Student Union and they were like, *what*?"

Laughter erupted in the room before someone called out. "It's like they think we're starting a Black Panther Party at Pembroke."

"Right?" Maya said through giggles. "All we want is a place to talk comfortably. No code-switching, no answering dumb questions about our identities. Just a place to relax." Victoria stepped back and let Maya take over. The girl was speaking truth and people were listening. Victoria admired her ability to hold a crowd captive with her enthusiastic energy. "We want to bring something different to this campus, right?"

The crowd confirmed this.

"This isn't just about us though," Maya said. "It's my hope that we'll partner with students who want to form a Latino Student Union and an LGBTQ Student Union. And we need to host events that welcome everyone."

Pembroke didn't have those groups yet. The university had a long way to go before reaching their diversity mission statement, but these students had enough enthusiasm to get the ball rolling. Hope bloomed in Victoria's chest.

"Yes," said a female student from the front row. Victoria recognized her from last semester's Composition class. "Because we need fun parties because this place *stays* boring."

"Oh my god, you guys, we could have a '90s dance party as our first event!"

"That would be so lit!"

As she watched the kids dissolve into excited shouts and laughter, Victoria fought the temptation to call the group back to order. This wasn't her classroom and it wasn't her place to control their conversation. She sat uncomfortably, waiting for some order to happen. There were no officers yet, so there was no one to keep Robert's Rules. Victoria pretended to be totally cool with the pandemonium even though it made her sweat.

"Okay, y'all!" Maya shouted. "Let's be cool for a second. This many black folks in one area shoutin' is gonna make people nervous."

The occupants of the room laughed and Victoria was relieved. *How did she do that and how can I be as chill as a nineteen-year-old?*

"If we're going to get any of these ideas off the ground, we're going to need a plan. Kerri is going to send around a clipboard for contact information. If you're serious about this, please sign up. In our next meeting, we're going to toss in nominees for officer positions. We need structure before we do anything else."

Victoria let out a small breath. Maya was teaching her a valuable lesson about guiding those around her with loose reigns. She gave her peers agency. She didn't need to get cross or micromanage them, she just let them express themselves.

"Girl, why don't you just be president?" said the young man in the wheelchair.

"Because democracy, Quinton," Maya replied. "We have to nominate and vote based on the people. Student Government also wants us to write up a constitution. Can I get a three-person committee to work with me on that?"

Several students raised their hands.

"Okay, which of you are Pre-law or English?" Maya asked. A couple students dropped their hands. "Right, Jaleena, Marcus, and Izzy; let's meet up tomorrow to sketch this out."

"What about money?" Quinton asked. "We need to raise money for events."

Maya's gaze flitted to him. "If you're nominating yourself for treasurer, please do." She smiled and threw him a cheeky wink.

"I'm majoring in Economics," he said with a shrug. Victoria could tell that the young man was a little smitten with their fearless leader. "I don't know, I think I could help."

"Well, we could use it," Maya said. "They're not going to throw money at us. Everything we want, we're going to have to work for it."

"Parties are great or whatever, but what about the shit we have to deal with on the daily?" said a kid from the back. People ahead of him shifted to give him the floor, all eyes on him. "Like, is this the group I can come to when I'm feeling..." he trailed off, sensing the room's full attention focused on him.

"Alone," Victoria said.

"Yeah," he said. "Alone."

She stood and addressed the room. "As I said, you guys are in control of all the day to day business, but you're also in control of how you take care of one another. Pembroke is prestigious, expensive, and lacking in diversity. Some of you are already used to this fact, while others might only be recognizing it now. Some of you are here on scholarship, the first of your family to get to this stage. Some of you have the hopes of an entire community on your shoulders, right?"

There were a few nods from the students. "I can't tell you that the pressure will ever let up. If you weren't asked to the table, you're always going to have to prove you belong there. For some of you that might never end. What's your name?" she asked the student in the back.

"Adam O'Neal," he said. "I'm a freshmen."

"Adam, you belong here. If you made it this far, you've got the strength to go even further. That goes for all of you. Some of you will have to have the strength to convince Adam that he belongs here on the days he feels isolated. Can you reciprocate the encouragement, Adam?"

The boy gave a wordless nod. Victoria's chest ached for him and his pensive expression. He was a small light-skinned young man with pale green eyes and tight sandy curls. He chewed on his lip and averted his gaze from Victoria. "Yeah."

"Does everyone promise to give each other the encouragement they need to make it through their time here? Because if you can't, a group like this cannot succeed."

Murmurs rippled through the group, some nodding, others clapping and saying "yes." The students closest to Adam clapped him on the back and pulled him in for hugs. When she saw his bashful grin, Victoria knew he'd be okay.

"I'm going to hand it back over to Maya," she said. "But I just felt like I needed to say that. You don't have to feel alone, any of you."

"Thanks, Dr. Reese," Maya whispered, her warm hazel eyes smiling. "We need to hear that."

Victoria nodded and sat back down. *The kids are alright.* The students knew what they wanted and were willing to work for it. That's all she needed to know. If they elected Maya as their president, they would be fine. She was reminded of what John had asked her when they spent the evening at his house. *What you bring to your work that wasn't there before?* This was one of those moments she would hold on to. The smiles of students who no longer felt alone… Victoria had helped, in a small way, to create this feeling of comradery.

After an hour of debating, brainstorming, and good-natured fun, the students were ready to break up the party and return at a later date. Victoria said her good-byes and slipped into the hallway while students mingled with one another. As she rushed across the quad, a phone call buzzed in her pocket, making her slow her pace.

She stopped short of Stevenson Hall and checked the screen. *Mother.* "Not now," she whispered. Victoria knew that her mother wouldn't stop until she got a reply. "Yes, ma'am."

"Victoria, you're still coming tomorrow?"

"Yep."

"Have you found a dress yet?"

Victoria rolled her eyes. "I'm going to find something soon."

"Please make sure that it's tasteful. Nothing busty, nothing too formfitting. Please don't look fast."

Fast? She squeezed her eyes shut and prayed her mother didn't need to prolong this conversation. "Gotcha."

"And you'll come to the house before we leave. You can unpack and visit with your dad before we head out. The ball starts at 18:00, so try to catch a 15:00 train."

"Yes, ma'am."

"Just make sure you keep track of the time," Katherine reminded. "We need enough time to get prepped before the event and I cannot worry about loose ends."

Victoria was counted in the loose threads category.

"I will be there."

"With bells on, I hope," her mother said in a cheery voice. "Are you excited to meet Matthew?"

"Still not interested."

"We'll see, little lady."

"Goodbye, Mom."

Chapter Thirty-One

"Hold your hand over your head, Johnny, before you bleed out!" Margaret shouted.

Baking Halloween cookies had been quickly put on hold in favor of a minor emergency. In the flurry of two panicked mothers hurrying around the kitchen for something to bandage his bloody hand, John chose to sit at Sandra's dining room table. A knife was in his other hand and a hacked pumpkin sat before him. Somewhere in the laborious process of carving a smile, John's knife had slipped and nicked his palm.

"Sandy, where's your first aid kit?"

"In the hallway bathroom," Sandra said as she pressed John's bloody hand with a tea towel. "Jesus, he's bleeding like a stuck pig."

"I'm fine," he said in a tired voice. "Really, Sandy, where are those knives I got you for Christmas? Why are you still using these dull blades?"

"Johnny, put that knife down and hush up," Margaret called from the bathroom. She came rushing back to the kitchen, blowing her hair out of her eyes. Locks of red hair had escaped the bun tied at the back of her head, making her already frantic appearance more witchy. John didn't have it in him to laugh at his mothers. He didn't have the heart to laugh at anything at the moment. "You need to save your strength."

John glanced at the thin rivulet of blood that snaked down his arm and back at his mother. "I'm not going to die."

"Good lord, I can't," Margaret said as she set the first aid kit on the table and backed away. "I never could see my own child bloodied. Sandy, you do it. Does he need stitches?"

Sandra removed the towel and peered at his hand. "Nope, just some butterfly bandages and gauze. Go wash your hand, kiddo."

John stood and took his mother by the shoulder, leading her to his chair. "Sit down, Mom."

Margaret's hand fluttered over her chest as she took a deep breath. "I just wish you were more careful, Johnny."

He stood at the kitchen sink, shoved the sleeve of his gray Henley past his elbow, and washed away the blood. The cut on his palm stung from the heat of the water, but he ignored it. He'd spent the last twenty-one hours ignoring his feelings, one more couldn't hurt. He hadn't heard from Victoria and it gutted him. John had to stuff his feelings down and carry on with business as usual. Becca was still his ward and she needed him. Library business still needed to be completed. Had he been any other man, he would have stomped over to Victoria's house, beat down her door, and hauled her over his shoulder. But he was raised with manners and going full alpha-male wasn't in his nature.

"That's good enough, kiddo," Sandra said, interrupting his thoughts.

He shook out his hand and returned to the table. "It's not that bad," he muttered as Sandra slathered ointment along the cut. She bandaged him up and tied the gauze in a neat bow at the outside of his hand.

"Clean that tonight so it doesn't get infected," Margaret said, shielding her eyes. "And wash that shirt with cold water."

"Fine."

"Alright, what's got you so bent out of shape?" Sandra said as she washed her hands and returned to the abandoned cookie dough. "You showed up claiming you'd help us with Becca's cookies and all you've done is stew."

"I haven't been stewing," John said.

"You have," his mother said. "And hold your hand up."

John raised his arm above his head and held it there while he addressed his mothers. "I'm not stewing, I'm just tired."

Sandra scoffed. "He's tired."

As he stood in the middle of the kitchen with one arm poised for a high-five, he prepared himself for a tag team interrogation. The odds were not in his favor. If John were more honest with himself, he couldn't handle just *one* of them on his best day. "No one told me that it was Becca's responsibility to bring cookies to school. I thought that ended when you got to middle school."

"Becca said she gave you a note from her class," Margaret said. "Did you lose it?"

He resented his mother's implication, but knew it came from a place of truth. John did have a habit of losing papers. "I don't know. I don't remember the conversation."

"Really, kiddo. Parenthood is full of permission slips and last minute demands."

"I'm not a parent," he reminded them.

"Of course," Sandra said. "But you're one for two months. Get with the program."

"I fail to see where the carved pumpkins fit into this afternoon," John said, changing the subject. "You said you needed cookies."

"Because it's a nice touch, Johnny," his mother said with an exasperated sigh. "I didn't show up to *your* school with the bare minimum, did I?"

John rolled his eyes as he remembered how Margaret had showed up to his own school with Christmas cookies and Santa hats for all of his classmates. It was just as embarrassing then as it was now. She may have been a hit with his friends, but at the tender age of nine, John had his reputation to consider. "Christ," he said.

"But this isn't about cookies or pumpkins," Sandra said. "Something else is bothering you."

"It's the good doctor Reese, isn't it?"

John could always count on the two of them to pounce on his weaknesses and pry them out of him. "I don't want to talk about that."

"Bingo, Maggie," Sandra said, sprinkling chocolate chips into the batter. "He's having woman trouble."

"I thought so," his mother said with a knowing smile.

"He's got John's glare when he's stewing," Sandra with a laugh. "Do you remember counting the wrinkles in his forehead?"

Margaret chortled into her fist. "God rest his soul, but that man knew how to pout!"

As old as John was, he could never get used to the two women talking about his late father. Long ago, they'd reconciled easily with the idea of being married to the same man. After all, the divorce had been his mother's idea. When he went on with his life, Margaret had been relieved. With no animosity on her end, she had welcomed Sandra and Jessi into the fold with an ease that John never understood. He still thought of his father as a rigid unyielding man who barely spoke to him as a child. Hearing his mothers describe his actions as reminiscent of John Sr., irritated him. John sighed and decided now was probably a good time to relent. "Alright, it's Victoria."

"We know, kiddo. Catch up," Sandra said, spooning mounds of batter onto a baking sheet. "Now just tell us the problem so we can dig you out of your hole."

"What makes you think it's my fault?"

"I just said you were in a hole, I didn't say you dug it."

John finally dropped his hand and sat next to his mother at the kitchen table. "The short version is that she's afraid of a relationship."

"I'm well acquainted with that," Margaret said, perching her chin on her fist. She narrowed her hazel eyes as she peered at her son. "The greatest thing that came from my marriage to your father was you. But we were incompatible from the start. I don't blame a girl for being a little skittish."

"Is there anything about me that should make a woman skittish?" John asked, gesturing to himself. Both women looked over at him and paused to think.

"Nothing comes to mind," Sandra said. "You're a perfect gentleman, kiddo."

"But, we don't know the full story," Margaret said. "Much as I love to defend my own, I really liked that Victoria. She seemed like a keeper."

"You're right, Maggie," Sandra said, wiping her hands on her apron. "She's a smart gal and cute as a button."

"Wasn't she though?" Margaret asked. "A tad nervous, but just as sweet as can be."

As far as the women were concerned, John wasn't even in the room anymore. "That's all true," he interrupted. "But that doesn't change the fact that she's not interested in me like that. I asked for more and she turned me down."

"Oh, I don't believe that," Margaret scoffed. "You're a lovely young man. Maybe it was something you said. Maybe the way you said it. Tell us the conversation."

John tried his best to relay the argument without revealing every scandalous detail. As he spoke, Sandra continued spooning batter on the baking sheet while Margaret nodded occasionally. When he'd finished, he made a useless gesture. "Now how am I the monster in this situation?"

The pregnant pause between the two women made him nervous.

"Well?"

"Do you want this one, Maggie?"

His mother sighed and shook his head. "You take it, Sandy."

"What is it?"

"These kids think they're the first at everything," Sandra said with a chuckle.

"I swear as old as he is, you'd think he could see it himself."

John pushed down his irritation and held back his growl. "What the hell are you two talking about?"

"And as well-read as he is," Sandra added. "Jesus, kiddo, have you *never* been in love? It's been two weeks and you're losing your damn mind over a girl. You never considered that you were just falling in love with her?"

John was dumbstruck.

Sandra put the first two pans of cookies in the oven and set the timer before starting on the next pan. "Surely someone told you that some opposites attract and stay attracted," she continued. "This Victoria needs someone like you to undo her tight little rubber band ball and you need someone like Victoria to keep you on the ground. This combination is hardly new, is it Maggie? He's looking at me like I'm speaking French."

His mother eyed him suspiciously. "I think he's coming to the realization, Sandy. Let him get there."

John finally opened his mouth. "I don't…"

"Girl, he's taking too long," Sandra said. "You should have just told her how you felt in the office. Had you said three simple words, she probably would have still ran away, but she'd have a good long think about those words. A clear firm hand isn't always a bad thing, kiddo."

"Are you getting it?" his mother asked.

He stared at them in disbelief. He didn't love Victoria…did he? "No, you've got it wrong. We're so opposite, it's a laughable cliché," John said. "I might be in lust, but I don't think we're in love. I've only just met her and we're supposed to be professional and…" He trailed off because the excuses were piling up and they didn't look good. The women weren't buying it.

"He's almost there," his mother said.

"And he doesn't want to get hurt."

"Will you two stop talking like I'm not sitting here?"

Sandra shrugged. "Alright then, now what are you going to do?"

John didn't know what to do. "I can't do anything about it until she comes back from her trip to Chicago."

"Showy gestures are lovely," Margaret suggested. "Women like something with flourish."

"Ugh, this isn't some movie, Maggie," Sandra said with a frown. "She's a professional woman who apparently *doesn't* care for flourish."

"And that's why my husband worked better for you."

Sandra's brow shot up. The two women exchanged knowing looks before dissolving into giggles. "I swear, Maggie…"

"Oh god, you two are the worst," John muttered.

Chapter Thirty-Two

Only when John left his mothers to pick up Becca, did he really have time to think about his predicament. *Love?* That required being with her in a long-term relationship, dating, learning everything he could about Victoria. All he knew was that she was a military brat with a deadly jab. And that when she was a child, she yearned for stability so badly, she dreamt of being a farmer. The crop wasn't important. He knew that she liked reading romance novels as much as she enjoyed living them with John. He knew that she was a hardworking woman who wanted to accomplish all her goals all the time. God, he knew that any day he spent not seeing her, not hearing her voice, felt as if he was being raked over the coals of ache and want.

John struggled to remember a time he'd felt this distracted and listless. He had woken that morning to take Becca to school and his mind had been somewhere else. Only when they got to the school parking lot, did he remember she was without lunch. His niece wasn't upset when he fished a twenty from his wallet for her. She kissed him on the cheek and skipped off. When John got to the library, he'd read books to the afternoon crowd of children, but his heart wasn't in it. The performance was dull to say the least. And now he had a cut hand to remind him what happened when he daydreamed about the woman who had quietly backed out of his life.

When he pulled up to the pickup curb, he waited for Becca and her gaggle of girlfriends to be released from their after-school detention. Seven girls were escorted from the building, all of them laughing and chattering about nonsense to be sure. John counted them again. *Seven?* He was certain that the feminist collective was only four. Becca walked tall with a confident grin as the girls huddled around her, gesticulating wildly and screeching. It dawned on him that one of those girls was probably Becca's nemesis, Megan or whatever. "Well, I'll be damned," he said with a low whistle.

As they approached his truck, she waved at him. He could overhear her saying in a nonchalant voice, "That's my uncle Johnny, he's a librarian."

The gaggle of girls glanced over at him and giggled. The three he recognized from the slumber party called out in unison, "Hi, Mr. Donovan."

He gave a half salute. "Ladies."

His niece continued to chat with her small cult following until John rolled his eyes and laid on the horn. "Time to go, Becca," he called.

"Hold on!"

"Call us tonight? I want to hear everything. Again."

"Me too! I just can't believe he would even."

"I will, we have to Skype earlier though," Becca said with a grin.

"Becca!"

"I'm coming!"

More giggles and a round of goodbyes later, Becca

flung open the door and climbed into the cab. "I had The. Best. Day. Ever," she screeched.

John waited for the rest of the girls to cross in front of the truck. "Who are all of those girls?"

"Jenny, Megan, Bridgette, Devon, McKenna, and Kelly," she recited as if it were common knowledge.

John looked down at her. "Didn't you get into a fight with them?"

"We're friends now," Becca said. "Catch up, please."

He frowned. "When did this happen?"

His niece returned his frown with her own. "Like, after the first day of after-school detention. We all had some group therapy or something and we learned a lot. Jenny was being mean to me because her parents just decided to get a divorce and she didn't know how to handle it. They apologized and we accepted."

Really? That simple? "And this is why you're having the best day ever?"

Becca scoffed. "No, that was ages ago. I'm excited because of Connor."

"Who's Connor?" John asked as he started the engine.

"The boy in fifth period P.E. He's so cute and amazing."

John swallowed his shock. There were a few ways to play this out and if he shot his mouth off too quickly, Becca would clam up. The first night they'd worked in the library, Victoria had told him to listen to his niece and she might continue to share. Instead of demanding the boy's address so John could drive there and wring his neck, he tried something else. "So what was so exciting about fifth period P.E. with Connor?" He tried to make his voice light as he gripped the steering wheel.

"Omigod, it was incredible," she crowed. "I was

showing McKenna the new kicks I learned at the gym and Connor just walked over and asked me if I wanted to sit with him at lunch tomorrow."

That's it? The kid hardly sounded like Romeo. A relief, but cafeteria lunch didn't sound like the greatest overture. "Yeah?"

"And then he said he liked the way I kicked and wanted me to show him how to do it. He's not really good at it, but he was trying it anyway."

"Okay…"

"I haven't even gotten to the best part. We started the square dancing unit in P.E."

John was lost. "They're still square dancing in gym class?"

"Connor asked to be my partner! He turned like, three shades of red and asked if I wanted to dance with him. He's terrible at that too, so I didn't feel like a klutz. We held hands and skipped and do-si-doed! It was *magical…*"

John glanced down at her to see if she was on the verge of swooning. "Huh, well that sounds okay, I guess."

"Okay? It was more than okay," Becca said. "It was—"

"—magical. Right."

"And now we're going to have lunch tomorrow."

"And that's what the girl gang wants to talk about tonight?"

"I have to show them the outfits I might wear tomorrow. I'm thinking about my purple jeans and the green sweater, but I know that Kelly is going to suggest the pink sweater. I think green pops more. Do you think I should keep my hair like this?" she asked patting her afro-puffs.

John shrugged. "Sure, your hair always looks cute."

"Man, I wish I had braids like Victoria. Do you think I could get them?"

He crossed the intersection before answering. "That's one of those 'Ask Mom' questions."

"Victoria's friend, Regina, did hers."

"I don't think that's happening any time too soon," John said, pausing at a stop sign.

"You could ask Victoria," Becca pressed. "When are you seeing her again?"

He did his best to control his breathing by twisting his hands against the steering wheel. He winced at the sharp pain in his injured hand. "Victoria and I are finished working together."

"But she's your girlfriend," his niece said. "I mean…" She screwed up her face as if she too were speaking French to him.

John was getting just a little tired of the women in his family treating him like a small boy. "She's not my girlfriend."

"You're in a bad mood," she said, with a suspicious expression that mirrored her mother's. "Did you guys break up?"

He couldn't wait to drop this child off at her grandmother's house. "What made you think that she was my girlfriend in the first place?"

Becca laughed, her large brown eyes twinkling with mischief. "That's easy," she said with a broad grin. "Because you looked like Connor when you talked to her."

"Excuse me?"

"When we saw her at the dress shop, you were all, 'Uh, hello, uh Dr. Reese,' and you turned three shades of red."

John didn't have anything clever to add to this conversation. His twelve-year-old niece had found him out. She had no doubt caught some of the Donovan women gossip as well. The four of them were becoming more and more insufferable as he traversed this…whatever the hell it was, with Victoria. He certainly didn't need a child to make declarations on something she didn't understand. "What did your grandmother tell you about grown folks' business?"

Becca crossed her skinny arms over her chest and stuck out her little pointed chin in defiance. "It's for grown folks."

"That's right. Get back to me when you're thirty and we'll talk. For now, just worry about this Connor boy and lunchtime chicken nuggets."

She went back to swooning in no time. "He's so cute, Uncle Johnny. And so brave too. Boys don't just walk up to girls and say they want to square dance with them, but Connor did. He's really shy, but he took a chance."

As John slowed down on Sandra's street, he peered down at his niece. She wore a dreamy smile on her face that accurately described "puppy love." She was smitten beyond repair. He hoped that this Connor was worth a damn because he couldn't very well punch a child. He also heard her words. Connor was brave. Connor square dances. Conner took a chance.

"Are you going to the gym?" Becca asked as she gathered her backpack.

"For a little while," he said. "I'll come back by and get you when I'm done." He stopped outside of Sandra's house where his mother's yellow Volkswagen was still parked. "Your grandmas are still making your cookies."

"Oh good." She was about to jump out of the truck

and run up the driveway, but paused to look at him. "Uncle Johnny?"

"Hmm?"

Becca pursed her lips as she examined him. "I could use a hug…how about you?"

John didn't think that trick could be employed on him, but he welcomed it immediately. "Yeah sure," he said, cracking a smile in spite of himself. "I could use one."

Becca caught him across the midsection with her arms and squeezed him tight. With her face pressed against his chest, she murmured, "Be brave."

John hugged her back, placing a quick kiss on her crown. "I'll try that."

Chapter Thirty-Three

Just ten minutes.

It had only taken ten minutes for Victoria to start eye-ing the front door as a means of escape. After setting down her weekend bag and hugging her parents, she was still in the foyer of their Lake View home, getting a tongue lashing from Katherine.

"When did you get these?" her mother demanded, running her fingers through the curtain of Victoria's braids. "And why are there so many…baubles on them?"

Victoria tucked her hair over her other shoulder, away from her mother's prying fingers. "I got them a couple of weeks ago. Reggi did them."

"Regina?" Katherine said with suspicion. "Are you still running with those girls?"

Victoria drew a breath and looked to her father for help. Archie patted her shoulder and gave a shrug be-fore making his escape into the kitchen. Once again, he sniffed out an incoming disagreement between his daughter and wife, and made himself scarce before he was asked for an opinion. Part of her didn't blame him for fading into the background, while the other part of her resented him for not taking her with him. "Yes, ma'am. We're all still *friends*."

Katherine narrowed her cat eyes. "Even Paula? The one who writes that filth?" She blew out a frustrated breath. "Ooh chile, that girl has even infiltrated my circles. Betty Anne actually had the nerve to suggest one of her trashy books for our reading circle. Can you imagine?"

Victoria didn't know who Betty Anne was, but she was grateful the woman had taste and was honest about it. She couldn't wait to tell Paula. "No, I cannot imagine," she said with irony. "How Betty Anne thought she could sneak something past you is beyond me."

"Where's your dress?" Katherine said snapping her fingers. "I need to see it."

"Can I at least sit down and have a drink, Mother?" Victoria only just arrived and now she was being put through her paces. Her mother was more drill instructor than her father ever was. Three hours before the event and Katherine was already in giant hard curlers that pulled her face and scalp tight. In her sixties Katherine Reese was still a beautiful woman with skin the color of burnt honey, full lips that were always painted a respectable mauve, and carefully shaded eyebrows that always appeared accusatory. Victoria stared into the face of her future and felt exhausted already. She didn't know how Katherine had the energy for any of it.

"The dress."

Victoria heaved a teenage sigh and went through her bag for her dress. It was a simple black satin shift with spaghetti straps, that reached her ankles. She had planned to wear her braids in a bun. Simple, black, and easy.

Katherine took one look at it and shook her head. "Absolutely not."

Of course not.

Victoria draped the garment over both her arms and extended it towards her mother. "What on earth is wrong with it?"

"It's too formfitting, Victoria. It's basically a night-gown." She clucked her tongue in disappointment. "What did I say about looking fast?"

She resisted the urge to roll her eyes. "This is not fast."

"And that is exactly why I told you to arrive a couple hours before the ball. I can't have you sashaying in the room giving away the milk when the lawyer wants to buy the cow."

Victoria bit the inside of her cheek as her face warmed. As old as she was, she should have expected this from her mother. "It's the only dress I brought," she said, forcing a calm tone. Hysterics could not be employed right now, she had to speak to her mother like an adult and not the angry teenager she used to be.

"Not to worry," Katherine said with a beaming smile. "I've got something upstairs that will look perfect on you." She moved towards the stairway and stopped. "You're still a size 12, right? It's hard to tell with that ghastly sweatshirt you're wearing."

Victoria stuffed the dress back in her weekend bag and joined her father in the kitchen. "Yes, ma'am," she called over her shoulder.

Archie Reese leaned against the kitchen counter waiting on her with a whiskey in hand. "Drink?" he asked.

"Please." She took it and emptied the glass in one gulp. The liquor stung her throat on its way to her belly.

"She doesn't mean to get at you like that," her father said in a soft voice. "She just worries, is all."

Victoria shot him a sideways glance. "She's been get-ting at me over this and that since I was a kid. That's a long time to be worried and a long time for me to feel hounded."

Archie held out the bottle of Dewers. "Another?"

"You know she'll get angry if we're tipsy before the reception," Victoria said, holding her glass under her father's liberal pour.

"You're pretty good at hiding things, honey," her fa-ther said with a wink. "I think you can manage this one secret too."

She sipped the second one with a little more deco-rum as she leaned against the counter beside her father. "I don't know about that."

"The hiding?"

"I'm getting worse at it lately."

"Might not be such a bad thing," Archie said tak-ing swig. "Is that the reason we haven't seen you since January?"

Victoria set down her glass and faced her father. "Dad, I'm in a pickle," she blurted out.

Archie cocked his head to the side and peered at his daughter. He was still a handsome man in his sixties: deep sienna brown skin, sporting a salt and pepper mus-tache. He kept his hair in the same high and tight style from his military days. He also put his glass down and placed his meaty fists on his hips. "Are you pregnant?" he whispered.

Victoria rolled her eyes. "Oh god, not you too…"

"Oh okay, sorry."

She would be in her forties and they'd still be con-cerned for her virtue. "Mom is trying to set me up with some lawyer and I need you to run interference. Make sure we're not alone for too long, glower at him, remind him that you're a Master Gunnery sharpshooter. Do the things that dads are supposed to do."

Archie's brow knitted at the center. "Is there a reason why I'm doing this?"

"Because you owe me," she hissed in a low voice. "You seem to forget that you're not supposed to be smoking, but I saw you light up outside when I was here in January. If Mom found out about the pack of cigarettes in the planter out back…"

"Okay, okay, I hear you," he said, trying to quiet her. "I'll terrorize the boy."

Light footsteps descended from the staircase as an airy voice rang out, "You two aren't getting drunk before we leave, are you?"

Archie and his daughter looked at each other with secretive grins before tossing back the remainder of their whiskeys. "No!" they called out in unison.

What better way to ensure a daughter meets a mother's high standards? A mother must pick out a ball gown herself. Victoria hadn't picked her own prom dress when she was in high school, so why should this event be any different? In her mother's full-length mirror, she stood erect, because the bodice wouldn't allow even a minor slouch. Victoria was convinced her mother had strapped and laced her into a medieval contraption. Katherine had tucked her breasts deep within the neckline several times before she'd been satisfied there was no trace of cleavage. Victoria just did her best to breathe through the pain of the tight bodice. Her only accessories were a pair of drop pearl earrings and a single strand of pearls at the base of her neck. And of course, she looked fantastic in the gown, the royal blue silk taffeta skirts swishing around her ankles. When her mother finally stepped behind her, gently lifting her chin and pushing her shoulders back, her eyes glittered with unshed tears.

"Oh darling, you look beautiful." Katherine sniffed. "You look like one of those duchesses from the old times."

Victoria caught her mother's eye and smiled. "Thanks, Mom."

"I wish you allowed me to dress you more often," Katherine said, quickly dabbing at her eyes. "Remember how much fun we used to have?"

Victoria paused before answering, remembering a different past that involved her mother shouting *"Archie, she's sweated out her curls!"* Archie would sigh and tell them both to stop sweating the small stuff. "Yes," she said, swallowing the truth.

By the time she sat in the grand ballroom of the Drake Hotel, sweating and unable to breathe, Victoria couldn't wait to make an exit. If she planned it right, she could call for a car right after the ceremony and just before the reception. She glanced at her phone, for the eighth time, and willed someone to rescue her. Her friends had wished her good luck before leaving, but their involvement was minimal as no one wanted to deal with her mother.

She wished John were with her.

Victoria had tried, in vain, to push him out of her mind during her train ride to Chicago. As much as she wanted his company, it was too risky for those worlds to collide. A quick visit with her parents was all she wanted. In and out, no muss no fuss. Had she brought John, it would have been a mess. Victoria was certain of it. Katherine would have made a big deal over his long hair, his tattoos, and the fact that he didn't make as much money as the lawyer. After all, her life was fine before she met him, she didn't forget things and she made her deadlines. She didn't have to depend on anyone to help her finish a task. She needed to return to an orderly existence where things made sense and she was in control. John was an obvious threat to that existence. Victoria should have known he was trouble when he'd first walked into her office.

So why did she stare longingly at her phone, expecting him to call?

She picked up the phone and began typing a message to him. And then she erased it. *No, no, no, just stop.* She set the phone back on the table and heaved a shallow sigh. Out of the corner of her eye, a flash of Katherine's ruby-red skirts came gliding to her table. Her mother wore a bright smile, but her eyes were judgmental.

"Victoria, what are you doing just sitting there?"

"Breathing, ma'am."

"Breathe on your feet and make the rounds with me," Katherine said as she took her by the elbow. She led Victoria to the first clump of partygoers she could spot. Victoria managed to snag a glass of champagne from a passing waiter before being thrown into the group. "Colonel Sheldon, Theresa, you remember my daughter, Victoria. The professor?"

An older man in full evening dress uniform inclined his head at her and smiled beneath a sandy blonde mustache. "Of course we remember Dr. Reese," he said with a chuckle. "I've quarterdecked her on more than one occasion. Fastest pushups I ever saw from a ten-year-old girl."

They all laughed, Katherine the loudest of them all. "Oh, Lionel. Do you realize how much work I had to do to undo all of the rough and tumble?"

They all laughed some more, while Victoria covertly finished her champagne. "Built up her arms didn't it?" the Colonel said as he gripped Victoria's biceps. "You couldn't ask for more out of a Marine daughter."

Victoria smiled sweetly at Colonel Sheldon. She'd been a fan of his since their family was stationed at Quantico. When Archie took her to base, Colonel Sheldon always had candy waiting for her. She just had to win foot races for it. "Thank you, sir."

"How is teaching, sweetie?" his wife Theresa asked. She wore a simple black gown, not too different from what Victoria had picked out for herself. *I bet she's able to breathe.*

"It's going well, ma'am," she said.

"Oh, that's good to hear," Theresa said with a genuine smile. "You've been at the private university, what is it called? Primrose?"

"Pembroke."

"Yes, Pembroke, for how many years? Three or four?"

Victoria was surprised. "Yes, about four years."

"Your mother tells us that you should be up for tenure soon?"

She nodded and glanced at her mother, who beamed at her. Sometimes her mother *did* listen to her. Victoria was surprised yet again. "Yes, that's right."

"We wish you luck, dear," Lionel said with a rough clap on the back.

"Please excuse us," Katherine said, taking her by the elbow again. "There's someone I'd like Victoria to meet."

Before she had time to say a proper goodbye to the

colonel and his wife, she was being whisked away by her mother. Victoria spotted another waiter with a tray of champagne and swiped another flute. Quickly, she tossed that one back and set both glasses on a nearby table. Two champagnes, maybe three, on top of the two whiskeys from home, on an empty stomach… Victoria was playing it fast and loose tonight.

She was definitely light-headed as she was shoved into the next partygoer's face. Gripping her mother's arms, she stood upright and focused her gaze on a man who spoke softly to an older woman, perhaps his mother. "Linda, I'm so glad I found you," Katherine said. "Victoria, this is Linda Cortez and her son, Matthew."

So this was Matthew. The divorced lawyer.

"Victoria." Linda extended her hand. "It's so lovely to finally meet you. Your mother has told me so much."

Victoria shook the woman's hand and offered a tremulous smile. "It's nice to meet you, Linda," she said in a loud voice. It was safe to finally admit that she was on the wrong side of tipsy.

"And this is her son, Matthew," her mother said, directing her attention to the tall man to her left. Matthew was quite handsome, with jet black hair cut like a European footballer and a glistening white smile. He wore a slim fitted black suit with two shirt buttons undone at the collar. She noticed a flash of a small gold cufflink at his wrist when he extended his hand towards her.

"Victoria," he said in a low smooth voice.

She shook his hand without grace. Tight with three rough pumps. Victoria almost jostled the man's arm right out of the socket. "Pleased to meet you," she said.

Matthew, unbothered by her manic handshake, slowed

her pumps and leaned over her hand to lightly kiss the back of her knuckles. "The pleasure is all mine."

Out of the corner of her eye, she could see her mother exchange grins with Linda. The two women were prepared to leave at a moment's notice, Victoria realized. And she would be left with a man who still kissed women's hands.

"Katherine, could you introduce me to the guest of honor? I haven't met him or his wife yet."

"Of course," her mother said, all too thrilled to continue the charade. "Let's leave these two to get acquainted." Before taking her leave, she pulled her daughter close and whispered, "No more champagne."

Victoria couldn't help the grin that spread over her face as her mother shot a departing glare. "Matthew, could you be a dear and get me a drink?"

"Sure," he said, grabbing two glasses from another passing waiter. As he handed her the drink, Katherine's eyes scolded her while Linda pulled her away.

"Thank you," Victoria said between sips.

"So you're a teacher?" he asked, peering over his glass at her.

The way his gazed roved down her body made her uncomfortably chilled. She gave an involuntary shudder and hugged her arms around her middle. "I am."

"What grade?"

"College students," Victoria said, finishing her last drink of the night. It would have to be her last; she was having a difficult time focusing her eyes on Matthew. The dim lights and smooth jazz were about to put her to sleep as she wove on her feet.

His mouth quirked into a feline smile. "That's hot."

Victoria frowned. "Is it?"

"Oh yeah," he said with an appraising nod. "If you were my professor, I would have showed up to class every day."

Gross.

"And what do you do, Matthew?" Victoria needed to steer the conversation anywhere else. She'd learned a long time ago, the best thing you could do at a party was make people talk about their occupations. Good or bad, everyone liked talking about their jobs. Matthew seemed like a man who liked to talk about himself in general.

"I'm in corporate law," he said with a little shrug. "It can get a little rough, but it has its perks. I've got a downtown loft on State Street. It's still mine after the divorce."

She nodded. "That's nice."

Matthew moved closer and whispered, "If you want, I could take you there when this is over."

She shrank away from his proximity and forced a smile. "I have to get up early in the morning."

He arched a perfectly threaded black brow and grinned. "I can have you back before curfew if you'd like."

Gross.

"How gentlemanly of you," she said with a fake laugh. Victoria searched the crowd for her father, who was supposed to rescue her from this creep, but he was nowhere to be found. "So have you had any interesting cases lately?"

"Well, I can't get into it too much." His smiled was dripping with a smug arrogance that made her miss John. *What is John up to tonight? And where in the hell is Dad?* "But you're just a teacher, so I don't think you're gonna blab to the papers."

"Mmh?" She was half listening.

"Some Podunk town, somewhere downstate, is suing one of my clients for negligence. I'm sure we'll settle out of court. I don't expect it to last longer than a few months. Besides, they can't prove that my client's medical device is giving them cancer."

Victoria heard that part. "What?"

He shrugged. "There's no causation that my client's inaction caused them bodily harm…or cancer."

Jesus Christ, who was this maniac Mom set me up with?

"Well, I guess that's good for your client?" Victoria said, searching for the words to disguise her disgust.

"And good for my bottom line. I'm thinking about taking a trip with my bros to Bali after it's over. Have you ever been to Bali in March?"

She shook her head. "I've never been to Bali ever."

"You gotta go right after the winter to score those off-season deals. I've been twice."

Victoria blinked. "I don't really have time for vacations these days."

He laughed. "Really? You guys get the whole summer off. What are you doing with your time?"

"Scholarship and course prep," she said through a clenched jaw. "If I'm lucky, I'm able to attend a couple conferences. I don't think any teacher, k-12 or professor, gets the summer vacation people think we do."

"Easy, tiger," Matthew held his hands up in defense. "People make plenty of assumptions about me too. Have you ever heard of lawyer jokes?"

Victoria, who was officially drunk and now past the point of caring, rolled her eyes and made a face. "I'm sure they make you laugh all the way to the bank."

He shrugged easily. "I am pretty rich."

"Lovely," she replied.

"Let's continue this cross-examination on the dance floor," Matthew said. "I'm also a fantastic dancer."

"Uh…"

Without waiting for her answer, he took her hand and dragged her to the dance floor where the smooth jazz had changed to a light bossa nova. Victoria followed because he was actually helping her to stay upright. Her head spun as he pulled her close to his body. One of his hands held hers aloft while the other rested on the small of her back, dangerously close to her ass.

"I don't think I know this dance," she said, clinging to his shoulder. The room tilted slightly as they swayed around the other dancers.

"Just follow me," he whispered in her ear.

Victoria followed him as best as she could, breathing heavily the whole way. She was certain that it was the tight bodice. The firm wires and plastic inserts not only kept her back straight, but they compressed her lungs, making it difficult to take a full breath. Her face felt hot and her chest strained against her neckline as she gulped for air. She regretted that last drink. The others put her at a comfortable buzz, but the last one shoved her over the line right into Matthew's arms.

"Your mom looks excited," Matthew said as if he were proud of his handiwork. Victoria glanced over her shoulder, seeking out her mother's ruby-red gown, and made herself dizzy in the process. She swiveled back to face Matthew and trained her eyes on the American flag pin on his lapel. She used the pin as an anchor and stared at it while Matthew prattled on.

"Let's try something else," Victoria said to the American flag pin. "What kinds of books do you like to read?"

"Books? I haven't had to read a book since college," he scoffed.

Before she had a chance to voice her disappointment, Matthew did the unthinkable.

He released her back and spun her away from his body.

Before she realized she was being spun like a top, Matthew jerked her arm, sending her spinning back to him. Victoria landed with her back against his chest. With the wind knocked out of her, she gasped, fighting for any last scraps of air. He twirled her around to face him just as the edges of her vision blurred and faded to black. Victoria lost feeling in her lips and fingers as her knees buckled under her weight. Matthew wasn't prepared for her body to crumple in his loose grasp, so when she slipped from his fingers and hit the floor, she hit it with a loud *thunk*.

"Oh shit," was the last thing she heard before darkness enveloped her.

Chapter Thirty-Four

Her father's face, bathed in a soft light, was the first thing Victoria saw when she came to. Her hearing was fuzzy and her vision was still blurred, but she knew it was him. The same concerned expression knitted his brows just as it had when she fell out of a tree as a girl. Soon enough, her vision cleared, revealing she was no longer at the hotel ballroom. She was in her parents' home, in her old bedroom.

"You alright, honey?" Her father was still in his evening dress uniform, metals gleaming in her eyes. He dragged a heavy calloused palm over her forehead, checking her temperature. He puckered his lips as if he didn't like what he felt. "Here, drink some water. You're gonna be dehydrated in the morning."

Victoria slowly rose up on her elbows and looked around her bedroom. "How did we get home?" she croaked. Her mouth felt like it was stuffed with cotton balls.

Archie brought a cup to her lips and tilted it. Water had never tasted so delicious and satisfying in her life. And she hadn't been so publicly drunk since college.

"Oh no, Mom…" she trailed off, remembering her mother's last words; *no more champagne.*

"Shhh," her father said, giving her more water. "Don't worry about that. Your mother is still at the party."

Victoria wiped her mouth and met her father's gaze. "How bad was it? Honestly."

Archie straightened up and placed the water on the nightstand. "Honestly? That boy, Matthew, said you took a dive like the mob had paid you off. Someone nearby, who didn't know you were drunk, said that it was probably your tight dress. Hell, it looked like it was cutting off your circulation. Some young cadet rushed in with a saber to cut it off and all the women screamed. Then Jeffrey volunteered to cut the back of it with the Bowie knife he always keeps on him. Your mother got into a shouting match with him over the cost of the dress, but Robbins won in the end because you were still unconscious."

Victoria cringed, but after a quick check, she noticed that she was still wearing the dress *and* had full lung capacity. She rolled over slightly and felt the back. Her fingers found a jagged cut of fabric along her spine. "Good lord," she murmured.

"So Jeffrey and I flipped you over like the suffocated fish you were, and freed you. I mean that dress was tighter than a tick. As soon as you were able to breathe, you woke up coughing and then you threw up."

Victoria flopped down on her pillow. "Oh no," she moaned.

"At that point, your mother damn near passed out herself. But don't worry, you threw up on Matthew's shoes. He jumped around crying about Italian leather and ran off before anyone could help him. Jeffrey told your mother that this was the best retirement party he'd ever been to and she told him to go to hell. Honestly, he was right. It was pretty entertaining."

Victoria's gaze slid over to his. "Dad..."

"As far as everyone else was concerned, the dress was trying to kill you. No one knows you overdid it on whiskey and bubbly."

She closed her eyes and pinched the bridge of her nose. "I'm never going to hear the end of this," she muttered. "Mom is going to wear me out."

"When are you and your mother going to come to an understanding?" Archie asked, resting his elbows on his knees. "I swear, y'all been at it since the'80s."

Victoria opened her eyes and shot up from the bed. Another wave of nausea hit her as she righted herself. "Oof." After another gulp of water, she pointed an accusatory finger at her father. "*We've* been at it? It's always been a one-sided fight, Dad, and you know it. Absolutely nothing I do is good enough for her. I'm never ladylike enough, I'm not organized enough, I can't find a husband. *She's* been at *me*."

"Okay, okay, then when are you going to assert yourself?" Archie asked. "You wore the dress and you met her idiot blind date; how did that work out for you?"

"Acquiescence saves us from the unnecessary arguments," she said in a stiff voice. "If I battled her on everything, I'd never get anything done."

"Like I said: How's that working out for you?"

Victoria opened her mouth and then snapped it shut. He had her there. In her anxiety, she drank to calm her nerves. To avoid conflict, she wore the dress and got propositioned by a creepy lawyer. Victoria was the one who bore the brunt of her mother's demands, and it rarely worked out in her favor. "I need to get out of this dress," she said.

"Sounds like a plan," Archie said as he rose from his chair. "Your mom ought to be back in an hour or so, would you like me to hold her off?"

"If you can, that would be nice."

As he exited the room, her father paused before closing the door. "Maybe you can come up with a plan of attack for tomorrow morning. You need to tell your mother that you're a grown woman."

From her bed, Victoria nodded. "Sure, Dad."

Chapter Thirty-Five

Just as her father said, Victoria was indeed quite dehydrated the following morning. It was around eight in the morning when she pulled herself out of bed and dragged herself to the bathroom attached to her bedroom. She drank directly from the sink until her belly was full, washed her face, and returned to bed. She would need to gather her strength if she was to go downstairs and confront her mother, who was still probably livid about last night's events.

Victoria went into her weekend bag and pulled out her laptop. No doubt, emails were piling up since she last checked. She decided to send off a few before getting dressed and facing the music like a grown woman. She absently deleted spam, campus-wide maintenance alerts, and events before one message caught her eye. She clicked on it and narrowed her eyes in confusion.

"Friends of the Farmingdale Library, you're cordially invited to the Halloween Masquerade Ball…" she trailed off and squeezed her eyes shut. "Oh, come on."

Another ball.

This time, John would be in attendance.

Victoria dragged her fingers down her face and groaned. She never wanted to go to another ball, gala, or black-tie party as long as she lived. Hadn't her mother already set aside enough parties for her to pass out at? She looked down at the email again. *Monday night?* That was only the day after tomorrow and last she checked, Victoria didn't have a costume for a masquerade ball.

Should she go or should she stay away? Victoria was technically a Friend of the Farmingdale Library; she had the tote bag to prove it. She would have to have the messy conversation with John one day, there was no putting it off for weeks on end. Farmingdale wasn't a large enough town for them to simply avoid one another. A fleeting memory of the short dance she'd shared with Matthew last night told her otherwise. In that moment, when she'd been in another man's arms, she had desperately missed John. Her head tilted back against the headboard with a dull thud. She needed to talk to John, she needed to see him. She had to apologize for her behavior.

Her gaze left the ceiling, where there were no straightforward answers, and landed on the wall near the door. The nearby bookshelf caught her attention. Victoria cocked her head to the side and squinted her eyes. *No, it couldn't be...*

She shoved the computer from her lap and slipped from her bed.

Are you kidding me?

A book sat amongst the literary criticism and theory books that she hadn't touched since her PhD days. A small worn paperback with lines tracing its old spine. As she knelt to examine the shelf, Victoria's hand flew to her mouth.

"G.D. it."

There, in all its glory, sat *For the Duke's Convenience*.

* * *

Fully dressed and ready to go home, Victoria marched downstairs with her weekend bag on her shoulder and a tawdry paperback romance in one hand. Her parents were in the dining room drinking coffee, when she stormed in and announced, "I'm going home."

Archie looked up from his morning paper, reading glasses perched on his nose. Katherine's pursed lips hovered over her coffee mug. She was still dressed in a silk robe and satin bonnet. "Excuse me?" she said, setting down her mug. Archie's chair slid from the table.

"Stay where you are, Dad," Victoria said. "I've got something to say to the both of you."

Her mother gathered her robe to her neck in disdain. "Archie, you better tell your daughter to watch her tone."

"Aw hell, Katherine, she's your daughter too," her father said, taking off his reading glasses. "What is it, Victoria?"

"You see this book, right here?" She waved *For the Duke's Convenience* in their faces. "This book is emblematic of how much of an idiot I am. This book proves what kind of stick-in-the-mud, prudish tight-ass I've been all these years. There's a man, a beautiful librarian, in my town, who has been hounding me for the last couple weeks over this book. I was so hardheaded and stuck in my ways that I convinced myself I couldn't make a mistake. But in reality, I don't return library books on time because I'm a normal person who's allowed to fuck up."

Her mother gasped and her father cleared his throat. "Young lady—" Katherine started.

"No ma'am, that's part of the problem. I'm not a young lady anymore." Victoria glanced at her father who gave her a slight nod. "I'm a grown-ass woman who is allowed to think for herself. And for the first time in thirty-four years, I'm finally understanding that. John Donovan is back in Farmingdale waiting on me to commit to a relationship and I couldn't because I was worried about you and your demands."

"Who the hell is John Donovan?" her mother asked.

"The beautiful librarian," Archie said.

"I was so worried about being perfect for everyone, in every situation, that I managed to drive off the one man who likes me when I've got him in a sweaty arm bar. I could have brought him here to meet you, but I was worried about what you'd think of him. Moreover, I worried about what you'd do to him," Victoria said, pointing at her mother. "If I couldn't stand up to you, I didn't want to subject anyone else to you."

Her mother's eyes watered up with alarming convenience as she turned to her husband. "Am I that terrible of a mother?" she asked. "Have I not done everything I could to ensure she was a successful woman?"

Her father chose not to answer. Instead, he placed his hand over hers and turned to Victoria. "Continue."

Victoria took a deep breath, and with a clear head, she addressed them both. "I love you both very much, but there is a reason why I haven't seen you in ten months. I can't be myself around you and that has to change if we're to have a real relationship. Mom, you have to stop dictating how I dress, how I stand, and who I date. It's got to stop. No more tight ball gowns, no more divorced lawyers." Victoria finished her tirade by kissing them both on the cheek.

"So, you're not coming to brunch?" her mother asked, stunned by her lecture.

"Absolutely not," she said, hitching her bag on her shoulder. "I've got 48 hours to get my librarian back."

"Go get 'em, baby," Archie said with a fist pump.

"Thanks, Dad."

"Archie, are you really going to let this girl leave here—"

"Katherine, let it go. She's got her own life and she's got to try living it." Her father picked up his paper and flipped the page. "Didn't you hear her? She's got a beautiful librarian to catch."

Her mother was a gaping fish. For the first time, in her own household, no less, no one sided with her in a dispute. She looked from child to husband, puzzled by the idea that she'd lost an argument. "I don't know what to say."

"We can talk about it when I get home," Victoria said, taking her mother's hand. "Just know that I love you no matter what, but you've got to stop running my life. Some of your decisions led me to vomiting at a retirement party." She gave a tender squeeze before releasing her mother's hand.

"Be careful getting home, baby," Archie said with a wave.

"Will do, Dad. I'll see you guys later."

Chapter Thirty-Six

"You should be Spider-Man," Becca said, pointing to the panel on the wall. She slung the bag with her Wonder Woman costume over her shoulder as she perused the adult costumes with keen interest. "We can be superheroes together."

Something about the spandex bodysuit didn't necessarily appeal to John. Chris, who stood beside him, must have read his mind and shook his head. "Nope."

"I don't think I'll feel comfortable," John said.

"But Spider-Man is the best," she argued.

If it wasn't for Becca and the Friends of the Farmingdale Public Library Halloween party, John wouldn't spend a Sunday in a crowded party store looking for last minute costumes. Unfortunately, Director Wegman required every library worker's participation, in full costume, to celebrate the community, the board of directors, and patrons. Becca just loved Halloween. Chris had come along to offer assistance, but John knew he was just curious about the latest gossip concerning Victoria.

He didn't have much to spill. It had been two full days since he'd last spoken to her.

"Why don't we go with a literary theme and do Sherlock Holmes," Chris suggested. "They've got the hats over here."

John shook his head. "No."

"How about Captain Ahab? We could wrap cardboard around your leg."

"How about Zorro?" Becca asked. "Since you have to wear a mask?"

John paused to think. "That's a possibility."

Chris sidled up beside him and asked in a low voice, "Will Dr. Reese be there?"

He sucked in a breath and ignored his friend. "Becca picked the perfect costume. I'll go with Zorro and it can double as that guy from *Princess Bride*."

"What's *Princess Bride*?" Becca asked, grabbing a cape and sword.

"She's obsessed with Alanis Morissette, but Jessi never taught her about *Princess Bride*?"

"Another reminder that we're getting old," John muttered.

"So what about it, man?" Chris tried again. "Is she going to be there or what?"

"I don't know," John growled under his breath. "I haven't spoken to her."

"So that's it? You're just going to let her get away?"

What he couldn't get his friend or his family to understand was that it wasn't up to him. At the end of the day, Victoria had the last word. As much as he wanted her, needed her, in his bed and by his side, she had to make up her mind. He had the patience of Job when it came to the ornery children in his department and he had tried to extend that same patience to the woman he desired. Victoria had shit to work on. She had to come to grips with her obsessive need to control everything in her life. In the meantime, he just had to wait. It didn't mean he was especially lovely to be around, but those were the facts. He was going to be a surly asshole until he knew that path was completely closed off. He just wished Chris would stop hassling him about it.

"Just so you know," Chris said in his ear. "You look like a mess. You look like you haven't slept in days."

He looked that way because he *hadn't* slept in days. "That's accurate," he said. John took the elements of his Zorro costume from Becca and let her explore the rest of the Halloween store. "You think this comes with a holster thing for the sword? Is that what they call it?"

"Man, who gives a fuck about the costume?" his friend whispered. "The love of your life is just floating out there waiting for you to pull her to shore."

"That's a little dramatic, don't you think?" Even as John said the words, he knew Chris was right about this too. He was lonely and hurting. If anything, Victoria was his lifeline and *he* needed to be pulled to shore.

"I saw you two at the gym; I know there's something between you," Chris said while playing with some toy guns. "I'm a little weirded out that you're just bopping along like it's not a big deal. Like you don't have something to lose."

John heaved a tired sigh. "I don't know what to tell you, Chris."

"Look, if I had that woman clutched between my thighs in a sweaty rear naked choke, I wouldn't let her go so easy."

John clenched his hands around his costume bag. "Chris…"

"If I had a sex arrangement with that woman, you know I'd keep every single appointment," his friend continued, moving on to the fake handcuffs. "Were you supposed to be with her today? Your place or hers?"

John sucked his teeth and stepped to Chris's face. "Shut. Up."

Chris raised a brow as he turned towards John. "Am I making you mad?"

"Say another thing about my girlfriend and I'll fuck you up," John said with a menacing growl meant only for Chris to hear. "I don't care if you're my oldest, dearest friend, I will rip you apart if you mention a sweaty Victoria ever again."

Chris didn't move away. Instead, he edged closer to John. "There's the energy I needed to see."

John blinked in confusion. "What?"

"You're walking around here pretending she didn't rip your heart out and stomp all over it, when I know damn well you're a fucking mess. You thought you could hide that from me?"

John backed up. He couldn't believe he'd been about to come to blows with his best friend in a party store. "I'm sorry," he muttered. "I didn't mean…"

"You said exactly what you meant," Chris said, leaning against a police officer costume stand. "You told me that she was your girlfriend and that you'd rip me apart for her. Simple as that."

John's shoulders slumped in resignation. He did just say that. In fact, he growled it. "I don't know what to do."

Chris clapped him on the back. "First step is admitting what you feel for her. It's not a situationship anymore. You love her. You have to tell her."

This was the third person to tell him the obvious. He was in love with Victoria and pride prevented him from saying so. "I don't know if she's going to show up at the party," he said.

"Fuck the party. You have to say something."

John looked down at his Zorro costume and frowned. Now or never was coming at him fast. If he was prepared to call Victoria his girlfriend, he had to make himself take other chances. John had to risk his dignity and go all in.

"We call this emergency meeting of The Write Bitches to settle the matter of Victoria's hot librarian," Regina said, holding a glass of wine aloft.

Paula was nearby, with her own wine glass, busily sifting through Halloween costumes. "Yes, yes, let's come to order."

For her part, Victoria had skipped the wine after her embarrassingly boozy weekend. She was searching through the Halloween costumes that Regina and Paula had been kind enough to bring to her home. There were feather boas, tiaras, and costume jewelry, some of which were from Regina's bachelorette party several years ago. "Whose are these?" she asked as she picked up a pair of real handcuffs.

Paula raised her hand. "The key is around here somewhere in a small baggie."

"What have you used them for?"

Her friend stopped her search to give her a look. "Really?"

"Gotcha," Victoria said, giving them another glance before tossing them back in the pile.

"Girl, you haven't lived until you've locked a guy up," Paula said with a giggle. "And then pretend you've lost the key afterwards. Oh, how they squirm."

"I'm not looking to lock John up," she said. "I just need to apologize to him."

"You need to do more than that," Regina said. "You left him without an answer to the biggest question: Do you want more?"

Victoria was aware of that. After her trip home, she'd made up her mind that she wanted John. She needed to know that she hadn't ruined everything with her neurosis, that he wasn't completely fed up with her indecision. She wanted to date John, and she wanted to do it with spontaneity. Before she could do any of that, an apology was in order. Victoria knew he'd be there to greet the "friends of the library," but she wanted to do it with a bit of flourish. She had hoped he might appreciate the extra step after her erratic behavior. Plus, she needed to return *For the Duke's Convenience* and pay the $30 fine she owed. She would have done it that day, but it was Sunday and they were closed. Monday night's party had to work.

"So what really happened at the military ball? Is it as bad as you described in your text?" Regina asked.

"Possibly worse," Victoria said. "But I managed to tell my mother the truth."

Her friends went quiet.

"I did," she insisted. "I told her that her days of ordering me around were over. I didn't go to the previously scheduled brunch and came home. My dad actually backed me up for once."

Regina glanced at Paula before speaking. "You told *Katherine Reese* off?"

Victoria nodded. "I did. And it felt great."

"And she took this…well?" Paula asked.

"I don't know how she took it," Victoria said. "The

point is, she took it. And now I'm ready to approach John like an adult. You guys were right; I can't keep treating relationships like a checklist. I have to take risks instead."

Paula nodded with appreciation. "Okay."

"Sounds good to me," Regina intoned. "So what are you going to wear to this party?"

Victoria looked at the assortment of costume pieces sprawled on her couch. Her eyes settled on a simple black eye mask. "I think I have an idea," she said as a smile stretched over her face. It was the first genuine smile she'd made in days.

"Yeah?" Paula said, finishing off her first glass of wine. "You're going with the handcuffs?"

"No, but you're not too far off the mark."

Chapter Thirty-Seven

It was difficult to steady her breathing as she pulled up to the library's crowded parking lot on Monday evening. Victoria sat in her car for a while, thinking of what words to say if she saw John. The paperback novel sat in her passenger's seat, a loud reminder of what she could have if only she just asked. Tonight she would ask, plead if she needed to. Victoria took a deep breath and adjusted the mask over her eyes. She tugged the black knitted cap over her head and tossed her braids over her shoulder.

"Good enough," she said to her reflection before leaving the safety of her car.

She scampered across the parking lot and paused before the entrance of the library. This was it, no turning back. Victoria took another breath, clutched the book to her chest and entered the building.

Inside, the party was already underway. Masked individuals passed by her as she crossed the threshold, making their way to a punch bowl. "The Monster Mash" blared throughout the building and the lights were dimmed. Farmingdale Public Library didn't resemble the same library she'd visited while shadowing John. It almost felt like a nightclub.

Victoria made a beeline for the checkout counter

where someone was actually working. Martha sat behind the counter wearing a Little Red Riding Hood costume and a red eye mask.

Victoria slid the book on the counter and shouted, "I need to return this book."

"No need to shout, dear," the woman said. "My hearing aid is back in business."

"Oh."

Martha opened the front cover of her book, scanned the barcode, and set it on the cart behind her. And then she went back to the novel she was reading.

"Excuse me," Victoria said. "I need to pay the fine."

Martha looked up. "What's that?"

"I need to pay the fine," Victoria shouted.

The older woman glanced at the computer and shook her head. "No, you don't."

Victoria gripped the counter, leaning forward to take a look at the computer. "But I do, it's been overdue for months."

The older Red Riding Hood swiveled the computer monitor to her. "No, you don't," she repeated. "There aren't any fines here."

Confused, Victoria looked through her account page. "What?"

"There's a note though," said Martha. She took a closer look at the screen. "Mmh. It looks like Mr. John Donovan left a message."

Victoria's scanned the message for herself and her heart bloomed. "Dr. Reese, is exempt from her fine as a token of my unwavering appreciation. She is not only a friend of the Farmingdale Public Library, but the love of my life."

"He shouldn't be leaving messages like that." Martha

made a *tsk* sound as she swiveled the screen back to her side. "It's not very professional."

It took everything Victoria had inside of her not to crumple into ugly tears.

The love of my life.

"Where is he?" she asked. "I have to find him."

Martha waved her hand over the crowded bottom floor. "John's around here somewhere," she said. "Good luck finding him in all these masks."

Victoria spun around and searched through the partygoers and their masks for a familiar body. Her heart pounded in her chest at the prospect of being close to him but not picking him out in a crowd. He could be anywhere.

Chapter Thirty-Eight

She came back to him.

John saw her as he descended the stairs from the Children's Department. It had to be her. Her braids swung from a black knitted cap, still adorned with the same gold cuffs and cowry shells. Victoria wore a black and white horizontally striped shirt and black pants. A simple black mask covered her eyes, but he recognized the bottom portion of her face right away. He remembered those lips, the curve of her neck, the slope of her shoulders, the flair of her hips.

She was dressed as a thief.

John would have laughed if his heart didn't ache from the very sight of her. As he ran down the stairs, he could tell she was looking for him. Behind her mask, she searched the melee for a sign of him. At the foot of the stairwell, he pushed back the edge of his cape and walked towards her, but there were too many people in his way. Before he could reach her, she left the checkout counter where Martha sat reading.

"Victoria," he called out.

She didn't hear him.

Slowly pushing herself through the crush of people,

Victoria made her way behind the checkout desk, towards his office. He blew out a sigh of relief as he followed her.

Something was different about his office. As Victoria closed the door behind her and surveyed her surroundings, the abrupt change made her smile.

John's desk was spotless.

Gone were the empty coffee cups and random stacks of loose paper. All that was left were framed photos, his computer, and a brand new desk calendar. Perhaps the desk calendar had always been there, but the mass of trash hid it. She slowly approached the desk, hesitant to disturb the perfection. A soft chuckle escaped her chest as she took it all in. He made an effort to keep some order in his life.

Rather than wade through a suffocating crowd to search for John, she had escaped to the comfort and safety of his office. Or the scene of the crime. As she ran her fingers along the newly cleaned desk surface, she remembered how frightened and desperate she must have sounded the last time she was here. His questions and probing had been harmless, yet she evaded him so messily. Victoria closed her eyes, remembering the pulse of energy surrounding him as he'd approached her for a kiss. He had wanted to take her in his arms and she had pushed him away.

"Here to turn yourself in," said a low voice from behind her.

Her head jerked up and her hand recoiled from his desk. Victoria slowly turned around and beheld a sight that was even more alarming than a clean desk.

Zorro stood at the threshold.

Her jaw fell open as she let her gaze wander over him. John's lean figure was dressed in all black, from his riding boots to the loose-fitting shirt that opened at the collar to reveal a deep V of tanned skin and sandy chest hair. His black cape fell to the side to reveal a saber and whip hanging from his belt. His face was impassive and stony as he stared at her from under the wide-brimmed hat.

Victoria felt like she'd pass out at yet another party. This time it would be from the sheer masculine beauty of a masked avenger. She groped for the desk behind her to steady herself. She wanted him to cross the room in three easy strides and crush her with a passionate kiss until she forgot her original purpose for visiting.

Instead, John stepped forward only to close the door behind him. He stood against it and, from the safety of his black mask, waited with the same placid expression, his gloved hands folded across his chest. Victoria didn't feel safe behind her mask.

"Hello, John," she breathed.

"Professor Reese."

Emotionless and straightforward. She'd asked for it. "I made a mistake."

The corner of his mouth quirked as his jaw tightened, but he made no reply.

Victoria was forced to continue. "I had the book all along."

John inclined his head a fraction. "I told you as much."

"It was at my parents' house," she said with a nervous laugh. "I forgot that I took it with me on my last visit and I must have left it on the nightstand. I think my mom must have put it on the shelf when she cleaned the room."

He nodded.

The gulf between them now seemed like an actual barrier. It was a test. If she was adult enough, she would cross the chasm and apologize to him. But she held back, expecting him to say or do something. Anything. "And now I'm dressed like a thief because it's appropriate," she said, gesturing to her costume. "I'm also a fool. And I'm sorry."

His Adam's apple bobbed in his throat.

"I'm sorry for not giving you credit," Victoria tried. "I projected my insecurities onto you while making these weird demands. I hid behind my fear because…"

"Because our relationship wasn't a haunted house," he finished. "And taking the risk with me was too real."

Ashamed, she ducked her head. He was right. The thrill of a haunted house was easy to walk through if it meant you could return to normal life. But for Victoria, normal life was dull and packed with rigid routine. There was no risk, no adventure, and more importantly, no way to get hurt. No, that wasn't true. It was painful enough to stand in the same room as John and not be able to touch him.

"I find it scarier to be apart from you," she admitted. "I'm unable to think of anything else when I'm not with you." Her breath came out in a shallow burst of air. "I'm lost without you."

He shifted his weight against the door, loosening his arms, just slightly, as his lips made a thin line. Victoria pulled herself away from the desk and ventured towards him. She kept her back straight and her voice steady as she approached him. "Last night, before I went to sleep, I told myself I would stop living a coward's life. That I would stand up for what I believed in. I believe in you and me, John."

John's breathing changed.

Standing toe to toe with him, Victoria fought the urge to reach out and grab him. She needed to say her piece before she accidentally forced herself on him. "And I don't think I've thanked you for believing in me when I've been busy trying to sabotage myself," she said, glancing at his bearded face. Beneath it, she could see his jaw clench as if he were struggling with his own self-control.

He gave an imperceptible shake of his head and cleared his throat. "No," he said.

"You told me that no man was in control of my destiny." Victoria reached out and laid her hand on the center of his chest, fanning her fingers out against his warm skin. His heart was pounding. "I don't think that's true. I think, in many ways, you're probably the key to my destiny."

Despite his unflappable demeanor, John's breath hitched. Victoria flushed under her mask and she hoped that wasn't the most embarrassing thing she'd ever told a man. Doubt made her withdraw from his chest, but John swiftly caught her by the wrist. His gloved fingers pressed hers back to his heart. "Do you mean that, Victoria? Do you really believe it?" His voice was a hoarse whisper that caused her knees to buckle.

Victoria's mouth fell open, unable to fathom her luck. His hands were on hers, he still wanted to listen to her. They were still connected by an invisible string, tugging them closer by the second. "Yes, I do."

"Tell me, Victoria," he said. "Meet me halfway."

She wanted him. All of him. This was another test,

another part of the courage she had to screw to the sticking place. *Just say what you want and he will give it to you.* He'd made that promise from the start. "I love you," she said in a hurried breath.

His grip tightened.

"I love you more than I can even articulate."

"Try," he ground out.

Victoria gave a shaky nod and swallowed. They stood so close now, connected by their hands. She wanted to fall into his chest and bury her face against the V of his shirt. Against the patch of skin revealed through the fabric. "John, I've been a professor for nearly a decade, but when I'm with you… I realize I have so much to relearn about life. Your mind is so much more open and inviting than mine. Your heart is full of kindness and patience. I love you, completely and without conditions."

There. She'd spilled her guts. Victoria didn't feel quite as nervous after telling the truth. As she stared into John's partially hidden face, she wanted to share all her secrets.

If she was going to make a habit of taking chances, Victoria decided to risk it and push her all of her chips to the center of the table. She stood on her toes, and went in for a kiss that she desperately needed. But John stopped her, just a short distance from his face, and he held her still by the shoulders. "No," he said in a firm voice.

Chapter Thirty-Nine

John knew what he was prepared to do and it killed him to stop her. Flush against his body, her curves threatened to sink against his hardness. It had taken everything in his being not to laugh when she'd admitted to having the book. *For the Duke's Convenience* was the least of his worries. But John had still wanted more. He wanted her to meet him halfway.

And she had. With the words: *I love you.*

As he held her still, merely an inch or so from his face, he tried and failed to not stare at her lips. They were full and inviting, made for kissing and sucking, the bottom one pouted in disappointment. The simple action ripped at John's heart just as it caused his blood to flow swiftly to his cock. His thin leggings were no match for what was straining at his waist. But instead of pulling her hips to meet his, he held firm to his principles.

"Take off your mask," he said.

Victoria lowered herself back onto her heels, her hands fell away from his chest. She watched him warily, her tongue darting out to nervously lick her bottom lip. John stifled the groan traveling up his throat. She reached up, slid her eye mask over her ski cap, and let it flutter to the floor. When her eyes met his, they were swimming in tears. Her face and neck reddened under his gaze, but her eyes were unwavering.

With her soul truly bared to him, Victoria was the most beautiful woman he'd laid eyes on. Contrition was etched on her face as her chest rose and fell in short panicked bursts. She'd done something more terrifying than touring McLean's Haunted Warehouse: she'd admitted she was wrong. The hardheaded woman had told him that she loved him. His mind, his heart, and John was fairly certain, his body was included in the package. John wrapped an arm around her waist and brought her close. A soft gasp escaped her lips as she fell against his chest. She felt what was throbbing just below his waist and shifted slightly, instinctively rocking her hips against his strained cock. "Jesus," he hissed, pressing his hand to the small of her back.

"Can I kiss you now?" she whispered.

His voice caught in his throat when she blinked. A single tear fell from the corner of her eye, towards her temple. Her face was upturned and so very close to his, waiting on him to say something. "That depends," he said sternly.

"Tell me," she breathed.

"If this is going to work between us, and god knows I want it to, I have rules."

She reached up and wiped her tear away. "I like rules," she said with a nod.

It took everything in him not to smile at her candor. "Be honest with me, tell me what's on your mind. Stop hiding away behind some day-planning armor."

"Okay."

"Stop pretending to be someone you're not for everyone you meet. You can be a rhetorician, but quit losing yourself in all of these roles."

She took a deep breath before replying. "Okay."

"Can you come up with a plan for working on that?"

A smile tugged at her lips. "I can actually do that."

While holding her, John felt proud of both of them. For the first time, they were truly honest with one another. The heaviness in his heart slowly disappeared, leaving him relieved and excited for this second chance. "Now, would you still like that kiss?"

She answered by pressing forward.

There was electricity in Victoria's lips as they made contact with his. The jolt stunned him and traveled throughout his body, from his arms and to the tips of his fingers. Her mouth shook him to his core so violently, he opened his eyes to make certain it was only a human woman kissing him. A human woman with a pagan goddess's tongue to be sure. John let his eyes fall shut as she eased her tongue through the barrier of his lips. She gripped his shoulders, then his neck, and finally the sides of his face, as she pulled him down to meet her. While connected, he whipped off his hat and flung it somewhere in the office before dragging his mask from his eyes.

"I'm so sorry, John," she whispered in between kisses. "I'm so sorry I hurt you."

He didn't ignore the admission, but he wasn't interested in replying. His tongue was busy battling hers, sparring and sliding against her in a feverish attempt to possess her. He devoured her like a man on his death bed. As if she were the last drink of water in the desert. Her lips were soft against his, pliant and lush, and the more she gave, the more he took. Her hands slipped behind his head, fingers raking through his ponytail. Electricity gathered in his scalp, traveled through his neck to his chest. Soft moans vibrated against his lips as she pulled him near.

John's hands traveled their own electric path. One stayed planted on her ass, squeezing and kneading her soft flesh, pushing her against his erection. The other swept up her torso and landed on her breast. He squeezed the full globe and cursed his gloved hands. He needed to feel all of her.

In frustration, he broke away from her lips and finally inhaled. With his teeth, he wrenched off his leather gloves and cast them to the floor with his discarded mask. "Victoria, I need to…"

Her eyes seemed to understand his strangled request. "Now?"

"Please."

She nodded and made quick work of undoing her belt. "Right."

"I mean, if it's okay with you," he said, watching her trembling fingers work.

"It's absolutely fine with me," she said with a chuckle.

John locked the door behind him. "I missed you so much." He came back to her and slipped the ski-cap from her head, tossing it to the floor. "I couldn't stop thinking about you."

As he reached up to remove his cape, Victoria's hand caught his. "No," she said, licking her lips. "Leave it on. Leave all of it on."

This time, he couldn't hold back the groan in his throat. Fun Victoria had come out to play. "Does it do something for you?" he asked, slowly backing her into the desk behind him. Their eyes locked as she moved backwards, her hands undoing her zipper.

"I don't know what you're supposed to be, but I like it," she said.

"I'm Zorro, I think." They stopped when the backs of her thighs hit his desk. Thank god, he'd cleared it off. "Or that guy from *The Princess Bride*."

"You look like a dangerous highwayman," she whispered, shoving her black jeans down. "Who's about to rob me of my valuables and virtue."

"Exactly," he said, leaning over to pull her legs out of her pants. "I like where this is going." On his knees, he hooked his thumbs through the waistband of her panties and pulled them to her ankles. When she stepped out of them and leaned against his desk, Victoria parted her legs, opening herself to him.

He could have lost it then and there.

John drew himself back to his feet and stared at the sexy women sitting on his desk. She was naked from the waist down, suggestively pushing her thighs apart, then closed. "You have something that I want, m'lady," he said, removing the belt holding his saber and whip. He reached into his pants and pulled out his straining cock.

With sultry hooded eyes, Victoria leaned back on her elbows. "Give me your worst, you dastardly blackguard."

John grinned as he moved between her thighs, pushing them apart with strong hands. "I don't remember that in the book," he said, giving her soft opening a teasing brush with his cock. Already slick with arousal and hot to the touch, he rocked his length against her clit.

Victoria hissed and squeezed her eyes shut. "I don't know where I read that," she panted, raising her hips to connect with him.

"Can you stay quiet, Victoria?" John asked, licking his thumb. Once he pressed it to her swollen core, she jerked and let out a long, deep sigh. As he moved his thumb in circles over her clit, he noted the movement of her hips as they kept time with his pace. A lovely deep red settled over her brown cheeks as her mouth fell open.

"Maybe," she breathed.

"Maybe?" He applied pressure as he leaned forward and cupped the back of her head with his free hand. He didn't want her to miss this show; their union.

"Yes," she said, though it may not have been a reply to his question. Her affirmative could have been something altogether different because it played on repeat the more he circled her sensitive flesh. "Yes, yes, oh god, yes, Johnny," became her new mantra and she recited it with a feverish whisper as her face contorted into an agonized expression.

Her Zorro, her Westley, her highwayman, assaulted her senses and made her see stars. Just with the touch of his thumb. When Victoria caught her breath and opened her eyes, she came face to face with her lover, John Donovan. His green eyes glittered above hers, growing darker with hunger. She had remained as quiet as she could, but he hadn't even gotten to the main event. Victoria was losing grip on propriety and damned glad for it.

John was waiting on her.

"Please," she whispered. "Now."

It was all he needed to hear. Planting one hand at her side, he leaned forward and pushed the tip of his penis past her folds. As he stretched and filled her with an achingly slow patience, hot tears pricked her eyes. She gasped at his pleasant intrusion and pushed against him in response.

"No, honey," he said, holding her hips still. "Let me go slow."

Victoria's gaze flitted to his pleading eyes, his flared nostrils, and relished in the pleasure she offered him. His hips moved in a slow and steady rhythm, rocking her gently against the hard surface of his desk. He whipped his cape back and wrapped her legs around his waist.

"I want to commit this to memory for as long as I live," he whispered, leaning down to run his hand under her shirt. When he found her breast, he fanned his long dexterous fingers over the smooth satin of her bra. Her nipple stood at attention, begging for more stimulation. "When you're not with me, I want to remember your soft skin, your beautiful curves, this wet heat surrounding my cock. Every fucking inch of you, Victoria."

She raised herself on her elbows to give him easier access to her breasts, and was thankful when he pulled down the cup of her bra to pinch her nipple. A low hungry moan forced its way up her chest and spilled past her lips. Her frenzied breath could not be controlled as John moved in and out of her. She wished she could say that the smacks of skin and muscle were the only sounds that filled John's office, but her pants of arousal joined the cacophony. Soon, his moans accompanied hers, keeping rhythm with the union of their bodies.

He pulled his hand away from her breast and clutched her hip, pulling her onto his cock with more force. "Faster," Victoria panted. "Don't stop." Heat climbed her neck as he drove into her. *All I have to do is ask for it.* John sped up the pace, cords stretching along his neck as he gripped her hips tighter. In her position, all she could do was let him control the rhythm. God knew her back would be sore from this desk. A deep throb mounted within her womb, pulsating throughout her body as she took John to the hilt. She clenched around him, pulling him in close with her legs. The deep throb soon turned into an arousing pressure, threatening to unfurl and set fire to her entire body. Victoria, on the verge of tears, reached down between their joined bodies and touched herself to release the building tension.

John's eyes followed her hand and watched as she caressed herself, plucking at the string that was holding the last of her sanity together. "Yes, baby," he groaned through clenched jaws.

Her pants turned into breathless moans with every slam of John's hips. Victoria's fingers worked her clit in small circles. "Yes, yes, oh god please..." The prayer died on her lips as her walls spasmed around him. Her back arched away from the desk as a keening wail escaped her. Grabbing a fistful of his shirt, she pulled John closer to her and rode the wave of pleasure that swept over her body until it left her thighs shuddering against his hips.

Without the strength to carry on, Victoria went limp in his embrace, breathing through the last electric currents of her second orgasm of the night. *Second? Jesus...* John took her exhausted legs, skillfully ducked under one, and crossed her ankles over his shoulder near his neck. With her legs pinned together, the friction intensified, as his free hand wrapped around her thighs. "My love," he muttered punctuating every thrust. "You are mine."

He was near the end of his own fraying rope. When he muttered an unintelligible curse under his breath,

Victoria finally opened her eyes to see him pull out of her. With an unexpectedly elegant sweep of his cape, he came on the black screen of fabric. His face flushed bright scarlet, from his nose to the tips of his ears, as he doubled over and emptied himself. "Goddamn," he growled with a ferocity she'd never heard before.

Pulling her tired body to a sitting position, Victoria became aroused all over again at the sight of him losing all control. She did that to him. "Well, you can't wear that anymore," she breathed.

He glanced up with brows knitted at the middle. A broad smile spread over his face as he straightened up. "No, I can't," he exhaled his laugh. He quickly adjusted himself behind the cape before unhooking it from his neck and tossing it onto a nearby chair. "Should I send your coach on its way, m'lady?"

"You can hand me my underwear," Victoria said as she primly crossed her legs.

John swooped low to grab her discarded panties from the floor. "No, madam, these are mine. Valuables and virtue, remember?"

"You *are* a dastardly blackguard."

He raised his arms as he approached her. "I am," he said, stopping right before her.

Victoria peered at him from under her lashes, suddenly bashful by their current state. "Did you mean what you wrote on my library account? That I'm the love of your life?" The words fell from her tongue before she could think them through. There was nothing like post-coital honesty.

She feared that it was a mistake to mention, but John planted his hands on both sides of her legs and leaned over her. He pressed his brow to hers and closed his eyes. "Of course I meant it,"

Victoria pulled away to search his face. "When did you wipe my record?"

John leaned closer and nuzzled her neck, his beard tickling her throat, making her nipples harden again. His promise to pay attention to every inch of her body was a serious one. "I did it the day you met my mothers." His lips dragged over her pulse, sucking the warm spot before leaving it for her earlobe.

She could barely think with his teeth gently tugging at the sensitive flesh, his hot breath fanning her face. "You did that..."

"I called you 'my love' on accident and then subjected you to Maggie and Sandy," he said, running his tongue along the curve of her ear. "Clearing your account was only fair, but I didn't add the note until this morning. I love you, Victoria."

Victoria angled her face to meet his. "After what I did?"

"My love, I would give you unlimited rental privileges if it meant you came back to me."

Chapter Forty

John meant every word. He searched her face to see if she understood that. Tears stood bright in her wide eyes, threatening to spill with a single blink. Victoria cradled his face in her hands and stared at him. "John," she whispered.

"I should have told you the last time we were together," he said, cupping her face in his hands. "Next time I won't wait."

Upon hearing that, Victoria crumbled into a quiet sob. She hung on to his face as she dipped her own, desperate to hide her tears from him.

"No, no, don't cry," he said, hooking a finger around her chin. "Baby, you don't have to—"

"I love you too," she said with a sniffle. "I love you, John Donovan."

Why the hell is she sobbing? John grinned and kissed her lips. "Say it again."

Tears flowed as she hiccuped. "I love you, John—"

He covered her mouth with a crushing kiss before she could finish her sentence. He laughed against her mouth and held her close. Her breasts pressed against his chest and her arms wrapped around his neck. As he dragged his lips away to brush his thumb against her tear stained cheeks. "Do you want your pants?" he asked.

Victoria wiped her eyes and laughed. "Yes please."

"You can't have your panties," he said, moving away from her and placing the garment in a desk drawer. "They belong with your other pair."

As she shoved her legs through her pants, she shot him a puzzled expression. "Other pair?"

"The pair I nicked from you at your office."

"I'm not giving you any more until you start paying for them. Undergarments are not infinite." She adjusted her clothes and pulled her knit cap back on her head.

"I know," he said, reaching for her mask on the floor. "That's why I keep taking them." She eyed her mask warily as he extended it towards her. "Would you like this?"

Victoria bit back a smile and shook her head. "No, no masks tonight."

All of their joking aside, he was relieved to hear her say that. Victoria was ready to participate in a real relationship with him and it made his heart swell with excitement. No more schedules, no more professional pretenses.

He was now her boyfriend, Johnny.

"Could you please put your hat back on?" she asked in a sweet voice. "I really like the whole ensemble."

John retightened his low ponytail and covered his head with the wide-brimmed hat. "M'lady." He offered his arm.

"Should we mingle?" Victoria asked as she took his rock-hard biceps in her hand.

"I'm under strict orders to party," he said, leading her from his office. "From the boss man himself."

"I can't believe Mr. Wegman would throw a party like this," Victoria said, lifting her voice above the blare of *Thriller*. "This is the first time you guys are doing this, right?"

John held her tight against his side as they maneuvered through partygoers. "It is, but sometimes the old man gets an idea in his head and tackles it with tunnel vision." He peered down at her. "Much like someone else I know."

Her head snapped up. "Sometimes tunnel vision is good," she said with a smile. "It brought me here."

God, she was so adorable when she allowed herself to relax. John wanted to tweak her upturned nose and kiss her forehead, but a sight caught the corner of his eye that made him cautious. "If you want to talk to the man yourself, you can," he said, pointing to the elderly Sherlock Holmes near the refreshments table. He was in deep conversation with a woman dressed as a standard black cat.

"Sure," Victoria said, squeezing his arm. "I've never met him."

He loved that little squeeze, how her breast pressed against his muscles and her fingers gripped him. It was difficult not to flex under her grasp. "Mr. Holmes, I presume."

The old man looked him up and down before replying, "And Zorro! John, have you met a friend of the library, President Kowalski? Mary Anne, this is John Donovan, the head of our Children's Library."

The cat-woman slid her mask to her chin. "Hello there."

Victoria's grip tightened around John's arm. "President of Pembroke University?" he asked, extending his hand.

"That's right," Mary Anne said with a strong shake. She glanced at Victoria who shrank against him in an effort to look smaller. "Professor Reese?"

"Dr. Kowalski," Victoria said, straightening up. Her hand was still wrapped around his arm, quite different from the time they ran into her nemesis on the street. "You're also a friend of the library?"

The woman smiled warmly and nodded. "Of course, I've been on the board for nine years, pestering Howard, here, the entire time. And yourself?"

"Only for two years," Victoria said. "I'm actually—"

"—wait a minute, now," Wegman interrupted. "Are you Dr. Victoria Reese? The professor who reached out about the internship?"

"I am," she said quickly. "I'm working with John on that right now."

"What internship?" Kowalski asked.

"I was going to pitch the idea to you," Victoria said as her body began to tremble. John snuck his thumb to her hand and rubbed her skin until she relaxed. "As a Four-Week Initiative project."

Mary Anne gave her an appraising nod. "Give me the elevator pitch now."

Pembroke's president was all business, even in a cat costume. No wonder Victoria constantly walked a tightrope at her job. John continued to stroke her hand with his thumb, quietly urging her to stand tall and assert herself. Surely some performances were necessary. Victoria cleared her throat. "My aim is to create an internship for the English students of Early Childhood Education and Children's Literature to work with John's department. I believe their chances of job placement will be increased if they've had one-on-one interaction with young readers. Of course, this is an internship that could extended to more than one area of study. Working for a public library is beneficial to all kinds of students." When she finished, she let out a shuddering breath.

"I've been working closely with Dr. Reese to ensure the work duties are aligned with your university's learning goals," John added.

President Kowalski's knowing stare flitted to their union. As they were connected at the hip, it was evident they'd been working close indeed. She pursed her lips and narrowed her eyes before announcing, "I like it. It's an inexpensive and simple solution to our community outreach problem. Unfortunately, Pembroke has a reputation for being elitist and aloof. We need to change that." With a decisive nod, she added: "I'd like to see a written proposal from you, Dr. Reese."

"Really?" Victoria croaked.

"The sooner the better. If we can get this started in time for the Spring Semester, we can see how well it works for students of other disciplines. For now, we should start with English, don't you think?"

Victoria was frozen. John nudged her to speak. "Of course," she blurted out. "I can meet with you tomorrow if you'd like."

"Email me this evening so I'll remember."

"Just one more thing," she said. "Does this need to be approved by the Curriculum and Policy Committee? I was told it would take a month to reach your desk."

Kowalski frowned. "Who's running that committee?"

"Dr. Kenneth Williams, ma'am."

The woman rolled her eyes and exhaled a mirthless

chuckle. "Oh brother. Just leave Kenneth to me. He's still golf buddies with the last president who nearly gambled away our endowment. No, Dr. Reese, we'll get this off the ground by January."

Victoria looked up at John, her eyes widened with excitement. "Okay, that's perfect."

"Let's hope that I get more Four-Week Initiative ideas as good as yours," Kowalski said against her drink. "Howard, you don't mind my people pestering your people, do you?"

Director Wegman clamped his teeth on his over-sized Holmes pipe and shrugged his narrow shoulders. "If John doesn't mind a Pembroke woman bossing him about, I'm fine. I'm used to it."

John's shoulders shook with laughter. "It isn't half as bad as you make it out to be, Mr. Wegman." He exchanged looks with Victoria, who hadn't separated from him since the start of this negotiation. "I find some of Dr. Reese's bossing delightful."

Her mouth quirked into an embarrassing grin.

"Is he just saying that because he's your boyfriend?" Mary Anne asked with a raised brow.

"It seems that way," Victoria said. "Johnny has always objected to my rules."

John almost lost his breath. Victoria stood tall beside him, asserting herself and laying claim to her own brilliant ideas. Claiming him. He wasn't an associate tonight, in front of her boss.

He was her boyfriend.

Epilogue

Christmas Dinner in Chicago

"I'm warning you now, so you don't get confused later," Victoria said, facing her parents' front door. "I will probably act and sound different around them. I might not touch you like I normally would, and I'll be saying ma'am and sir a lot. Again, I'm really sorry about this."

John winked in response. God, he actually winked.

"I need you to tone that down when we get in there," she added.

His hand settled on the small of her back. "Baby, you're getting wound up," he warned. "What did we say about being open and honest?"

Victoria hadn't seen her parents since Uncle Jeffrey's retirement party, but she had increased the frequency of phone calls with them. While there seemed to be a change in her mother's tone, something softer and less demanding, she still dreaded the eventual visit with John in tow. She relied on a couple of mantras to give her strength: Teach people how to treat you. Set your boundaries from the start.

For his part, John wore a gray suit, kept his hair in a respectable ponytail, and held flowers for Katherine.

However, that didn't take away from the fact that he looked like pure sex. Or that they'd almost missed their train because of an ill-timed quickie. The whole two-hour ride was spent on her smoothing down her hair, adjusting her make up, and telling John to stop saying "calm down, honey." God, she'd been worried about her mother... What about her dad?

As the door swung open, Victoria held her breath. Archie revealed himself, dressed in an apron that read: "Grill Master." He saw the both of them and beamed. "Hey honey." He grabbed her for a tight bear hug before peering over her shoulder at John. "Is this the beautiful librarian? Did you get your book back, son?"

John gave a throaty chuckle. "Yes, sir," he said, holding out his hand.

The two men shook hands while Victoria looked on in trepidation.

"Archie, let them in for godsakes," Katherine's voice rang out. "It's too cold to be mingling on the porch."

"You heard the woman," Archie muttered under his breath.

They pulled their overnight bags inside and closed the door behind them. The Reese household was humming with activity and brightly lit with her mother's "sensible" Christmas decorations. There was a tree in the foyer, and if Victoria guessed right, there would be two more in the living room and the study.

"Go 'head and set your bags over there and Vicki will show you your room later," Archie said.

Victoria held her tongue. As long as they stayed at her parents' house, she knew they'd have to sleep in separate rooms. Even her father was insistent on that.

Her mother sashayed into the foyer, wearing her own

apron. Upon spotting John, her eyes widened and a broad smile slid over her face. It actually appeared genuine… "Dear god, you are a large man," she said. "How tall is he, Victoria?" Katherine touched John's arm and fluttered her lashes. "He positively dwarfs everyone in the room."

"I'm only six five ma'am," John said with a genial grin. He leaned over her extended hand and kissed the back of her fingers. Her mother reddened in the face as she lifted her free hand to her chest. Once he released her, John handed Katherine his bouquet of flowers. "Thank you for inviting me to dinner, Mr. and Mrs. Reese."

Chris was right: John was good at this. Her mother was a puddle of pleasantries at the mere sight of the young Viking. Victoria openly rolled her eyes at the scene. "Oh my, you've brought me gardenias," her mother crooned as she inhaled the warm scent of the full blossoms. "How on earth did you manage it?"

"I know a guy," John said.

Victoria was that "guy."

She'd made certain to drill him full of Katherine Reese facts a week before their arrival. So far, he was doing well enough, but Victoria wanted her mother to release her boyfriend. "Well, let me get these in a vase and they'll serve as a beautiful centerpiece for tomorrow's breakfast." She turned to Victoria and gripped her arms. "Darling, you have such a glow about you! School is going well?"

"Uh…yeah, actually it is," she said, meeting her mother's gaze. "The internship that John and I created just got approved for January. And I'm also halfway through tenure portfolio…" she trailed off because she wasn't used to her mother asking about her work. Victoria didn't know what else to say.

"Oh, wonderful," Katherine said, gathering her in her arms. Victoria wrapped her arms around her mother and cast a confused expression at John. "My baby is going to have some job security!"

"John," Archie said. "Grab yourself a beer from the fridge and join me on the deck. We've got a turkey to smoke."

"What kind of smoker you got, sir?" John asked, moving towards the kitchen. "I hear the Weber Smokey Mountain's pretty good."

Archie laughed. "Pretty good, but the Nordic Season is better, let me show you the specs on this baby."

With her boyfriend tied up with her father's smoking project, Victoria was left with her mother in the kitchen. She sat at the counter and watched Katherine bustle around. "So what's for dinner?"

Her mother pulled a large casserole of macaroni and cheese from the oven and fanned an oven-mitt over it. "Oh, honey, I've made everything. I didn't know what your John would like. You didn't tell us he was white."

Victoria held back the laughter that bubbled in her chest. "He'll eat anything," she said.

"Well, we've got greens, macaroni, dressing, ham, turkey…" Her mother trailed off as she counted the items left out on the counter to cool. "And you're sure he's not one of those vegans?"

"He's not," Victoria assured. "Thank you for going through all the trouble, Mom."

"And did you already have dinner with his people?"

"We did, I met his sister, who just got back from Sweden," she said. "It was really nice."

Her mother stopped busying herself long enough to stand on the opposite side of the kitchen island. "I did a lot of thinking since your last visit."

Victoria bit her lip and glanced down at the white tile of the island. "I'm sorry for coming off too aggressive."

"And I'm sorry for being so bossy," Katherine said.

Mother and daughter paused for a moment to stare at one another. Victoria's mouth tugged at the corner, trying to decide whether to cry or smile. Katherine took the first step, reaching out and taking her daughter's hand.

"I just want you to know that I'm going to do a better job of butting out. After all, you're a grown-ass woman," she said with a twist of her mouth.

"Thank you."

Their moment ended just as quickly as it began, with her mother returning to the oven. Yeasty bread rolls were next in line to be loaded up. "He's good to you?" Katherine asked over shoulder.

Victoria nodded. "He's good to me."

"That's all I need to hear."

Only when she sensed everyone had gone to bed, Victoria crept to John's guest bedroom, in the cover of darkness, and opened his door. "John?" she whispered.

"Victoria?"

She quietly closed the door behind her and tiptoed to where she remembered his bed was. "I just wanted to check on you."

"Is that a fact?" he asked in a low purr. "You're not allowed in here, young lady."

Victoria felt his body shift as she climbed into his bed. "Can you stay quiet, Johnny?"

"I absolutely can," he whispered. "In your parents'

home, I'm not going to do anything that would warrant noise."

"You're no fun," she said, snuggling up against his bare chest, his arms wrapped around her, pulling her close.

"You know what's fun? Not getting in trouble with the Master Gunnery sharpshooter and his wife."

"I want to know what you talked about with the Master Gunnery Sergeant while you were outside smoking the turkey."

In the darkness, she could barely make out his body, but felt him shift to his side and lean on one elbow. "We talked about you, my love."

"What about me?"

With his thumb, he rubbed the curve of her cheekbone and stopped at the corner of her mouth. "We had a good long talk about my intentions, my five-year plan, and how I'd allow you to spread your wings," John continued. "I told him that my intentions were to be the best boyfriend I could be, every single day. My five-year plan included the library and the university, us moving in together, me marrying you. You know, the normal courting process," he said with a soft chuckle.

Even though her heart pounded, Victoria found herself grinning. They were only just getting around to "normal" courting, but his mind was on the future. Marriage. She could see the same future and, instead of panic, she felt excitement. "What else did you say?"

"I told him that your wings were already unfurled. His daughter was already flying, I just needed to catch up with her."

She was too thrilled to know what to say.

John continued without her input. "He nodded, took

a swig of beer, and checked the turkey even though he had checked it five minutes previously. He said all of that sounded fine to him but to check with you because you're a 'grown-ass woman.'"

Tears slid from the corners of her eyes and down her temples. "I am," she managed to say.

John's hand left her face and traveled down her arm, to her hand. He brought it to his lips and kissed her fingers. "I thought as much, but I wanted to have one of those man-to-man talks with him. Marines like ceremony and tradition. Their daughters aren't too far off the mark."

"That was lovely of you," she said with a grin.

"So how about it, my darling? Does your five-year plan include being with a librarian?"

Victoria pulled away from him and groped for the nightstand. Once she'd switched on the light and saw him clearly, her heart melted from the sight of the G.D. Viking who lay beside her. With the blankets at his waist and muscles stretched taut, his beauty was still breathtaking. "I have one condition."

A dark brow arched. "Yes?"

She swept the back of her arm across her wet eyes and sniffed. "Promise me that we'll continue our sordid affair."

His face broke into a wide smile. "I promise, Dr. Reese," he said, throwing his arm over her middle and dragging her close. As he moved over her, pushing a thigh between her legs, he kissed her deeply. His promise to remain chaste in her parents' house quickly unraveling as he placed light kisses around her mouth. "I promise to be here at your convenience. All you have to do is ask and I will give you anything, baby."

Victoria was left breathless.

"Goddammit, Johnny Donovan, I love you," she said, planting a kiss on his lips.

* * * * *

Reviews are an invaluable tool when it comes to spreading the word about great reads. Please consider leaving an honest review for this or any of Carina Press's other titles that you've read on your favorite retailer or review site.

To purchase and read more books by Charish Reid please visit Charish's website at:
https://charishreid.com/

Acknowledgements

To my husband, Noah, whose patience is boundless: thank you for being the perfect hero and the inspiration for my books.

To "The *real* Write Bitches," Katherine and Courtney and my Writing Buddy, Sandra: thank you for solving puzzles with me, exchanging manuscripts, and communicating through gifs. All of it helped create this book.

The Lady PhDs who show up to school every day, with the sole purpose of changing the world: thank you for hustling through that 4/4 load. *Dr.* Pompili, *Dr.* Chansky, *Dr.* Green, *Dr.* George: you are heroes.

I want to thank my sister, U.S. Marine Master Gunnery Sergeant, for pulling up her *own* seat at the table so she could sit tall and speak clear. You've shown me I can do the same.

Special thanks must go to my editor, Kate, and my agent, Saritza: your support and guidance makes this road less bumpy.

Lastly, thank you, Normal Public Library, for giving me my first librarian job. I got to smooch my now-husband in Dewey decimal class 800.

About the Author

Charish Reid currently lives in Sweden with her professor husband, who enjoys walking and biking way more than she does. While he walks and bikes, she writes contemporary romance featuring sexy academics, who are trying to find love and adventure from under stacks of student papers. While she was born in Little Rock, AR, she has lived all over the United States observing people and taking notes for poetry, essays, and novels.

After earning her Masters in Literature, she went on to teach English and Rhetoric at several universities before penning her first book. Cashiering at a major discount retailer, being a menswear salesperson, and bartending were fairly easy compared to class prep, performing for students, and grading. When she's not writing or teaching, Charish enjoys watching movies and talking to folks in other countries. Travels to Thailand, Latvia, Estonia, Finland, Ireland, and Sweden will probably find their way into future books.

You can catch up with Charish here:

Website: https://charishreid.com/
Twitter: https://twitter.com/AuthorCharish
Facebook: https://www.facebook.com/
    CharishReidAuthor